BLUELINE OF LIFE

&

DEATH:

Chasing the Money

STUART CANNOLD

DEDICATION

I dedicate the second book in the Blueline series to my wife Jo. Without Jo's prodding, cajoling, and nagging, this series would be a bestseller only in my mind. Thanks, Jo. I'll love you forever.

My publicist, J Michael Parker, told me writing the novel is the easy work, getting it "out" is tough. Son of a bitch, J Michael, you're right on the money! I used to be a gambler. I'm betting I make a few bucks on this book if not on the pair of novels.

I want to thank Frank Ricci, PhD, whose review on Amazon literally brought tears to my eyes. Thanks for your critiquing and your valuable suggestions. It's time for you to write your life story.

Billie Batchelder, what can I say? I found out the hard way that many people in this business will tap you on the shoulder with their right hand and stuff your money in their pocket with their left hand then run like hell. You picked up the pieces and made Blueline of Life and Death: Chasing the Money reality. (Book three: The Beat Goes On, is READY! Thanks Billie). The "family" is going to make this book a winner!

I worked Huntington Park Police Department in California from September 1996 to June 2011. Never, absolutely never, have I worked alongside finer people. The men and women who wear the badge, and those who watch their backs are the very backbone of our society. You leave the house for the job. You may not return. God Bless the Blue!

Finally, and this is tougher than seriously burned steak to write, I dedicate Blueline to the Police Officer who carried serial number 5172, Loy D. Cleveland, my FTO, my partner, my friend. Damn you, Loy, you died too soon. Save me a seat in that black and white you're pushing around up there. I'll be sitting next to you in it one day soon. I'll buy you a pack of cigarettes.

Lastly, if you like the book, or if you don't like the book, I'd love to hear from you. Call me at 661-944-7539, or email me at 5tompublishing.com or at furrycuffs4two@yahoo.com.

Thank you

ABOUT THE AUTHOR

The author was born in Brooklyn in 1946. He grew up on the streets of New York and New Jersey and created his own chaos early on and damn near didn't graduate high school. At age 28, Stu started to turn his life around with the help of some amazing people who refused to throw in Stu's cards.

Stu earned a BA from Franconia College in New Hampshire. While attending Franconia College, Stu, a journalism major, spent a semester as an intern for a southern California newspaper. Although he turned down an offer to work for the newspaper, he returned to California years later and made it his home. He went on to earn a Master's degree in education, attending Oakland University, which was then affiliated with Michigan State.

He earned his administrative credential from Pepperdine University and his Doctorate in Educational Administration from United States International University in San Diego. He graduated from the Cerro Coso Police Academy in 1996.

Stu taught classes for many years for the University of Redlands and Phoenix University. He spent 33 plus years as a teacher and school administrator in Detroit and California.

Stu and his wife Jo, who reside in southern Arizona (and love it), collect classic cars. Three of their vehicles are in the Riverside Resort and Casino's car museum in Laughlin, Nevada. As you might have guessed, one of those cars is a 1930 Ford Model A, police car. Another is an authentic 1978 Harley Davidson Police Motorcycle with Sidecar, and the third is a 1957 Ford Thunderbird E Bird with overdrive, a rare bird, and a Gold Medallion winner in the 2019 Thunderbird Concours in Flagstaff.

The Camaro B4C CHP car pictured at the beginning of this novel belongs to Jo and Stu. Stu and Jo's 1974 Cadillac Miller-Meteor Criterion ambulance is a rolling memorial for September 11, 2001. **WE MUST NEVER FORGET!**

Stu is terrified of heights. Second, to publishing a novel, Stu wants to overcome the fear of heights and jump out of a plane. Years ago, Stu attempted this feat in California but chickened out. Stu doesn't know the meaning of the word quit and one day promises to make a second attempt at skydiving, this time with a jumpmaster.

Stu and Jo share their house with Princess and LT or Lieutenant, two Norwegian Elkhounds. It's actually their house. Princess and LT rent space to Jo and Stu. Years ago, a female friend gave Stu a piece of advice that he swallowed and digested: *you never fail until you quit trying.* From an unhappy kid growing up on the streets of New York and New Jersey to a young adult battling the "elements," in California, Stu's skin fits today. He and Jo couldn't be happier; life is great. Stu is *Happy, Joyous, and Free.*

Table of Contents

LOSERS

As Jack Webb would say, it was June, it was hot in Los Angeles. It was about to get hotter. I sat on the couch in my apartment. I had a half empty or half full fifth (depending on your mood) bottle of Seagram's and a shot glass on the cocktail table. I poured another double shot into the glass and downed it.

I watched Justin Turner on the big screen TV take a called third strike that appeared to be high and outside. I didn't give a shit. The fact that I wagered $500 bucks that the home team Dodgers would beat the Giants meant little to me. These days not much mattered to me. Since Mac had lowered the boom on my cop ass, I was in a sort of shock that I had never known before.

She and I hadn't spoken in several days. I didn't want to talk to her. I needed to think. I needed to take the edge off. You couldn't write shit this unbelievable. I took another shot from the bottle which was now three quarters empty. I downed it, put my head on the pillow, left the game on, and dozed.

When I awoke, the game was in the Dodger half of the thirteenth inning. The bases were loaded with two outs and the game tied. Corey Seager was batting with a 0 and two count. Corey slammed a fast ball into center field. The Dodgers won. I won $500.

I swallowed another shot from the diminishing bottle then went back to sleep. Rest was a turbulent plane flight. I dreamed of strange sexual encounters with women without a face. I dreamed of a guy sitting next to me on a barstool who repeatedly tried to buy me a drink. I put up with his shit until he put his hand on my shoulder. I decked him with a hard right cross knocking him off the stool onto the floor.

It was zero seven hundred hours when I awoke in a sweat. I met with Judge Karma in my nightmare. He again warned me that I played poker with Karma and lost. Now I had to pay the price. I wiped away the sweat. I knew what I had to do.

ROCKY, GIVE ME A BREAK!

I knelt at Rocky's grave site. "Give me a break, buddy. This isn't funny. If you laugh, I'll dig you up and kill you again myself. I swear I will." I placed a pack of Marlboros on Rocky's headstone. "If you were here this never would have happened. As a matter of fact, you and your better half helped put this thing together. What the hell am I gonna' do? Yeah, yeah, I love Mac. But she's not the Mac I knew. She's not.... And she lied to me. There is no way in hell I'm going to make this work. All the Viagra in the world couldn't get me hard with the image I have of her. I'm so fucking confused I know I'm not making sense." I must have knelt for fifteen minutes talking to Rocky. My knees ached when I finally stood up. "I gotta' get out of here buddy. Rest well and stop your freakin' laughing."

I turned. Walking toward Rocky's grave was Mac. "Shit," I thought. Just what I need now. I hadn't seen Mac since the Meadowlark. We talked briefly on the phone, but I refused to meet with her. I didn't want to see her. I nodded. "Hey."

Mac returned the favor. "Hey. We need to talk."

I nodded. "I don't know if I'm ready for that." We stood half a dozen awkward feet apart.

"I don't care what you're ready for or not ready for. I," Mac stressed the, "I need to talk." Mac half turned. "Follow me to Naomi's, you can buy me breakfast."

Naomi's was formally Denny's. When Denny's closed shop in Amity, a young husband and wife turned the eatery in to Naomi's. For some reason, the name change seemed to resuscitate the coffee shop. We were immediately seated. I sat across from Mac. The first sound I uttered was a sigh. I wasn't happy to be here, but the meeting was inevitable.

Mac broke the silence. "Tony, my AA program tells me I must continue to take personal inventory and when I'm wrong, I have to promptly admit it. I was wrong, Tony, very, very wrong. For that I am sincerely sorry."

I didn't hesitate. "Your program also stresses honesty. What the hell happened to that?" The waitress interrupted a very awkward conversation.

"I'm sorry, Tony. I screwed up big time. I'm as sorry as I can be."

"I'm curious about something. How the hell did you get into the department?"

"Believe it or not, it wasn't all that difficult. During my background investigation, I made it clear that if they disqualified me because of my…my operation, I'd sue. That and my connection got me in. They assigned me a very small backwoods area in northern California. When the fire burned out, I transferred."

I had a friend who worked for the Los Angeles County Office of Education, where teenaged gang bangers were locked up. She taught in their schools. If a teacher screwed up, most of the time a threat of a lawsuit would scare the shit out of the suits, and they'd fold quicker than the Dodgers in post season. The waitress brought coffee. I looked down at the cup not because I wanted the joe, I wanted to avoid eye contact.

"Tony, I think I taught you that there are two acronyms for F-E-A-R in the program that help me. One is Fuck Everything and Run. The other is Face Everything and

4

Recover. We have to face this sooner or later. Let's make it sooner." I was at a loss for words. I wanted to run. I was in pain. My heart said one thing; my head said something else. A shot or three would clear the fear. Unfortunately, Naomi's didn't serve alcohol. "You talk, I'll listen."

"Can we go someplace more private? Your place or mine?"

I shook my head. Big bad cop was afraid to be alone with Mac. The fact was I was afraid of the unknown. Put yourself in my shoes. The situation was a bitch. She was really a he. I was a he. I had been slam dunking Mac all over hell and back, even in a cop car. Jesus H. Christ. I made eye contact from across the table as the waitress set food that I didn't even remember ordering on the table. As Mac's eyes met mine, I quickly looked down at scrambled eggs and ham. I wasn't really hungry.

I had nothing against any lifestyle as long as it was between two consenting adults and it didn't have a negative effect on anyone else. I was an adult, but I wasn't consenting; at least not yet, and maybe never.

Mac picked at her breakfast. I sipped coffee. The white top she was wearing showed plenty of her ample breasts when she bent over to fork her eggs. I started to get hard then I conjured up a very negative image. The hard on died. That led to another image: me on top of Mac with a quickly fading erection. I scooped up scrambled eggs, put them in my mouth and chewed slowly.

Mac smiled. "Listen, how about we go to one of your favorite watering holes tonight? I'll ply you with liquor and maybe we can sort this out."

My head and eyes were hovering over my breakfast plate. I bit my lower lip, a new nervous habit. "I don't know...."

5

"Let me make it easier on you. I want to make this work. It takes us both to put this together. I'm not going to beg; I'm not going to grovel. I'm going to say this one more time. I'm so very sorry for not telling you the truth from jump-street. My bad. I love you with all my heart and all my soul. My panties are wet just sitting here talking to you and not because I have to pee. You got a decision to make, Tony. Think about it while I go to the lady's room."

I didn't even look at Mac's tight ass in her body-hugging blue jeans as she walked to the bathroom. I did notice her panty lines! She was right. The ball was in my court.

When I arrived home, the first thing I did was call my bookie. I told him to take my $500 and the original five and let it ride on tonight's game. Kershaw was pitching, which gave me a good feeling.

I turned on the news. COVID-19 numbers were flattening in some states, increasing in states like New York, New Jersey, and Arizona. Oregon was replete with rioters daily. The presidential race was heating up. Trump couldn't stop tweeting, and Biden was hiding. Great world. It was too damn early for a shot, but I poured one anyway. Since I poured one, I tilted the Seagram's bottle and downed a second shot. The ringing of my cell temporarily ended my desire for a third. It was Sully. "Hey buddy. What's up?"

"Rumor has it there are major changes at the Amity PD."

I shook my head into the cell. "Haven't heard a thing. What kind of changes?"

"My sources tell me Chief Payne took some kind of position in Cochise County, Arizona. Don't know if it was with a department or not. I guess he decided to get out of Dodge before the entire state blows up."

I looked at my cell as if I could see Sully through it. "Smart move. He can take his retirement then start a second retirement in Arizona. Do you know where in Cochise County?"

"Haven't the slightest. But I hear he took Jimenez with him."

I was silent. That was no great loss. Actually, neither was a great loss. "Is Rolando acting boss?"

"Yup. Rolando is Acting COP."

I wondered how that would impact our present assignment. I walked back to the coffee table. I poured that third shot. I turned off the television. "Very interesting. Is our meeting still on for tomorrow morning?"

"0800 hours in the detectives' briefing room."

"Okay. I'll see you at 0800 tomorrow." I sat down to think about those changes.

I wasn't in the mood to do much thinking, at least about the changes in the department. I started to think about Mac, about our scheduled meeting. I gave that fifteen minutes of my time then turned on the TV.

I watched two reruns of T.J. Hooker. I liked William Shatner. I liked Heather Locklear. The show was a bit over the top but there were some great car chase sequences. I missed shows like Jack Webb's Dragnet and Adam 12. I often taped Blue Bloods, probably my favorite cop show.

I finally gave in to the urge to close my eyes. I downed a double shot of Seagram's then the lights went out with my head on the pillow and the rest of my body stretched out on the couch with the overhead fan creating a cool breeze. I didn't wake up until the phone rang.

"Tony, Gigi from the station. The WC asked me to call. We got a call up. Black Lives Matter is demonstrating on the Boulevard. So far, it's semi peaceful but we want to be prepared so the troops are being called in. WC wants to know your ETA."

Ninety something fucking percent of Amity was Hispanic. Now they're going to demonstrate for Black Lips Matter. Horseshit. Any excuse to damage and loot. "What time is it?"

"Thirteen hundred."

Damn, I slept for quite a while. "Tell the big guy I should be in and ready by fifteen hundred. Riot gear?"

"No. Regular uniform. Throw your riot gear in the van. It'll be out on or near the Boulevard. The WC said you could partner with Mac or Sully, your pick." There was hesitation on the other end of the line. "I pick Mac," Gigi said.

"Funny. Tell the boss I'll partner with Sully." I hung up.

I drove south bound on the five-freeway thinking about the state of affairs in this country. I would have bet Mac's panties, which I didn't like playing with anymore, that the shit that was going on could never have happened. BLM and their proponents were burning stores, cars, and even police stations. They were looting. We were standing by and watching this shit happen. We weren't making arrests. When a couple defended their property, they were arrested. What kind of bullshit was this? We had a president whose hands were cuffed as much as our cops' hands were cuffed. We were giving in to socialists which was really communism. Statues were being torn down which was part of our history. Right or wrong, these statues represented the growth of our country. I was disgusted.

I turned off the five-freeway with time to spare. These so-called protesters were a pain in the ass. Most of them had no idea what the fuck they were protesting. And many of them were paid agitators or shit holes who were looking for an opportunity to pillage and create havoc. The only way to deal with these assholes was to one up them. If they came at you with a rock, baton, or asp them until the dirt bag was withering on the ground in pain, severe pain. If they broke a store window, break the baton across their head. If they burned a car, rubber bullet or tear gas 'em. If they obstructed traffic, arrest them.

I was sick of hearing black lives matter. All lives matter equally. One damn rule should apply to all across the board. It was that simple. But this world had turned softer, gentler. It didn't work. There was a small percentage of this population that wanted to game the system, that wanted something for nothing, that was chasing socialism. I was sick of it.

I saw a cartoon on Facebook. A pretty white girl in a short shirt, wearing no panties, flashed her bare butt to a big uniform cop who was standing behind her. He admired here ass then pepper sprayed it. Way to go Kojack!

It was going to be a long night. The minute it got dark and these puke buckets thought they could hide in the dark, all hell would break loose.

Sully and I dumped our riot gear in the van in the back lot. We grabbed an unmarked unit and hit the street. Sully was, of course, in plain clothes. I was in uniform, although unbeknownst to me, that was about to change!

The Boulevard was already packed with slow moving, horn honking, sign carrying vehicles that made it impossible for shoppers to spend their hard-earned money in the Boulevard

9

stores. Then there were the sign carrying lunatics chanting, "NO JUSTICE, NO PEACE." One asshole carried a large sign lettered in red that read, "No Justice, NO PIECE." Pure fucking genius. I guess that meant he was sleeping on the couch tonight.

We were reassigned to walk the Boulevard. We were to be "alert, reasonable, tolerant, and ever present," according to the watch commander, whatever the hell that meant. I looked at Sully and shook my head. "This country is going down the crapper. We're going to put up with this shit."

Sully said, "We could stop it before it starts. Issue two orders to leave the area. After they ignore the second order, tear gas the hell out of them."

I observed Hispanic kids who couldn't have been more than eight carrying Black Lives Matter signs. Some carried signs that read, "Defund the Police." One girl, who may have been seven or eight, carried a sign that read, "FUCK THE PIGS." I pointed the sign out to Sully. "Great parenting." The parents should be arrested for child neglect. "Piss pots. They're pieces of shit." Sully took out his cell then snapped two quick pictures of the kids carrying the obscene sign.

That picture should be front page news in tomorrow's paper. You'd never see it unless you stole Sully's camera. But if someone had snapped a picture of a cop "roughing up" a rioter, it would be front-page news for days.

We had earpieces so we could hear the radio. We weren't about to hear it over the screaming crowd without the earpieces. The major action seemed to be on the south end of the Boulevard where Sully and I were slowly meandering through the throngs of assholes.

We walked, talked, and observed. I watched a short, thin Hispanic teenager with his jeans below the crack of his ass take a spray can out from under his dirty, sweaty t-shirt. I elbowed Sully. We watched.

The punk was so engrossed in the "artwork" he was about to create on the store front window that he had no idea we were a few feet behind and on either side of him. I was curious if he was going to scrawl BLM, Defund the Police, Fuck Cops, or some other shit on the window. I wasn't going to find out.

As asshole aimed the can, I caught his right arm, grabbed the can, handed it to Sully then slammed asshole against the brick façade. His brown face turned white. "Sorry to interrupt you, Van Gogh, but the owner of that business doesn't want your crap on his window."

Adam Henry looked at me quizzically. He ran his hand through his short black hair. When he recovered, he asked, "Can I get my can back?"

"The only can you might see is one with bars on it. Let me see some ID."

He shook his head. "No ID."

"How old are you?"

Sully was tossing the can up and down as if it was his night stick.

"Twenty-three."

The punk didn't look twenty-three. "When's your birthday?"

He told me without hesitation. I did the math. It added up. Apparently, the kid was quick thinking, or he was telling the truth. "Do you live in Amity?"

He shook his head. "Maysville."

"Why are you causing trouble here?"

11

He shrugged his shoulders. I looked around. The crowd was thickening. Sully looked at me. I shook my head. "C and R," I said. "Catch and release." I shoved the punk against the wall. Quickly, methodically, I patted him down. Nothing.

Sully shook up the spray can. The twenty something year old was still leaning on the wall. Sully sprayed the punk's white t-shirt. He wrote, "I LOVE AMITY POLICE" on the shirt. The writing was sloppy but legible. We continued walking the Boulevard.

We made our way through the increasing throng of protesters the six blocks to our "war zone" the area where our van and units were parked. We had a black unmarked Ford Mustang that had been seized from a drug dealer a few years ago.

The WC commanded us to cruise the outer perimeter of the Boulevard looking for signs of serious disturbance such as gang activity, setting cars on fire, breaking windows, and looting. And I thought we called these felons, these rioters, protesters. They were fucking thugs, hard core criminals. Assholes. Idiots, puke pots.

Sully climbed in the Mustang which wasn't a bad looking car for an undercover unit. It beat the shit out of pushing a Crown Victoria around the city.

The area immediately around the Boulevard was quiet. But it was still light. The rats came out when the sun set, and darkness set in.

Sully stopped for a light. "How's Mac doing?"

I stared straight ahead. I nodded. "She's good."

"Is she working tonight?" I nodded. "Mac's working. I'm not sure of her assignment but she is working." I wanted to change the subject. "Any new thoughts on the money?"

Sully pulled away from the light. "As a matter of fact, yup. I've been giving it a lot of thought."

I wanted to mess with Sully. Since we had "patched" things up, we were becoming a team. He was still fun to mess with. "You're obsessed with that money. You would think it was yours."

Sully took his eyes off the road. "I'm not obsessed but it is a challenge. I think the best way to handle this is to go back to the beginning. We've got to start searching through the paperwork again. I want to go back to day one. I want to re-interview the wits. I want to talk to all the cops who helped in the investigation. I want to talk to anyone and everyone who was involved. We're missing something. We have to be."

Sully was right. The search for the money was a cluster fuck. The minute the he/she took a bullet, our money source disintegrated. I was in no mood to revisit the case. As Mac would say, I had to get into the now and stay in the now. The now was the bullshit on the street tonight.

Sully drove north to Mission Street an east west street with railroad tracks running between the two lanes in either direction. When trains ran east or west on Mission it was a television commercial in the middle of your favorite show. You thought it would never end.

I heard the train, heard the train's whistle then observed the arms come down blocking the tracks from cross traffic. I settled in for a wait. "You know Sully…." I didn't get to finish my sentence.

"14 Adam and X-ray 7, a 459 silent at the Mission Bank, Boulevard and Mission."

"14 Adam, we're at Fountain and Mission. We're held up by a freakin' train."

"X-ray 7," I shouted into the mic so I could be heard over the damn train. "We're waiting for the train to pass at Mission and the Boulevard." I slammed my fist on the dash.

"One Robert, we're northbound The Boulevard from Franklin. We're in pursuit of a black Chevy 2 door, California license plate 3 Adam Boy Boy 741. The vehicle is occupied two times by male Hispanics wearing ball caps. They ran out of the bank. They could be our 211 suspects. Both subjects are armed. Speed is 50 to 60."

"All units clear the air. Robert 1 is in pursuit."

"Son of a bitch. That's a reserve unit. Marci Garcia and Royola Flussh are in that unit." Marci had been a reserve for 3 years. She was good and she spoke Spanish fluently which helped when a non-Spanish speaker needed a translator or a female for a search of a female subject. Royola Flussh, or Royal Flush as we called her, was a newbie black female.

"Robert 1, we're northbound Seventh crossing Adams. Suspect ran the light at Seventh. Speed is 55 to 60."

The train finally passed. Sully burned rubber and hit the overheads. Several units were attempting to catch up to the pursuing units. I half expected the WC to tell Robert 1 to terminate the chase.

Our level one reserves receive the same training as full-time officers. They are fully certified by POST, Police Officer Standards and Training. But they're not on the street every day. They're mandated to put it a minimum of sixteen hours

14

a month. Their skills maybe sharp but they're still reserves. Some of them go full time; some of them quit; some of them remain reserves. They do this for free. That's right, they receive a uniform allowance twice a month; they receive not one penny in pay.

Sully was driving like T.J. Hooker. He drove into opposing traffic to get around an idiot who either didn't hear the siren and didn't see our overheads or didn't give two shits. I didn't have my seat belt on.

"Robert 1, we're still northbound Seventh crossing Stewart. Speed is 60." There was a pause, then I heard, "They're probably headed for the freeway. Dispatch, please notify CHP."

"Copy that," dispatch said. "We have an airship on route."

"Damn," I said to Sully who had better things to do than listen to me blabber. "I know full timers who aren't as calm and cool as these two in a pursuit. So far so good."

"We're northbound Seventh crossing Linden. Speed is fifty-five. Stand by. They're slowing down. The passenger tossed what I think is a gun out the window; now a second gun out the passenger window. Can I get a secondary unit to find those weapons? Be careful with them. We want to preserve the perps' prints."

Sully and I were the closet unit. We were less than three blocks away.

"Suspect vehicle has rolled to a stop northbound Seventh just south of Ramone. I'm going to need units to block traffic north and south bound."

I could hear the airship overhead. These two female reserves could teach at the academy. Up to this point, they were textbook.

When four units were in position behind the primary unit, when the cops took their positions using the units for cover, Garcia said into the mic, "Please clear the area for a felony vehicle stop." Garcia took a position behind her opened door, gun drawn and aimed at the back of the driver's head. Flussh took a position behind the passenger door, her Glock aimed at the back of the passenger's head.

"This is the Amity Police Department," Garcia shouted crisply, clearly. "Listen closely to my directions. If you follow my directions to the letter, you will not get hurt. If you deviate from my instructions, you might leave the scene in a body bag. Is that perfectly clear?"

We were the secondary unit. We were in position ready to take each suspect into custody as Garcia called each out of their vehicle, which came back stolen. Sully looked at me. "Garcia sounds more like you than you do." He smiled.

I flipped Sully off.

"I got it bitch. Let's get on with it."

Garcia continued in slow deliberate language. "Listen punk, crack-wise one more time and...." She didn't finish her sentence. There were too many people standing around including bystanders off in the distance. Three helicopters hovered overhead, a Sheriff's unit, an LAPD unit, and a news chopper. There was so much noise it was amazing anyone could hear anyone else.

"Driver and passenger put your hands behind your neck. Interlace your fingers." She repeated her instructions in

Spanish. "If, when you exit the vehicle, I even smell a weapon, you're inviting trouble."

"We don't have any weapons cop. Never did."

"You can go to hell for lying to cop, punk," Royola said dryly.

Garcia hoped the weapons were recovered and the prints were preserved. "Again, when you're ordered out of the vehicle, you are going to come out one at a time, as directed. Is that crystal clear?"

"Yeah cop."

The driver had an attitude. Garcia had enough of it. "Punk, my name is Officer Garcia or ma'am to you. If that's clear, let's try this again. Driver remove your left hand from behind your neck. DO NOT, I repeat, DO NOT remove your right hand. With your left hand, remove the keys from the ignition. With your left hand, throw the keys out the window. Make sure they land at least three feet from the vehicle. Is that clear ass wipe? Be very respectful with your answer or I will charge you with serious and willful disrespect of an officer, a serious felony."

Sully was grinning from ear to ear. "Did you train Garcia?"

"I wish." She was damn good, damn good. I wondered why she didn't go full time.

There was hesitation from inside the vehicle. Then, "Ma'am, I hear you loud and clear. I apologize for my mouth. Please, no more charges." The keys came out of the vehicle. The perp had a good arm. The keys landed five feet from the car's door.

"Driver, and driver only. With your left hand, open the door. Do it slowly."

17

"Yes ma'am." The door opened.

"Driver step out of the vehicle. When you step out, when ma'am tells you to do so, face away from me. Is that instruction clear?"

"Yes, ma'am."

"Step out now."

Ass wipe was facing away from the officers. His hands were behind his neck. His fingers were interlaced.

"With your left hand, lift up your shirt then do a 360." Quickly, Garcia added, "Turn all the way around. Stop when you are facing away from me, let go of the shirt and put your hand back on your neck."

Flussh had her gun directly on the passenger who stared straight ahead. He was probably too frightened to even shit.

Ass wipe followed ma'am's direction perfectly. "Keeping your hands behind your neck, slowly," she emphasized slowly, "start walking backward toward the sound of my voice." More cops than there were fans in Dodger Stadium eyed the action. Guns were trained on the suspect just in case.

Joe Citizen doesn't realize that in a situation like this, gun fire is "contagious." Supposing the perp suddenly reaches for his waistband whips around and points a weapon in the direction of the backing officers. One officer opens fire. Every other officer fires. In court the defense attorney says to his witness in blue, why did you fire at my client? The response should be your client pointed a weapon at me, sir. I wanted to go home to my family, in one piece. Let the attorney chase that answer around the court room.

I took a weeklong hands-on officer safety class. One of the scenarios was a robbery call. My partner and I jumped into a unit, then drove to the scene. Upon arrival, we took positions that afforded us cover. My partner went to the right, I to the left. I found cover behind the side of a building, my partner behind a block pillar. Within seconds, out of a store walks a man with a bag in his left hand and a gun in his right hand. We're all wearing protective gear. The guns are loaded with soap pellets which hurt like hell if they catch you. Even though this is training, the rest of the class is watching, your adrenalin is pumping.

The guy, still a good twenty-five or thirty feet from me, is walking toward me. The gun is sometimes pointed at the ground; at times he raises the gun slightly but never points it spot on at me.

"Drop the gun. Do it now." Numb nuts keeps walking. He keeps raising and lowering the gun. "Drop the mother fucking gun or I am going to light you up like a fucking Christmas tree. He keeps walking and screwing with the gun. Now, maybe fifteen feet separate me and asshole. "Drop the fucking gun asshole."

He takes another step and I fire three rounds. Our mentor sergeant blows his whistle which signals a stop to the exercise. Weapons are holstered. The "bad guy" recovers and gets up dusting dirt off his pants. MY partner, the "bad guy," our instructor and the shooter (me) gather in front of the stands where the rest of the class is awaiting our "sentencing."

"Tony, you fired three units. You struck the suspect three times in the left leg. Were you aiming for the leg?"

"No sir. I was aiming center mass. Bad shooting."

"Actually no. You were three for three. He was a distance away; he was moving, and your heart is pumping. My question is to your partner. Why didn't you open fire?"

"He had the angle. He hit him."

"But Tony's rounds didn't take him out. It was the third shot that took him to the ground, and at that he still had the weapon in his possession. You should have fired. The suspect could have taken one or both of you out. You fire until the weapon is down, the suspect is down or both. If eight cops were present, if there is no crossfire, I would expect eight cops to fire. The taxpayer will buy you more ammo."

Garcia continued to bark marching orders (literally) to suspect one. When he was next to the front of the unit, an officer cuffed S/1 (suspect 1), walked him to the trunk of one of the backing units, searched him, read him his right in English and Spanish and put him in a unit. The officer remained with S/1.

Flussh followed the same procedure with S/2. Suspect 2 was put in a different unit. This way they couldn't talk with one another and conjure up some BS that we'd have to untangle later at the station.

The recovered weapons were turned over to Garcia and Flussh for tagging, booking, documenting, and sending off for fingerprinting.

After the suspects were safely on their way to the station for booking, after the scene was code four and the crowd, the cars, and the airships started to disperse, there were high, high fives for the ladies who had made the bust. I was sure well-deserved commendations would be in order.

A thorough search of the stolen vehicle recovered no money. "Sully," I yelled. "More missing money."

"Fuck you." In their haste to get out of the bank, Manny and Mo dropped two money sacks. These clowns were real losers

ACCEPT THE THINGS I CANNOT CHANGE!

My cell rang. Sully and I were grabbing coffee at the 711. It was night. The crowds had multiplied as had the damage. So far it was broken store windows, tagging, fights, and an occasional bottle thrown at us, minor looting, and a lot of arrests. Most of the arrests were citations written in the field and the arrestee was released and told to go the hell home. If it remained this way, we be able to handle it without mutual assistance from surrounding departments.

My cell rang. I didn't have to look at the caller ID. "Mac, what's going on?"

"You found a way out of our date. Now what?"

"You gave up on foreplay, huh? You cut right to the chase."

"Tony, I'm hurting."

Sully sensed I wanted privacy at least as much as one can get outside a 711 when the city was being turned upside down. "And you think I don't hurt? Who are you partnered with?"

"I'm not. I'm not working the call out. They've got me responding to calls. It's quiet. I think the entire city is on the Boulevard. If we get a break, can we have breakfast?"

"Probably not. That would be awkward. I can't break away from my partner. We have an early meeting tomorrow. How about after the meeting?"

"Okay. Be careful."

"You do the same."

"Tony, I.... I'll see you tomorrow."

"Mac?" Sully proved his value as an FBI agent.

I nodded.

"Everything good?"

"As good as can be expected when two cops are in a relationship." I tossed my coffee cup into a trash can. "Let's go find some trouble and stomp it out."

Sully and I continued to cruise the perimeter. When we got tired, bored or both, we parked the unmarked unit and walked the Boulevard. "Things" remained quieter than I had anticipated. As a matter of fact, there appeared to be less foot traffic now that it was dark than there was during daylight.

I heard the crackle of my radio. As was too often the case, I thought too soon. "Any unit in the vicinity, a possible armed robbery in the alley to the rear of 7100 Boulevard Jewelers. The suspect is a male Hispanic 20 to 30 described as 5'9" to 5'11" 155 to 165 pounds wearing all dark clothing and a blue Dodger baseball cap with LA on the front."

Sully and I were half a block from the incident. He bought the call as we trotted through a walkway to the alley. We found the victim on the ground against a green trash dumpster. Sully called for an ambulance as the guy was bleeding from the head.

"Can you tell me what happened?"

"I was in the Oasis Bar. I had a couple. I decided it was time to leave. I walked out. I saw this guy trying to break into my car." He pointed to a blue Chevy that was probably a couple of years old. "I yelled to him as I was running to my car. The guy pulled a gun. I nearly shit myself. I backed off. He followed me back here, hit me on the side of the head and

23

told me if I didn't give him my money, he'd kill me. I gave him about forty-eight dollars."

"Did he take your wallet or anything else?"

"Nope. My wallet's in my other pocket."

"Can I see your ID?"

Two patrol officers not assigned to the protest, arrived on scene at the same time as the ambulance. We turned the robbery over to them. Sully and I went back to the car. Sully drove. I thought about Mac.

I needed to talk with someone about Mac. That was tricky. The department shrink was out of the question. No matter how many times I was told a meeting with the department doc was confidential, I had seen leaks too often. That was out of the question. I had good insurance. I could meet with a shrink provided through my insurance. That idea was better than the department shrink. Or I could put my big boy pants on and make my own decision.

I loved Mac. No argument there. I could imagine Mac and I back together, seriously back together. What I couldn't imagine was what the hell would happen if somehow, someway someone finds out about Mac. I'm done in so many ways my life is over. I didn't even know if I could get it up with Mac since she shocked me with the news.

Since it was quiet, I called dispatch on my cell. I told her to tell the WC that we were clear for calls unless the Boulevard got hot. The WC approved, and I had an FBI agent for a squad car partner.

Sully said, "I have a new theory on the money."

"Go with your theory."

"Do you know how drug dealers sometimes launder money?"

"They funnel it into a legitimate business."

Sully nodded. "What do you think?"

"Anything's possible." My mind was only half where it should have been. "How would you launder that kind of cash without drawing someone's suspicion?"

"I haven't gotten that far yet. I'm playing with possibilities. I guess we'll sit down as a team tomorrow and see what the team thinks."

We cruised the north east end of Amity, the home of the bangers and dealers. Even that was quiet, a bit eerie. I was waiting for all hell to break loose. It didn't happen. By twenty-three hundred hours I was on my couch watching the news and drinking shots. I had an early call in the morning.

The good: thanks to the Dodgers I was up two grand. The bad: I had a tentative meeting with Mac after our morning meeting. I went to sleep on the couch with the TV on.

A MEETING TO REMEMBER

ACOP Lee Rolando stood at the podium at the front of the Detectives' Briefing Room. "Let's get this show on the road folks, please. We're still cleaning up from yesterday's demonstrations if you will." Rolando paused to let everyone settle down.

"You're probably wondering why some faces are missing. I don't want to keep you in suspense. For those of you who haven't heard, Chief Payne accepted a position in southern Arizona. He took Detective Jimenez with him. It was sudden but it was a good fit for the Chief, so he seized the opportunity. I am Acting Chief of Police. We're down patrol officers. As a matter of fact, as the result of budget cuts we are seeking to hire three officers to fill six vacancies. If that doesn't make sense to you, join the club. On the other hand, if you know of anyone who'd like to lateral over, or if you know of anyone interested in joining up, have them contact Sergeant James who's in charge of recruitment.

"We're working on Flussh and Garcia to come over full time. Flussh and Garcia are two of the coolest reserves I've ever seen in action. They don't want to take a major pay cut to join up full time. Can't blame them.

"That leaves us with Agent Sullivan whose been graciously extended and will spend most likely the next year in beautiful Amity. Dee Mackenzee will also remain with us for an extended stay.

"That brings us to our own Tony Kano. Tony, Dee, and Sully will be pulling double duty. The threesome will handle, at least temporarily, patrol duties. Sully is POST certified. When time permits, they will be working the SafeGuard

Armored Truck heist. We may still be down one perp. We are down the cash.

"Any questions?"

"Sir, can you give us more details about our patrol assignments?"

"Sure Tony. Until we fill our slots, and once we hire, our new hires still have to go through FTO training. So new hires are about a year out of being on their own. We need rubber on the road. You three will be rubber on the road. In short, you can and will work the case. When needed you're in a unit, marked or unmarked on the street. When needed, you will respond to calls. You will be in soft clothes unless ordered otherwise. Does that answer your question?"

I looked at Sully then shot Mac a quick glance. With our breakfast upcoming, I felt like I was a death row inmate about to walk his last mile. "Thank you, sir. Question answered."

"Any other questions?" Acting Chief Rolando looked at his three stooges. "We have one more order of business before we adjourn and allow you to dig into the missing money. This is normally done at a city council meeting but because of time constraints, I'm going to do this here and now. Kano, front and center please."

Rolando walked out from behind the podium. I stood next to him. "As of this date, I hereby promote you to Acting Detective." He handed me a detective's shield incased in a leather holder. I reached for the shield, took it, and shook Rolando's hand. I was surprised to say the least. Sully, Mac, and the rest of the team applauded. Talk about bittersweet. "That concludes our meeting. Congratulations Tony. Go get the money boys and girl."

BREAKFAST SPECIAL

I knew the meeting with Mac was going to be awkward; I just didn't know how awkward. I'm rarely at a loss for words. Today, this minute, I didn't even know where to begin.

We were sitting across from one another in a booth seat. We had coffee in front of us. We were waiting for the server to bring us breakfast.

I asked Sully to give me an hour; I told Sully I had something important to take care of. I was certain Sully figured I was meeting with Mac. He just didn't know why. At least I hoped to hell he didn't know why.

"Congratulations, Detective Kano. Do I get to see the new detective's badge?"

I took the encased badge out of my pocket and handed it to Mac. "It's acting detective."

"It may become permanent. You never know." Mac looked at the badge. She smiled then rubbed her hand across it. "Carry it with pride. Carry it safely." Mac handed it back to me.

"How was last night?"

Mac smiled. "Quiet. I backed a couple of loud music calls and one 273.5 call. It turned out to be a lot of yelling. No arrests. A frightened neighbor called it in. How was your night?"

"Mostly uneventful. We walked the Boulevard. When we got tired, we grabbed the unit and patrolled."

"Where do we go from here, Tony?" She didn't waste any time getting to the point.

I picked up my coffee cup buying a few seconds. "I honestly don't know. I'm confused, really confused."

"Tony, give me an honest answer to a straight question."

I nodded across the table.

"If I had been born a female, would you still be running from our relationship or would you solidify it?"

I felt like I was being cross examined by some high-powered mouthpiece. Mac asked a fair question. She was entitled to an honest answer. I owed her that. "I loved you, Mac."

"Past tense."

I nodded again. "Past tense. If you were the "you" I first got involved with, you know we'd at least be engaged. I proposed. Remember?"

"I'll never forget, Tony." Mac dabbed at the corner of her eye.

"I want this to work, Tony. I want this to work with all my heart. I love you more than you can know." Mac raised her voice. I was sure half the eatery could hear her. "Step aside and get out of your own way, Tony. Together we can make this work."

I took a deep breath. I let it out slowly. This was training for tense situations. This was as tense as leveling my Glock at some asshole who was moving toward me with a knife, getting closer and closer. Do I shoot or do I risk my life trying to talk him into putting down the knife? "What do you suggest?"

I was used to making the decisions. I was putting the ball in Mac's court. Hell, I was giving her the opportunity to be judge and jury. Judge Karma took a position in my mind's eye.

The waitress brought our breakfast. "Obviously, we can't go on as if nothing happened. But we can accept it and move on." Mac bit into her ham and eggs. "Do you want it to work?"

I didn't hesitate. I surprised myself. I was shocked when the words came out of my mouth. "I do. I really do. I'm scared, angry, and…. I care, you know that. I love you. I can't be any more honest than that with you, Mac. I'm not sure I can work through this."

I felt like I was back in the hospital trying to accept the fact that half my leg was gone, and Rocky was dead. This was painful. I hurt deep down inside. I wanted to be part of Mac's life. I didn't know if I could accept what I couldn't change. I could understand why she didn't tell me. I didn't like it, but I could accept it. I believed her when she said she fell fast and hard. I'm loveable and addicting. Had she told me from the gate, I know I would have run from her, no question. "What do you suggest?"

"I suggest I come over to your place after work. We can talk more." Mac smiled.

There was mischief in those eyes that I loved to look at, stare at, smile at. Again, my words surprised me. "Date."

"Should I pick up dinner on the way over?"

"Your call." I finished my coffee. I asked the server to refill my cup. Our hour was almost up. I didn't want to keep Sully waiting.

A PLAN FOR TRACKING DOWN THE CASH

There was a small office on the department's second floor. It was sometimes used for meetings, sometimes for interrogations, sometimes for disciplinary actions. It was empty. Sully appropriated the room while Mac and I were feeding our faces. He also appropriated a white chalkboard and several markers.

"Glad you could make it." Sully teased. "I hope I didn't keep you waiting."

"Actually," I lied, "we formulated a plan. Let me spell it out."

Sully walked to the chalkboard at the head of the oblong table. He wore a blue suit, white shirt sans tie. "Go with your plan, Detective Kano."

I smiled. "I think we need to go back to the very beginning. We need to re-interview the cops who were on scene when the robbery and killing went down. We need to review the paperwork of the SafeGuard employees who were interviewed. We need to visit SafeGuard and interview anyone who might be connected who may not have been interviewed. We need to interview any of our own who might have even a remote connection to SafeGuard or a relative who might be connected to SafeGuard. I don't want to leave any rock unturned." I caught a breath of air. "Speaking of rocks unturned, I want to take a closer look at the fucking Jew attorney Jerry Kline. He smells, and the smell is all bad."

While I spoke, Sully condensed all this on the chalkboard. Mac copied it off the board onto notebook paper.

"Anyone else have anything to add?" Sully ran his fingers over his lips. When neither Mac nor I spoke up, Sully said, "I do. I'd like to dig deeper into Myra's background, her family, her friends."

"There's a helluva' lot of work here. Maybe Rolando will let us borrow a couple of reserves to assist us at least with background digging. And maybe while we're asking for favors, we can allocate this room while we're working the case. I'll text Rolando." I took my cell phone out of my pocket. Rolando was in my contacts. I texted him.

I had an answer in under a minute. "You got them both, detective. As long as the room is unoccupied. I need a deposit and a first and last on the room. As far as the reserves go, that'll be great training for them. Tell them to log their hours as training time."

I went to hang up. "Detective Kano, quid pro quo."

"What?"

"I need something in return."

"You got it, sir. What do you need?"

"I need two of you on patrol. We're down crew this morning. Seriously understaffed. I don't care how you work it out, but I need two of you in an unmarked unit. You three decide then let dispatch now. You'll be X-Ray One."

"Copy that, sir."

I hung up and explained the situation to Mac and Sully. Sully looked serious. "How about you and I take the patrol duties? I need to talk with you anyway." Sully looked serious; that frightened me. What the hell could Sully want to talk with me about? I had visions, ugly fucking visions. I observed Judge Karma in my mind's eye.

32

"That's fine," Mac said. "You boys go have fun playing cop. I'll stay back and start digging into the SafeGuard crew."

"Listen," I said, looking directly at Mac. "New rules. If anyone leaves the reservation, the other two are to always know your destination along with dispatch. 10-4?"

Sully nodded.

"10-4, Detective. Do I have to salute?"

SULLY, SULLY, SULLY

I drove, Sully was in the passenger seat deep in thought. Mac was at the station digging into possibilities. I was dying to know what Sully wanted to talk to me about; I was also scared. There was no way in hell Sully could know about Mac, about Mac and me unless Mac had turned to Sully with help convincing me to give our relationship a chance. I seriously doubt Mac would do that. (I had never been so damn wrong in my life). I didn't want to ask Sully what was up, so it became a waiting game. I drove around the city aimlessly, alternately thinking about Sully and about Mac, about Mac and about Sully, about Mac, about Mac, about Mac.

I really wanted to talk with someone, but I had to be careful. I could screw up my life and Mac's if her secret got out. It was amazing it had been this quiet this long. How, if our government could keep conspiracies quiet over the years, Mac's secret should be child's play. At least two government cover ups came to mind. The Kennedy assassination and Roswell, New Mexico.

I did a lot of reading about Roswell. Something landed there that wasn't from this world. Weather balloons my big fat baton. The government changed its story too many times. There were too many witnesses. There was physical evidence. The government had proof. They were keeping it from the public.

As far as JFK's assassination, sure Lee Harvey Oswald took Kennedy out but was there a second shooter? The Warren report was horseshit. Then Oswald gets taken out by Jack Ruby, the result of sloppy police work to say the least. Finally, Ruby dies in prison of cancer.

Ruby had mob connections. Oswald had ties to the Soviet Union. My best guess is that it was a mob hit. It was payback because JFK shined a red light on organized crime. He hired his brother who was a bulldog, and this pissed off the mob. Hell, it was the mob who helped put JFK in the White House. Payback is a bitch.

Dr. Lopo, the shrink who interviewed me for my fitness to return to duty would be my first choice to talk with about Mac. Dr. Lopo, as sincere as he came across, was too deeply connected to the PD for me to trust. I really needed someone to talk with but that might not happen.

Sully turned toward me as I stopped for a light. "You've never been married, have you?"

I bit my lower lip. "No."

Sully nodded his head. "I've had over ten mostly good years. I have a nice house, two great girls six and eight and a damn good career."

I wasn't sure where this was going. Sully suddenly made it clear.

"My wife wants a divorce."

"Wow. Sudden or did you see it coming?"

"I'm away from home so much if my wife sold the house and bought another, I probably wouldn't even notice the change of address."

"What are you going to do?"

"She's resolute. There's no changing her mind. I'll get an attorney to start with. I'm still in shock. I'll give it a few days to sink in, feel Amy out and see how amicable we can make this."

"I'm sorry, Sully. Life can sometimes be a real bitch."

"Shit happens. Maybe if I had been home more, I would have seen it coming and could have done something about it. Who knows, maybe she'll have a change of heart.

"The bitch is going to be not coming home to the kids. I'll probably move into an apartment. No way I can afford two mortgage payments."

"Maybe they'll be a reward if we find the money."

"Maybe if we find the money, we keep it. That's our reward."

Old habits die hard. I watched a guy in a black Lincoln Continental Mark run a light. Red light runners were always a good traffic stop. "I'm going to pull that idiot over. He ran a light."

"You're a detective now, son," Sully joked. "Let the traffic units do their thing."

"Not all of us are Feds, Sully," I countered. "Some of us work for a living."

"I'm glad you work for a living because you sure the shit wouldn't make it as a standup comic."

"I'm bored. Besides, you never know what you're going to find."

Sully was wearing his seat belt. I guess he didn't trust my driving. I didn't blame him. I put out the stop. "X-Ray One, show us 1038 at Victory and Boston on personalized plate TOM VICTOR SAM TOM ADAM ROBERT. It should come back to a 1969 Lincoln Continental. We'll advise on a back." Everybody in California has a personalized license plate.

I lit the guy up. Before I got out of the car, dispatch came back with the return on the plate. The plate come back to a 1969 Lincoln Continental. The R/O was Lamont Montel. Lamont was second banana on a weekly situation comedy. Just because his bought and paid for license plate read TV STAR, didn't mean he had the right to run a light, not in my city.

I approached Lamont's Lincoln on the driver's side. I identified myself and held out my badge for the lone occupant of the "gangsta' car" to see. Sully, in his grey suit, stood back by the rear of the passenger side of the Continental. The black-on-black Lincoln was a tank, but it was a gorgeous car.

"Sir, I need to see your license, registration and proof of insurance please. I'm stopping you because you ran a red light." Lamont smiled. His teeth were white. Nothing else about him was white. He was dressed casually in tan slacks and white pull over shirt.

"I'm late for a shoot. You do know who I am don't you?"

"Yes, sir. I do know who you are. License, registration, and proof of insurance, please."

"Listen friend, I'll give you an autographed picture and a couple of tickets to a taping of our show. Cut me some slack."

"I'll take the autograph, but I still need to see your license, registration, and insurance." I glanced at Sully. He was shaking his head grinning from cheekbone to ear and back again. Sully knew what I was up to.

Lamont handed me his license.

"I also need the reg and the insurance card."

He pulled them out of the glove compartment then handed them to me.

"Thank you, sir." I put out a code four.

"If I were a white tv star would you have pulled me over?"

"Sir, from the back, I have no idea what color you are. Sir, I pulled you over because you are in violation of 21453 of the California Vehicle Code; you ran a light, a red light, a very red, red light."

He waved his hand at me. "Whatever." Then he added, "An autographed picture and four tickets to a taping of my show. Front row seats." I started to walk back to our unmarked unit. "I'll be back in a moment for the autograph, sir. Please sit tight."

Lamont smiled. He took out his cell as I backed up toward the unit. I stood behind the opened passenger door as I wrote Lamont's citation. Sully stayed in position still grinning.

When I finished scratching the ticket, I walked back to Mr. Montel. I held the citation book out for Lamont and handed him a pen. "Your autograph in the box next to the red X, please. It's not an admission of guilt, it's a promise to take care of the ticket. Your court date is under your signature. If you choose to fight the ticket, I'll get you a front row seat in court."

"You're a real comedian," he snapped, looking annoyed.

"Not according to my partner, but thanks for the compliment."

He signed the ticket. I pulled the citation book back, pulled his copy and handed it to him. "Please drive careful in Amity, sir."

He stuffed the ticket in the glove compartment. "Here." He handed me four tickets to a taping of his show. "I know you're doing your job. I also know I ran the light. That black shit was just my anger rearing up. I respect the police, and I respect the fact that you protect us and do one hell of a dangerous job. Stay safe."

I nodded, thanked Lamont for his show tickets, and walked back to the unit feeling bad for writing him the fucking cite. If there wasn't so much paperwork involved in voiding the ticket, I would have trashed it. Lamont was a nice guy. Maybe Sully and I would go to the taping of Lamont's show. Hell, I could take Sully's wife and Sully could take Mac!

I walked back to the Continental. "Listen my friend. Go to court on your court date. I won't show up. The judge will toss the case."

ON THE ROAD AGAIN

We got back in the unmarked. I looked at Sully instead of the road. The guy in front of me stopped for no apparent reason, at least I didn't observe a reason. I skidded to a stop inches from his bumper. I eyed the guy looking in his rear-view mirror shaking his head. "Been driving long?" Sully asked.

"I was thinking…."

"That's your problem. You should be driving not thinking. Have you had that problem all your life?"

I realized Sully was fucking with me, but he was, in fact, correct, at least to a point. Unless I had a Glock leveled at some asshole, a shot glass in my hand, or my head between some broad's legs, I had a difficult time concentrating on one subject. My mind liked to jump around. Mac tried to get me to focus on the NOW; another one of AA's little tricks that seemed to work for her.

"I think," I said to Sully, "we need to revisit the two guards who were driving the armored van." I scratched at my head but this time I kept my eyes on the road. "Could it be possible that one or both of these guys were in on the robbery, and that they were killed so there would be more money and less people to divide it between? I'd like to take a long, hard look at these guys.

"I also think Mac's idea of going back through the paperwork is a great idea. Something could have been missed. There has to be a tie in someplace that we're missing.

"Since you're riding shotgun and not doing a whole helluva' lot but feeling sorry for yourself, give Mac a call and ask her to take a look at Manny and Mo."

"Yes, Detective, sir. Immediately if not sooner, sir." Sully made the call.

MIND FUCKING

I knew what was rolling around in Sully's head. He had no idea what was rolling around in my head, thank God! "How does an FBI man adjust to patrolling the streets of Amity?"

"Believe it or not, I like it. Most of my work is in the office playing with papers and beating the telephone lines to death. I dig into peoples' pasts and try to build a case against them for federal offenses. At least we're out and about here. I like it. I could get used to it. In my business you pretty much know what's going to be on your calendar each day. Here, all hell can break loose at any time."

As if on cue, what the old timers used to call a squawk box told us we had a hot call at 3687 Clarence. It was a silent alarm in a condo unit. We had two apartments and one condo hit within six weeks. The M.O. was two male Hispanics would knock on the door. When the door was opened, they'd force their way in at gun point, tie up the occupant or occupants and take anything of value that could be pawned quickly for cash. One victim was pistol whipped; another had a mild heart attack. Because they wore ski masks, we had little to go on other than height, weight, age, and one had an ugly scar over his right eye.

We figured these clowns cased their targets and the residence. They knew when to strike, and always did so during daylight hours. They weren't making big money, but they had a steady stream of tax-free cash coming in until we could get lucky and close down their operation.

"I know the condo complex," I told Sully, as I hit the overheads but not the siren. I stepped down on the accelerator. This time Sully buckled up. "Don't trust my driving partner?"

42

"A few minutes ago, you almost ran up some jerk's ass, and you weren't even rolling code. I'm taking my life in my hands just letting you drive, detective!"

I shoved my foot down hard on the accelerator and swerved around an imaginary vehicle. Sully grabbed the dashboard.

We arrived at the condo complex the same time the backing unit arrived. They covered the back, Sully and I walked to the front of the complex guns drawn and at the low ready. We were at the side of the house when the front door suddenly opened and a male Hispanic, dressed in gray slacks and white t-shirt came running down the stairs. Sully was on him like bees on honey.

"On the ground now, dirt bag. Put your hands behind your neck and interlace your fingers." Sully raised his voice. "Do it now."

I got on the radio. "X-Ray One, we're holding one at gun point to the rear of the complex. Dispatch, please clear the air and please call the condo."

"All units clear the air. X-Ray One is holding one at gun point. I'm making the call now."

The subject, face down on the concrete, looked up at Sully. "I'm the owner of the unit. I think I accidently set off the alarm."

"And I'm the queen of Sheba," Sully said. He was picking up my good oral habits.

"X-Ray One, no answer."

"Copy that. My partner is going to remain outside with the subject. The Adam unit and I will clear the house." Hopefully, I thought silently.

43

"Let's go guys." I turned my radio down. We made entry. We carefully went from room to room searching for another suspect. We came up empty.

When Sully observed us exit the condo unit, he allowed the subject to stand up. Sully patted him down. Carefully he told the suspect to take his wallet out of the pocket of his slacks. "Show me some ID."

The Adam unit cleared. The condo owner WAS the condo owner. He had indeed set off the alarm, accidently. Sully cleared us. We got back in the unmarked car. Sully slid behind the wheel. Fuck him. I guess he really didn't like my driving.

"Did you ever think of coming over to Amity?"

"I gave it serious thought when you were busting my hump. I figured that would be a great way to get back at you. I thought, for our family's sake, for sanity reasons and for financial reasons, the Feds were a better fit for me than the PD. I would have preferred a PD. If Amy and I split, maybe I'll let you put in a good word for me. Hell, you might have a new partner. My legs might not be as shapely as Mac's, and I don't have much of an ass, but…."

My cell phone rang. It was playing the National Anthem. That meant it was my bookie. "Sol, what's up?"

"I know I'm up two big ones. Sure, why not. Let it ride on tonight's game. All or nothing. I want to see how many games I can run up in row. You know that 500-dollar bill you keep hidden in your wallet; I'm going to get that one of these days. Okay buddy. Thanks. I think."

"I hope you're paying taxes on your winnings?"

"When Uncle Sam says I can write off my losings, I'll declare my winnings. Truth be told, I've lost a hell of a lot more than I've won."

"Since we're making small talk, when are you and Mac going to tie the knot?"

I shook my head and sort of laughed. "You tell me your wife has had enough of your ugly ass, and in the next breath you want to know when I'm getting married. I don't think so. I'll take that one day at a time if you don't mind. In the meantime, I'm going to teach the agent here how to pull traffic. That guy in the red Mustang busted that stop sign. Let's see you do a traffic stop."

Sully grabbed the radio. He made contact with dispatch. "X-Ray One a roller, please."

"X-Ray One, go with your roller."

"6 Robert Mary Edward 331. 6 Robert Mary Edward 331."

Dispatch came back with the plate in less than fifteen seconds. "That plate comes back to Conrad Vega, this city. Registration is current to a 2011 Mustang."

"Thanks, dispatch. We'll be 1038 Clayton and Robinson. We'll advise on a back."

"Copy X-Ray One."

I nodded my approval. "Not bad for an FBI agent. There is hope for you after all."

Sully opened his door. "If the guy's a fag, you can have him."

"Sorry Sully, the way things have been going at your house, you might want him." I watched Sully approach. I stood back on the passenger side of the Ford. The guy had his hands on the steering wheel. He was alone in the car.

I heard Sully explain to the guy why he was being pulled over. I heard the driver respond. "I know. I reached for the radio and realized I didn't make a complete stop." Sully asked him for his license. The driver complied.

Sully walked back to the unit. He slid in behind the wheel and ran the guy's license on the computer. I maintained my position. The guy came back clean. Sully walked back to the Mustang, handed the driver back his license and told him to drive carefully. "X-Ray One, we'll be 10-8 with a verbal warning issued."

"Not bad for a Fed."

"This is almost more fun than watching you damn near rear end a car."

THE SADDEST SIDE OF POLICE WORK

We were very much into a conversation about Sully's failing marriage when my cell rang. We were summoned back to the station for an emergency briefing in the second-floor briefing room. We drove directly to the station, ending our conversation, with Sully accepting the blame for his decaying marriage.

I gave Sully credit for taking responsibility for the failure of his marriage, but I disagreed with him. Most of the time a relationship that failed was the result of both parties. Maybe one had more to do with it than the other, but the relationship still involved a pair of people. I was also convinced that most relationships fell apart the result of lack of communication and/or financial problems.

I, who had never been married, I, who was in a failing relationship came to this conclusion. My mind was deep into Mac as I punched the gate code into the security box and drove into the lot thinking how I rarely got a hard on now when I thought about Mac.

Sully made a stop at the downstairs men's room. I took the stairs two at a time, entered the briefing room and took a seat in the second-row center so I could hear the briefing sergeant loud and clear when he started the show. I didn't have long to wait.

Sully had just entered the briefing room accompanied by Mac when Sergeant Estoban Valencia stood front and center behind the podium. The Sergeant had transferred to Amity from San Diego. He had been with us for just over a year. He was easy going, knowledgeable, friendly, and likeable.

His uniform was freshly laundered, and neatly pressed. He had a full head of dark black hair. Sergeant Valencia stood six foot tall and probably weighed in at 185. When he wasn't supervising the troops, he was in the basement of the station working out.

"Okay team let's get to the business at hand. This is serious. A young girl's life may hang in the balance."   All eyes focused on the Sergeant behind the podium. No mouth moved.

"We have a report of a missing Amity 15-year-old who has not returned from school. This young lady is a cheerleader, an honor student, has a part time job as a tutor and according to mom and dad is not into drugs or booze. She has a boyfriend and they're on good terms. She attends church regularly. The BF also attends Amity High. He writes for the school newspaper, is also an honor student and he plays sports at the high school. She's only four hours late…." The Sergeant looked at his watch. "Four hours forty minutes now."   He held up a stack of papers. "We have her picture here. It will be at the back desk. Grab a copy on your way out. We have reserves going door to door. We have a call out to neighboring departments. You know the name of the game. The longer she's missing, the less chance we have of finding her.

"Her name is Ricki Montego Valenzuela. She's 15 with long black hair. She stands five foot two and weighs 115 pounds. She speaks English and Spanish fluently. She has no tatts and no distinguishing marks on her body. She was last seen at school at 1330 hours in the lunchroom. She never showed up for her honors English class nor did she show up for cheerleading practice. She's an only child. We've questioned several of her friends to no avail. We've broken you into teams and grids which are marked on the paper containing Ricki's photo. In a couple of cases, we've assigned you to question teachers and students who are still at the school. A couple of you have been assigned to question neighbors or visit her known hangouts and friends. The rest of you are assigned by grid. We can't track her on her cell. Her cell was found in her locker. Any questions?" Sergeant Valencia scanned the room.

"Okay, you know the drill. Unless it's an emergency, nobody goes home until Ricki is found. Hit the bricks." He paused. "Oh yeah, one more thing. Two tickets to a Dodger or Angel game of your choice if you find her, including parking and a fifty-dollar certificate for food. Good luck team."

The ugly side of police work is a missing juvenile. There are some very sick people in this world. Unfortunately, all too often when a youngster is missing the end result is tragedy. In other words, the victim is found dead.

When a child is reported missing, we pull out all the stops. All available staff is held over until we reach results. I was well aware that there were child predators living in and around Amity. Our first field of focus, after eliminating immediate family as suspects, would be sex offenders.

If nothing else, this would most likely get me out of dinner with Mac. Sully, Mac, and I walked downstairs to the parking lot. Being with Mac, near Mac, was now awkward as hell. I was very uncomfortable.

"I guess you guys are a team for now. Sergeant Valencia wants me to go out to Ricki's house and revisit with her parents to see if there is anything they remembered following the initial visit."

If Ricki was as clean as Valencia made her sound, this didn't look like it was going to have a happy ending. Ricki didn't sound like your normal runaway.

Photos of Ricki in hand, Sully and I drove to East End Park. He took the north side of the park; I took the south end. We stopped anyone we could. We showed them pictures of Ricki. A few of the kids at the park knew Ricki from school. No one admitted to knowing her whereabouts. It was getting dark when we left the park.

I said to Sully, "This is not going to have a Hollywood ending. I'm liking this less and less." Missing kids was not an unusual occurrence in Amity. Kids stayed out pass curfew, if they had one, and were afraid to come home. Some made up stories, some spent the night at a friend's house, still others walked the street all night until he or she grew the courage to come home. Ninety percent of these kids had "spotty" behavior. Ricki was as clean as freshly polished furniture. It had to be a kidnapping and/or rape or…."

Sully made a U-turn. "Let's check out the movie theater on the Boulevard. We can stop and check with ticket sales. It's probably a dead end but worth a try." It was a dead end.

I called the WC. "Was Ricki's boyfriend interviewed?"

"We spoke with him by phone. If you and Sully want to give it a shot, drive over to his house. I'll have dispatch text you the address."

Twenty minutes later we were in front of a very small white house with a patch of green lawn that had been recently cut and manicured. There was an American Flag flying off the tiny front porch. Sully and I climbed three steps, took two large steps, opened the screen door then knocked on the front door.

A short, squat middle-aged lady with black hair opened the door. I immediately identified myself as Detective Kano. (I liked the sound of that; I really liked the sound of Detective Kano). "This is my partner Agent Sullivan."

"I'm Mrs. Vega-Chapa."

"Is Roberto home?" Sully asked.

Mrs. Vega-Chapa shook her head. "He's out looking for his girlfriend. Would you like to come in?"

She held the door ajar for us. We stepped into the tiny house which was about the size of a small one-bedroom apartment. It was clean. It smelled fresh. Sully and I walked four steps. We were in the living room. "Sit down."

Sully and I sat on the couch. Mrs. Vega-Chapa sat in a recliner across from us. A glass topped table separated us. "Is your husband home?"

"He's at work. He works as a foreman at the Cosmo Plant on Silverton. He's been there for almost eighteen years now."

I knew the place. It had a good reputation.

Sully took out a notepad. He placed it on the glass top table. He took out a pen and held it between his fingers. "How well do you know Ricki?"

Mrs. Vega-Chapa shook her hand before she replied. "She's been here for dinner a couple of times. The sweetest girl Roberto ever brought home. They've been together since eighth grade. They were very close."

"Did anything Ricki did or said strike you as strange?"

Mrs. Vega-Chapa shook her head. "Never. A mom couldn't ask her son to go out with a nicer young lady. She often tutored students free of charge."

"Do you think she was into drugs or abused alcohol?"

"No, not at all."

"Did she and Roberto argue a lot?"

"I only heard them fight once. Roberto bought her an expensive diamond cross. She loved it but Ricki knows money is tight. She thought he should have given us the money for groceries and not spent in on her."

"Did they ever fight physically?"

"I raised my son to respect women. My son would never raise his hand to a woman. He's big and strong but no, never a woman."

I piped in, "Were Ricki and Roberto having sex?"

"I think so. I found rubbers in his dresser when I was putting his clean laundry away."

"Could Ricki have been pregnant?"

"I think Roberto would have confided in me. But I guess it's possible. If she was pregnant, she wasn't showing. Can I get you gentlemen a cold drink?"

"We're good," Sully answered for both of us. "Is there anything you can think of that might help us find Ricki?"

"I can't think of anything."

"What time does your husband get home? We'd like to talk with him, too."

"About eight thirty."

"Here's my card. When Roberto talks to you, ask him to call us, please. I'd also like your husband to give me a call later."

Mrs. Vega-Chapa stood up. "I hope you find her safe."

"So do we. Thank you for your time, ma'am. If you think of anything else, anything at all, please call." She walked us to the door.

When we were back in the unit Sully asked, "What do you think?"

"I don't think there is any question. I think it's foul play or she was pregnant and ran away. I want to speak to the boyfriend. Something isn't adding up."

"About five years ago the FBI assisted a local police agency in the disappearance of a teenage boy. Parents were questioned, neighbors were questioned, school authorities were questioned, friends were questioned. Nothing. Not a damn thing. The home appeared to be the Cleaver family. Finally, we brought in a cadaver dog. Guess what?"

"The dog found the body."

"In his family's back yard. Guess who?"

"I remember reading about the case. The teen kid was adopted. He was a football player and a body builder. Stepmom liked his body. Stepmom liked his cock. She admitted she'd fuck his brains out. When the kid turned driving age, he naturally wanted a car. He told stepmom either you buy me a Dodge Challenger, or I go to stepdad. She flew into a rage. She gave him a long, slow blow job. When he fell asleep, she took a belt, put it around his neck and choked him to death. The backyard was a pond because of all the rain. She dug a deep hole and buried him. Dad was none the wiser. If it weren't for the cadaver dog, we never would have found him, and stepmom would have gotten away with it."

"You think she's dead?"

"If not," I said, "she's being held hostage and probably being used for some asshole's satisfaction. Ricki won't be found alive. Bet on it unless she's pregnant and ran to Mexico to get an abortion."

"I hope you're wrong."

"I hope so too. I'll bet you Roberto is somehow involved." I drove aimlessly. There was one positive. I didn't have to meet with Mac, yet.

ROBERTO: VICTIM OR PERP

Roberto called at 2030 hours. He agreed to meet us at 2100 hours at a coffee shop a couple of blocks from his house. "I think this is about to get interesting," I told Sully.

"No reports on Ricki?"

"Not a damn thing. I'm telling you Sully; Ricki is either dead or will be when we find her. This wasn't a kidnapping for ransom. The mom and dad have no money. I doubt it was a crime of opportunity. Somebody didn't just stumble on her and decide to grab a pretty girl off the street. Somebody wanted her for sex. You know how that usually ends."

We drove around Amity for a few minutes to kill time. It was dark. That decreased our chances of finding Ricki. "How do you want to play this?" I asked Sully.

"By ear. Let's see where the kid takes us. I'm going to go out on a limb and say the girls pregnant, and they both got scared and they have her in hiding. Or maybe they found someone here or in Mexico to abort the fetus."

We waited another ten minutes then drove to the coffee shop. We parked in front, walked in, and seated ourselves. Ten minutes later Roberto strolled in.

I motioned for Roberto to join us. "Roberto, my partner over here is Agent Sullivan. I'm Detective Kano." (It slid off my tongue. I was getting use to Detective Kano).

The waitress walked over to our table. Sully had an iced tea. I had an ice coffee. The waitress asked Roberto, "What can I get you?"

"I'll have an iced tea."

"Would you gentleman like a menu?"

There were no takers. When the waitress walked away, Sully asked Roberto, "How are you doing?"

He sighed. "I'm worried sick. This isn't like Ricki. I know something's happened. She doesn't even have her cell with her."

"And you know this how?" I asked.

"Her mom went up to the school. They opened Ricki's locker. Her cell phone was in the locker."

"Does her mom have the cell phone now?"

"She took it to the police station. They told her they were going to 'dump' it whatever that means."

"Is there anyone you know who might want to harm Ricki? Maybe a guy who likes her or even one of the girls who's jealous of her. Maybe a teacher who likes her more than he should?"

Roberto looked at me. He looked exhausted. "No. Nothing like that. If anyone fucked with her...." He caught himself. "Excuse my language."

I said, "Don't worry about it. I promise I won't blush."

The waitress set his drink on the table. "You sure I can't get you gentleman anything?"

"We're good, thanks."

"Has Ricki ever done this before, ever disappeared like this?"

"Never. She's an excellent student, a cheerleader, someone who wants to help others and asked nothing in return. She's one in a million."

"How many times a week do you and Ricki have sex?" I watched his face, his eyes. Nothing.

He shook his head. "We've never gone all the way. Neither one of us a lot of free time. When we are together, we make out a lot. She gives me a hand job through my pants until I come. That's as far as we've gone. She's a virgin."

I thought to myself I've heard that one before. "You're sure she's not pregnant?" That struck a high note.

"I just told you Ricki's a virgin. When you find her, ask her yourself. You'll see."

I'd seen good liars before both on and off the job. If Roberto was lying, he was damn good.

Sully spoke up. "Would you be willing to take a polygraph test?"

He sipped his drink through a straw. "You think I had something to do with it?"

"No," Sully said. "But the more people we can eliminate as suspects the more we can focus on finding Ricki. If we can rule you out as a suspect, we wouldn't be here. We'd be out on the street looking for Ricki. Does that make sense?"

Roberto nodded. He rubbed his hands on the cold glass. "I'll do it."

"Call the station tomorrow." I handed Roberto my card. "We need to get your parent's approval in writing. We'll set it up. We appreciate your cooperation."

Sully finished his iced tea. "Is there anything, anything at all you can think of that might help us? Maybe a place that Ricki liked to hang out when she was by herself?"

"The couple of places she might go, I've checked. I've called everyone I can think of. If she'd just call...."

Ten minutes later we walked out of the diner together.

AN UPDATE FROM MAC

My cell rang. Sully was driving. The ring tone was Hail to The Chief. That meant Mac was on the other end of the line. "What's up?"

"Have you and your partner taken code seven yet?"

I shook my head. "No."

"How about buying me dinner and we can update each other?"

"Sully, you hungry?"

"If you're buying, I'm hungry."

"Actually," I said to Sully and into the phone, "Mac invited us. She's buying."

"How about the PIG's Pen on Melrose?"

I told Mac that worked for us. Before you go all crazy about the name of the restaurant, the place was named for the retired cop who owned it. His name was Paul Ivan Gants, hence PIG's Pen. In addition, Paul, when he was a cop and detective, was a neat freak. He was a bit obsessive-compulsive. The guys were always calling him a pig because he was such a neat freak. Like calling a short guy biggie!

What made the PIG's Pen even more attractive was that any first responder got twenty percent off their meal. A cop received a fifty percent "thank you" for your service from Paul.

We took our time meandering over to the PP. I was hungry, but I dreaded meeting up with Mac even though Sully was with us. I didn't expect Mac to get into anything heavy in the presence of Sully.

As one might expect, The PIG'S Pen was immaculate. The dining room walls were decorated with framed police pictures, newspaper articles about famous cases. A framed picture of O.J. with Johnny Cochran and photographs of past and present police cars. One picture depicted a female cop sitting on a fifties Ford LADP unit. The car was fully dressed. She had on a uniform. The top had no buttons. Her breasts were half exposed, nice knockers, very nice. She was wearing a half-cocked LAPD hat. She had a straight stick (a baton) between her legs. I hoped she didn't get splinters.

To be fair to the gentler sex, Paul posted pictures of male cops. One showed an officer working out in the LAPD gym. He was topless and sweaty. His black gym shorts showed a bulging crotch. Another showed a uniform cop half in and half out of his unit. His fly was unzipped.

The PP was always packed. It was a fun place to renew friendships. You never knew who might show up. If you were working, it was a great place to relax and lose some of the stress of the shift.

I wanted a drink, but I was working. One drink and one incident and I would be on Paul's wall. "What the hell," I said across the table when the waitress walked over. "Get me a double shot of Seagram's please." I wasn't in uniform. I was a detective. Nobody at the table was in uniform.

Mac spoke up. "Cancel my partner's drink, please. We'll have three ice teas."

Sully looked at me then at Mac who was seated across from us. He smiled. "How much is his bail?"

"He has a no bail warrant. One more bust and he makes the career criminal list. We put him away for life." I felt something between my legs, it was Mac's shoeless foot. It felt good but it didn't get me hard.

I looked up. Paul was at our table. He was wearing a white apron with LAPD stenciled all over it. In the center of the apron was a picture of a uniformed cop standing over a suspect who was prone out on the ground. The caption read, "You have the right to eat at the PIG'S Pen."

"Long time no see." Paul was still in great shape. He still had a full head of black hair, a thin moustache, and muscles. Retirement from the department was treating Paul well.

"Introduce me."

"Paul meet Mac and Sully. Mac works for Triple A, and Sully is Full Blooded Italian."

"I've heard a lot about both of you. Mostly good." Paul smiled. "Can I get you something from the bar, on the house?"

That made my thirst for a shot or three more acute. Just then, the waitress appeared with three ice teas.

"Question asked and answered," Paul said when the drinks were on the table. "How is the department treating you, Detective Kano?"

"News travels like a canyon fire around here. I can't complain." Mac moved her toes. She was right on target. I felt a growing erection. I was alive down there to Mac's touch. That was a good thing. I hadn't stopped taking those little blue pills.

Another waitress, this one dressed as a western sheriff from the eighties, the eighteen eighties, handed each of us a menu.

"I'll give you a few minutes to look over our menu. I'll be back."

"You guys be safe out there. We're busy as hell tonight so I've got to check on the food. If I get a chance, I'll be back, if not, see you soon. It was great meeting you." Paul looked directly at Mac. "Ma'am, if you're searching the dick for weapons, I think you've missed the mark!"

AND NOW THE NEWS

We ordered, sipped iced tea, made small talk, and finally got down to cases. "I pulled the files starting with SafeGuard employees. The investigators appear to have done a thorough job of vetting people of interest. I have three subjects I want to revisit.

"I made a list of people we should be investigating or reinvestigating or interviewing during our screening. Included on the list are Tony, who maybe after all this time can remember something that had been previously locked away in that sick mind. I want to dig into the background of our attorney friend, Jerry Kline. I want to talk to Interpol about the out of the country sightings of Myra Williams. Anybody have anything they want to add?"

Sully remained silent. "I don't"

"What have you and the newly anointed dick had to report on Ricki's disappearance?"

"Not a whole helluva' lot," Sully said. "We know Ricki is supposedly as innocent as they come. I don't buy into that. We met with Roberto, Ricki's boyfriend. He claims to know nothing about her disappearance. The jury's still out on that one. Other than that, I'm enjoying letting the new detective chauffeur me all over Amity."

"In summary," I said, "there's little to report." Mac's right foot again found its way between my legs. It amused me more than it turned me on. The server in the cop uniform interrupted us to take our order.

We were halfway through our meal when my cell rang. It was the watch commander. He wanted to know what we had learned in the disappearance of Ricki. I updated him. He sounded annoyed. "Remember you're on the taxpayers' dime. I've got personnel working who aren't even on the clock. I need you back on the street as soon as you finish eating. Tell Mackenzee I want her to grab a unit and hit the street too."

I wanted to tell him to go fuck himself, but I had enough negative karma. "Yes, sir." I had to get in at least one jab. "Can I bring you something?"

The WC hung up. I was certain that remark would pay dividends later.

DAMN YOU, MAC

I had four grand riding on the Dodger game after letting the two-grand ride. I decided one last bet was in order. So, I let it all ride. The Dodgers gave the game away on a bases loaded walk in the thirteenth. Easy come easy go.

I may have lost a few bucks, but because of conflicts in working hours, I managed to stave off an extended "visit" with Mac. I just wasn't ready for a sit down with her.

If anything confused me more than the disappearance of Ricki, it was what to do with Mac. I had even cut back on my drinking so that my thinking was clear when I tried to reason my way to a solution; you know I was serious.

I loved Mac. I could not dispute that. At least four glaring facts red flagged the situation. One fact was obvious: Mac was not who she said she was. If she lied or mislead me once would she do it again? Two, could I accept the fact that Mac was born a man? And three, could I even get it up knowing I was making love to what was once a guy? Then there was the outside possibility that someone would discover the truth about Mac. Could I deal with that?

My mind works in strange and mysterious ways. On the one hand, I wanted this relationship to work. On the other hand, I was walking in to the unknown.

AA taught Mac when she runs in to a difficult situation to write about it, to pray about it and/or to talk with someone about it. A closed mouth friend or a sponsor. I wasn't about to share that little secret with anyone. I didn't know anyone short of a priest who I could share that secret with, and I didn't really care to talk with a priest. Hell, other than weddings and funeral services, I hadn't been in a church in years. This was a decision I had to make on my own; at least I thought I did.

I sat at the kitchen table after finishing two slices of cold pizza which were left over from last night's late dinner. I was working on my third cup of coffee. I drew a not so straight line down the middle of a piece of typing paper. On the left side of the page, I wrote 'pros; on the right side I wrote 'cons.' It came out to be pretty much what I already had in my head. The difference was I was able to look at, study it.

On the positive side, I really did love Mac with all my heart. Most woman could not put up for an extended time with the profession of a cop. The sometimes-crazy hours, the dealing with the scum of the earth, the not knowing if your mate was going to come home or you were going to get a call telling you your spouse was in the hospital on the operating table; that doctors were unsure if he would make it. Or you get the visit at your door at three in the morning telling you some piece of shit took your husband out while he was having breakfast at Denny's. Mac was a cop. Mac would accept this.

Another plus was that we were two apples from the same tree. Both of us were lively spirits. Both of us were fun loving. Together we brought home enough money to do pretty much anything we wanted to do. The sex, at least to this point, was incredible. Maybe my mind was sicker than most, but on the negative side I wrote that I didn't know if I could get a woody with Mac anymore.

The negatives were the lie, the fact that Mac was born with a faucet and the unknown possibility of someone finding out. For some reason, seeing it in writing seemed to force me to come to a conclusion: this decision would be a two-way street. I had to, I absolutely had to discuss it with Mac.

RICKI OR NOT?

I had gotten out of the shower and was toweling off. The phone rang, Hail to the Chief. "I was just thinking about you."

"I've been thinking of you non-stop. Were you thinking of what you'd like to do to me in the back of a police car?"

"Actually, I was thinking about what to do with you. You're right, we have to get together."

"We do. I got a call from the station. They found a body several hours ago off Old Sierra Highway in Santa Clarita. It's the body of a young girl. It appears she was strangled. There's no definite on the body yet, and no positive on the cause of death. I want to get in touch with Sully and drive out to the scene. Let's meet at the station. Can you be there by 0830?"

"Yeah. You want to call Sully?"

"Done." A brief pause. "Tony, I love you with all my heart." Mac hung up.

Mac, Sully, and I met at the station at 0830 hours. We commandeered an unmarked unit, then started the forty-minute drive to Santa Clarita. Sully drove, I was riding shot gun, and Mac was sitting behind me.

"Anybody want to speculate on whose body we're going to find in Santa Clarita?"

"I think that's almost a given," I said to Mac. "Unfortunately, I think we're going to find the remains of Ricki. The more burning question is who the hell killed her? My best guess at this point is Roberto. The odds in a case

67

like this is almost always someone who was close to the vic. Roberto fits that description."

Sully slowed to let a red Corvette change lanes. The Vette came closer to Sully than he should have come. "I agree with Tony. Odds are Roberto is our guy but let's see how this plays out."

"I'm not so sure. There is the possibility," Mac said, "that his was a crime of opportunity; that some Adam Henry observed a cute young girl and he decided to grab her for fun and frolic. Just saying…."

Sully jumped back into the conversation. "Your boyfriend gets a promotion to detective and everyone wants in on the action." Sully's tone was friendly. He was having fun with us.

"Not everyone has the skills of an FBI agent," Mac said. "And what's the boyfriend crap? I don't go out with dicks."

"Are you two an act? If so, don't give up your day job, you'll starve."

Sully was approaching the San Fernando Valley. We were a few minutes from Santa Clarita and the crime scene.

The weather was mild with a few clouds in the sky and light wind. The wind would pick up as the day wore on. Santa Clarita was known for the wind and sudden fires. Because of the sometimes-heavy wind, there was almost always fire danger. A wind whipped fire was the most dangerous. In recent years, wind-swept fires took a toll on property and people. Nonetheless, ass holes driving the freeway would toss lit cigarettes out the car window onto the grass, or some moron would throw a firecracker out the window. That's all it took.

Because Santa Clarita was minutes from the San Fernando Valley, and half an hour (a few minutes more in traffic) from L.A., the community grew. There were some gorgeous houses in Santa Clarita including acreage and horse property. If you could afford to live in SC, the crime rate was low and housing prices were on the increase.

Sully entered the fourteen freeway, the gate way to the Antelope Valley, and minutes from where I expected to find the body of Ricki Montego Valenzuela. The question we had to ponder was who and why?

In a murder case, you start eliminating suspects by starting with those closest to the victim and working "outward." That would be spouse, siblings, close relatives, more distant relatives, neighbors, friends, enemies and so on. A prime person of interest would be the person who was last to see the vic alive.

Detectives had their work cut out for them. Even if they had a suspect, they needed to prove it and they needed to build a case. But before that could take place, they needed an autopsy report. The autopsy would indicate approximate time of death, cause of death, trauma involved in or after the killing such as rape, torture, and/or staging of the body.

If it were a "rage killing," if someone was close to the victim and she attempted to break off a relationship with the subject, he might fly into a rage and stab her numerous times or beat her to death with a hammer or even his fists. If the latter be the case, the dicks would be looking for a suspect with bruised or bandages hands. If the murder weapon were a hammer, they'd get a warrant for a suspect's house and name the hammer in the warrant. If the weapon were a knife, they'd be looking for the knife.

Sharp detectives would also get on the computer and search for suspects who had priors, (prior convictions) and had similar M.O.s, modus operandi. That is, they used the same weapon in a similar crime. For example, if a murder victim had been raped and her body "staged," placed on its back after death with legs spread apart, and the victim was stripped of all clothes, a good detective would search the computer data base for similar crimes. Next, if a suspect jumped off that data base, the investigating detectives would look at crime proximity. Did the suspect live in the general area of the victim or in the general area of the victim's place of residence? Did the suspect work in that general location? Did the suspect know or have a relationship of some kind with the victim?

Discovering a victim's body then nailing down the suspect did not happen in thirty minutes or an hour as depicted on television. Lots of leg work, finger pounding on computer keys, interviewing people. Listing suspects, eliminating suspects took time, weeks, months, sometimes years. With the advent of DNA and computer data bases, a cop's task may be daunting but criminal science made the "hunt" a bit less daunting.

Let's say a perp leaves a tire track in soft mud or snow. A composite or mold of that tire track can be lifted from the scene. There is a possibility that the tire is an unusual brand or fits only certain vehicles. Now the detectives have something to work with. The computer can tell them which tire stores handle that brand of tire, which shops in the area sell that tire. Footwork may be able to trace the tire to a shop. More leg work may pin down the subject who purchased the tire.

Tracking a suspect isn't always the fun and games you see on television. It takes hard work and dedication to nail a suspect who doesn't want to be caught. Then the work really begins. You have to build your case. For every top-notch DA and prosecuting attorney, there are a dozen attorneys who will fight with balls to the wall for their client.

We clearly observed the narrow two-lane road that was surrounded by a mountain on one side and a steep downhill slope on the right as we pulled up to the crime scene conspicuously evident by police cars, marked and unmarked; by over a dozen cops walking around with more behind the yellow crime scene tape than in front of it; by newspaper reporters; by constant chatter; and by the voice of dispatchers over the police radios. The scene was surreal. What made it a nightmare was that we were certain the body, covered by a white sheet, half concealed by thigh high grass, was that of Ricki Montego Valenzuela.

We remained behind the crime scene tape. I walked over to a sheriff dressed in a tan shirt and green pants. He looked young, in good physical shape, and annoyed.

I took the lead. I flashed my dick badge. "Detective Kano. Investigator Mackenzee and Agent Sullivan are behind me. Have they identified the body?"

He shook his head. Mr. Annoyance smiled, just a bit. "Peterson," he said. "No, but the whole world thinks it's the Valenzuela girl. What a shame. So young, so pretty."

I agreed by nodding my head. Mac and Sully remained behind me. They observed but said nothing. "Anything you can tell us?"

"Apparently, and all this is preliminary pending the coroner's report, they believe she was strangled with the belt off her jeans. They're putting out an APB for the boyfriend, Roberto Vega-Chapa. Other than the belt, her clothes are intact. Again, this is all preliminary pending an autopsy report. She doesn't appear to have been raped."

71

I thought Ricki and Roberto got into it for one reason or another and he strangled her. He had someone drive him to Santa Clarita where he dumped the body, or he "borrowed" a car and drove her here. "Does it appear she was killed here or elsewhere?"

"Don't know. They haven't said."

I nodded, thanked the sheriff and we walked halfway to the unmarked unit. We stopped to offer our thoughts. Sully said, "I'll wait for further from the coroner before I make a call. Roberto didn't have a license. If he killed her elsewhere and drove the body up here, he'd be taking one hell of a chance. Even if he had the body in the trunk he'd be gambling. If they stopped him for driving without a license, they'd impound the car. Before the car was towed, they'd inventory it. He'd be dead in the water." Sully looked at Mac. "Your guess."

Mac shook her head. "I have the right to remain silent. I'll take the right."

"Chicken shit," Sully said.

"Yeah, you're probably right. If you're forcing my hand, the boyfriend." Then she added, "Do we want to hang here to see if anyone comes up with anything else or do we want to take it back to the reservation?"

Sully jumped in. "Let's take it back to the station and review your findings on the missing money."

"Here we go again," I chided. "You and the missing millions." We headed to our home away from home.

REVISITING A CLUSTER FUCK

We stopped in Van Nuys at a fast-food drive through just off the freeway for a cold drink to take with us on the rest of the drive back to the station. Across from Teddy's Drive Up was a car dealership. In front of the dealership, annoying the hell out of people walking around the dealership, and causing a minor traffic jam because drivers were rubber necking, were about twenty protesters. Some carried signs saying "BLM, No Justice, No Peace." A couple carried signs reading "Defund the Police." Three carried signs that read "FUCK COPS."

Not all were adults. Some were kids. Some of those kids weren't even ten years old; great parenting. I know I sometimes have a big mouth and a smart mouth. But very few things political piss me off like Black Lives Matter.

"What a crock of shit." I said as we sat in the unmarked unit waiting for our turn to order. "If these assholes had a job, they probably wouldn't be out here causing shit. Every damn life matters equally. I didn't cause your problems. Half of you caused your own problems. Go to school, get an education, get a good job and help yourself to the American way of life. Why the hell is it that when your protest turns to rioting, when you start spray painting police cars, burning buildings, and breaking windows, you don't steal food, diapers, and work boots? You steal sunglasses, cell phones, televisions, and beer. If you don't break the goddamn law, you won't end up in handcuffs. If you don't break the fucking law, you won't go to jail. Don't tell me that there are more blacks behind bars than whites. I'll tell you, here are more blacks committing crimes than whites."

I turned to look out the window. Across the street some fat black bitch was holding a white cardboard sign that read, "FUCK ANYTHING WHEREING A BLUE UNIFORM." "Look at that shit. The piece of garbage can't even spell wearing. Put a nine mil in each ass cheek and you'll see how fast that shit stops."

Sully pulled up to the speaker. "What do you guys want? I'm buying."

"I'll take a medium iced tea," Mac told Sully.

I was still on my high police motorcycle. "I'll take a double shot of Seagram's." I forced a smile still looking at the asshole protesters. "I'll have a medium iced tea, too."

"Three medium ice teas and three winning lottery tickets, please."

The voice shot back, "You're five minutes too late. I gave our last winning lottery tickets to those protesters across the street. Now maybe they'll go home."

"At least someone was on my side."

Sully said, "Tell us how you really feel."

"I feel like this great Country is going to hell. We're upside fucking down. Look at what the fuck is going on in Oregon, in Washington, and in New York, to name a few. People are afraid to go out of their own homes. A couple stands on their property after so called protesters kick down a gate at a gated community and they get arrested for threatening these protesters who are now rioters in my opinion."

"Didn't the female point an AK something or another at a demonstrator?" Mac asked.

74

That was all the ammunition I needed to set me off. "In the first place, and the leftist fucking press doesn't tell you this. That fucking AK something or another wasn't loaded. In the second fucking place there is a Castle Doctrine that gives them the right to protect their own property which was threatened. And if they are convicted, and I seriously doubt any jury in the land will convict them, the governor said he'd personally see to it that any conviction is vacated. Their house is inside a gated community. These pieces of shit kicked down the gate to gain access."

Sully gave us our iced tea and headed back to the freeway onramp.

"My point is we're buckling to this shit. The defenders of their property are not the criminals. The so-called fucking protesters who kicked down the gate are the criminals. We're arresting the wrong people."

Before I had a chance to go on Mac said, "You need a great blow job!"

I damn near choked on my tea. Was this an act of desperation or was Mac as horny as I. I knew the answer. "Are you volunteering?"

Sully's face was red. He stared straight ahead at the cars in front of him on the freeway. I knew he was listening.

Mac's face was beet red. I couldn't see her face in either the rear-view mirror or the side view mirror. She wanted to play; I'd play. What the hell, I had nothing better to do. "Do you want me to climb into the back seat or do you want to wait until we get back to the station?"

"If Sully won't arrest us, start climbing."

Sully slowed down to 65. He was watching the rear-view mirror and smiling from ear to ear. "Don't forget, my wife just kicked me out of the house. I'm so horny I could cum in my slacks watching you two kids."

I climbed into the backseat. I was sure Mac wouldn't dare give me head with Sully in the car watching. I hadn't gotten comfortable when Mac unzipped my pants. Fortunately, the windows in the unmarked are heavily tinted.

Mac reached inside my pants. She rubbed me through my tighty whiteys. She licked and kissed me through my undies. Then gently, she reached inside my underwear, caressed me then kissed me. She kissed first the head of my cock then all the way down the shaft. She was working it for all she was worth. Any thought of not being able to get hard was a thing off the past. I was beyond rock hard. If there was a driver behind the wheel of the car, I didn't see him.

Suddenly, Mac stopped. "I need a drink." She grabbed her iced tea. She downed a mouthful. Next, she went back to work. I could feel the piece of ice from the tea on my bulging cock. It felt good and it didn't even begin to kill my erection. Damn, I was in ecstasy.

Mac continued to work my cock with her lips and the ice in her mouth. If Mac was trying to prove to me that she could still get me rock hard, the game was over. She won hands down; or cock up!

As Mac was licking, kissing, and sucking, I remembered back to an incident in college. An older woman, an awesome looking older woman, a great looking older blonde woman, and I had a couple of shots together in the bar that had pool tables in the backroom. The place was clean, crowded, and the pool room was filled. There were people standing on the sidelines waiting for a table.

Sharon and I kept drinking. We were, to say the least, feeling no pain. One thing led to another and I bet her twenty bucks she wouldn't blow me on the pool table. Without a second thought Sharon took my hand. She led me to the pool room. The first table was in use. Sharon pushed the balls aside. The two shooters stood watching cues in hand. I pulled myself backward onto the table. Sharon undid my belt, unzipped my pants then began to pull down my underwear. "Stop, stop. Stop. You win." I got myself back together, got off the table, paid Sharon twenty bucks. We had a few more shots then went back to my place to finish the frolicking. I'd love to have that moment back again. I'd be twenty dollars richer.

Mac didn't miss a beat except when she stopped to ask Sully, "Are you taking this all in, Sully? Too bad you don't have a camera!" Mac went back to our pleasure. My throbbing cock was three quarters of the way down her throat. With her free hand, she held my hand. She stopped long enough to whisper, "If you cum, cum in my mouth. I don't want you all over my clothes."

She sucked and swallowed until I couldn't hold back any longer. I came and came and came. Every drop went in Mac's mouth. She didn't lose a drop.

Sully pulled into the back lot at the station. He didn't say word one! The car was parked in a rear stall when I awoke. "Did you have a nice nap?"

"Damn. How long have I been asleep?"

"Since we got the drinks. Here's your iced tea?"

I was rock hard when I got out of the unit.

We climbed the stairs to the detectives' briefing room. It was clean, tidy, and ready for us to get to work. Mac took the lead. She had a white board at the head of the table divided into three sections. I couldn't wait to see what Mac had in mind.

"While the two of you were screwing around on the streets of Amity, I was hard at work trying to make heads or tails out of what we should do next. Here's my suggestion."

The air conditioning in the room was on full blast. I was beyond cool. Mac was wearing a very light blue shirt with t-shirt underneath, and apparently no bra. Her nipples were straining at the material of her shirt. That was a pleasant distraction for me.

Mac held in her hand a black marker. She wrote: SafeGuard Drivers in the first section. She wrote SafeGuard Employees in the middle section, and Attorney Jerry Kline in the final section.

"To begin, I dug up all the old reports on the case. A good chunk could be discarded as the officers and dicks did a great job interviewing those who might have been involved. Some, and those are listed at the top of the white board, deserve a second look.

"It's a long shot but perhaps the two SafeGuard employees who drove the armored truck were part of the robbery? They could have been taken out at the scene to increase the cash distribution to the remaining felons."

Mac was trying to make her case; she was trying to lay out a plan of action. So far so good.

"That said," Mac continued, "I suggest we take a look at these two players and see if they tie in at all to anyone at SafeGuard."

I looked at Sully. We both nodded.

"I think we also need to take a long hard look at the SafeGuard employees. There is a possibility that someone on the inside orchestrated this rip off. We had discussed this before and agreed it was a possibility. The detectives have interrogated those they thought might have been involved. I believe a second look is in order here too."

Sully and I look at Mac. We nodded. "Great work," Sully said.

"Finally, for now, as this is by no means the end of our digging unless we hit pay dirt, we have Tony's buddy Jerry Kline. If anyone deserves to be dissected, it's JK, esquire.

"I suggest each of us pick a curtain and we start digging. What do you think?"

There was no reason to disagree. It was a solid starting plan. Sully was the first to stake a claim. "I'll take the two guys in the armored vehicle and start digging into their backgrounds."

"I'll take Jerry the Jew." I had a strong dislike for ambulance chasers. The fact that he was a Jew made him even less palatable.

"That leaves me with the SafeGuard employees," Mac said. "I got some of the paperwork you're going to need tucked safely away in the downstairs closet. I suggest, since it's lunch time, that we adjourn for lunch then come back to work."

We agreed. I had just slid my chair away from the table when my cell rang. Lunch wasn't meant to be.

ANOTHER DAY AT THE OFFICE

Sergeant Valencia wanted us downstairs and in his office code three. We took the steps two and three at a time sans lights and siren. We entered his office without bothering to knock.

"Close the door. Have a seat." As always, his uniform was neatly pressed. His hair was trimmed and combed. His government issued boots shined. He was seated behind his desk which damn near hid the sergeant from view because files were piled high. "We have a 'situation' and APEST call out."

Very recently, Amity PD had trained a half dozen officers to take on the role equivalent to LAPD's SWAT. APEST, Amity Police Employing Special Tactics was made up of five male cops and one female member. They were highly and specifically trained in hand-to-hand combat, hostage negotiation, sharp shooting, use of deadly force, humane tactics, and dirty tricks. Their motto was: "The innocent shall survive."

"Here's what we got," Valencia said. "A black teenager walked into the First Community Savings and Loan Bank on the Boulevard. I think you all know the place. Apparently, he was by himself. He pointed a gun at a teller and had her fill a paper sack with cash. He made it just outside the bank when a unit happened by. They observed the gun. The kid observed them. He ran back in the bank. The bank has little foot traffic at this hour, but he is holding hostages and is threatening to take one female hostage with him. He's demanding a vehicle be brought to the bank with a full tank of gas and police radio.

"He maybe high, desperate, deranged or all of the above. APEST is assigned to free the hostage and get everyone out of the bank in one piece. If APEST has to take him out so be it."

"What do we know about the kid?"

"His name may be Avory. He's about 15. He's heavy set wearing blue jeans, white pull over shirt and tennis shoes. He's also wearing a blue L.A. Dodger cap. His weapon of choice appears to be a black semi-automatic handgun.

"We've got a command post set up south of and across the street from the bank. APEST is in telephone contact with the kid. Two APEST sharp shooters are on the roof across from the bank. Obviously, we rather not take the kid out. But the innocent lives come first. If we even think a hostage may go down, we'll take the kid out.

"Understand that if a black kid is killed by a white cop, all hell might break loose within a couple of thousand miles of us not to mention what might happen to Amity."

Sully jumped in. "Do we have a black sharpshooter on the team?"

"No. And black face is out of the question," Valencia quipped. "Of course, all the news outlets are out there. The crowds are swelling. If at all possible, we want the kid in one piece. But we're not risking an innocent life for the sake of some punk with a gun." Valencia drew a breath. "I want the three of you to report to the command post and to Commander Edison. Give him any and all the support you can. Questions?"

We had none. Valencia wished us luck and we were on our way.

A hostage situation is always a bitch. You never know what the perp might do. He's desperate. Couple that with the fact that today, anytime a white cop shoots a black person, the press roils up the waters. I'm a cop. I'm saying that white cops have shot blacks when they should have attempted other means to resolve the situation. That's a rarity. I am saying in damn near every shooting, black, white, or otherwise, the perp has failed to obey a lawful order by police which increased the severity of the situation.

Let's say a police officer is making contact with a suspicious person on the street. The cop asks for his identification. He takes off running down the street with cops in hot pursuit. The fleeing subject suddenly stops, turns, and points something at the pursuing cops. It could be car keys, a cell phone, a gun. The gun could be loaded with one round in the chamber. The gun could be empty. Make the call, joe public. What the fuck do you do? If he's black do you hesitate to pull the trigger? You may not go home. Had the mother fucking perp not run, the situation would never have escalated, NEVER!

Are there racist cops on the street? Absolutely. Are they few and far between? Yes. Do we need to get rid of them? Of course, and as soon as possible. But the vast majority, the very vast majority of cops are hardworking, dedicated individuals like you and me who have a mortgage payment, bills, a spouse, and kids they want to see at the end of their shift. Make no mistake about it, defund police and we are FUCKED. Spend seven days in Oregon, in San Francisco, in parts of New York then come home and tell me you want to defund the police department.

Commander Edison was an easy-going guy. He was fifty-two years old but sure the hell didn't look it. Somehow, he was happily married with three daughters and lived half an hour from the station. He almost always had a smile on his

82

face. One of his major strengths was teaching recruits and wanna-be APEST candidates. He could correct you and work with you without making you feel uncomfortable or out of place.

I knew firsthand of Commander Edison's ability to motivate newbies. Within the first month that I was kicked lose and patrolling the streets on my own, I pulled a guy over for running a red light. It was broad daylight. The guy was the only occupant in the vehicle. I ran the plate. It came back clean. So, at this point, the only offense was a traffic violation.

The guy was east bound on Berry Drive. The light was clearly red at Broad Street. It wasn't a "gimme." He ran the damn light. Technically, I was out of Amity. The light "belonged" to the Sheriff. I put out the stop. He pulled into an adjacent apartment complex parking lot.

I approached carefully. His hands were on the steering wheel until I reached the car's post where I stopped. The guy was Hispanic. He had tatts and plenty of gold around his neck. He suddenly took his right hand off the wheel. He looked back at me and said, "Amity. What do you want?"

I stayed put. I kept my eyes on both his hands. His left hand remained on the steering wheel. His right hand was flying around the car as if he were a 727. I couldn't get a close look at his eyes and I probably wasn't close enough to smell his breath. I suspected he was on something other than grass. "License, registration and proof of insurance, please." I stood my ground. I imagined his neck must be hurting by now from turning back to glance at me.

"Why?"

Most cops get irritated with Adam Henrys who like to make a difficult job more difficult. "License, registration, and proof of insurance and we'll talk about it."

Adam Henry didn't move. "Aren't we out of our jurisdiction?"

"Now I was getting pissed off. Trying to hammer home my point with a bit of humor, I said, "Make you a deal. If you can spell jurisdiction, I'll let you off without a ticket. If you can't, I get the license, registration and insurance papers without any more argument."

He looked at me and grinned. So far so good. "Jur...." He hesitated. "esdiktion." He knew he blew it. Without saying a word, he opened the glove compartment. I observed carefully taking a step and a half closer to the car. He took out what I assumed were the registration and the insurance papers. "Here." He threw them at me.

I knew better than to make a move for either the registration or the insurance papers. I let the wind blow them all over hell and the parking lot. If I even tried to catch them, and the jerk had a weapon, I was dead meat. "Want to throw your license away too?"

"You belong in Amity not Village Point."

"I belong anywhere I want to belong, sir. I can stop you anywhere in California I want to stop you." I stepped back a foot. "I'm guessing your license is suspended."

"I'm guessing I'm going to get out of this car and kick your ass into next week."

That was 422 of the penal code, a terrorist threat. When he attempted to open the door, I reached out with my left foot and kicked it closed. I took a step forward, drew my taser and leveled it at his chest. I had Adam Henry dead bang. "Next spelling test. Can you spell taser?"

Just as he said, "You know you're a real asshole," another unit pulled into the lot. It was Edison. He got out of his unit. "Everything code four, Tony?" He looked at the papers on the ground. "Looks like temper tantrum time. What's going on?"

I explained the situation to Edison. He smiled. "May I?"

"Be my guest."

Edison stepped forward. He looked at the driver. He stopped smiling. Edison looked menacing. "Put out a code 4, Tony, then call paramedics."

I looked at then Senior Officer Edison quizzically.

"I'm going to open his door, drag his ass out of the car and beat him into the ground with my night stick." S/O Edison took out his club.

Adam Henry changed his tune. He held up both hands. "Hang on man. I was only playing. I didn't mean anything. I really didn't."

"Okay" Edison said, still holding his straight stick in his right hand. "Let's play Let's Make A Deal. You get your ass out of the car like a good boy, pick up all the papers you tossed on the ground and we won't give you a littering ticket."

He was out of his car faster than Uncle Sam takes your money on pay day. He chased down most of the papers then got back in the vehicle.

Edison stepped back. "Your stop, Tony."

"Do you have a license, sir?"

He shook his head. "No. It's suspended for failure to pay child support. I have an ID card." He handed it to me.

A California ID card looks almost like a driver's license. It has the same numbers on it. It says California Identification on it instead of driver's license. I ran him. He was clean except for driving on the suspended. I handed him back his ID card. "I think we both had enough entertainment for one day. When you get home, look up jurisdiction."

The three of us shook hands and Adam Henry left the scene smiling. S/O Edison and I went to lunch. He critiqued my stop.

"Everything looked great from what I observed. The reason I rolled out to the scene was that you didn't put out a code 4. If I were you, I would have called for a back the minute Adam Henry got froggy. It's much better to be safe than sorry. Don't believe that if someone hears you put out a request for a back that you're a pussy. It means you want to live to go home so you can get some pussy!"

Commander Edison came out of the command post when he observed us. He held out his hand. "How are you, Tony? Looking to promote to APEST? We're always looking for great candidates."

I shook his hand. "I'm still working on traffic stops." I introduced him to Sully and Mac.

He introduced me to the Assistant Commander, A.C. Pollack. "Junior here," he smiled at Pollack, "wants my job so we're breaking him in like you'd break in a new car. We make sure his water and oil are checked regularly. We know he's full of gas. Most importantly, we make sure he keeps his foot lightly on the accelerator, so he gets where he's going slowly."

Pollack, with crew cut and baby-faced features, seemed embarrassed. He didn't look like he was me when I was twenty-five years old. "Nice to meet all of you."

"Tell 'em what we've got, Assistant Commander Pollack."

He stepped toward us nodding. "A black kid apparently took down the bank. He's got a small grocery bag stuffed with cash. The kid is a frightened teenager or higher than a kite or both. He has a semi- automatic handgun black in color. He started to exit the bank. A cruising unit happened by the bank as our suspect exited. He observed the unit and thought they were coming for him. Bad thinking. He went back into the bank. He has hostages. He wants a vehicle with a full tank of gas and a police radio. When he gets what he wants, he says he'll leave with a hostage and drop her off when he's certain he's not being followed.

"We have made telephone contact. As of last update, we have his first name as Avory. Our primary goal, of course, is the safety of the hostage and of everyone in the bank. Two caveats. One is that the kid is just a teenager. I know he's a teen with a gun, but he's still a teen. I'm not soft. I am human. The second caveat is this fucked up world we're dealing with today. If a white cop takes down another black, not only does Amity explode but so will cities near and far."

The four of us nodded. "That said," Edison began, "if the plan of attack were your call, what would you do?"

Pollack thought it over, briefly, very briefly. "The same thing you're doing, sir. I have sharp shooters in position, and I'd be negotiating for a safe surrender. At some point, we're going to have to make a call." He breathed a heavy sigh.

"Would you give him the car?"

"I'd bring in the car but only to get him out of the bank. Once out of the bank, the game has changed."

"How so?"

"Now we're dealing with only one hostage. We have three cops at the rear of the bank. Once he comes out the front door with the hostage, we shuttle the employees and the customers out the rear door to a waiting bus who will get the hostages out of the area.

"I'd rig the gas gauge in the car to show full. It would have a tenth of a tank of gas. The police radio would be a fake."

"Do you let him take the car with the hostage?" Edison asked.

"Of course not. One of our guys should be able to drop him if that becomes necessary."

I looked at Pollack. "If it became necessary to neutralize the sub, could you make that call?"

His eyes glazed over. His half smile disappeared. "As much as I would hate to make that call, I would. We're trained to look at it this way: We're not taking a life, we're saving lives. He called the game. We're ending it as safely as we can."

Edison's cell rang. He took the phone out of his uniform pocket. He listened. "Great. Great work. See if you can get a home address and phone number. Thanks, Charlie."

Edison put the phone away. "Good news. Charlie got a last name out of the kid. The kids from Compton. He probably took a bus here. He still won't come out. He still wants the car. He won't release any hostages. We're going to buy time and see if we can make contact with a parent or relative."

MOM LOVES HER SON, PUNK
LOVES MONEY

The situation was far from resolving itself when day turned to night. At 2045 hours, Avory Chapman refused to give himself up. He refused to release even one hostage. He was steadfast in his demand for a car with gas and a police radio. He was determined to take one hostage with him and release her only when he was sure the posse wasn't in hot pursuit.

Our progress: the negotiation team managed to track down Mom. She was in the crowded mobile command post with us. Like most moms would be in this situation, she was dazed, confused, and really loved her son. She wanted the situation to be resolved without any further harm to anyone, so did we.

Pollack made a phone call. "Listen," he began. "We've got a growing crowd out here. Some of these onlookers are relatives of the hostages in the bank. Some are bored and curious excitement seekers. Others are troublemakers. There's also the not so friendly left leaning press. I don't care how the hell you do it but push them back, way the fuck back. If this pot boils over, I don't want to deal with a secondary situation. Explain to them we're moving them back for their own safety. If that doesn't work, if you have to make arrests, bring in the bus and make arrests. If you have to kick ass, kick fucking ass. We'll deal with the consequences later. I want to resolve this situation before Avory goes off the deep end."

A hostage negotiator was on the phone with Avory. "We're willing to give you the car with gas and a police radio. We'll even let you take the money with you. We want you to let the hostages go." The negotiator was sitting in the mobile command unit, which was a converted grey hound bus, in front of the computer.

"I won't let anyone go. I want the car."

"Give a little, Avory and you'll get a lot. We need you to show us good faith. Let half a dozen hostages go. Just half a dozen."

"No way. I'm tired and hungry. I want the car."

"We'll send in a dozen pizzas. And soft drinks. Let a dozen hostages go."

"No way. It ain't going to happen."

The negotiator had one more card to play: mom. Mom said she had a good relationship with her son. She said the kid got himself into drugs when dad left. They had money problems. She said this was Avory's way of helping out mom.

That was bullshit. It was Avory's way of filling his head with fantasy. It was Avory's way of putting life out of his mind. There was no way to soften the blow. Avory was a felon digging a hole so deep he'd never shovel his way out. He was a dead man walking unless he capitulated.

The negotiator shook his head. He fingered a switch. "Talk to your son, mom."

"Avory, you need to listen to these men. You need to do what they tell you. You don't want to get hurt. You don't want to hurt anyone. You're in trouble; don't make it any worse. Please don't." She swallowed hard. "Let the people go. Let them go. Nobody is going to hurt you if you let them go." She turned to Edison and Pollack. "I'm so sorry."

Edison said, "You have absolutely nothing to be sorry for, ma'am. Avory is old enough to make his own decisions." Both Edison and Pollack knew what was next. So did Sully, Mac, and I. They had no choice but to give Avory the car.

Mom wiped tears from her eyes. "Please, please don't hurt my son. He's all I have. He's really a good boy. He just wanted to help. Don't hurt him, please."

I thought to myself, she's not a black mother, a white mother, or a Hispanic mother, she's a mother. It took three times as much money to incarcerate as it did to educate. Why weren't we building more schools, hiring more teachers, and raising teachers' salaries instead of building more prisons? When will we ever learn?

We were still crowded in the mobile command post. Avory's mom sipped a glass of water. Mom sat. Mac stood next to mom her hand on her shoulder. Commander Edison stood very close to his assistant. "Assistant Commander Pollack, this show is yours. The call, if necessary is yours. I'm here as backup. It's your game."

Pollack nodded. The stakes were life and death. Pollack turned to the negotiator. "I want to talk with Avory."

The negotiator flipped a switch. He slid the mic to Pollack. "Avory, this is Assistant Commander Pollack. You need to come out now with your hands in the air. It's over. Come out now and we'll move on from here." You could read the consternation on the Assistant Commander's face. "C'mon, Avory. Give it up. Your mom's here. She's getting sick to her stomach with fear. Work with us, Avory. Please work with us."

"Car, gas, and radio. I'll release the hostage when I'm sure you're not following me."

Pollack was not happy. There was one move to go. It was his move. Reverberating like a fucking steel ball in a pin ball machine were the words, "Please don't hurt my son."

I watched Pollack's face. The pain in his eyes was haunting. This was a nightmare that would wake him from a sound sleep for years. "Give it up, son. We'll do all we can to help you."

Assistant Commander Pollack got on his cell. "Is the car ready? Have our shooters moved to the bank building? Are the uniforms in the rear of the building ready to shuttle the hostages to the bus?" Pollack nodded after each of his questions. "Move the car into place."

"Copy that, AC."

"Are we ready at the rear of the bank building?"

"That's affirmative, sir."

"Shooter one, are you in position?"

"In position and holding, sir."

"Shooter two, are you in position?"

"Affirmative, sir. Waiting further instructions, sir."

Pollack looked over at Mac. "Escort the mom out, please. She can sit with you in a unit."

Mac nodded. Mom was in tears. Mom was shaking so badly, water spilled from the plastic cup. "Please don't hurt him. Please. He's only a child."

Mom was right on. He was only a child. A child with hostages, a child with a gun. A bullet fired by a child kills the same as if an adult pulled the trigger.

Pollack took a deep breath. He waited until Mac and mom disappeared out the mobile command post door. "Shooter one, do you know the code for the day?"

"Yes, sir."

"Shooter two, do you know the code for the day?"

"Affirmative, sir."

We observed a green Crown Victoria slick top police car rolling into place. It stopped directly in front of the bank. The cop behind the wheel killed the engine. He left the keys in the ignition. At the same time as he turned the ignition off, he stepped on a concealed switch on the floorboard high up on the floor. It was a kill switch. If Avory made it behind the wheel of the car, there was no way in hell he was going to start the car.

"Avory," Pollack said, almost pleading. "Give it up. Let the hostages go and come out with your hands in the air, son."

"Is their gas in the car?"

"As you asked."

"Is there a police radio in the car?"

"Yes." Pollack was truthful to both questions.

"I'm coming out. If I have to shoot the hostage, it's gonna' be on you."

"Shooters one and two, Elvis is in the building. I repeat, Elvis is in the building."

"That's a copy."

"Copy that."

The front door opened a crack, then a bit more, then far enough for the female hostage to be observed. She was wearing brown slacks and a tan button down top. She looked to be in her thirties. Right up against her was Avory. He had her by the neck, a gun to her right temple. He wasn't a black kid, he was a kid, a fifteen-year-old kid who didn't know what life was all about, and yet he was wise beyond his years, street wise and desperate.

Pollack was sweating. The air conditioners were running full blast in the mobile command unit. "Shooter one, do you have a fix?"

"I have a lock, sir."

"Shooter two, do you have a fix?"

"Partial, sir, partial."

Slowly Avory and the hostage walked toward the car. Six feet separated the two bodies from the bank's front door. Two dozen feet separated Avory and his female hostage from the green Crown Vic slick top police unit. "Update me on the hostages in the rear of the bank."

Instantly a voice came back. "Everyone is out and boarding the bus, sir."

Pollack breathed a sigh of relief. He was running out of time. Maybe eight steps separated Avory and his hostage from the cop car. He couldn't let Avory and the hostage get into the car. If Pollack allowed that to happen, it could well mean death for the hostage.

Seven steps and they'd be at the car. "Give it up kid. Let her go. For mom's sake, Avory. Let her go and put the gun down. Do it now, son."

Six steps. His eyes were locked on Avory, the hostage, the gun.

Five steps. Assistant Commander Pollack heard, "Please don't hurt my son. Please don't."

Four steps. "C'mon kid," Pollack said softly. "Don't throw your life away. Please don't make me do this."

Three steps. "Shooters one and two, Elvis has left the building. I repeat. Shooters one and two Elvis has left the building."

Before you heard the shots, Avory's head exploded like a goddamn pinata. The hostage screamed and ran. Avory was dead before he hit the sidewalk. He never knew what hit him.

Pollack heard, "Please don't hurt my son. Please."

A TIME TO WEEP

Mac ordered a Diet Coke. Sully ordered a scotch rock. I ordered two double shots of Seagram's. The bar was dimly lit. Off to the side was a fairly large well-lit room that housed four pool tables. All were occupied. The bar itself ran almost the entire length of the room. We were seated at a table in the quiet corner of the TAP ROOM. "Anyone hungry?"

Sully shook his head. "Maybe after a couple of drinks."

"Mac?"

"I second what Sully said. Being Triple A with a gun, I haven't seen anything like you two have, although working here the short time that I have been, I'm catching up with you guys. What I witnessed tonight is going to be with me for quite a while. It's disturbing to say the least. To watch a fifteen-year-old child do what he did, with a damn gun that he never should have had in his possession, is bad enough. To rob a bank, to hold people at gunpoint, to attempt to orchestrate an escape, as he did…. Then to try to comfort his mom…."

"That was a tough one," I offered. "At least the life of the hostage was saved. In that regard the operation was a success. It's horrific."

"Can you imagine," Sully began, "going home to your wife and kids after that and trying to act as if it was another day at the office?"

Mac jumped in. "I can't even imagine having to make the decision to take the kid out that Assistant Commander Pollack made. I'm sure he'll live with that for years to come. How horrible."

"Here's to keeping the peace," I said as we hoisted our drinks. "Sometimes the job is a bear." I downed my double. The other double was in front of me. "I've thought about trying out for Amity's new APEST. Now I'm not so sure I'd want any part of it." I kept seeing Avory's face in front of me.

Mac looked at me. "I've been offered a position at Amity."

I downed my second double. "Did you accept?"

"I've got a couple of days to make a decision. I thought maybe we'd talk about it later."

Sully smiled at Mac. "You'd make a helluva' addition to this department. Your smarts, your sense of humor, your diligence and your shapely legs are what this department needs. Can I buy you a drink?"

"I'm allergic to alcohol but thanks."

"I know," Sully said. "I'll have one for you. I meant a soft drink?"

"I'm good. Thanks."

"Tony?"

I nodded. "Sure. Thanks."

"I'm moving into a one-bedroom apartment in Glendale next week. That should be an interesting adjustment from a twenty-eight hundred square foot two story home."

"It's really over?"

"Yeah, she's as serious as a bullet in the back. We're working out visitation and finances. This is going to be murder emotionally and financially. Now I know what wops mean by divorce Italian style."

I quickly added, "A bullet to the woman's head. I can help you move."

"I'll join in."

"I may take you both up on that. Excuse me while I go to the little boy's room." Sully got up.

I really didn't want to be alone with Mac. How quickly a situation can change. In the very recent past I couldn't wait to be alone with Mac. Now I was scared. Mac smiled. Her blue eyes were soft and inviting, loving.

"You can run," she said softly. "You can't hide."

I knew Mac was right. The real bitch of the situation was that I loved Mac. I never loved a woman the way I loved Mac. We had a blast together. We belonged together. There, I said it. But in order for that to happen, I had to accept things I couldn't change. I didn't know if I was capable of that kind of acceptance. Hell, I didn't even know if Mac could still get me hard.

"How about we go back to your place later. Maybe we can sort things out?"

I had a few second to mull that over in my mind. I nodded. "Deal."

DOES PETER WANT TO COME OUT TO PLAY?

We were seated in my living room on the couch. We were separated by several feet. Mac was sipping coffee. My full attention wasn't focused on a quart bottle of Seagram's on the table in front of me. A piece of my attention was focused on Mac. I was more relaxed now, not relaxed but more relaxed. I should have been relaxed. I had enough booze in me.

My head was fucking with me. I was wondering when Mac would make a move on me. I knew she would. My question was would Peter respond? Men are funny animals. I knew the more I worried about getting a hard on the less chance there was I'd be able to get it up.

Mac pulled her feet under her, sans shoes. "Tony, this is the very last time I'm going to say this. I'm not about to grovel, even though under the proper circumstances it might be fun. My program tells me when I screw up, I have to make amends as soon as I realize I wronged someone. I didn't tell you I was born a male from the start. I should have been honest with you. I should have told you before I fell hard, very hard. Not an excuse. I was wrong, very wrong, and for that I apologize. I sincerely apologize. The Big Book of AA tells me I have to quit fighting everything and everybody but that I am nobody's doormat.

"I want our relationship to continue. I want us to be together always. I cannot be more honest than that."

I started to take the double shot in my hand. I pushed it away. Mac deserved a straight answer. I admired her honesty. One problem was that I didn't know what I wanted. That wasn't true. It was a lie. I did know what I wanted. I wanted a future with Mac. The question I had to answer was could I deal with the situation. My next words surprised me. "I want what you want, Mac. I really do. The question is can I deal with it?"

Mac looked me in the eye. She took my hand and held it in hers. She caressed my fingers. If you're willing to try to work through it, let's give it a shot."

"Speaking of shots…." I picked up the shot glass. I downed a double. I wasn't feeling any pain.

Mac slid closer. She slid her hand from my knee to my thigh. She put her hand on my crotch and rubbed me softly through my slacks. Peter wasn't home.

Mac kept rubbing me through my slacks. She stopped long enough to take off her top. She didn't take off her black bra. She looked hot, burning hot. I wanted to respond. I pressed her fingers down harder on my crotch. Mac kept rubbing, first softly then more aggressively. She unbuttoned my pants, unzipped my slacks then reached inside and caressed me through my undies. Peter walked in the house. But he apparently didn't realize someone was knocking at the door.

I hadn't stopped taking the pills that thrill. There was only one answer and I knew what that was. If Mac and I were going to go anywhere together, I had to get through this. All guys at one time or another have trouble getting hard. It could be high blood pressure, obesity, too much to drink, too tired or a combination of all of the above. In my case I kept seeing Mac as a guy.

Mac put her soft hand inside my underwear. She rubbed the tip. Peter heard the knock at the door. He was trying to decide whether or not to answer the knock. He started toward the door then backed away. Mac continued to caress me. She slid closer. Mac leaned down and pulled off my shoes. She slid my pants completely off and let them fall to the carpet. I helped her remove my underwear.

Mac pushed me onto my back. She removed her bra. Mac crawled between my legs. She licked Peter's head. "He tastes good. Mommy wants more."

Peter walked to the door. He opened it a crack. Quickly, he shut the door. He didn't recognize the caller.

Mac took Peter in her mouth. Peter peeked through the window. He pulled his head away.

"I'm enjoying this," Mac said. "Let's see how it cums out."

Mac licked and sucked from top to bottom. Her tongue found my balls. She licked my balls as she caressed Peter. She slid the tip of her finger in my ass. Most men won't admit they like that stimulation. I liked it. Mac knew it. She was licking my balls, caressing a dead Peter, and fingering my asshole. What more did Peter want?

Apparently, it wasn't enough. Peter wouldn't, couldn't didn't respond. I thought about a poem I had read, or someone had told me a long time ago. "Some relationships last forever, others peter out. Ours will last forever, Peter in or Peter out!" I had a demented mind. It fits Mac's license plate: DCZDMND.

TOMORROW IS ANOTHER DAY

Mac gave Peter one final attempt at resuscitation. She bit down gently on his head. At the same time, she buried a finger in my ass, with her free hand she reached up and squeezed my nipple, first gently then with urgency. Peter slammed the door and walked into the living room probably to watch TV.

"Listen, it's not a big deal…."

"Bad choice of words. Try again." What the hell could I do in a situation like this? It was embarrassing, to say the least. I was used to being in control.

"We'll work through this too."

"It's not you, it's me."

"It's both of us, Tony. In your mind, you're picturing me one way.   That's   keeping   your…   keeping your…ugh…performance skills…ugh…below par."

"Below par. Hell, I didn't even make it to the green."

"So what?" Mac smiled. Her head was on my chest. "No hole in one tonight. Look at the fun we're going to have getting us back in the saddle."

I saw that mischievous twinkle in Mac's baby blues. "Have you ever had a strap on in your ass?" She held up her hand to stop my response. "It's getting late. Let's go to bed. Tomorrow is another day."

We went to bed. Mac fell asleep. It was no wonder I tossed and turned. I finally fell asleep. I dreamed of Mac. She had on several faces. Need I say more? I even dreamed of Judge

Karma warning me that things aren't always as they appear. I awoke; I fell back asleep. I awoke. I looked at Mac next to me. So peaceful, so beautiful. I reached down to feel Peter. He was hard. I had to piss.

THREE DAYS LATER, A
PRELIMINARY AUTOPSY REPORT

The only situation that wouldn't get hard was my damn cock. Chasing the cash was becoming a pain in the ass. We were digging and re-digging into interviews of persons of interest. We were creating persons of interest. We were talking to detectives who did the initial interviews of witnesses. We were tracking detectives who did follow-ups. We were coming up broke.

Ricki's boyfriend turned himself in accompanied by an attorney for whom someone footed the bill. The attorney was from out of town and came at an expense Roberto Vega-Chapa sure the hell couldn't afford; interesting to say the least. His name was Martin Edleman. He probably attended the same fucking synagogue as Jerry Kline.

Roberto was released following questioning to no one's surprise. The DA had no grounds to hold Roberto. This was going to turn out to be a shame. Although Roberto had told us he would take a polygraph, Edleman advised to decline the test. Roberto now declined.

Ricki's preliminary autopsy report showed strangulation at the hand of another. The murder weapon was her own thin black belt from her pants. It had been wrapped around her neck and tighten and tighten and tighten until she stopped breathing. Preliminarily there was no evidence of drugs or alcohol in her system; NONE! There were bruises on her wrists, as if she were forcibly restrained but that was the extent of any other marks on her body. She had not been robbed. She had not been raped. She WAS a virgin.

Mac, Sully, and I sat around a beaten up old wooden table in the unoccupied reserve office. I tossed the report in the middle of the table. "Can you believe that shit? Someone, give me a goddamn motive."

Sully came up to bat first. "She seriously pissed someone off or she wouldn't put out for Roberto. His frustration got the better of him and he exploded. Rage ala O.J."

"A possibility," I countered. "That would mean he would have had to borrow a vehicle to transport her."

Sully asked, "Was she killed at the scene?"

"The medical examiner isn't sure yet. He thinks so." I looked at Mac. "You can play in this game."

"I agree. It's most likely Roberto. Sully could be right on. The kid was probably sick of hand jobs and maybe a blow job or two. He wanted in her pants." Mac smiled. She looked at Sully. "When you were Roberto's age, did a hand job satisfy you? Did even a blow job keep you cooled down?"

Without thinking I said, "Sully saved himself for his wedding night." The second those words came out of my mouth I said, "Sorry Sully."

"I refuse to answer on the ground that the answer might show how shy and reserved I was as a teen." Sully looked at me. "You're close, detective. Actually, the first person I had sex with was my wife, before we were married. She's the only person I've had sex with."

Mac looked at me. "There is no way I'm going to ask Tony that question. Our mission is to find out what motivated Roberto to kill Ricki. If we can do that, we can seriously assist the investigating dicks."

106

"Hell, Mac, if we can do that, we'll solve the fucking case for them."

Sully said, "I'd like to know who foot the bill for the kid's mouthpiece. Judging from the house they occupy, the car they drive, the clothes they wear, there ain't much money left over at the end of the month."

"Let's take a look at Roberto," I suggested. "We know he's a good student. We know his dad works. We know Ricki was his steady girlfriend. He has no record. He's well liked. He attends church regularly. His teachers say he's respectful and friendly. His attendance record is excellent. He's involved in after school activities. No blemish on his school record. He apparently doesn't smoke. If he drinks, it's negligible. Anyone else want to chip in?"

"Yeah," Mac said. "A stiff cock has no conscience. I'm telling you; the kid was sick and tired of not getting any. He wanted in Ricki's pants and finally had enough of being denied. He probably went off the deep end. She told him to take a hike and he killed her. Hell, he might have had the belt off her pants before he ever thought of putting it around her neck."

"I won't argue with you," Sully said. "Now all we have to do is prove it."

It was getting near lunch time. There wasn't much we could do with Ricki's killing at the moment. We could go back to looking at the money. Before I could say anything to Mac or Sully, Rolando called me. The conversation was one sided. It was short, sweet and to the point. After I hung up, I turned to my partners. "We've inherited more work."

"And that would be…...?" Sully asked.

"And that would be this case. It's now ours. I have no idea why, but per Rolando, it's our case."

"Trial by fucking fire," I said.

"We didn't have much else to do anyway," Mac smiled. "Patrol, looking for stolen cash, digging into a homicide."

I cut in. "A homicide that's practically solved itself. A couple of days and this one should be in the history books. It wouldn't surprise me if Roberto and his high-priced Jew attorney walked into the station later today and copped a plea." I was getting hungry and thirsty.

"While we're talking about Jew attorneys, I'd like to dig into Jerry Kline's background. I'd like to follow JK, Esquire and see where his fucking Ferrari takes us. What do you think?"

"I need to break away for about an hour and a half sometime today. I need to run up to Glendale to sign a lease on my apartment." Sully looked sad. "We do have some loose ends to tie up first. We still have a few interviews left."

"How about we break for lunch? After lunch Sully can jump on the freeway, take care of his business, then meet us back at the station. While he's taking care of personal business on the taxpayer's dime," I kidded, "we can start tying up loose ends." Then I added, "I'm starting to enjoy this more than patrol."

"I think I'll let you two kids go to lunch. I'm going to grab a bite before or after I sign the lease. Then I'll get back to the station. I'll make it as quick as I can.

"Hey buddy, would you like company?"

Sully shook his head. "Thanks friend. I'm good. Just one more adjustment in the scheme of life. I'll adjust. Had I seen it coming, I might have handled it differently. I never saw it coming. All the time I wasn't home, I guess she couldn't take it anymore. She and I talked. There is someone else. That hurts but I guess I asked for it. The divorce, she says, will be as friendly as a divorce can be. Like the man said, she'll get the elevator, I'll get the shaft. The girls, and making ends meet will be tricky. Maybe when we find the stolen cash, I'll help myself to a reward."

LUNCH WITH MAC

Mac and I drove out of the city to a diner called Black Jack's Gamble. Judging by the crowded parking lot, Jack's gamble paid off. The story behind the name was that Jack liked to play poker and he also liked to play the ponies. According to the story, Jack won the diner in a poker game.

Mac and I walked into the diner. The hostess, dressed as the ace of spades, escorted us to a table. The walls were decorated with classic cars and pictures of Jack either behind the wheel of those cars or standing in front of those beauties. Other pictures showed Jack raking in chips at the poker table and standing at the winner's window at the track collecting his winnings.

"I'd like to open a place like this when I retire. I'd call it The Cop Shop. The walls would depict our cops and other first responders. The menu would be made up from the penal code. For example, a 211 p.c. (robbery) might be a sausage sandwich with side salad. A 273.5 p.c. (spousal abuse) would be a chef's salad. A 422 p.c. (terrorist threat) would be a chicken plate, and so on."

Before I could continue my creative assault, the waitress came over. She handed us menus, took our drink order then took a deck of cards from her apron. "Pick a card. Jack said he'd be over to the table when he gets a chance. He said, if your card is higher than his, he buys. If he wins, you pay double. The money goes to the families of fallen officers." The server was dressed as the seven of diamonds.

Mac picked a card. She picked the ten of clubs. When the waitress walked away, Mac asked, "Have you given any thought to us?"

"I haven't given much thought to anything else."

We were seated across from one another. I felt Mac's bare foot between my legs. "You're full of shit. You probably think of everything but."

"Not true. I've been thinking a lot about the cases. I've been worried about Sully. But I have been thinking a lot about us. I'm still confused." I hesitated long enough for the queen of clubs to come by and drop off our drink orders and take our food order. I took a sip of ice coffee.

"Your program tells you one day at a time, one thing at a time. Your program teaches you do the foot work and let God handle the results. My first thought is to be able to get it up when we're screwing around."

Mac didn't hesitate to scold me. "You don't hear me complaining. That's numero uno. Next, we'll work that out. That's my promise to you." Finally, she pointed to my crotch, "I'm getting a...a...a rise out of you, I can feel it."

I was getting a bit hard. But I should have been rock hard.

"How about we go to your place after work. I'll throw something together or pick up take out. Maybe we can watch a ballgame. I'll pitch and you can take a couple of swings. I haven't changed my panties in three days. That should get you going."

It did. Picturing Mac's dirty panties, her toes dancing between my thighs, images of the recent past, stirred Peter. Hopefully, it was the start of things to come.

As we were about to leave, Blackjack came over to the table. He was dressed as a blackjack with a patch over his eye. I introduced him to Mac. "The queen of hearts," the tall, slightly overweight gambler said. "A very beautiful queen of hearts."

"Thank you, kind sir. I like your establishment."

Jack nodded. "Sometimes gambling pays off. Not always, not often, but when it does, the rewards are sweet."

Mac looked at me. She raised her eyebrows and smiled. Her foot never left my crotch.

From Jack's pocket came a deck of playing cards. The back of each card pictured a black and white Crown Victoria police unit. The shield on the unit's door read Black Jack's Police Department. The motto over the rear quarter panel read: "TO SERVE UNTIL YOU'RE STOMACH'S FULL." I loved it.

Jack plucked a two of diamonds from his deck. "Lunch is on me and goes to the families of the fallen, my friend."

Mac and I each pulled out a twenty and handed it to Blackjack. I dropped an additional ten on the table for the seven of diamonds who was not only a damned attractive card, but also an excellent server.

MORE SAD SURPRISES

We reconvened at the station in the same meeting room. I asked Sully, "How'd it go?"

Sully sat down. His tie was loosened, the top button of his blue shirt was undone. He looked annoyed. "As good as can be expected under the circumstances, I guess." Then he threw in, "As bad as things are for me right now, I've got to put up with you two." Sully forced a smile.

What Sully didn't know, what Mac didn't know, what I didn't know was that "things" were going to get worse, a hell of a lot worse and even more complex and confusing.

Mac suggested we start digging into the armored car heist as she had outlined it. We agreed. Before we got to reviewing our respective tasks, my cell rang. It was the watch commander. I listened. What the WC had to say was quick and to the point. "Holy shit," I said into the phone. "You've got to be kidding."

The second I hung up two voices came at me from opposite angles. "What?"

"Roberto hung himself in his parents' garage."

"My God," was Mac's reaction.

"That wraps that one up. Roberto knew we were closing in on him for the murder of Ricki, so he did himself."

"Sounds like it."

I had to agree. I shook my head. What a waste of two young lives, I thought. But it made sense. He had an attorney, so Roberto knew he was in deep shit. His attorney probably

113

advised Roberto that he'd try to cut a deal but no matter what, Roberto was going to do time. Roberto was a juvenile. Under today's rules, with today's liberal courts, no way in hell would Roberto be sentenced to other than Camp Snoopy as the incarcerated gang bangers called it. He'd be out in a couple of years. So why the rope around his neck?

I had no doubt that Roberto was Ricki's killer. Nothing else fit, although we really hadn't looked hard at anything else. As a matter of fact, we really hadn't looked at anything else period.

"I want to do some follow up on Ricki. I want to know who she was last with prior to the killing, what she was doing and anything else that might solidify Roberto as the killer. Roberto may have put a noose around his neck, but I don't want to put a sheet over him until we've thoroughly vetted Ricki and Roberto. Tomorrow I want to visit with Roberto's parents."

Sully came out swinging. "Do you have any doubt that Roberto is the killer? Give a guy a detective badge, and he thinks he's Columbo."

"Who the hell is Columbo?" Mac asked.

The only reason I knew was because I watched the reruns occasionally. "I want to be thorough. I want to exhaust all possibilities. If you guys want to start unpacking the armored car heist, I'm going to call Ricki's mom and see what she can give me." I took a note pad out of my pocket and retrieved Ricki's mom's phone number. I called. She answered on the third ring. I took copious notes.

Twenty minutes later, when I hung up, I had a few phone numbers of Ricki's girlfriends. Other than those numbers, I had a handful of nothing.

Since I had nothing else to follow up on, and while Sully and Mac were digging deeper into the money grab, I called Ricki's female friends.

DIG UNTIL YOU HIT BOTTOM

I spent two hours seventeen minutes talking to Ricki's girlfriends on the phone. The day Ricki died she spent time with three of those five friends. Before noon, the day she died she had a soda with Terry Grover on the front stoop of Terry's house. At twelve thirty their friend Fran Stevanson joined the two on Terry's front stoop. According to both girls with whom I spoke, Ricki left alone at approximately one in the afternoon.

The meeting that interested me most was Ricki's meeting with friend Cassie Toya. According to Cassie, Ricki lived four and a half blocks from her. Cassie stated to me that Ricki called her and asked her if she wanted to go to church with her. Ricki normally went to church with her family and Roberto on Sunday. Occasionally, very occasionally she attends a service during the week. This day offered was one of those occasions.

Cassie agreed. At two forty-five, Ricki appeared at Cassie's door. They walked three streets to the Church of All Faiths. Cassie and Ricki entered the church together. Cassie took a seat in the pew. Ricki walked over to the confessional.

They departed the church fifteen minutes later. From the church, they walked back to Cassie's house. Ricki left Cassie at her house as Cassie had to baby sit, and Ricki had a tutoring appointment at her house. The student was an eight-year-old boy who she had been tutoring in Spanish for nearly a year.

The nearly two and a half hours I spent on the phone gained me zilch. I wanted to talk with the priest Ricki visited. I bet my last bottle of Seagram's, and the hard-on I couldn't

116

achieve with Mac, that the visit to the priest would gain me naught.

Then a thought hit me. Mac learned in AA that God sometimes worked in strange and mysterious ways. The priest didn't know me from a fucking Chinese fortune cookie. Maybe I'd talk with the priest about my problems with Mac.

A SECOND CHANCE TO GET IT UP

Mac stopped off and picked up Chinese food to go, then drove to my place. We sat on the couch eating Chinese, watching the Dodger game, which I didn't bet on, and talking about things personal. The quart bottle of Seagram's was new when I cracked it open. I was working on my fifth shot.

"I keep this up," I said to Mac as I downed that fifth shot, "I may join you in AA."

"You don't listen well. It's got nothing to do with how much you drink. It's got to do with what happens to you when you take a drink. Winston Churchill was a heavy drinker, but he could stop when he wanted to. I've watched you. You drink a lot, but you can stop when you want to. The doctor's opinion in the Alcoholics Anonymous Big Book says we alcoholics are bodily and mentally different from our fellows; that we have an allergy. The minute we take one drink, a phenomenon of craving sets up and we have to have another. I don't think you have that allergy."

The sound was muted on the television. I could see the screen clearly. There was no score in the top of the fifth with the Mets batting. The Mets had runners at the corners with one out.

Mac picked up the empty food containers. She dumped them in the trash. She took a Coke out of the fridge. When she sat back down on the couch, she sat close. She took a long sip then set the bottle on the table in front of her. She placed her hand on my inner thigh. "Batter up."

She was driving me crazy with these innuendos. There was enough pressure on me. I couldn't ignore Mac's come-on. I

118

fondled her ass. Her hand found Peter. She stroked him. He started to rise. I ran my hand inside the waistband of Mac's slacks. I found her panties. Those damn panties were a turn on.

Suddenly Mac stopped stroking me. I hadn't noticed but apparently when Mac got the Coke out of the refrigerator, she also brought a paper bag with her. It was sitting on the table next to the Coke bottle.

"Close your eyes."

"What?"

"Damn it! I said close your eyes. Don't you damn listen?"

Peter responded positively to Mac's stern voice. "I need one more drink." I hurriedly poured myself another shot. I was oblivious to the fact the on a long double the Mets scored two runs. I didn't give a mad fuck. I had no money on the game, and if I did, it's only money!

"Close you damn eyes. Now!"

I did as ordered. Peter was still misbehaving in a good way. Maybe, maybe I was over the hump; no pun intended. I heard the crinkle sound of Mac reaching into her bag of tricks. The rustling noise faded, then stopped. I was still excited; Peter was still hard!

I sensed her moving closer. I could smell her perfume. She leaned forward. "Here." She put a blindfold over my face. "Can you see anything?"

"Sometimes," I said, "it's easier to see the light when you're in the dark. I can't see shit."

"That's good. Put your hands out in front of you. Do it now, do it fast."

Again, I did as ordered. Peter liked Mac's tone, her orders, the blindfold.

I felt something cold against my wrists. Mac slapped handcuffs on my wrists. I was now blindfolded and cuffed. I was damn near helpless. I was excited. The best was yet to come.

While Mac was screwing around with the blindfold and the handcuffs, she had wiggled out of her slacks. I knew that because she let me feel her slacks. Next, she let me touch her blouse.

"Before we continue, I'm sitting here in a black bra and pink panties that I've been wearing for three straight days, you're going to need another shot." Mac poured it for me. She held it under my nose. I opened my mouth and tilted my head back. As I swallowed the shot, Mac said, "Look out teeth, look out gums, look out stomach, here it comes." The she added, "Let the games begin."

Mac managed to get me out of my pants with a little help from me, very little help. Blindfolded and handcuffed makes it very difficult to take one's own pants off. We managed that minor miracle in short order.

I could feel Peter straining against my briefs. Good boy, I thought. Very good boy. I was wondering what was next in Mac's bag of tricks. I didn't have long to wait.

"I'm sliding out of those filthy pink panties that have the scent of me, my pussy, my cum, even my pee on them." I could hear the sound of the panties sliding off Mac's ass, her legs, her feet. I had a clear picture of those panties coming off Mac's tight ass. I felt Mac straddling my leg. "Sniff this, bitch." She held the panties under my nose. I inhaled deeply. Peter liked the scent. He loved the scent.

"Lick them, bitch. Lick that filthy crotch." I didn't resist. I didn't want to resist. "Can you smell my pussy?"

"Yes, ma'am." I was getting into this. I was liking it. So was Peter.

"Lick my piss off the crotch of my pink filthy panties." Mac held them as I sniffed and licked, licked and sniffed.

"You are now my bitch. Is that clear?"

"Yes, ma'am."

"Fuck this ma'am crap, bitch. From here on out it's mistress. Is that very clear?"

"Yes, mistress. That's very clear mistress."

"Good bitch. You've earned a reward. Hold these." Mac handed me her very dirty pink panties. Even with handcuffs on I was able to fondle those panties. I held them up to my nose. I sniffed them. I licked the crotch. I tasted Mac.

"Open your damn mouth, bitch boy. You've earned another shot." Of course, I did as I was told. I felt Mac's hands near my thighs. I expected her to caress Peter, who was dying to get out from inside my briefs. She didn't touch Peter. "Scoot your ass up, bitch boy. Now."

I lifted my butt off the couch.

Mac slid my underwear off. I was wearing a button-down shirt, shoes, socks, t-shirt, and nothing else. "Let's get those shoes off, bitch boy. Now the socks." As Mac finished sliding my socks off, she suddenly snatched her panties from me.

I was naked except for my button-down shirt and t-shirt. Unless Mac cut it, with handcuffs on, the shirts weren't coming off. Mac had other ideas.

I felt her reach out and touch Peter's head, softly, lovingly. "What a good little bitch. Peter is growing. He's almost as large as my clit." Suddenly Mac grabbed her filthy panties from under my nose. "You want these so badly bitch boy, you're going to get them. Oh, you are going to get mistresses' panties, mommy's dirty, dirty panties."

"Tell mistress what it is you want, bitch boy. Go ahead, tell mistress."

"I want your panties, mistress."

"Say, "Please mistress, can I have your panties?" Say it."

"Oh mistress, may I have your panties, please, please, mistress?"

"Why do you want my panties, bitch boy?"

"Because they have my mistress's scent on them. Her cum, her pee, her…."

"Your reward for being such a good little bitch boy is mommy's panties. Scoot your ass up off the couch for mistress. That's a good little bitch boy."

I felt something crawling up both legs. It was soft and nylon. Instinctively, I knew Mac was sliding her filthy pink panties over my ass.

"Now bitch boy, you have what you've wanted for such a long time. Don't you, bitch boy? Don't you?"

"Yes, mistress."

"And what do you say to your mistress for giving you such a present?"

"Thank you, mistress. Thank you so much, mistress."

"What are you going to do with mistresses' panties?"

"I'm going to cherish them, mistress. I'm going to…."

Mac leaned over and patted Peter on his tip through my pink panties. Peter was rock hard.

"Mistress is so proud of her little bitch boy. So proud. You can't forget that your mistress is the boss." She slapped me hard across the face. The open-handed slap stung. "That, bitch boy, is so you don't forget that mistress is the boss. Mistress is in charge, always and forever. Is that clear?"

"Yes, mistress."

"Mistress wants you to touch yourself through your panties. Do it now."

I did exactly as I was told. I was excited beyond words. Mac could see Peter's love of the game.

"You've earned another shot, bitch boy. Then bitch boy will thank mistress for her gift. Is that clear?"

"Yes, mistress. That's crystal clear, mistress."

"And what, you sorry little bitch, are you going to do to please mistress?"

"Absolutely anything mistress wants me to do for her. Anything, mistress. I love my mistress. Peter loves his mistress."

"Mistress wants you to get your sorry ass off the couch. Mistress wants you on all fours on the floor at mistresses' feet code three."

Handcuffs and all, I was on the carpeted floor at my mistresses' feet immediately.

"Take off my shoes, bitch boy. Suck and lick my toes, one foot at a time."

Sucking toes wasn't my "thing." Doing as I was ordered, so it seems, was my "thing," or at least one of them. I cupped mistresses' right foot in my hands the best I could while wearing handcuffs. I started with mistresses' big toe. I licked and sucked and sucked and licked. I think what made me rock hard was that mistress was forcing me to do something I didn't want to do.

"Don't stop you little bitch toe sucker. Your mistress likes that. You might get a reward." Mistress looked down at me. "I see from the bulge in your panties that you're enjoying my toes. Don't stop licking and don't stop sucking." Mistress kicked me in the side with her bare foot.

"Thank you, mistress."

"You're welcome, bitch boy. Now start on the other foot. You are a fast learner. Now slowly, very slowly, very gently, lick up my leg."

I immediately did as I was told.

"Higher, higher. Now go down to the other leg to the ankle and lick your way up, you pathetic piece of manhood. That's a good little bitch. Now between mistresses' legs. Lick my pussy. Nibble on my cunt. That's a good little bitch. She how hard my clitty gets when you lick it right. My clitty is larger than your pathetic dick." Mistress laughed. "That feels good. Get your tongue in there deeper, deeper, yes like that. Mistress is feeling good. You may earn your reward."

Peter was straining against my pink panties. Mistress was pleased. "You're getting mistress wet. Mistress likes that. Give me your hands, loser."

I picked my head up. I didn't want to. I was enjoying my feast. Mistress grabbed both my hands. She quickly undid the handcuffs and tossed them on the carpet behind the couch. "Don't you dare touch that mask, bitch!" Mistress slapped me across the face again with an open hand. It stung. "You've earned a reward. Head back, mouth open." Mistress poured a shot down my throat. It heightened my sense of pleasure.

"Take off your panties."

I did.

"Rub yourself with your panties."

I did.

Mistress grabbed the panties from me. She threw them near where the handcuffs landed. Mistress lay back with her head on the arm of the couch. Her legs were open, and her arms told me to come to her.

I did.

"I want you inside me, you little bitch. Let me see you get harder than mistresses' clitty."

I slid between mistresses' legs. I felt the moistness, the wetness as Peter ventured inside mistress. I put my hands under mistresses' tight ass. I pulled mistress close. Peter died a sudden death. He wilted like a flower in winter. He went to sleep like a sedated dog. I thought I was going to die on the spot, or on top of mistress.

CHASING THE MONEY

While Sully dug deep into the two armored car drivers, Mac took a whack at any SafeGuard employee who deserved a second look. I, in the meantime, took a swing at my second favorite pastime: Jerry Kline. I found an available laptop, commandeered an empty office then went to work. That was easier said than done.

I kept thinking about Mac. Not being able to finish what I started was not only embarrassing it was painful emotionally. Peter had been doing so well until it came time to throw the first pitch; he balked!

I enjoyed the hell out of Mac's B and D games. Obviously, judging by how wet she got, she enjoyed it too. I was sicker than I thought but I fooled the department shrink twice.

Mac's AA program taught her that if something or someone was renting space in your head and you didn't like it, raise the rent, and evict them. Mac being in my head I could deal with. Not being able to maintain a hard-on was a different story. To date, that story had a very unhappy ending. Being alone with my thoughts put me in a bad neighborhood, a very bad neighborhood. I was about to take it out on Jerry Kline.

Jerry Kline liked the limelight. The Harvard Law School graduate was a popular student. He came from wealth. His dad was a criminal defense attorney, as was his mom. They had not only earned a small fortune, but they inherited a larger fortune. According to my research, Jerry wanted for nothing. He donated to charities. His favorite charity was St Jude's. He was also an animal lover and donated to all sorts of animal charities. I was an animal lover. Jerry scored a point or two with me. The question that had to come to mind was, if he had all that money, why would he get involved in a risky heist? The answer simple: he wouldn't.

I ran him every which way. The guy was clean. He hadn't even gotten a ticket in years until I came along; or I should say Lancaster's finest came along.

Jerry Kline was divorced without kids. He was too damn clean for my liking. I kept digging. He was on the board of an import business. He imported high end cars. Cars like his Ferrari. As Sully had intimated, this could be one hell of a way to launder dirty money: armored car dirty money. That made no sense.

I ran his credit with the big three. All his credit scores were above eight hundred. His offices were in Beverly Hills, Woodland Hills, and Agoura Hills. My guess was he liked hills. My best guess was that I was barking up the wrong law firm.

I sat. I thought. I didn't think any more about JK; I thought about Mac and my inability to keep it hard. All those freakin' pills I took daily. I wanted a refund. Mac said fear meant Face Everything and Recover or Fuck Everything and Run. I wanted to face everything and recover. But how? I was about to find out.

WHAT THE FUCK DO I DO, ROCKY?

I decided to take a break. I needed to talk with Rocky. I drove to the cemetery. I placed Rocky's usual gift from me, a box of Marlboro cigarettes, on his headstone. I got on my knees. "Hey, buddy. How's it going? I need some help here with Mac. I don't know what the hell to do."

Mac's AA program taught her to write out problems; that helped her to focus. She was also taught to talk "issues" over with a sponsor or some other tight-lipped person. Rocky sure the shit was tight lipped. Talking about it out loud might be therapeutic.

"Listen, buddy, I love her.... She's not who I thought she was. I'm having man problems. What the hell should I do?"

A voice said, "If four people are coming at you with guns, and you figure you're about to die, don't freeze. Make a decision and act. At least you might be able to take one or two of them with you. So, if it were me, I'd make a decision and live with that decision. Either go full speed ahead and do everything in your power to make it work or tell Mac it's over and move on. Mac would tell you, let go, let God. Remember, you're not alone in this. Mac is part of this, and Mac has issues too. Besides, for some dumb reason she loves your ugly ass. I'm not about to tell you what to do but if it were me, I'd.... Sorry buddy, that's strictly your decision."

I stood up. I rubbed Rocky's bracelet. "Take care, buddy. Rest well. I'll see you soon."

A GATHERING OF THE MINDS

I drove back to the station. It was eleven o'clock. Damn near lunch time. I walked to the reserves' "office." Mac and Sully appeared hard at work shuffling papers. "Good morning," Mac said. "Nice of you to join us."

I nodded. "Don't give me too much shit. I've been hard at work. I dissected Jerry the Jew. I've been pounding the computer and I've been to the library. You can cross the rich ambulance chaser from the list. As much as I hate to admit it, JK ain't our boy."

"I'm finishing up on the armored truck drivers. I talked to their supervisors. I had employment files sent over. I read through those files. They're not who we're looking for. To round out my morning, Amy asked me if I could get my ass out of the house by this weekend. I guess she wants to play house."

"I've got nothing going this weekend. I can help you move."

"Put me on that short list too." Mac said. She looked at me and smiled. I was thinking she was telling me don't let last night bother you. We're going to work through it. Male ego, right? Rocky told me to make a decision. I was determined to take his advice.

"How far have you gotten with the SafeGuard employees?" I asked Mac.

"I have files stacked higher than a 747 trying to land at LAX in the fog. I'm weeding them out one at a time. I'm looking for any connection of any kind. So far zilch."

"I'm going to take a break from the money chase. I'm going to drive over to Ricki's place and talk to mom. Then I want to go over to Roberto's house and see if mom and dad are around. As piss poor as the timing might be, I want to dig deeper. I want to search cell phones and computers. I doubt mom and dad will have a problem with that."

Mac said, "I'm going to stay here and keep digging. If I leave the reservation to drive over to SafeGuard, I'll let you know."

Sully said, "I'll tag along with Dick Tracy. Maybe he can teach me the art of investigation."

THE ELECTRONIC AGE

On the drive over to Ricki's place, I listened to Sully vent about his failed marriage. Sully wasn't the only one deep in thought. "I'm going to come on over to Amity if they'll have me. I've had more than enough of pushing papers for the Feds."

"Excellent. Come over here and push paper for Amity. Sounds fair to me."

"At least I have you to mess with."

"I was thinking of joining the Feds so I could distance myself from you."

"Not to change the subject, but what's you're thinking on Ricki and Roberto?"

I could see Sully looking at me out of the corner of his eye. "We've been over this ground before. For whatever reason, Roberto killed Ricki. He took himself out of the picture when he realized we were closing in on him."

I shook my head up and down. "Most likely. But I want to be thorough. This one needs to be tied up tight. Two kids are involved."

We parked down the street from Ricki's house. Several cars were at the curb. My guess was friends and relatives were at the house to support mom. We walked to the door. Sully knocked. A neighbor invited us in, walked us to the living room and pointed to mom. Half a dozen people were in the small, clean living room. Sully and walked over to Mrs. Montego Valenzuela. We showed our badges and said our introductions. We extended our condolences. "Is there somewhere we can talk in private? It should only take a few minutes."

Mrs. Montego Valenzuela nodded. She said something to another lady in Spanish then she led us to the bedroom. The bedroom was also neat, tidy, and spotless. "What can I do to help you?"

"We're sorry to do this at such a bad time. I apologize for that. But the best time to do this is when things are fresh in everyone's mind."

We were invited to sit down on the edge of the bed. We said we'd stand. "Is there anything you can think of anything at all, maybe something you remembered since the detectives last talked with you, that might help us. We're trying to put all the pieces together."

"I told the other detectives everything I could think of." She had a tissue in her hand. Mrs. Montego Valenzuela dabbed at her eyes. They were red. Obviously; she had been crying. "It's hard to me to believe Roberto would have killed her. I can't understand that."

Sully stepped closer to Ricki's mom. "I can't understand what you're going through. I can assure you we are going to do everything we can to sort this all out."

I quickly asked, "Did Ricki have a computer?"

"She has a laptop."

"We'd like to take it to the station and go through it. It may help us with the investigation. Would that be okay with you?"

She nodded. "I'll write down the passwords. I'll be right back."

133

Mrs. Montego Valenzuela returned with the laptop. Taped to it was a piece of paper with the codes we needed to access the computer and any useful information that might be in it. We escorted Ricki's mom back to the living room and said our goodbyes. The next stop was Roberto's house.

ROBERTO, ROBERTO, ROBERTO

The Vega-Chapa's were alone in the house. They both came to the door when I knocked. I made the introductions, offered our sincere condolences, and explained to mom and dad why we were paying a visit at such a bad time. We followed the Vega-Chapa's into the living room.

"Have a seat. Can I get you something drink? Coffee, tea, a soft drink?"

We declined. Sully and I wanted to get this finished as quickly as possible. The situation was awkward for all. I apologized for the questions I was about to ask. "Do you have any idea why Roberto did what he did?" I couldn't bring myself to say hung himself.

Mom and dad shook their heads at the same time. Mom said, "He couldn't handle losing Ricki. He couldn't deal with it. He loved her so much. He really, really loved her."

Dad quickly added, "I know what you think. I read the papers. I listen to the talk at the shop. I guarantee you Roberto didn't kill Ricki. I guarantee it. He loved her. He really loved her. My hand to God, sir. Roberto did not kill Ricki."

This wasn't going to get us anywhere. The questioning could be reserved for another day. "Can we take a quick look in Roberto's room?"

Mom and dad led us to Roberto's tiny bedroom. It was small but clean. The single bed was tucked away in the far corner. A bureau stood against the opposite wall. Three framed pictures of Ricki were on the bureau. Certificates, some framed, earned by Roberto for academic and sport

135

achievements were on the wall above his bed. His laptop was on a small desk by the window. I wasn't about to do a thorough search. We could do that later if necessary. The first cops on scene likely didn't search the room. I finished looking around. Sully looked at me. He raised his eyebrows. I looked at dad, then mom. They waited for me to finish in silence.

"We'd like to take Roberto's computer and his cell phone if that's alright? We want to see if there is anything in either that might help with the investigation."

Dad said, "That's fine."

"Roberto and some friends would meet at Kevin Duffmann's house a couple of times a month. Are you aware of that?"

"Yes," Mrs. Vega-Chapa responded. "The group would participate in church activities, sometimes design volunteer programs, sometimes have a choir practice."

"Do you know when those meetings started?"

Mrs. Vega-Chapa thought for several seconds. "About three years ago. It was suggested by Father Patrick Strayhan at the Church of All Faiths, and then it built up over time with the help of Kevin Duffmann, whose house they met at. Then Mrs. Vega-Chapa added, "Both those kids were great kids. They weren't lazy and uncaring like too many kids are today. They understood that it took hard work to get ahead in this world, but that there were plenty of opportunities for those who wanted it. We raised them that way. Roberto took after his dad. We don't have as much as some people, but what we have, we worked for. Roberto was the same way; Ricki was too. They both worked hard and were happy kids." Mrs. Vega-Chapa broke down. She sobbed. Her husband wrapped his arm around her.

I nodded. "Does the computer need a code?"

"Ricki and Roberto," mom said without hesitation. Roberto's cell had no code. She continued to cry.

PHONE, COMPUTERS AND
POSSIBLE DAMNING EVIDENCE

Sully and I hadn't heard anything from Mac, so we assumed she was still at the station buried in paperwork. We stopped at a fast-food restaurant. We picked up assorted sandwiches and drinks and headed for the barn. Since Sully had all but finished clearing the armored car drivers of any wrongdoing in the heist, he could help me dump Ricki's cell phone, revisit Roberto's cell, and examine what was in both computers.

"Pick a sandwich, any sandwich. Pick a drink, any drink."

Mac looked at me. "Did you hit the lottery while you were out? You're awfully cheerful."

"Nope. I was wrestling with a decision. Thanks to Rocky, I think I came to a conclusion."

"Do tell."

Sully grabbed a ham and cheese sandwich and a Diet Coke. "It can wait. I think you'll be happy." I pulled an Italian sub and fries out of the pile of food. I reached for a soft drink. "I'm buying," I teased. "What do you want?"

Mac smiled. I had a damn good idea what she wanted. The question was could I give it to her. "I'll take what's left."

I handed Mac a roast beef sandwich, a can of Sprite and fries. "Anything new to report?"

Sully was busy munching on his food. "Not a damn thing. When I get finished with what you call lunch, I'm going to start digging into the hiring reports and the applications. I'm going back five years. That should keep me busy for the next two years."

"We picked up Ricki's cell phone and her laptop. We already have Roberto's cell. His folks gave us his laptop. After that delicious lunch Sully and I bought you, we're going to get busy on the phone and the laptops." I took a bite out of my wop slop sandwich.

We left Mac to continue going through the files of present and former SafeGuard employees dating back five years. Sully and I went to work. We started on the computers. I had Roberto's computer; Sully had Ricki's.

I started with Roberto's emails. There were exchanges with teachers about school assignments; there were emails to school friends; there were plenty of emails to Ricki professing Roberto's love for his sweetheart.

What I didn't find was anything incriminating. Specifically, I was looking for an email to a friend, probably a male friend, asking for help with the loan of a car or help with moving a body, Ricki's body. I didn't find it. I kept digging.

I found an email to an apparent friend asking what time dinner would be served. The responder wrote, "When you arrive." The email address gave no clue as to whether this was a male or a female. I made a note on the legal pad sitting next to me to check this out.

People who watch cop shows on television have absolutely no idea of how much "trudging" is involved in police work. If you don't have the patience for paperwork, sometimes mounds of paperwork, police work is not for you. Leg work and sifting through paperwork, cell phones, and computers is often the key to solving a case.

Case in point, true story. A middle-aged woman of apparently good health is found dead in her bed by her husband of thirteen years. No obvious signs of death are noticeable on her body. The autopsy report pinpoints a four-hour window of death. The husband was at work during those hours. Relatives say the marriage appeared happy with the usual arguments; neighbors mirror that image of the couple.

Digging into paperwork shows that eighteen months earlier, each spouse had taken out large life insurance policies on the other. The beneficiary stood to gain half a million dollars in the event of the other's death unless dedicated detectives could prove murder for monetary gain.

Detectives kept digging. They asked the husband to voluntarily surrender his three computers, two at work, and one at home. He agreed. Detectives also asked for his cell phone. He complied.

Often, people think you can wipe a computer clean; you can't. Same with a cell phone. Same answer. You can bury the damn things in a backyard, but if they're found, you might be in trouble.

The investigating detectives dumped the cell phone and had experts "open" the computer. When all was said and done, hubby had a twenty-two-year-old bimbo he was banging. Hubby liked to gamble. He lost, he lost big. He was into two loan sharks for major money. Here was clear motive.

But he was at work when his wife died. The preliminary autopsy showed zilch. Rule hubby out? Not so fast. While the cell phone pinpointed numerous phone calls between bimbo, bettor, bookie and loan shark, the computer, which bright boy thought he wiped clean, showed several searches for ways to kill your wife. He dug into poison. Now detectives had motive, means and opportunity. A search warrant was signed by a judge and served by the detectives. A search of the house providing nada. The husband was brought in for questioning. He declined an attorney. It took twenty-three minutes of "soft" questioning for him to admit he had administered a small amount of poison over a period of time. He claimed the bimbo had no knowledge, but he copped a plea.

Instead of half a million dollars tax free, he got LWOP, life without parole. Paperwork, dedication, and hard leg work by our fine detectives solved that murder. More often than not, that's how cases are solved.

If you know how to do it, you can trace an email address. If you know what to do, you can come up with the address. I punched extension 714 on the phone. "Claudia, Tony Kano. How are you?"

She responded cheerfully.

"Glad to hear it. I need a favor. I need you to find me a name and address and anything else you can find on the following email address. When you get a chance, and when you find anything, give me a call on my cell. It's regarding a 187 within our city and a suicide. Thanks. I owe you."

I went back to work. I spent damn near an hour searching for anything. I found nothing else of interest. I decided to "dump" the phone. Once I had the phone numbers Roberto called, I could cross reference them not only to Ricki, but to anyone else he might have called. From the phone, I could also pull Roberto's whereabouts around the time Ricki was strangled. I jumped back on the phone.

THREE DAYS LATER

Anybody who says cops get fat eating donuts and drinking coffee should have watched Mac, Sully and I bust our collective asses for three solid days. We barely had time for a piss break. For three solid days it was telephone, computer, telephone interviews, computer, and telephone. It didn't let up.

Mac's three days were no different. She compiled records on SafeGuard employees. She went through names; she cross referenced those names against arrest records. She dug, and dug, and dug. She stopped when she thought she hit bottom. Slowly but surely, we were making progress.

Sully and I compared Roberto's telephone calls to Ricki's. He called her numerous times each day. The calls were almost always brief maybe a minute to two minutes. Was this the pattern of a jealous young lover or just their way of expressing love?

That one call that jumped out at me was a local phone number that stood alone on Roberto's call list. I had a department buddy run the number for me. I was waiting for his call back. "Sully, what time did the medical examiner put on Ricki's death?

Sully rubbed the stubble on his chin. "I believe it was sometime between three and eight p.m."

I studied my notes. "Interesting?"

"What makes it interesting?"

"We were able to tower track Roberto's whereabouts from the pings off the towers. He was consistent in walking the area around the school, her house, his house, the park, the library. I'm not saying he could not have done it; I'm saying it would have been difficult especially without a vehicle. I will go on record saying if Roberto did it, he had a helper."

"Interesting." Sully paused. He looked down at his notes. "There isn't anything, absolutely nothing that makes Ricki standout negatively. All her calls are verified up to the time she left school the day of her death. At that point, we lose contact because the phone is in her locker."

I was satisfied. "We're making progress. If Roberto did strangle Ricki, we know he had help. If we can nail down the help, we can connect the dots." I was mentally fatigued.

I looked at my watch. It was lunch time. It was beyond lunch. I said to Sully, "Let's get a hold of Mac and go get something to eat. Mac can tell us about her adventures over lunch. Sound like a deal?"

"Sound good to me. I'll call Mac."

While Sully was making arrangements with Mac, I, of course, was thinking about Mac, and Peter. No pun intended but they went hand in hand. As long as I kept busy with the cases, I was good. The minute I stopped for even a minute; Mac came to mind.

Usually, when I thought I had an insurmountable problem, I could "logic" my way through it, talk to someone about it, write about it, or compare my situation to someone I knew who had worked through a similar problem. I didn't know a damn soul who had gotten involved with a woman who turned out to have been born a guy!

MAC IS ON TRACK

We drove out of the city and dined at Fred's Fine Foods which was a police friendly diner. The eatery's "attire" was the fifties complete with Doo Wop tunes from the nostalgic fifties' jukebox, to fifties attired waitresses (not on roller skates) to fifties car pictures on the walls. My favorite picture was that of a 1957 Ford black and white with gumball machines and fifties copper posing in front of fender in period correct uniform including over the shoulder holster.

We wasted no time ordering because we were anxious to get down to business. Sully and I shared with Mac our findings on the Ricki strangulation. In turn, Mac shared her progress with us.

"I reviewed all the employee files that I could get my hand on dating back approximately five years. I also reviewed the job applications from those hired and those rejected over a five-year period. Anyone who jumped out at me was run for wants and warrants. I have a short list of possible conspirators. I also have half a dozen more files to peruse." Mac drummed her fingers on the tabletop to the beat of PRETTY LITTLE ANGEL EYES. "Any questions?"

"Just one. Does anything look promising?"

"Not really." Mac answered my question. "As I've said before, this is a process of elimination so it's not a waste of time. We're narrowing down the search field."

I didn't understand how we were any closer to finding the money, but I didn't want to get into that in front of Sully. He had enough problems with his pending divorce.

My cell rang. It was my buddy tracking Roberto's dinner email. He had the information I asked him to get me. I scribbled it on my notepad. "If I wasn't married, I'd kiss you." I said into the phone. "Oops," I added, "I'm not married." I heard a sharp click as he hung up hurriedly.

Our food arrived. Suddenly there was silence at our table. Mouths were quiet and full of Fred's Fine Foods.

ANOTHER STEP FORWARD, ANOTHER STEP BACK

After lunch we went back to the office. We spent several hours chasing down more information. At 1645 hours we decided to call it a day. Sully drove back to his new apartment in Glendale. Mac and I drove to my place.

I poured myself a shot of Seagram's, then another as I stripped down to my underwear. Mac did likewise. We got into the shower. Mac soaped me up from toes to head, back to front and every place in between. It was the in between that felt great. I returned the favor. Mac was wet, very wet, and not just from the water.

We took our time washing away the mental odors of the day. Twenty minutes after we stepped into the shower, we stepped out of the shower refreshed. We toweled each other somewhat dry and lay on the bed for fun and frolic.

"No cuffs or blindfold today, mistress?"

"Nope. Today you take it straight." Mac went to work on my almost dry body, on my stiffening Peter. She rubbed lotion on her hands. She pushed me back against the pillow. She took off everything but her tan panties. She stripped me naked. She sat between my legs then she rubbed her lotion hands all over Peter. Peter could not have been happier. He got hard fast, real hard, real fast. "No problem here."

Just what I needed to hear; just what Peter needed to hear. Up my anxiety level, why don't you?

Mac kept rubbing. I watched Peter grow in appreciation. "Peter likes your hands. So do I."

"He'll like my mouth even better, so will you." Mac got up and walked to the sink. She dampened a towel. When she came back to the bed, she bathed Peter in warm water. She dried him off. Next, Mac swung around so that her head was facing my feet. She kissed Peter hello. He responded. I buried my tongue in Mac's warm, moist pussy. Don't let anyone tell you sixty-nine is just a number.

Mac licked and sucked for what seemed like, felt like, an eternity. I licked and sucked. It couldn't have tasted any better had it been a triple shot of Seagram's. Peter was at his finest. "Peter seems happy."

"He is. So am I. How about you?"

"Do you hear any complaints from mistress?"

"No, ma'am."

Mac took every inch of Peter in her mouth. She was unreal. She stopped sucking and licked and kissed my balls. The three of us were in heaven.

My tongue dug deeper into Mac's pussy. My finger found her asshole. Slowly I teased it. I kept licking Mac's pussy. I nibbled on her clit. My finger went slowly deeper. When I felt Mac relax her muscles, my finger explored deeper. I made small circles with my finger.

We played for a good thirty minutes. Finally, Mac pulled away. She climbed on top, gently stroked Peter then put him inside. She tried to put him inside. Peter wasn't having any of it.

You only come to bat so many times in a ballgame. If you keep swinging at the ball and don't make contact, ever, you're going to be shipped to the minor leagues.

ANOTHER DAY AT THE OFFICE

Mac called me in the morning. She called for two reasons. One was to reassure me that Peter's early demise would soon be a thing of the past. She reassured me that we, and Mac the WE, needed time. Then she informed me that she would be going through the rest of the computer files from home. If she decided to interview any of the employees at SafeGuard in person she would call before she leaves her place.

Sully and I set up a game plan. I wanted to visit the person who had emailed Roberto about dinner. I was certain nothing would come of it, but I had a need to be thorough. I wanted to go to the church Ricki and Roberto and Ricki's family attended regularly. The church she went to with her girlfriend during the week before she was murdered. I wanted to talk with the priest.

FATHER, I HAVE SINNED

Sully and I drove to the Church of All Faiths. This was the church Ricki attended and visited the day before she was murdered. On the drive to the church, it hit me like a cinder block. I could talk to Father Strayhan about my situation with Mac. Hell, he didn't know me, had never seen me before and would probably never see me again. Couple that with the fact that he was bound by his oath to protect my privacy, as is an attorney bound to client attorney privilege, and I had my confidant.

Sully parked the unmarked police unit in front of the church. We walked inside. We identified ourselves to Father Patrick Strayhan who stood about five foot ten, was average build, with black hair and was probably in his late fifties. Father Strayhan invited us to the office. We sat at his desk. The man of the cloth sat behind his desk.

Father Strayhan was friendly and cooperative. I asked him if he recalled seeing Ricki Montego Valenzuela recently. He did. As a matter of fact, he recounted precisely what we already knew. I asked Father Strayhan about Roberto. He also confirmed what we already knew. A dead end for progress for us in both cases.

"Such a shame," Father Strayhan said. "They were both such sweet children. Terrible. Just terrible. May they rest in heavenly peace."

"Anything you might be able to tell us that might assist us in the death investigation of either child," Sully asked.

He looked us in the eye. "I'm sorry. I wish I could. If you leave me a business card, and if I hear of anything that might

149

be helpful, I'll certainly call. If I hear any talk from anyone that I can share, I'll be in touch."

"We appreciate that, Father." I shook my head. "I believe if we spent time in church and less time chasing the almighty dollar, this world would be a much better place."

"Amen to that" Father Strayhan said.

We had one more stop to make. I had the name and address of the man Roberto emailed. I wanted to talk with him if for no other reason than to satisfy my cop instinct even though my gut told me it was another dead end.

We were fifteen minutes from the address my cop buddy had traced for me from Roberto's email. Sully drove. I thought about, what else, Mac and Peter. We arrived at the address, parked the car, and walked to the door. We didn't know if the subject would be home.

Sully knocked at the heavy brown stained wooden door. A short man, about fifty years of age, neatly dressed in a blue suit, white shirt and matching tie answered the door. I immediately flashed my detective shield. I made the introductions. "We're looking for Kevin Duffmann."

"That would be me." He flashed a smile showing clean white teeth that might have been bought. Kevin Duffmann opened the door wide. He held out his arm. "Come on in, gentleman. Unfortunately, I think I know why you're here." Duffmann escorted us into the living room. The house, although older, was remodeled obviously at great expense. The house was an entertainer's delight. It boasted high ceilings and was open to accommodate as many guests that one would want in his dwelling. Duffmann pointed a finger at two matching brown ottomans. "Have a seat. Would either of you like a drink?"

We declined. I liked Duffmann. He appeared genuine and friendly. I was going to find out I had a lot to learn as a detective.

Sully stepped in. "You said you thought you had an idea as to why we are here. Please tell us about that."

Duffmann was seated on a couch that probably came as a set with the two ottomans; at least, if it didn't it could have fooled me. Above the fireplace I observed a picture that appeared to have been taken outside the church we had just left. In the framed picture was at least two dozen people, kids, young adults, and adults. Duffmann was obviously a church member.

"You're here investigating the deaths of Ricki and Roberto. Tragic, tragic, tragic. I knew them both rather well. We attended the same church."

I nodded.

"We hold regular church gatherings and dinner gatherings here. It's a way to get to better know each other." Duffmann asked again, "Are you sure I can't get either of you gentlemen something to drink?"

We declined.

Sully asked, "Is there anything you can tell us that may help us in our investigation? Anything at all? Some small detail that may mean nothing to you but that may help us to get to the bottom of this?"

"I've been giving this a lot of thought. After all, we were friends. We attended the same church. We were active in the community. I'm sure not a detective, but it would appear to me, from what I've read in the papers, that Roberto, for whatever reason, killed Ricki, then took his own life."

"So, it would appear," Sully said. "But that is not a given." Sully quickly added, "Yet."

Kevin Duffmann looked at Sully. "I can't think of anything at all that could be of help in your investigation."

"How well did you know Roberto?"

Duffmann smiled. "Well enough to tell you that I was shocked when I learned Roberto took his own life. He was a sweet young man. He was active in church. He was a fine student. He played sports. He was part of our private church group."

"When was the last time you had contact with Roberto?"

Duffmann thought about that. He played with the knot on his light blue tie. "He was over here with the rest of the church group that belongs to our little clan about a week ago. He contacted me about our once in a while dinner to find out the time." Duffmann looked me in the eye flashing those white teeth. He shook his head. "Such a tragedy; such a shame."

Sully stood up. I got up and handed Duffmann a business card. "If you think of anything…." I didn't finish the sentence.

On the drive back to the church, Sully and I discussed our brief meeting with Duffmann. "Nice guy. I love the house."

Sully took his eyes off the road momentarily to look at me. "I like the house. I think Duffmann is as phony as a politician."

I was surprised. "What makes you say that?"

"Gut feeling. And why are we going back to the church, detective?" Sully enjoyed baiting me. I didn't bite.

"I've got some personal business. I'm going to need twenty or thirty minutes. Would you mind?"

"Hell no. I'll drop you off and go get a cold drink or take a quick nap in the car. I didn't know you were religious."

"I'm not, buddy. It's just something I need to take care of."

"No problem. No worries." Sully dropped me off at the Church of All Faiths.

I can only assume it was Father Strayhan who met me in the confessional. And although it really didn't matter, I hoped he wouldn't know my voice from our earlier meeting.

"Father," I began awkwardly, "I haven't been to confession in God knows how long." The minute those words came out of my mouth, I wanted to change them. I continued. "I have a problem and I'd like you to hear it."

"Of course. I would be happy to hear it. I would be happy to help in any way I can help. God and I are with you. Go on."

I spelled out my situation with Mac as carefully and as clearly as I could. I was nervous but once I got into it, I was more comfortable. How do you explain to a priest that the woman you love isn't, by birth, a woman?

Father Strayhan had an immediate answer. "Son, you do know what the Bible says about marriage, about marriage being between a man and a woman? I can understand that you didn't know from the very beginning. I understand that. Now that you know, you have a tough decision to make. When you make that decision, think about what the Bible says about marriage. I can't make that decision for you. I can give you guidance. Is that helpful, my son?"

"It is, Father." I thought about as helpful as a match in a windstorm.

153

"Then that should put this matter to rest." Father Strayhan paused to let his words sink in. They sank alright, right down to the pit of my stomach. "I hope to see you at church Sunday."

Sully was waiting in the car for me when I left the church. "Did you get your business taken care of?"

"Yeah, sort of."

"While you were chipping away at the taxpayer's dollar on company time, I was hard at work." Sully started the car then pulled away from the curb.

"And that means?"

"And that means I ran your buddy Kevin Duffmann."

"Tell me he's got a record?"

"Not exactly."

"Okay Sherlock, give it to me."

"He has an arrest record out of Connecticut dating back seven years."

That surprised the shit out of me. I really misjudged the guy, maybe. "For what?"

"Indecent exposure, soliciting a minor, a male minor."

"You're shitting me."

"Nope. No conviction. They cut him loose. Lack of evidence."

"Anything else?"

"Nothing so far. Still like Duffmann?"

154

"Jesus. Any possibility it was trumped up bullshit?"

"I'll call back to Connecticut later or tomorrow and do a bit of digging. Let's head back to the barn."

TWO FUNERALS

We attended two funerals in two days. From a distance we observed Ricki's funeral. We were looking for anything, anyone out of the ordinary. Occasionally, the killer will attend the victim's funeral. Sully, Mac, and I set up shop in our unmarked with binoculars and camera. We did the same at Roberto's funeral. At first look it appeared fruitless.

We didn't have enough direct evidence to say that Roberto strangled Ricki. We did know that Roberto took his own life. There were absolutely no marks on Roberto's body, no drugs or alcohol in Roberto's system to indicate foul play. We could say with the strongest certainty that it was suicide; he took his own life. The question became why? Did Roberto hang himself because he realized we were closing in on him? Did he take his life because he was heartbroken that someone had killed the love of his life? It sure the hell, by all outward appearances, looked like Roberto was Ricki's killer.

When we got back to the barn we walked to our temporary office. Mac was at her desk working away and buried in paper. "I'm going to run over to SafeGuard. There are a couple of employees I want to interview."

"On your way out, let dispatch know what your twenty is going to be. When you leave SafeGuard, let dispatch know you're on your way back to the reservation."

"Yes, sir, detective, sir. That's a big ten four, sir." Mac smiled and nodded.

I returned the nod and the smile. "Do you think you have something?"

Mac shook her pretty blonde head. "Just following up on possibilities. You?"

"We talked to the priest where Ricki and Roberto attended church. I went to confession. We talked to a guy who attends the church and who has church members over on a regular basis. The guy's been arrested for indecent exposure and a possible soliciting charge. There wasn't enough evidence to hold him. Sully's going to follow up on that."

"I'm going to call Kevin Duffmann and ask him for the names and phone numbers of those from the church who regularly meet at his house. I should have asked him for those names when we were at his house."

Mac left the office presumably for SafeGuard.

"Now what?" Sully asked.

"See if you can dig anything else up on Duffmann. I'm going to get on the phone and build a timeline on Roberto's movements the day Ricki was murdered. We've got approximate whereabouts and time frames but nothing conclusive that can eliminate him as a suspect. Mac taught me that sometimes elimination is as good as damning evidence. The lady is correct."

Sully took out his notepad. I tossed my notes on the table. We both got on the phone. There are two things I hate about police work; they are report writing and interviewing people on the phone. I was in for a long day and possible long night of telephone interviews, or so I thought.

I called Kevin Duffmann. "Sir, I meant to ask you when we were at your gorgeous home for a list of names and phone numbers of the people who attend church meetings and dinner gatherings at your house. We'd like to reach out to these people as part of our investigation."

157

There was dead silence on the other end of the line, then a sigh and, "Detective, I think that might be breaching a trust issue. If you were one of my guests, would you want your name and number given out willy-nilly?"

Duffmann had a valid point. He also had been arrested and probably didn't know I knew about that arrest, conviction, or no conviction. Lying wasn't my strong suit but I was learning. "Sir, let me tell you that at this point, you're obstructing an investigation." That was, to say the least, a stretch. "I can get a court order. It might take days to do that. In the meantime, we're wasting valuable time. I could come to your house and take you to the station for hours of questions under the pretext that you might be harboring a criminal." I was getting better with each lie. "The best way to do this is to comply. Most, if not all of your church group, will never know you gave up their names and numbers. You said you were friendly with Ricki and Roberto. Help us solve her killing."

"Detective, how about I call my attorney? We can all meet at the station."

The son of a bitch called my bluff. I had played a hand or two of poker in Vegas. I always lost but I played. "Have it your way, Mr. Duffmann. In the meantime, I'm going to send a black and white to pick you up and drive you to the station for questioning. The unit will be there within half an hour. That should give you plenty of time to contact your attorney. Hang on, sir." I held the phone a few inches from my mouth. I was certain Duffmann heard me yell to no one, "Joe and Harris, grab a unit and go to this address. You're going to pick up Kevin Duffmann for questioning. Thanks. I owe you."

"Okay, okay. I've got a file box with everyone's name and number. I'll get it to you in an hour or so."

"I'm also going to need the approximate age of each person on that list. Email it to me, please. My email is on the card we gave you. And sir, thanks for your cooperation." I hung up very pleased with myself.

Sully wanted to know why I was doing what I was doing and how I expected to use it to delve into Roberto's apparent suicide. "I'm not sure. How's that for an answer?" I wasn't being "smart" with Sully. The fact was if all this needed to be put into juxtaposition, I wasn't sure how it would fit, if it would fit. I certainly didn't like the fact that Ricki was murdered and shortly thereafter Roberto took his own life. In a situation like this, there is usually something called a "trigger," something that sets off the subject or suspect. For example, a serial killer may "go off" each time he is rejected by a girl who denies his advances. The trigger is the girl's rejection so, he goes out and kills. A subject may have been severely abused by his mother who had blonde hair and blues. The sighting of a blue-eyed blonde who resembles his mother might trigger his "buried" emotions and bring them to the surface. This triggers his angst to kill. Something triggered Roberto to place that rope around his neck. This newbie detective was determined to find out why. If, in the course of that piece of the investigation, I could tie it into Ricki's killing, so much the better.

"I'm thinking," I said to Sully, "that once I get the list of names from Duffmann, I can either make phone calls or we can make house calls. One more thing while we're on the subject of why Roberto took his life. Do you remember his mom said she found rubbers in his draw?"

"I do."

"Think about this. If Ricki died a virgin, why did he have rubbers?"

Sully rubbed his chin. "Maybe she was blowing him and didn't want him to cum in her mouth. Maybe he had a girlfriend on the side. I'm sure what was between Ricki's legs was on Roberto's mind and on his wish list. Maybe he was a good boy scout and was keeping the rubbers around just in case he convinced her to give in to his stiff dick."

Stiff dick was my trigger. It brought to mind my latest "session" with Mac. More frustration. It was a damn good thing I wasn't a killer, although some say there's a real thin line being a cop and a crook or a cop and a killer.

I checked my email. Duffmann had kept his word. I ran off two lists of names, phone numbers and approximate ages of those on the list Duffmann had dutifully emailed me.

Name Age	Number
Tom Landoff 15	713-8076
Scott Wilson 45	688-4231
Brett Chernov 50	879-2014
Bill Thompson 50	412-9074
Peter Johnson 13	678-0569
Matt Paulson 15	341-1514

Rick Mellowman 14	215-4387
Frank Delvo 15	632-9076
Kevin Duffmann 55	448-7034
Father Patrick Strayhan 55	672-5575

Quickly, I perused the list. I slid a copy across the desk to Sully. "Just in case you're bored."

We both studied the list. "Thoughts?"

"My first thought, of course, is that it's a church group that meets on a regular basis at Duffmann's house for dinner and church related activities. Do you know how often they meet?"

"According to Duffmann, they meet monthly, and it's not always the entire group."

"It appears to be a men's only meeting. Nothing unusual about that," Sully said.

"And the good Father is on hand to give spiritual guidance."

"Yeah. Sounds like legitimate business to me," I offered. I needed a break. I needed a drink, or two, or three.

TOMORROW'S ANOTHER DAY

I started my day at 0730 hours visiting Rocky. I brought him his cigarettes and placed a book of matches on his headstone. "Listen, buddy. I'm more confused than ever. The priest tells me marriage is between a man and a woman. Peter tells me he has a problem with Mac. I love her. What the hell am I supposed to do?

"And what about the killing of Ricki and the suicide or apparent suicide of Roberto? I seem to be at a fork in the road here. I don't know which way to turn." A thought occurred to me. Rather than call or meet individually with the people on Duffmann's list, Sully and I could meet with them all at the next scheduled meeting at Duffmann's house if the meeting wasn't too far in the future. I'd run that by Sully later at the station.

"Mac is digging into the money case. She's revisiting SafeGuard employees. So far, she's at a dead end also. See what happens when you leave us to fend for ourselves; everything and everybody falls apart. We're so fucked up even Sully's wife left him for someone else. Speaking of Sully's wife, how's Paula doing? I hear via the grapevine; she's not coming back to California. The way this state is going, that's probably for the best. As bad as it was, Newsom has managed to fuck it up even more. Pretty soon he'll tax you on your final resting place and call it a motel tax." Rocky was becoming not only a sounding board for me but also cheap therapy. Hell, I was only "paying" him a pack of cigarettes per meeting!

I sat and visited with Rocky for another twenty minutes. "I'll be back buddy. I'll keep you updated. Don't smoke all those at one time. Rest well my friend. Rest well."

I had the radio on an all-news station on the way to the barn. A news flash told me two Los Angeles County Deputies were ambushed as they sat in their unit in south central Los Angeles. According to the newscaster who had preliminary information, one deputy was male, one female. Both had been with the department fourteen months. They were in surgery and fighting for their lives, he said. According to the newscaster one shooter ran up to the driver's window. He opened fire. The deputies didn't stand a chance. A group of scumbag protesters stood outside the hospital chanting, "I hope they die."

Several thoughts entered my mind. First, I said a silent prayer for the injured officers. Second was when they catch this piece of shit, and they will catch him, I hope they kill him. Next was why is there so much hate for police who are out there to serve and protect. How the fuck could you walk up to a car and open fire? Being on the street, in uniform, was like being in a damn war zone. I well knew that. But this isn't Afghanistan. We live in the United States. If I had my way, I'd run over each and every fucking protester at that hospital. And yeah, say what you will, I'd sleep very well.

I arrived at the station at 0835. Mac and Sully were in the room drinking coffee and eating donuts. "We saved you a couple of donuts and coffee. As a matter of fact, I just made a fresh pot," Mac said. "I'm buying. Can I get you a cup?"

They had already heard about the ambushed deputies. A collection had been taken up within our department for flowers for the officers. I pulled a twenty out of my pocket and handed it to Sully. Then I nodded and smiled. "You're buying, I'm drinking. Anything new from your interviews?"

"Nothing yet. I have more interviews scheduled for later today. You and Sully?"

163

I brought Mac up to date on the church meetings at Duffmann's place and my idea to meet with all of them at one time. "If you're after comparing notes, I don't think that's a good idea. It may save you time but you're not going to get what I think it is you're after. If one of those on your list was involved in Ricki's murder, you really want to interview everyone one on one and up close and personal. Then you can compare notes. If you find a liar in the briar patch, you may have a jumping off point."

Of course, Mac was on point. "You're right. That'll make Sully's and my day. What time is your first interview at SafeGuard?"

"Nine thirty."

"We'll be in the office scheduling interviews. We'll call in to dispatch and let dispatch know our twenty."

Mac freshened Sully's coffee, poured a cup for me, and put a head on her cup. I forced myself not to think about Mac, Peter, and me. The word "head" sure as hell was a trigger.

ANOTHER DAY, MORE
INTERVIEWS, MORE POSSIBILITES

Scott Wilson was the second name on Duffmann's list. He agreed to meet with us when I called him. We set a time of nine thirty in the morning. It was nine twenty. It was another warm day in southern California. It wasn't too hot, and it wasn't going to get too hot, at least weather-wise.

As I pulled to the curb in front of the Wilson house Sully asked, "How do you want to play this?"

"By ear. If it gets to it, we can play good cop bad cop. But for now, my focus is trying to see if we can get one of these folks to lead us in a direction that will tell us why Roberto did himself. We can get a lead on Ricki's murder, all the better."

"Works for me." Sully said, "I'm having trouble adjusting to coming home to an apartment, and an empty apartment at that. It's not good, buddy. Last night I stopped off and bought myself a bottle of scotch."

"That'll get you through those lonely nights."

"Talking about lonely nights, what's the next step for you and Mac?"

"If you're writing a book, leave that chapter out."

"C'mon, buddy. You two belong together."

I had no idea what got Sully off on the tangent, but I wanted to put a plug in his jug in a hurry. "Mac said we should take it a day at a time," I lied. Then I lied again. "I always do as Mac tells me." I checked my watch. We were right on the money time wise. It was exactly 0930 when my right hand made contact with Wilson's door.

As Duffmann wrote on his list of names, Scott Wilson was about 45. He was also short, slightly overweight, wore glasses, and his blond hair was thinning. He wore a pair of old grey chino pants and a blue pullover shirt that was in need of ironing. I badged Scott Wilson then introduced Sully and me.

"C'mon in. I made a pitcher pf iced tea." Scott led us into the living room. The house was small, old, and in need of paint. Trying not to be obvious, I scanned the walls. I saw absolutely nothing that stood out.

"Have a seat." Wilson sat in a beat-up brown leather chair. Sully and I sat on opposite ends of the non- color matching couch.

I smiled. "I told you when we set up the appointment on the phone why we're here. Have you given it any thought?"

Scott nodded. He pulled at his right ear. "I have. I don't think I can be of much help. Outside of church, and outside of the meeting at Kevin's house, I didn't associate with either Ricki or Roberto. I can tell you they were the best of people. They were true givers. They were both spiritual, honest as the day is long and always willing to help. I can't say a negative thing about either. I know that's not what you want to hear…."

I cut in. "Actually, we want to hear the truth. If that's the truth, that's exactly what we want."

"That's the truth."

"Did you ever see Ricki and Roberto together?"

166

Scott thought for a couple of seconds. "Outside of church, no. After church they'd sometimes walk off to the side of the building together holding hands, talking and kissing each other on the cheek."

"Did you ever see them argue?"

Wilson shook his head. "Never. They were always happy, always smiling."

Sully jumped in. "How often do you go to Kevin Duffmann's house?"

"Usually once a month unless there's a dinner in between meetings at Kevin's house."

"What goes on at those meetings?"

"We talk about God, about things spiritual. If someone has a problem, we attempt to help. Sometimes we read from the Bible."

"When you say if someone has a problem we try to help, give us an example please."

"When my air conditioning unit broke down, it turns out two of our guests had been in that business. They repaired the a/c, which I couldn't have afforded to do. They even paid for the parts. When Ricki's mom couldn't afford the mortgage payment one month, those of us who could help, ponied up enough cash to make the payment for her."

Nice group of people I thought. I looked at Sully, he shrugged. "How long do the meetings at Duffmann's house last?"

"That's interesting. If it's not a dinner meeting, some of us leave after about ninety minutes, an hour and a half. If it's a dinner meeting, the meeting concludes at seven thirty."

"Do you do anything different at the dinner meeting?"

"No, we discuss problems. Things we can do for the community such as volunteering to read to kids at the library, helping to clean up parks; that sort of thing."

Sully asked, "Are you one of those who stay behind after the dinner or after the regular meeting?"

"No."

"Do you know what goes on at the after meeting, meeting?"

"The usual. People sign up for volunteer jobs. That sort of thing."

I nodded. "Are you and Kevin close friends?"

"Acquaintances would be more like it."

"How well do you know Ricki's mom, Mrs. Montego Valenzuela?"

"Not well at all. From church mostly."

"How did Mrs. Montego Valenzuela and Ricki get along?"

"Fine, I guess. Like I said, I really only know them from church."

I turned to Sully.

"I can't think of anything else. Can you?"

Sully shook his head. He handed Scott a business card. "If you think of anything else, please give us a call. We thank you for your time and your help."

I reached in my pocket for my cell. "I've got to call the station." I eyed Sully. "Damn, my cell's dead." I looked at Sully. "My phone is at the station."

"Here, use mine." Scott handed me his phone.

I walked out of eyesight. I pulled up Scott's previous calls. Quickly, while pretending to talk with the watch commander at the station, I photographed Wilson's previous calls with my working cell.

The second name on the list was Peter Johnson, a 13-year-old youngster who also attended the same church as Scott Wilson and who also attended the church meetings at Kevin's house.

When we got back in the unit, I called the Johnson house to schedule the meeting. I spoke to Peter's mom. I explained why we wanted to meet with Peter. I asked that if possible that both Mr. and Mrs. Johnson be present when we interviewed Peter. She explained that she and her husband were separated, that he was in Vegas with his girlfriend. She assured me that she would be present when Sully and I interviewed her son.

On the drive to the Johnson house, Sully called St. Francis hospital to check on the condition of the wounded officers. He identified himself as an FBI Agent. Sully was told they were both still in surgery. He was also informed that one officer has been shot in the face the other in the head. Not good news!

I knocked on the door of the big white two-story house in a gated community. A black BMW convertible sat in the driveway with the top down. The sprawling lawn was recently cut as were the shrubs. I guessed the house to be at least three thousand square feet.

Sully knocked on the door. A very young-looking Mrs. Johnson answered the knock. "I'm Detective Kano. This is Agent Sullivan." I showed Mrs. Johnson my badge.

Peter's mom was wearing a very low-cut brown tank top. Her bra hid little of her ample boobs which I didn't hesitate to mentally lock in my mind. Hell, Mac wasn't around.

Mrs. Johnson wore skintight jeans that accentuated her tight little ass. For those who remember what eating at the Y means, I looked at the outline of her tight jeans. I worked up an appetite, and not for food. She weighed maybe one hundred ten pounds if she had rocks in her pocket. The little cutie stood five foot one in her tennis shoes. Her blonde hair was cut short. She was nothing short of a fox.

My gut told me her husband left her for another woman. The way she was dressed told me her self-esteem had been shattered. When she held her hand out, I squeezed it gently making longer eye contact than was necessary. She gave me a knowing smile then quickly shook hands with Sully. "Please call me April, and let's go in the dining room. We'll be able to talk comfortably there."

Sully and I followed April. We sat on matching chairs with a teak table between the upholstered recliners. Someone either had big bucks or was deep in debt.

"Peter," Mrs. Johnson yelled, "please come down. The gentlemen from the police department are here."

I heard Peter on the stairs. I watched a tall thin thirteen-year-old, with mom's blonde hair, dressed in jeans and t-shirt bounce his way down the carpeted steps. He walked over to Sully. "Sir, I'm Peter."

"I'm Agent Sullivan."

Next, he stepped toward my chair. I extended my hand. "I'm Detective Kano, Peter. It's nice to meet you." Peter sat next to his mom.

"Before we get started gentlemen, I'd like to inform you that I will be recording this interview." Mrs. Johnson placed a Sony tape recorder in the middle of the table. She poked the on button. "Let the recording begin."

I reached over and turned the recorder off. "We have absolutely no problem with that, Mrs. Johnson. I'm curious, what do you do for a living?"

She smiled. "I was a driver education teacher at the local high school before budget cuts put an end to that elective. I know what you're driving at. To answer the question you haven't asked, my husband is an attorney, a criminal defense attorney. Richard Thomas Johnson. Have you heard of him?"

Another fucking attorney. At least he wasn't Jewish. "No ma'am, I haven't heard of him. Sully?"

"He was one of the attorneys who got serial rapist and murderer Brandon Holton off on a technically, a police error. A year later the son of a …. Gun raped a seventeen-year-old in her backyard. Her father came home from hunting early, caught him in the act, and blew his face off with a shotgun."

"Yes. My husband was good at his job but a lousy husband. He couldn't keep," she hesitated, looked at her young son then continued. "He couldn't keep his dick in his pants. Mark my words he'll pay for that in more way than one. He'll pay dearly for that.

"I apologize. I didn't offer you gentlemen anything to drink."

We declined.

"Let's get the interview going, Mrs. Johnson."

"April, please."

"Let's get the interview going, April. We still have several other interviews to get through."

April made eye contact. She smiled, then ran her tongue over her shiny white teeth. That tongue was inviting. She turned on the recorder then said with a smile, "Let the games begin."

I looked at Peter then at Sully. From the look on everyone else's face, mom was the only one not taking this seriously, at least so it appeared. Enough with the shadow boxing. I started the interview. "Peter, we're here because we are investigating the killing of Ricki Montego Valenzuela and the probable suicide of Roberto Vega-Chapa."

"I understand, sir."

This kid was either more polite than most thirteen-year-olds in California or was frightened beyond words; or maybe a combination of the two. I softened my approach. "Peter, we're here hoping you can help us in the investigation. In no way do we think you are in anyway involved. Does that make sense?"

"Yes, sir."

I looked at April. She nodded. I interpreted that to mean my statement was not over the top. "How well do you...did you know Ricki?"

He turned his hands over showing open palms. "Not well. Mostly from church. Sometimes I'd see her in school. We were in different grades."

I nodded. "Did you know Roberto well?"

"About the same as I knew Ricki."

172

I watched Peter's eyes, his face. I'd bet a quart bottle of Seagram's the youngster was telling the truth. "What do you want to do when you get out of school?"

He looked at mom. "I want to be a criminal defense attorney like my dad."

April smiled. Sully and I smiled. "Did you ever see Ricki with any other guys besides Roberto?"

"She sometimes talks with other guys either before or after school or at lunch."

"Did this piss Roberto off?"

Peter leaned back in the chair. "No. Roberto knew that Ricki really loved him. He wasn't jealous."

The kid had good instinct. "Was there any one young man who may have shown more interest in Ricki than any other?"

Peter was becoming more comfortable with me and with my questioning.

"No. Like I said, Roberto was sure Ricki loved him and he loved her. They had trust in each other."

I nodded. "Why do you think Roberto killed himself?"

Peter scratched his head. We locked eyes. "You don't know for sure that he took his own life."

The kid would make a damn good attorney. "No, we don't. But it is pointing in that direction. Do you have any idea who might have wanted to kill Ricki?"

"I know what you think. You think Roberto killed Ricki, and then killed himself. Can I ask a question?"

"Go ahead."

173

"Why would Roberto kill the girl he really loved?"

The young man would make a damn good attorney. At thirteen I was shooting craps in a back alley, in many back alleys. Hell, at thirteen, I would have shit my pants if two investigators sat me down to question me in front of my mom. This kid had poise. He came across sincere and thoughtful.

"If Roberto didn't kill Ricki, he killed himself because he lost Ricki. Why else?"

Peter had completely turned the tables. I turned to Sully and nodded. "Mrs. Johnson, did you know Ricki?"

"I never met her." She didn't ask Sully to call her April.

"How about Roberto? Did you know Roberto?"

"Never met him either."

"Do you go to the same church as Ricki and Roberto did?"

"No. I don't go to church. Peter did."

I turned to Peter. "Do you know Kevin Duffmann?"

"Sure. We go to church meetings at his house sometimes."

"What goes on at those meetings?"

"We talk about church related matters. Sometimes we read from the Bible."

"Did you ever have dinner at the Duffmann residence?"

"Sure, many of us did."

"What was discussed at those dinner meetings?"

"We talked more about church related matters. Sometimes we'd ask if someone had a problem we could help with."

"Did anyone bring up a problem?"

"Sure."

"What kind of problem?"

"Sometimes someone needed help with a project from school or was having difficulty with a sibling or a parent and asked for advice. Sometimes someone would need money."

"Did Roberto ever bring up a problem?"

"No. Roberto was always one of the first to offer his help."

I reached for my phone. "Damn, my phone's dead. Sully can I see your phone?"

"I left it at the station."

Before I could ask Peter for his phone, April handed me hers. I stood up. "I'll be right back. Thank you." I returned three minutes later and handed April her phone. "Listen, if either of you think of anything that might be helpful to our investigation, please don't hesitate to call us." I handed April my business card. Sully handed his card to Peter.

As I shook hands with Peter, I said, "If I had it to do all over again, I'd go to law school." That was a lie.

We thanked April for her hospitality. I asked her to make sure to hang on to the tape in case we needed to review it. I was being sarcastic. We left for our next appointment.

Sully was behind the wheel. We weren't on the road ten minutes when my cell rang. "Kano," I said.

"Detective Kano, it's April Johnson."

"You've thought of something else?"

"No. I thought your phone was dead?"

"I've got it on charge in the car. It may die any time," I lied. "What's up?"

"I thought you might like to come over for a drink after work. I didn't see a ring on your finger. And if there was one, I really wouldn't care."

"I'm flattered. Let me see what time we wrap up at the end of the day. I'll call you either way when I have an idea of when the interviews will end today."

"Deal."

"Have a great day." I thought about having dinner at the Y.

"It will be if you show up after work."

I really was flattered. She was hot. I was horny. Here was my chance to see if I could keep it up inside a woman other than Mac. Now I had another decision to make. Did I want to screw around on Mac to prove to myself that it was the situation and not me?

"Hot date tonight, huh?"

"I have the right to remain silent. Maybe she's got a hot looking girlfriend."

Sully smiled. "I'm old fashioned. And I'm not ready to get back on that horse yet."

I knew exactly how Sully felt. "I seriously doubt I'll go over there. That wouldn't be right."

"I agree. What you do is strictly your business."

THREE STRIKES AND YOU'RE OUT: ANOTHER INTERVIEW

Brett Chernov, fiftyish, according to Kevin Duffmann's list, lived in Canyon West which was a twenty-minute drive from Amity. I questioned Sully as he drove. "What do you think so far?"

"I think it's a nice day for a drive."

"Be serious."

"Okay, what's with the phone crap?"

"I wanted to see who Scott Wilson called recently. I also wanted to see who Peter called. I didn't get Peter's phone, but I got Scott's. I took a quick look at Scott's calls. He's called mainly a few people from the church who were on Kevin Duffmann's list. Nothing incriminating."

"Okay, Sherlock. Let's not let your promotion go to your head."

"Sully, somewhere, somehow, someone in Amity knows what the hell happened to Ricki. We need a starting point. This is as good as any."

"Calm down, detective. Just because you're now a dick, don't be a dickhead. I'm just jerking you around."

"You need to get laid."

"Hell, in the last four years of my marriage I can count the number of times I got laid on your fingers and three of mine. What does that tell you?"

"That's a loaded question. Ever cheat on the wife?"

"Never. I have old ideas." Sully stopped for a light. He looked at me. "I guess Amy didn't have the same ideas."

I sighed. I felt for Sully. "It's going to take time, buddy. Remember, I'm here for you." I had to give Sully credit for not cheating on his wife. I too, believe it or not, had scruples, and old ideas. That was one of the reasons I was so confounded and confused with my situation with Mac. I wanted to prove to myself that I was still a man and could still get it up; but I didn't particularly want to cheat on Mac even though I didn't know where the hell we were in our relationship.

"I know and I appreciate that." Sully pulled away from the light. "Let's see if we can rattle a few cages starting with this cage."

"I'll second that partner."

Brett Chernov lived in a condo in not the best part of Canyon West. When we pulled up to the complex, the first thing we observed were half a dozen gang punks spray painting the north wall of the complex. We had other things to do besides bust these idiots. I called it in. "Shit. We might not have a unit when we come out."

"Good. Maybe they'll buy us something less than a hundred years old with the insurance money."

"Yeah," I said dryly. "A tandem bicycle."

Sully found the safest parking space in the visitors' area. We looked around as we walked, looking for unit 667. There was more discarded crap in the parking lot than there was in the trash cans. This told me some of the tenants didn't give two shits.

We located unit 667. I knocked. We were a few minutes late. The man who came to the door was short, heavy set, wearing wrinkled slacks and an old Hillary Clinton t-shirt. I already disliked the guy. "Brett Chernov?" Sully asked.

"That's me. You are?"

"I'm Agent Sullivan. My partner is Detective Kano. Can we come in?"

"Actually," Chernov pointed to four chairs and a small round glass topped table. "I thought we might be more comfortable out here." The balcony was small but cozy. The table was small and round. The black, high back metal chairs were comfortable.

I didn't want to swim upstream at this point. "That'll work." Sully placed a note pad on the table then took out his pen. "I gave you an idea of why we came out here today. We're looking into the killing of Ricki Montego Valenzuela and the possible suicide of her male friend Roberto Vega-Chapa." I watched Chernov's eyes. I couldn't read him.

"Did you know either of them?"

Chernov put a finger in his ear. He was either scratching an itch, searching for wax, or seeing if his finger would come out the other end. He didn't answer my question. "My wife died suddenly six months ago. Expenses and her bills were high. Way too high on my retirement. I retired from janitorial work with Vista Janitorial Supplies and Services two and a half years ago. Paying off everything took its toll on me financially. I was forced to move here from Amity." He stuck a finger in his other ear. "Do you have any idea how much it costs to bury someone these days?"

He was worse than Bill Clinton, or Hillary for that matter. That wasn't even close to answering the question I had asked. That shit goes with the territory. As Mac might say, "God is trying to teach you patience."

Both Sully and I shook our heads at the same time. "No, sir." Sully said for both of us.

"Even with social security you're not nearly covered for funeral expenses; not nearly."

I changed the subject. "Did you know either Ricki or Roberto, Mr. Chernov?"

"I knew Roberto. Once or twice, he mentioned Ricki in conversation. I never met her."

"What was your impression of Roberto?"

"Nice young man. I liked him."

"Are you a member of the Church of All Faiths?"

He nodded then put the tip of his ear finger in his mouth. "Yes, still attend every Sunday."

"Do you go to meetings and dinners at Kevin Duffmann's house?"

The democrat paused. It was a long pause, too long. That gave Sully an opening and it was a cue to start playing good cop bad cop.

"My partner asked you a question, Chernov. Not a difficult question. How about you answer it this week."

We woke up a sleeping midget.

"Who the hell do you think you're talking to, agent or whatever the hell you call yourself. This is my house, my porch, my time. You have no warrant, and the only reason you're even here is because I said it's okay to be here. Either be civil or get the hell out of here."

"Let's take him down to the station, Kano. We can continue the interview in Amity."

I held up my hand. "Now wait a minute. I know we can take him in for questioning without a warrant, but I really don't think he wants to spend the day at the station. I'm sure he just got excited, maybe frightened by us. Let's give him a second chance." I watched the little puke pot's eyes. He licked his lips.

"I'm sorry. Maybe I did get a bit overheated. I liked Roberto. He was a sweet kid. The fact is I didn't know Ricki. Roberto did loan me money for the burial of my wife. I'm sorry. No need to go to the station."

I continued my "soft" questioning. "How much money did Roberto loan you for your wife's funeral?"

"Two thousand dollars."

"Do you know where he got the two thousand dollars from?"

Chernov's face turned whiter than a freakin' polar bears. He raised and lowered his shoulders. "I guess he borrowed it."

I sat up straight and leaned forward. I stared into Chernov's lying eyes. "Where the fuck did he get two grand from?"

"I don't know."

"Agent Sullivan, let's go the station."

Sully stood up. I stood up.

"Is that necessary?"

"Where did Roberto get the money?"

181

I was on to something. I was going to keep tugging until Chernov snapped. "Answer the fucking question numb nuts or to the station we go."

"I want an attorney."

Something jumped into my mind. Something Mrs. Vega-Chapa said when we were interviewing her about the two deaths. Jesus Christ. Jesus H. Christ. It couldn't be, could it? If I was right, Chernov was going to need an attorney. If I was right, a lot of people were going to need an attorney. "You'd better hope Perry Fucking Mason is available. About the only thing that is going to help you is a small miracle; make that a major miracle; better still make that a major league miracle. Come clean now, and we'll do what we can to help you. Fuck with us you little piece of trash and we'll bury you." I stopped to let that sink in. I looked at Sully. Sully's eyes, his face told me he didn't have clue.

"Get off my porch. The interview is over. I want an attorney."

We did as we were ordered. I didn't want to fuck up this case. If I was correct, this thing would be bigger than the blow job that Clinton lied about. This was beyond big.

We walked to the car. It was still where we parked it. All four tires had air. The windows weren't broken. I let Sully drive so I could sit in the passenger seat and put this together. We had half an hour before our next interview. We could go into the next interview with ammo. I thought about the phone calls Chernov would make if I were right. "Sully, let's talk on the way to the next interview."

The fourth and last interview for the day was Frank Delvo. Frank was fifteen and lived with both parents in Amity. I knew what I was going to do upon arrival at the Delvo home.

I briefed Sully on my thinking, and why I was thinking it. He was skeptical.

The Delvo home was in the upper middle-class neighborhood of Amity. As Clint Eastwood had said this was the VFW of Amity, very few whites. The family was apparently Italian. I liked them already. The house was two stories. My first observation was the American Flag flying high on a pole with a solar light attached so that the Flag would illuminate in the dark. Now I liked this family more. The porch wrapped around the entire house. The house was brick and colored stone. The windows were wide with a view of the neighborhood. I was impressed. Sully and I walked to the front door admiring the shrubbery and the manicured lawn. I guess that they had at least an acre, unheard of in Amity. Outside of Amity this house would command a million and a half dollars. At one time within the confines of Amity this house would sell for close to a million. Today you could probably buy it for half a million, give or take.

Sully rang the bell. A pretty woman, not beautiful but pretty, opened the mostly stained-glass door. "We're early," I said. "I apologize."

"No problem." She was small, was well proportioned height and weight-wise, and dressed in a grey skirt that fell below her knees. She wore a neck high white button-down men's white on white shirt complete with gold initial cuff links.

I made the introductions then flashed my badge.

"Come in, please. My husband and Frank junior are in the living room. Please follow me."

The living room was almost larger than many apartments I've been in. A mirror ran the length of one wall. A television half-filled another wall. Pictures of little Frank in many uniforms, high school baseball, football, basketball, and swimming were neatly framed and hung on another wall. Still another wall held framed pictures of what I guessed to be pictures of Frank senior behind the wheel of a race car. I was, to say the least, impressed. This didn't fit my scheme of things.

My thoughts were interrupted by the entrance of two Franks. Senior Frank stood six foot one if he stood an inch. He was built like a damned bull. His hair was thick, wavy, and black. His eyes were sparking blue. If I had his money my eyes would sparkle too. He was dressed in freshly ironed black slacks, red pullover shirt and black loafers which probably cost more than my new Glock.

A few feet behind the senior man of the house, was the junior Frank. He was neatly attired in brown slacks, a lighter brown button-down shirt, and brown loafers. He had to have been six feet tall, put together like dad with a crew cut and blue eyes. He appeared nervous. If I was on the mark with my theory about the cases, junior had plenty to worry about.

We made introductions. Senior Frank took command of his ship. "Let's sit at the dining room table. We'll be more comfortable. Anita," senior Frank said, referring to his wife, "made a pitcher of lemonade, and a pitcher of iced tea." As dad led us to the dining room table, mom walked to the kitchen to bring out a tray with glasses, two pitchers and four glasses.

"You have a beautiful home here. Have you lived in Amity a long time?"

Senior Frank nodded. "We bought this home twelve years ago when Amity was… how should I put it… a better area. We sunk a fortune in it in upgrades. We're very happy here."

"If you don't mind my asking, what kind of work do you do?"

184

"I own a piece of a sanitation business, a big piece."

I grew up on the east coast. The garbage business was Teamster controlled. It was run by the mob in New York and New Jersey. You didn't fuck with the mob or with the Teamsters. As a matter of fact, I had a friend who got into an argument with a garbage truck driver over his dumping his trash can in the middle of the street. When he was done chewing the driver out, he couldn't get over himself. He bragged to his neighbors and his wife how big and bad he was, and how the driver was too chicken to get out of the truck. My neighbor got no trash pickup service for two weeks. To get his service restored he had to apologize to the driver and promise the driver an expensive bottle of Scotch for Christmas. I carry a gun and I won't fuck with the Teamsters.

"Where is your accent from?" I smiled.

"Detroit. And yours is from New York?"

"Good ear."

"Hard to miss."

"I'm in the wrong business."

"If you're happy and you can make a living, you're at the head of the pack."

I nodded. "You're so right."

Anita poured drinks. She didn't ask if we wanted a drink. "Who wants an iced tea?"

When the drinks were poured, Sully said, "Frank junior, Detective Kano, and I'm Agent Sullivan. We are here to discuss the investigation of two deaths. Ricki Montego

185

Valenzuela and Roberto Vega-Chapa. I understand," Sully lied, "that you knew them both."

Junior looked nervous. His eyes gave him away. His parents were oblivious. "We hung out some. Mostly with Roberto. Occasionally the three of us."

"Not the four of you?"

"I don't understand."

"You said you sometimes hung with Roberto and Ricki but mostly with Roberto. Did your girlfriend hang with you guys too?"

"I don't have a girlfriend. I'm too busy with school, sports and church."

"I see," Sully said. Sully got down to business. "Why do you think Roberto took his life?"

Junior shook his head. The parents were expressionless. "I don't have any idea. I didn't think...never would have thought he'd do that. Except for money problems now and then, he had everything going for him. He had a beautiful, loving girlfriend, he did well in school, he was liked by everyone. I don't understand it."

Junior said Roberto had money problems from time to time, yet he loaned Chernov two grand. I thought that didn't make a helluva' lot of sense, unless....

Sully continued. "Who would have hated Ricki enough to kill her?"

Junior sat up straight. "I know what you guys think. You think Roberto killed her then killed himself. That's wrong. I know...knew Roberto well enough to know that he wouldn't kill Ricki. He loved her. He couldn't kill anyone. Not Roberto."

"Any idea who might have killed her?"

Junior Frank shook his head. "Hell no."

I jumped in. I asked the parents if they had ever met either Ricki or Roberto. It turns out that Roberto had done some light yard work for them to earn a few bucks. Roberto and junior hung out at the house sometimes. Other than that, the Delvos had little to add.

"Did Roberto mess with drugs or alcohol?"

"No. Neither do I. The school is very strict about that. I'd get kicked off the team for that stuff."

Sully wouldn't let up. "Do you go to the same church that Ricki and Roberto attended?"

"Do you attend the meetings at Kevin Duffmann's house?"

Frank junior looked at his father then his mother. He shook his head up and down. "Yes."

"What is the purpose of those meetings?"

"It's church stuff. We talk about problems…if we have any. We try to help each other. Sometimes we read from the Bible."

I thought, four interviews and four people who gave pat answers to that question. Coincidence? I think not. It was my turn to ask a question. "Sometimes at Duffmann's house some of you stayed later than the others. Why?"

Junior didn't hesitate. "Some of us had other things to discuss."

"What kind of things?"

"Maybe we'd talk about school, sports, part time jobs."

"Did you ever attend a dinner at Kevin's house?"

"Yes."

"What did you discuss at these dinners?"

"Church stuff."

I wanted a look at this phone. With both parents at the table, I'd be taking a risk. Sully moved in for the kill. He did it indirectly with practiced precision and skill. Sully made an end run. "Did Ricki also like girls?"

There was a deafening silence at the table. If you listened closely, you could hear a piece of trash hit the ground. Junior turned beet red. Whether he was sharp enough to know the direction Sully was headed or whether we were in the right church, but wrong pew was up for grabs. I'd grab the former.

Frank junior's color returned to his face. "I told you, I didn't know Ricki well at all but if she did, I don't think Roberto would have been able to keep it a secret." Frank was either annoyed at the question or frightened at what might be coming with Sully's next pitch.

Sully's next pitch was a high hard fast ball right under junior's chin. "Do you date girls, boys or both?"

Frank senior snapped to attention. I thought he was going to spill the tea from the glass that was in his right hand. "Wait a minute! What the hell kind of a question are you asking my son; my son who will letter in three sports?"

I held up my hand. "Please relax, Mr. Delvo. This is standard. We're asking this of all the individuals we're interviewing. Let me explain." I was getting good at lying. I was about to get better. "Although we found no semen at either death scene, we did find DNA, and an item we can't talk about. It is an item that will link the killer to the victim." I was making up this shit as I was talking to Mr. Delvo. "In other words, this is a process of elimination. There may be a sexual element to the killing of Ricki. Under California's exclusionary law, not only is this acceptable questioning, it's also ethical and necessary for the report I am going to write at the station to substantiate PC, sir, probable cause." I was so full of shit I could smell myself. I watched Delvos faces. He was nodding as though he digested and swallowed each and every lying word. His wife was also nodding in agreement. I guessed junior was tightening up to keep from shitting himself. If I was right, we were closing in on a killer. If I was wrong, some fucking attorney could make a tidy sum, tax free, for the Delvos.

I was on a roll. I kept moving. "I know you understand everything I'm saying, Mr. Delvo. Does your wife?"

Frank senior looked at the misses. "I understand."

Without blinking I turned to junior. "Frank, do you understand the consequences of not coming clean with us at this very minute? You can be held to answer to the judge and a jury if you withhold evidence. I'm certain you are not directly involved in Ricki's killing but I suspect you have evidence that can and will lead us to her killer. I'm asking that your parents, who want nothing but the best for you, tell you to be one hundred percent honest and forthcoming with us in this felonious investigation."

Frank senior said, "Son, this is a time to show these gentlemen how you've been brought up. Be honest with them. This is as serious as life gets."

189

Mrs. Delvo chimed in. "Go ahead son. Don't hold back."

Sully didn't want to be left out. "Frank, you're a juvenile. While we can't guarantee it, we can do our damnedest to keep anything you tell us out of the paper. As far as your so-called friends are concerned, we're not going to tell them anything. If they get information on this case, it's going to come from you and only you. The less you tell them the better for you and the better for our investigation." Sully was not as full of shit as I was, but he was running a damned close second. He continued, "You're in a difficult situation. What you've done, is of your own making. What you do now, today, this very second, can put a mark on your future. The size of that mark is up to you. Here's the best part of what you have to do. The moment you come clean with all of us at this table is the moment you will start feeling better about yourself. Even better than that, is that the healing process will start to begin for your parents as well. Tell us everything. Don't leave out anything."

Sully looked at the Delvos. "I know this is difficult for you. It may become more difficult before the pain decreases. But it's for the best." Sully took a Sony tape recorder out of his pocket. "I'd like to record this for the record. Because Frank junior is a minor, I need your permission. Is recording this session with your son okay with you?"

If there ever was a three two pitch with the bases loaded and the score tied in the bottom of the ninth, this was that pitch. If one of the Delvos, anyone of the Delvos objected, that three two pitch was going in the dirt: game over. If anyone attorney ups, we were fucked with a capital F.

Sully went into a stretch position. He came to a rest, hands at his belt. He lifted his leg and fired a fast ball.

Mr. Delvo swung. He hit it high and deep to straight away center field. The center fielder ran back, back to the track, to the wall; he looked up the ball was high in a stand; grand slam. Game over. "I think we need the advice of an attorney. Do not turn on your recorder. I want this interview to end. I hope you understand. Frank junior is our son. I'm not one hundred percent on what's going on here but we're going to protect our son. I don't want to interfere with your investigation but at this point, our boy comes first."

We almost had it; almost. Close counts in horseshoes and hand grenades the man said. We just got blown to pieces. I handed each of the Delvos a business card. "If you change your mind, or if you think of anything that might help us, please call. Also," I looked directly at Frank junior, "if you call your friends and warn them about anything, not only will it impede our investigation but depending on the course of the investigation, you can be charged." I had to throw one more pitch. Mr. Delvo was at the plate. "Your attorney can verify the validity of that statement, sir." I drew a disappointed breath. "By the way, who is your attorney?"

Frank Delvo senior swung at the pitch and replicated the grand slam. It went over the same fucking center field wall. It traveled farther than the grand slam. "We retain Jerry Klein for our business. I'm sure Jerry would be happy to help us with this."

Head down, Sully and I walked to the dugout. We both had the same one-word comment when we got in the car, "FUCK!!!"

Sully put the key in the ignition but didn't start the car. "Son of a bitch. I thought we were there."

191

"We were and we are. I believe we're on the money. Sherlock over here was in the right church and the right pew."

Sully's hands were on the wheel. "I think I've got it all but spell it out for me."

I nodded with a smile. "Roberto's mom's comment about the rubbers she found in his room set me on the right track, or what I believe is the right track. Unless Ricki was giving Roberto blow jobs every other day, why the rubbers? Couple that with the two grand he loaned Chernov, the meetings at Duffmann's house, and the dinners, all this shit adds up to one thing for me."

"Sex parties," Sully said.

"Sex parties with kids, or something like it. I was thinking more like these kids were getting paid to get these gay adults off. How does that work for you?"

Sully started the unmarked unit. He put us ten eight, back in service. "You're talking about an organized sex ring of underage kids?"

"I am. I think Frank junior was about to unload when big Frank attorneyed up."

Sully pulled away from the curb. "Now what?"

"I think our next move is to stake out Duffmann's house. If I'm right, and I think I am, this thing is going to get dirtier and scarier."

"When do you want to start the stakeout?"

"Let me call Mac. I'd like to meet back at the station. We can update Mac and Mac can update us. Then we can set up a plan. I'd like all three of us to be in on the stakeout."

"And don't forget your date with April."

"Are you the keeper of my social calendar?" I called Mac. She had an hour left of interviews. We agreed to meet at the station.

"I can't believe Delvo has your favorite attorney on retainer."

"I don't need to hear it. That's how the fucker affords his expensive imported automobile."

"Do you hear much from Paula, Rocky's widow?"

"No. My understanding is that she's with her folks. I can't even remember the state and at this stage of the game my head is so filled with this case I can hardly think straight." Mac would tell me to raise the rent and evict whoever was renting space in my head. Maybe easy for her to do, she worked a program.

"Other than April, what's on your mind?"

"April's the least of it, trust me. I guess I wouldn't make a professional poker player. Actually, the priest, Father Strayhan. If it is a sex ring of some sort, how can the Father be attending these meetings and not know or at least suspect?"

"Are you inferring….?"

"You're the experienced fed. We're taught to dissect all angles. That's what I'm doing."

"Just saying," Sully remarked.

"Listen, we've got time before we have to meet Mac at the station. Let's take a ride. There's someone I'd like you to meet." I gave Sully directions.

As he drove, I thought. Thinking these days put me in a bad neighborhood. I knew priests did things that were sick. Cops sometimes killed when they didn't have to shoot. I killed a guy because I thought he shouldn't be breathing our air. I didn't lose any sleep over it. But if Father Strayhan was involved in this shit, he deserved whatever he got. I wouldn't mind being the guy who gave it to him. I looked up. I thought, forgive me.

Why the hell the church wouldn't let priests marry was beyond me. Marriage for priests would solve all sorts of problems.

Sully parked the car. I led Sully to Rocky's grave. "Rocky, meet Sully. Sully is my new partner. He isn't you. He's got a lot to learn. But at least he doesn't smoke."

"Sully meet Rocky. The best partner, the best friend a guy could have. Rock, I didn't have time to stop to get you cigarettes, next visit, I'll get you two packs."

Sully looked at me like I had a loose lug nut. "You know something, Rocky, your partner is no winner either. He flirts during interviews, he can't drive, he thinks he's Sherlock Fucking Holmes, and he drinks too damn much."

I cut in. "But I have," I pulled out my detective badge, "this." I held the gold badge so I was sure Rocky could see it.

"Now we add braggart to his other strengths."

I smiled. "I miss you, partner. One of these days we'll be back together. I'll make you a deal here and now. I'll cut back on my drinking if you cut back on your smoking. It'll

194

be good for both of us." I looked at my cell phone. "We've got to go, partner. Duty calls. See you soon, real soon."

I made one call on the drive back to the station. I called St. Francis Hospital. Both officers were still in surgery. The protesters were still chanting, "I hope they die."

We arrived back at the station just in time for the briefing with Mac.

SURPRISES, SURPRISES, SURPRISES

We filled Mac in on our adventures with our four interviews. Mac looked a bit more than surprised. "Are you telling me that you suspect a child sex operation is going on right here in Amity, under our noses; and nobody's been the wiser?"

"It's a theory."

Mac laughed. "You really are the devil in disguise."

"Me? A damn priest could be involved, and I'm the devil in disguise?"

"Let's change the subject."

Sully looked at me, raised his eyebrows and smiled. "Guess who owns the couch tonight?"

"Fuck you, too. Listen, I want to stakeout the Duffmann place later tonight. Anyone want to keep me company?"

I had two takers. "Let's clear it with the WC, and let's take two unmarked units." I asked Mac, "Get anything on your interviews?"

"The jury's still out on that. But like I've told you a couple of times if nothing else we're eliminating possibilities."

"I've got a few things to take care of. How about we meet downstairs at 1830 and see what we shakeout at Duffmann's? On my way out, I'll clear things with the WC, and get us call signs."

APRIL IN THE SUMMER

I drove home. I had a couple shots of Seagram's then hit the couch for thirty minutes of R and R. I showered, shaved, changed clothes, and drove over to April Johnson's house not knowing what to expect. My knock was answered by none other than April. She was wearing a white t-shirt that read Blue Lives Matter. She wasn't wearing a bra. She was wearing darker white slacks that didn't show panty lines; I was disappointed. But those slacks hugged her body like mom hugs her newborn. "C'mon in. For the record," April smiled, "Peter is at his friend's house." She took my hand and led me to the somewhat familiar living room. "Do I need to search you for weapons?"

"I'm armed. But a hands-on intrusion is welcome."

April licked her lips. "Sit down. What would you like to drink?"

I sat on the couch. "I'm working later but a shot or two of Seagram's, if you have it, would cool me off."

"If you're hot, I can adjust the air. Or" she leaned forward and kissed me lightly on the mouth. "Does that do anything for your thermostat?" She turned. "I'll be back with drinks in a minute. Please keep your weapon holstered until I get back."

She sure didn't waste any time. Neither did Peter. He was showing respect and there was not a Flag to salute. The sign was a damn good omen. What wasn't so good was that I was thinking of Mac. Did I really want to do this to prove a point? And if I did prove a point, what the hell did it prove? Mac and I weren't married to each other. We had no claim to each other. April was cute, clever, clean, and probably

197

contagious. Hey, with that kind of alliteration I could be a writer, another Joseph Wambaugh. Maybe I had a second career.

Most guys would give their middle finger to be in the position I was in. (Sans Mac's change of "dealership"). I was troubled. Do I, or don't I? Should I or shouldn't I. I looked down at the bulge in my pants, just as April came back with the drinks on a coca cola tray.

She caught me looking down. "Did you lose something? Is that where you carry your baton?"

"Actually, I think I found something," I said honestly, knowing she didn't have any idea what the hell I was talking about. I was as confused as a child on his first scavenger hunt.

"Here." She set the tray on the table in front of the couch. I took the drink. She held her glass to mine. We tapped glasses. "To new beginnings."

"To new beginnings," I said. I downed the shot. She brought the Seagram's bottle with her. "You can have another. It's happy hour."

"Any hour with you, I suspect, will be happy hour." I poured myself a second shot. "Are you trying to get me loaded so you can seduce me?"

She took a second sip of whatever the hell was in her glass. "Am I that hard to take stone cold sober?"

I laughed. "Quite the contrary. I'd never have to wear glasses even if I keep looking at you until I'm 105."

"Keep throwing compliments my way. You're softening me up."

And I keep getting harder and harder. This time April stole a glance at my crotch. We were both silent. There was no need for words. April leaned over. I leaned sideways. Her lips met my lips. Her lips parted. My lips parted. My tongue met April's tongue. My head was spinning. It sure the hell wasn't from a couple of shots of Seagram's. WOW! We drifted to the couch; our lips locked in longing.

MORE SURPRISES

We rendezvoused at the station at 1830. I commandeered two unmarked units. There were three of us. Two of us would partner up. One would ride solo. I assumed Mac would ride with me. I didn't know if I was in favor of that. I didn't have a choice as it turned out.

"Who's who in the zoo?" I clowned.

Mac spoke up immediately. "I'll ride with Sully."

I was surprised. I had mixed emotions about her decision. It was a control thing. Why the fuck did Mac want to ride with Sully, and not me? I was damn sure Sully hadn't told her about April.

"Okay. Let's saddle up and get in place at Duffmann's place. There is no need to get too close to the house. Our mission tonight is to observe and track who goes and who comes, no pun intended. Sully and Mac, you guys are X-Ray Two Adam. I'm X-Ray One. We each have portables, so we don't need to tie up the radio. We also have our cell phones. Giddy-yup."

Just before 1900 hours we were in place at the Duffmann house. The X-Ray Adam unit was parked east of the house. I was on the west side. There was already a black Ford Fusion parked in front of the house. I jotted down the license plate.

I called Mac on my cell still feeling uncomfortable that she was riding with Sully. I updated her on the black Ford Fusion. "Give me the plate. I'll run it for you." It was customary that on a stakeout a two-man car would handle computer business. If I, a single man unit, got on the computer, I'd be blind to street traffic, foot traffic, any and all activity on the street while I was on the computer. I could not safely watch the street and punch keys on the computer, especially with my low-level computer skills. Cops died that way. It was too long ago that two New York City detectives, on stakeout in the city that never sleeps, were drinking coffee and bullshitting with each other. One was playing games on his cell phone. A "hitter" walked up to the car and emptied his gun into the car. One cop died instantly. The other detective died the next day at the hospital. You never know.

I did make one call. I called dispatch to check on the status of the two deputies who were ambushed. One was out of surgery. The other deputy was still in surgery.

I gave Mac the plate on the Ford Fusion. "Stand by."

It took three minutes for the return. "Wanna guess?"

"What do I win if I'm right?"

"Me." Mac didn't miss a beat, but she still chose to ride with the fed.

"Father Patrick Strayhan, from my favorite church."

"Yeah. You're right on. You're earning that badge."

"That said. One can only hope he's just...." Another car pulled up behind the Fusion. There were two people in the car. I didn't recognize either, but it was getting dark and I was a distance from the car. I got on my radio. "Can either of you make either of those guys who just exited the dark colored Cad?" I stuck my binoculars where they'd do the most good. I focused. The license plate was clear as clean glass. I wrote it down. "Here's another plate for you, Mac." I gave her the plate.

When the return came back, it came back to Bill Thompson who was on our interview list. We hadn't gotten to interview him yet. There was a teenager walking with Thompson. I couldn't identify the teenager.

The question I had to ask myself was if Frank Delvo junior spilled the beans, would the group be meeting at Duffmann's house? The answer was twofold. Probably not, on the one hand. On the other hand, if they had nothing to hide, they'd go ahead with their regular meeting dates. I opted for curtain one. Delvo junior kept quiet. He had more to lose if he shot off his mouth. Further, if his dad did lawyer up for him, Klein would advise the family to clam up tight.

We sat. We observed. There was little to observe. Even with my binoculars, I couldn't see into the house. Sully and Mac were too far from the house to be able to get a visual. I tried to make sense of this in my mind.

If there was sexual activity going on in the house, there was good odds, no great odds that Ricki's killer, if not Roberto, might be in the house now, or if not in the house was on our list. It was plausible that more than one individual could be responsible for the murder. If Frank junior opened his mouth, he could be in danger.

Carrying out another scenario, I could be way off base. The activity in the house could be innocent church teachings. I doubted that; especially after interviewing junior. If that be the case, the killer of Ricki could be an opportunist who saw a beautiful young girl and decided to take his shot.

It was twenty-one thirty hours when the house emptied of everyone but Duffmann, who we could only assume was in the house because not one of us could actually positively identify him as being in the house. We couldn't see into the house. Thompson and his charge got into the Caddy and

202

drove off. Father Strayhan got into the Fusion and took off. I thought about tailing the two but with one unit on each we were gambling on being spotted. The two of us could tail Thompson in his Cadillac. If we did, we could find out who the teenager was with him. Chances are the teen was on our list. I made the not so hasty decision to call it a night. Somebody said, "Tomorrow's another day."

I drove and I thought. Good detectives did their best work with their minds. I believed there was at least a fifty-fifty chance (you couldn't get those odds in a Las Vegas casino) that there was more than Bible study going on in Duffmann's house. I had a strong suspicion that more was being served during dinners at Duffmann's house than food. The big problem was that I needed proof.

A good detective needs patience. A great detective needs patience, determination, and the courage to be wrong. More cases are solved by a detective's gut feeling. I had a gut feeling.

MORE SURPRISES: I WANT AN ATTORNEY

When my cell rang at seven thirty in the morning, I was about to get into my car to head for the station. Without looking at the ID, I would have bet on Mac, then Sully, then the day's watch commander. I would have lost three times. At the other end of the phone was Jerry Kline.

"Officer Kano. This is Attorney Jerry Kline. How are you?"

Not one to play with words so early in the morning I said, "Surprised counselor, to say the least. Somehow, I don't think this is a social call. What can I do for you?"

"What can we do for each other? As you already know, I represent the Delvo family."

"Correct."

"I'd like to have a meeting."

"And that meeting would include….?"

"You and me, for now."

"My two partners are part of this investigation. It would be more appropriate if the three of us met." The fact of the matter was most attorneys intimidated the hell out of me. If cops were honest, they'd tell you attorneys frightened them. Cops will tell you war stories about how they fucked over some counselor when the attorney had them on the witness stand. The fact is that nine point five times out of ten it's the attorney who shoves it up the cop's ass raw. That's just the facts, ma'am.

Further fact: If a cop thought he had the smarts; he'd be an attorney. Many cops do have the smarts. Some even go to law school while still on the job. Most want to play cops and robbers on the street. It's a second childhood.

If I thought I could handle all the hard work and studying to get through law school, I'd bite the bullet. Then I'd bite an even larger caliber bullet to take the bar exam. Finally, the biggest bite of all would be setting up my practice. I'd love to be driving a Ferrari ala Jerry Kline.

"How about you and I meet, Officer Kano, then we can decide if we want to proceed, and if you do want to proceed, we can set up guidelines. I think you'll like what I have to tell you."

I knew I had the advantage here. Kline called me. I had something he wanted. "I'll split the difference with you, counselor. Sully and I will meet with you."

"You and I meet in my office. Whatever it is you drink; I'll have a quart of it."

"Counselor, this is one time I think I'm holding the winning hand. You tell me the time. My partner and I will be at your office. Otherwise, I rest my case."

"You should think about law school. I'd be glad to lend a helping hand. My firm can use someone with your balls. What do you drink?"

I felt my face flush. If he was fucking with me, he was a good lay. "One day I may take you up on that." We agreed on a time. He gave the address. It was game on. "Seagram's."

HE WHO THROWS THE FIRST
PITCH

I stopped to grab breakfast at Kenny's, solo. Kenny's was "cop friendly," not that it mattered, I was in plain clothes. I wanted to think through the meeting with Kline before we met. His client was a juvenile. As far as I knew at this point the junior Delvo wasn't in any legal trouble. If my guess was accurate, the kid couldn't be charged with anything. If my thinking was on target, the adults could obviously be charged. Thinking way, way out of the box, if Kline was looking to protect the family, I had to ask myself could the family be involved. That was a stretch. I wanted to cover all possibilities before I met with Kline.

I ordered one of Kenny's many specials, a sausage omelet. I also ordered coffee, and a winning lottery ticket. I got the omelet, and the coffee. The waitress told me she was keeping the winning lottery ticket for retirement. She was probably twenty-three.

I was so deep in thought I didn't even see her place the food on the counter. I didn't trust Kline any more than I trusted Bill Clinton when he said, "I didn't have sex with that woman." Kline was an attorney. The only pocket he wouldn't put his hand in was his own. What the fuck could the guy want? I sipped coffee, cut into my sausage and eggs, and thought more. The more I ate, the more I thought. Unless I was a terrible judge of people, there was no way mom and dad Delvo were involved in a child sex ring. Wops had a reputation for a lot of things; that wasn't one of them. I could still be way off base.

I asked for another coffee. I bit angrily into my dry toast. I ran through the Delvo interview again. The kid was about to give it up when dad interceded. If it wasn't child sex, the only other answer was drugs. They could be doing drugs in the house. They could be using the kids to deal drugs, to buy drugs. That would make more sense. If that be the case, Kline had at least one client to protect. The kids could be charged for dealing drugs.

I finished what I wanted to finish of my breakfast. I downed the last drop of coffee. I left a hefty tip, paid my bill, and exited Kenny's. I had a short drive to the station.

I met Mac and Sully in "our office." Before I sat down to join them, I said, "Take five, maybe ten." I sat. "You'll never guess who called me."

"A Seagram's CEO," Mac said, a poor attempt at being funny.

Sully said, "Tom Selleck. Since you're an acting detective, he wants to offer you an acting job on Blue Bloods."

"You guys amaze me. You could be a team, a comedy team; the two stooges."

"The suspense is killing me," Sully sulked. "Who the hell called you?"

"Jerry the Jew."

"Attorney Kline?"

"None other."

"Why? For what?" Sully was half out of his chair.

"He wants to meet this morning. We spared on the phone but all I can get out of the mouthpiece is that his clients are the Delvo family. He wanted to meet one on one. I told him I had two partners involved in the investigation and we all meet or no meeting."

"I like your style," Mac threw in.

"He beat me down without a stick. We split the difference. We agreed Sully and I would meet with him."

"What time?"

"Ten thirty this morning."

Sully shook his head. "No can do, partner. Mac and I have a follow up interview at SafeGuard at 10:30."

"You can call the counselor and change the meeting time, or you can go it alone. Sully and I had to bite nails to put this interview together. We can't change the time."

What the hell was that all about? I swallowed. I didn't want to fuck with the counselor. "I'll put my big boy pants on and meet with Kline all by my lonesome. Keep me posted and I'll do the same." I drew a breath. "Would someone like to bring me up to speed?"

Mac took charge. "We can't. There's really nothing more than speculation at this point. If something pops, you'll be the first to know."

MY HEADS IN A BAD NEIGHBORHOOD

Sully and Mac left me alone at the station to ponder all this new bullshit. Why was I cut out of what was going on in Mac's investigation? Why did she choose to go it with Sully and not me? Was this her idea of some kind of revenge, a vendetta? What did she know, what did they know that I didn't, and why didn't they want to let me in?

I had to clear my head. I had a meeting with Kline. I had to organize my thoughts. Mac was taught in AA to live in the now. She called it NOW: NO OTHER WAY. I had to get my head in the NOW. In this case it was Mac, Sully, and this fucking case, and the missing money that were invading my head. I had to raise the rent and evict the renters.

I grabbed a sheet of paper out of the computer. I focused on my upcoming meeting with the Jew attorney. I wrote notes which is difficult to do when you're not sure of the direction the conference is geared toward. Kline bothered me. He was not only a brilliant attorney, but he didn't care what he had to do to score a win for his client. One on one, he'd shred me into pieces. I reminded myself to get back into the NOW. Projecting that being chewed up and spit out was making a loser out of me before the first pitch was thrown. I was in a bad neighborhood. I had to move out.

Beverly Hills was the home to movie moguls, stars like the late Johnny Carson, Joan Rivers, Martin Sheen. Wilshire Boulevard boasted high end jewelry shops, dress shops, imported car dealerships. You had to have major league money to walk in BH. Kline's office was in a high rise on Wilshire Boulevard.

There was a doorman in full uniform standing under the awning. He eyed me suspiciously. "Your name sir, please."

I had on my best suit, which I had purchased for court appearances. The suit, with tailoring and tax, ran me two hundred fifteen dollars. It was off the rack at Suits R Us in Woodland Hills. The doorman's hat probably cost more than my suit. Capitalism at its finest. With tax free tips, the damn doorman probably netted more than I did.

I explained to Danny Doorman why he was meeting me, and with whom I had business. He said, "very well, sir," turned sideways, used his white gloved hand to push the intercom button, then spoke into the speaker so softly I could barely make out his words. This was a different world. "You may enter, sir." He told me the floor.

"Is there an office number, Danny?" I was being a smart ass. Even Danny Doorman one upped me.

"Sir, Mr. Kline, Esquire's office is the entire floor."

I rode a pristine elevator up to the eighth floor. The elevator must have been read its rights. It didn't make a sound from ground floor to door opening on floor eight. I hoped this wasn't coming attractions.

When the elevator door opened, the opposite wall, just above eye level, in large gold print letters read, HOME TO JERRY KLINE, ESQ., ON THIS FLOOR ONLY THE BEST WILL DO. Under that greeting, in smaller gold print was Jerry's motto: I GET YOU OFF.

The arrow on the wall pointed to the criminal defense attorney's office. I was prepared for almost anything but what I observed. The fucking oval office had nothing on Jerry Kline, ESQ. The president's desk probably cost less money than the receptionists. The white carpet was so thick

210

you could sleep on it comfortably. It was so deep, if you were short, you sink in the carpet up to your neck. It must be nice.

A dozen chairs were spaced along the wall. The brown leather high back chairs probably cost more per chair than Sully's mortgage for his former house and for the rent on his apartment combined. I swallowed hard. I was impressed.

No wonder the mouthpiece drove a Ferrari. Hell, I'm sure he wrote it off. Maybe I would let Kline sponsor me through law school. We could form a partnership after I passed the bar. Instead of DOO WOP, we could call the firm, JEW-WOP.

The pretty receptionist spoiled my dreams. "Sir, you are?"

"Detective Kano. Tony Kano. I have an appointment with Mr. Kline."

"Attorney Kline will be with you in a few minutes. Have a chair, please. Can I get you something to drink?"

Hell, it was ten thirty. "I'll have a double shot of Seagram's." Of course, I was joshing.

Rhonda Receptionist stood up. She was tall. Her white dress appeared more for a night out than a day at work but that was Beverly Hills. I watched her heels disappear into the carpet as she walked across the room. She disappeared. When Rhonda reappeared, she did so with a glass of Seagram's, ice, and the Seagram's bottle all three on a tray. How she balanced it all on that damn carpet was beyond me. She set everything down on the table in front of me. "In case you are really thirsty, I brought the bottle."

I was sure had I called the meeting; the booze would be on my bill. I'm sure Jerry wrote that off as he did his Ferrari. I looked at Rhonda. "Care to join me?"

211

"Maybe when I get off."

If I took her up on that, I wondered if she'd bill me. I didn't respond to her offer. I had enough trouble with Mac, and now April. I downed the drink, then quickly poured another, and downed it. Now there was no stopping me. I was a match for Jerry the Jew.

I tried to act cool as I entered Kline's office. If his receptionist's desk resembled that of the president's desk in the oval office, his desk was cut from the same mold only larger, much, much larger. It was mahogany with silver leaf all around. His high back brown leather chair had his initials on each arm. The thick pile brown carpet buried two to three inches of that desk. The wall behind Kline, repeated what I observed when I exited the elevator, "I GET YOU OFF."

His desk was piled with files all neatly stacked on one corner of the humongous desk. Two lap top computers sat in the opposite corner of the desk. He had a simple name plate in the corner of the desk. It said, JERRY KLINE, ESQ.

The wall behind the criminal defense attorney boasted pictures of Kline and OJ Simpson, each with a golf club in his hand. The picture next to it was of Kline with his arm around Johnny Cochran. More pictures showed Kline in or near expensive Ferrari imports. One picture displayed Kline at the podium in Scottsdale, Arizona at a Barrett Jackson Auction. I remembered that from a newspaper article. Kline auctioned one of his Ferrari's for cancer research. They let him drop the gavel when the car sold. In front of his desk, were five chairs, each of them shaped like a Ferrari.

Kline walked around his desk. He was wearing a grey double-breasted suit with a white-on-white shirt, highlighted by French cuffs and custom Ferrari cuff links. His grey tie showed Kline's initials in red script. That suit had to of cost Kline more than my car.

We shook hands. "Let me buy you a drink."

I nodded. "Seagram's No ice. Thanks."

"Have a seat."

I chose a 308 Ferrari. He walked over to a bookshelf, hit a button and the wall opened to a full mirrored bar. I couldn't believe this shit. The mirror was a Ferrari. This guy had a hard on for Ferrari's like I had a fetish for panties, Mac's panties.

"Were you born a Ferrari?"

Kline turned toward me. "Family tradition." He poured drinks, hit another button that closed the wall, then walked back to me. He handed me a drink. "Here's to getting off on the right foot. Let's not make this adversarial. We each have something the other wants. Let's see if we can get this done."

I drank. Kline took a seat next to me. "First order of business. On or off the record."

I didn't hesitate. I didn't want this meeting recording in any way, shape, or style. "Off the record." I drank some more. "Ground rules?"

"Let's make them up as we go. Obviously, I'm going to protect my client, and his family."

"I'm confused, counselor. As far as I know, your client hasn't committed any crime."

"We'll get into that. But no, he hasn't. He is a star athlete. He's well thought of in school, church, and community. His mom and dad are upstanding members of the community.

Negative publicity can drill down deep and ruin them not only socially can also wreak havoc on them financially."

As Kline and I played "ping pong," I tried to stay a shot ahead of him. That was most difficult as I wasn't sure what the hell his client was involved in. "Can we cut to the chase?"

"Can I get you another drink?"

"Sure."

"We'll cut to the chase, as you put it, in a minute. There are some things I need to confirm." He walked as he talked. "Can we keep any negative publicity out of the newspapers?"

"First of all, I don't even know what we're trying to keep out of the papers. Secondly, your clients a minor. As such, he's afforded certain protections under the law."

Kline came back drinks in hand. "Not so his family."

"I can't guarantee that. I'd be a lair if I said I could. I am only one mouth. You know how reporters are. Anything for a story no matter who it hurts." I wasn't sure if I should have used who or whom. I couldn't remember that English class. I didn't want Kline to think I couldn't speak the King's English.

I took another drink then went to slam the little white ping pong ball off the end of the table and over his attorney head. "Enough happy crap. You said we'd cut to the chase. Let's do it. What the fuck is your client involved in?"

Kline caught shot and volleyed it right back at me. "What do you think he's involved in?"

I didn't hesitate. "Sex or drugs or both. Your move."

"I'm impressed, Detective. I'm telling you; you'd make an excellent attorney."

"Shit or get off the pot. Stop fucking with me. This is all off the record. Let's get down to cases. I'm sure we both have better things to do than bat this thing back and forth." Then I offered, "Even though you have one hell of an office."

"A few years, all this could be yours."

"Are we done screwing around?"

"As far as I know," Kline said, "he's involved with a sex ring. Drugs are possible but I don't think so. I'd bet my yellow Ferrari that drugs aren't involved, at least not in my client's case."

That much was on the table. It was my serve. "Is it an all-male sex ring?"

"I don't know that I call it a 'ring.' Let's say sex is involved. Let's also say adult males are paying, one way or another, for services per and by minors."

"How long has this shit been going on?"

"To my knowledge, at least three years in Amity." Kline sipped what I guessed to be Scotch rocks. "Understand this all comes from my client. Your part in this is going to be to verify it. That's going to be a tricky business. Individuals with community standing may be involved."

Point Kline. My serve. "Do the upstanding members of Peyton Place include a priest?"

"Very possibly."

"Jesus H Christ."

"I don't believe he's involved."

215

"That's funny."

"Actually," Kline said, "it's sad, very sad. When this breaks free, it's going to be a sad day for Amity."

"What do you want to do next, counselor, beside pour me another drink?"

Kline stood up. I hadn't noticed how tall he was. He was probably six foot one. The guy was well put together. He walked over to the wall to buy me another drink. "I'd like to set up a meeting. The Delvo family, you, and me. What do you think?"

"The purpose of the meeting would be to get everything out on the table. If there is a child sex ring operating in Amity, it needs to be shut down. My client can help you do just that."

"And in return for your client's cooperation he gets what?"

Kline brought me my drink. He was still working on his. "In exchange my clients," he underscored the 's' in clients. "In exchange, the Delvos get complete immunity."

"Are you telling me that the Delvo family is involved?"

"I don't think Anita Delvo is involved. As far as the old man, not that I know of. I'm a forward thinker."

I rubbed my chin then I downed my drink. "This damn thing could go deep."

"I'm sure it does go deep, detective."

"Call me Tony." I was still rubbing my chin. "I need to get a hold of a layout of the house where they hold their meetings."

"The Duffmann house."

216

"The Duffmann house," I echoed.

"Why a layout of the house?"

"I'm also a forward thinker." I wanted to explore all avenues. I wanted to cover all possibilities. Depending on what the Delvo boy had to say, I might get enough to bug the place. I sure the hell should get enough from the meeting to score a warrant. However, I didn't want to play my hand too soon. "I don't want to ask the kid to wear a wire. That's too dangerous and a jury wouldn't approve. If Frank senior is involved, it wouldn't bother me one bit to shove a wire up his ass."

"Listen, Tony. I know I have earned a reputation as a sometimes-dirty dealer. But for me this is over the top."

"It sure the hell is."

"And call me Jerry. And for the record, we have something in common."

"No shit. What would that be?"

"We're both Italian."

"When the fuck did Kline become Italian?"

My real dad, who was killed in an auto accident when I was seven was Andrew Lesola. When my mom remarried, she asked me to take my stepdad's name. He was a good guy. Out of respect to both of them I took his name, Kline. My first name is actually Alfonzo. Can you see yourself hiring an attorney who name is Alfonzo Lesola?"

"If I become an attorney and join your firm, we can bill ourselves Two Wops from Beverly Hills."

"You gotta' do better than that to join this firm."

217

"I gotta' run this by the big boys at the station. This is above my pay grade. How about I give you a call and we see if we can set up a meeting for tomorrow?"

"Get back to me later today."

We shook hands. The handshake was warm. I left Kline's office disliking him a bit less. Rhonda Receptionist smiled when I walked out of Kline's office. She walked out from behind her desk. "In case you forget where you've been, my phone number is on the back of this business card. I'll help you find your way in." She handed me a multicolored business card which, in addition to Kline name, address, and phone number, had a red three oh eight Ferrari on it. You can't write this stuff!

I got in my car. I sat behind the wheel without putting the key in the ignition. I had a lot to swallow and digest. I had a lot to think about. I had plans to make. If nothing else, I apparently had a teammate, a wop teammate.

I also had the possibility; probability of a juvenile sex ring being operated by Amity community members. There was also the possibility that drugs were involved. Sex and drugs usually were a tow horse parlay.

THREE DEAD PERPS

My next move was SOP. I was supposed to notify my lieutenant. He in turn would contact the captain. The captain would touch base with Rolando who was acting chief. I went above and beyond. I called Lee Rolando directly; a no-no. Fuck them if they can't take a joke.

We set up a meeting for later in the afternoon. That gave me two and a half hours to kill. Number one on my agenda was to check in with Sully and Mac. I decided to return the favor. I phoned Sully. Screw Mac. She doesn't want me along for the ride, she doesn't get a phone call. Nothing childish about me when I'm pissed.

"Partner," he said, "I can't talk now. I'll call later."

I had free time on my hands. That's dangerous when I'm in the mood I was in. I needed to qualify for the quarter. I could drive out to the range, shoot, clean my Glock, grab lunch, and make my meeting with Rolando.

I could call April and get laid if I could get it up. That would necessitate my giving her a full explanation for walking out on her yesterday. I didn't want to do that.

I also didn't want to get my suit dirty at the range. Each of the four qualification shoots for the year are different shoots. You don't just stand static and fire your duty weapon. Sometimes you roll on the fucking floor and shoot; other times you duck and cover then shoot; sometimes you beat the shit out of a dummy with your baton or asp and shoot. It depended on the range master.

I opted to meet my range qualification. I drove to the freeway. I was a multitasker. As I drove, I thought. Most of my brain space was awarded to Mac. Whether it was intentional or not, she had me going. She had turned the tables on me.

Our indoor range was a few miles off the freeway in Santa Fe Springs. Traffic was heavy but I "borrowed" the diamond lane telling myself I was on police business. Fortunately for me, the range wasn't crowded. I didn't have to crawl on the floor to qualify. I did have to take out three perps holding three waitress's hostage in a crowded restaurant. I had to do this from a seated position.

The scenario: I'm seated across from a female friend enjoying dinner when these three assholes attempt to rob the eatery. After being given the demanded cash, they grab three servers and attempt to drag them outside to their car. They pass within ten feet of my table, so my window of "opportunity" is slim.

If I don't shoot, the slime balls have three hostages. If I shoot and miss, everyone in the restaurant is at risk. I have a relatively clear background. There's the possibility if I fire and hit my target, a round could go through one of the perps and hit an innocent. I have no choice. I have to take action. I have seconds to make the call. "Everyone down!" Now! "Do it now!"

The cardboard perps and hostages are on a wire line and are moving. I draw my Glock which is loaded with hollow points. A head shot, my only option because of the way the idiots are holding the hostages by the neck, is my only option. I have less than two seconds.

I point and shoot. Without looking to see the results, I fire off three rounds. The scenario is stopped by the shrill sound of a whistle. The range master and I check the results. I was three for three. I took out three bad guys.

"Great shooting, Kano. You saved three cardboard lives."
Timberman stopped, turned, and asked me, "Have you been
drinking?"

"Are you kidding me? You know I don't drink. One drink
and I wouldn't be able to find my Glock."

"Kano get out of here. You're done. Clean your Glock and
go back to what you were doing. See you next quarter buddy.
Well done."

I cleaned my Glock carefully. I didn't want to get any oil on
my cheap suit.

Timberman told me I saved three cardboard lives. The other
night I was watching a ballgame while downing shots. I have
no idea who was playing. The game was a laugher, a
lopsided ballgame. I think it was fourteen to three in the
eighth. Someone hit a three-run home run that just cleared
the wall, making it seventeen to three. The left fielder,
smiling, started yelling to the ump that it was fan
interference, that a fan reached out and touched the ball
making it difficult for him to make the catch. That was pretty
funny since all the fans in the stadium seats were cardboard.
I drove back to the station, in heavy traffic, thinking this
would be a better world if we were all cardboard!

PAIN IN THE BRASS

Acting Chief Lee Rolando decided it would be best if we met away from the station. We drove, in separate cars, to Martin Luther King, Junior Park in El Monte, a twenty-minute drive from Amity. We found a secluded area. The wooden bench was comfortable.

"It seems whenever we're together sir, it's bad news."

"Not your doing, Tony. It's the way things are. You're responsible for cleaning up some of our garbage. I'm grateful for that. If I become chief, you'll see just how grateful. What have we got?"

I crossed then uncrossed my legs. This could get messy.

"What have we got, Tony?"

I spelled out the meeting with Kline. "It's very possible community members are running a child sex ring in Amity. We're not yet certain how deep it goes nor are we sure of those involved. It might or might not involve drugs. It might involve a priest."

Rolando squeezed his upper lips with two fingers. He closed his eyes. "Mother of God when does it stop?"

"When it stops, you and I are out of a job."

"That wouldn't be so bad. You and I will never be out of a job. How long do you think this has been going on?"

"According to one source, at least three years."

"How the hell can something like this go on for three years in Amity without us hearing something about it?"

"If I'm on the money, and I think I am, there's a tight knit clique that has kept it hush hush. There are less than a dozen members. Half are adults, half are teens. All are male as far as we know at this point. I want the go ahead to meet with Kline and the involved family probably this afternoon. I didn't run it up the chain because I didn't want anyone else to know. The more people who know the better the chance the newspapers will get ahold of it, then goodbye case. This one needs to be put to bed quickly. The longer it drags on the more chance it's going to get out."

"What do you hope to accomplish at the meeting?" Rolando tightened the knot on his tie.

"I want to firm up what we think we know. Once we have all the facts, we'll set up a plan. Once we have the plan down, we'll bring it to you for approval."

"Who else knows about this?"

"Attorney Kline, the involved family, Sully and to some degree Mac."

"Who is the family?"

"The Frank Delvo family."

"I know the family. Not well but he supports our department." He stopped playing with his tie. "Obviously, Frank junior is involved. How about Frank senior?"

"We're not sure."

"Who's the priest? And don't tell me Father Strayhan."

"Okay. I won't tell you."

"My wife and I attend the Church of All Faiths. I hope to hell you're wrong."

"That makes more than two of us." I told the Acting Chief about the stake out. "If this afternoon's meeting gives us the evidence we need, I want to move quickly on a warrant. We're going to need to put a crew together to get this done damn fast."

"You have my complete backing. I know a judge who will give you the warrant." Lee Rolando stood up. "Let's get out of here. I want to know what time you're going to meet. Will Mac and Sully be at the meeting?"

"No. They're still chasing down the money from the armored car heist."

"Keep me in the loop. Good luck, Tony. Watch your back."

I walked around the park track to clear my head. I loved my country. We lived in the best country going, no doubt about it. But some people were so fucked up it was unbelievable. How sick could we get? As bad as it was, it was going to get worse.

FROM BAD TO WORSE AND THEN THE WORST

I called Kline. We set the meeting for three forty-five in his office. I went home to take a shower and wash some of the stench off me. I didn't know that the stench was going to turn to pure shit.

The initial meeting in Kline's office included the Delvos: Anita, Frank Senior, Frank junior, Kline, and me. For the meeting, the five of us sat at an oblong mahogany table in the corner of the room. There was a tape recorder on the table, but it wasn't turned on.

Attorney Kline opened the meeting. "Everyone here knows everyone else. While this is going to be awkward and difficult at times," his eye went from one Delvo to the others and stopped with junior. Kline looked directly at "little" Frank then continued. "I am here to protect the interest of the Delvo family. Our goal is to shut down the illegal activity quickly and with as little fanfare as possible. Are there any objections to that?"

Nobody objected. "I do have a question."

"Shoot detective."

I had been trained to never ask an attorney, who was fighting for the other side, 'would it be possible.' The answer would be no. Instead, I said, "I'd like to open the meeting with three of us present. The three would be Frank junior, Attorney Kline and me." I looked at Kline, then at the adult Delvos.

Kline's answer was immediate. "Not only doable but advisable."

My guess was that Kline knew where I was headed. The only way we were going to find out if the old man was involved was to separate dad from son. If dad objected, that was a tipoff. If dad didn't object, I got to question the boy without dad being in the room. I liked Delvo. I liked the Delvo family. I could only hope only junior was involved.

Kline said, "That might take some time. I would suggest you and Anita grab some coffee or an early dinner. I'll call you when we're finished. Before you go, and for the record, I am going to turn on the recorder and ask for your approval to interview Frank junior without you or Anita present."

A FAIL OF ONE CITY

Frank junior was nervous. He was more nervous when Kline explained to him that everything said in the room was being recorded. "Your job is to be honest, Frank. If you don't know something, tell us that. If you are unsure, tell us that. If you don't know what to say, ask me. I'm here to represent you and your family. In actuality, all of us here are on your side." Kline switched on the recorder. "I need each of you to identify yourselves by first and last name. Spell out your last name. I need an address, who you work for, the date and time. Frank, start us off." When those formalities were out of the way, it was game on.

I nodded. I appreciated Kline's opening, especially telling junior we were all in this together. "Let's start from the beginning, Frank. Tell us how you came to know the group that met at Duffmann's house."

Junior first looked down at the table, then his eyes met Kline's. The attorney nodded.

There was a pitcher of water on the table and glasses. Frank poured himself a glass. He took a sip then began. "I'm friends with Peter Johnson. One day after school we stopped at Martin's Malt Shop, just Peter and me. We were talking school, sports, the Dodgers, girls, whatever. He mentioned that he belonged to this group that met at Mr. Duffmann's house a couple of times a month. He said they talk about church, school, problems, volunteer opportunities and a chance to earn a few extra dollars. Pete said sometimes Father Strayhan from our church was at the meeting."

"I was interested in making extra money. A few days later, Pete mentioned it again. He said they were going to meet Thursday evening, the next day. I told my mom about it. She

227

got in touch with Pete's mom. She told me it was fine. I could go."

"One of the guys from the group picked us up. I don't remember who. We met in the big living room in the back of the house. He had two living rooms. We sat around a fireplace on the floor and talked about the things Peter said they talked about. That was about it. I guess we were at the house for about an hour and a half. A different man drove us home. I don't know who that man was."

I asked junior, "Was Father Strayhan present."

Frank shook his head. "No, not that time."

Kline said, "You're doing great, Frank. I need you to speak up so the recorder can hear you."

"Father Strayhan wasn't at the house; not that time."

"What happened next?"

"About two Thursdays later, Peter said there was another meeting. He said he was going. I said I'd go too. The same man picked us both up. He drove us to the house. It was a smaller group. There were only eight of us. I noticed there were four of us kids and four adults. Father Strayhan was there. We were in the back living room. We sat on the floor in front of the fireplace; all except Father Strayhan."

"Father Strayhan was standing in front of the group. He said, "Today is game night. "We have a new member, so I want to explain for our new member Frank, what game night is all about. Game night is about having fun, winning prizes, including money, and making your partner feel good and your partner making you feel good." "Father Strayhan said everything we say and do at our meetings absolutely must be kept confidential. We cannot talk about it to anyone outside these rooms. If we do talk about it outside these rooms, we'd lose points, money, feel good time, and we'd certainly be punished by God. Father Strayhan said we are specially chosen for this mission by God. So, it's most important we keep this mission top secret. Then Father Strayhan said everything we do here is God's business, and it's good."

"Last month we had members win an amusement park trip, a camp out trip, a bicycle, and money."

I was starting to get the idea. I looked at Kline. He was frowning. I was boiling. "You're doing great, Frank. How do you feel?"

He nodded. "I'm okay."

"Do you want to take a break?"

He shook his head. "Not yet."

"You're a brave man, Frank." Kline said softly.

I'm not a religious person. I respect men of the cloth like I respect cops. This made me sick. I was soon to get sicker.

Frank junior continued. "Because this is Frank's first time at game night, I'm going to be his partner tonight. The others will go with whoever taps you on the shoulder. Remember, when you go to a room, don't forget to hang the do not disturb sign on the outside door handle."

"I was nervous but because I'd be with Father Strayhan, I relaxed a little. I knew whatever Father Strayhan said, was the word of God."

Father Strayhan didn't miss a thing. He must have had a lot of practice. I felt sorry for Frank junior. The worst was yet to come. And it was going to be far worse than either Kline or I could have imagined.

229

"After the others were gone and it was only Father Strayhan and me in the living room by the fireplace, he explained to me that we were given points on how well we did. I was confused. He said each adult graded the teens on how well they did. The higher their point grade the better their prize. He said this month's prize was a bicycle, a trip to Catalina Island, an outing to Dodger Stadium, or fifty dollars. He asked me which one I'd choose if I won enough points. I thought about that. I wanted the trip to Catalina. I'd never been. I thought it would be great if I could take my parents."

Frank junior poured himself another glass of water. "Father Strayhan led me to a room. It was a small bedroom with two chairs and a bed. It wasn't totally dark, but it was dim. He didn't turn the lights on. He told me to hang out the do not disturb sign. After I did, Father Strayhan told me I earned a point for following directions."

"We sat on the floor against the bed. He told me since he was a priest, it was okay to tell him deep dark secrets; that he wouldn't tell anyone. He asked me if I ever read dirty magazines." Frank looked down at the table. "I told him I had. I told him I had some hidden in my closet."

"He asked me if I masturbated." Frank swallowed hard. He paused. Frank junior finally said, "I told him yes. He asked me how often." Frank's face was red.

"It's okay." I said. "We all do. Nothing to be ashamed of."

"I told him almost every day. He asked me if I read the magazines when I masturbated. I told him sometimes. He smiled. And placed his hand on my thigh. He asked me if I ever had sex with a girl. I said no but I wanted to. I asked him if that was wrong. He said no, not at all as long as the girl doesn't have a problem with it."

"He asked me if I ever touched a boy. I asked what he meant. He said did you ever touch a boy between the legs like this. He put his hand…. he put his hand on my penis."

Kline interrupted. "Where you dressed?"

"We were both dressed."

"What did you do then?"

"I was scared. I didn't move."

"Father Strayhan said I earned two more points for being a brave young man. He asked me if it felt good. I nodded. He rubbed me. As he rubbed me, he told me if I didn't earn the points I needed this month, I could carry them over to next month."

As Frank junior took a breath, I said, "Do you want to stop for today, Frank. You must be tired?"

"I want to go on."

"Before you continue, I need to ask you two important questions. They may embarrass you and they may be painful, but we need an honest answer. And as we told you earlier, we'll protect you in every way we can."

There was confusion in Frank's eyes. In his heart there must have been pain I could not imagine. I thought I had it tough with my decision over Mac.

"Did you ever tell anyone about this?"

"No. But Peter and I discussed it."

"Did your mom know about this?"

"No. It was a church meeting to her. When we went on a trip, it was a church trip."

231

"Did your dad ever touch you?"

There wasn't a second of hesitation. "Of course not."

THE HIDEOUSNESS CONTINUES

I didn't say a word to Frank. Neither did Kline. I looked at Frank. It was like he was reliving those past events. I was certain he was. I was just as certain he would relive those events the rest of his life. He'd probably need long term therapy, at the very least. I wondered if he'd ever have a normal relationship. All this because he trusted a man of the cloth.

"Father Strayhan continued to rub my penis through my pants. He took my hand and placed it on his penis. He showed me how he wanted me to rub it. I did. He didn't stop until I came inside my pants. He had me keep rubbing him until he finished in his pants. He kissed me lightly on the lips. He told me I could never tell anyone; that this was our secret. He also told me that for a beginner I did fine, that I earned a lot of points. I was confused because he was a priest, and even though I thought it was wrong, it felt good, and Father Strayhan said it was okay."

I kept shaking my head. Kline kept shaking his head. "Was that the end of it?"

"No. The following month we.... we.... we went into another room. This time we undressed. He had me touch him all over. He touched me all over. Then we rubbed each other until we finished. He kissed me on the lips. This time I could feel his tongue touch mine." Frank paused for a drink of water. "I liked it. It made me feel good."

I was getting sick inside. I've seen some horrible crimes. I've done some terrible things. Now I wanted to kill a priest, a so-called priest. No doubt I was going to hell. I had trouble keeping my stomach settled. "Do you want a break?"

"Please."

Kline turned off the Sony recorder.

There was more. I knew there had to be more. I didn't want to know about. I was a cop, a detective. I had to know about it.

"Let's take twenty minutes," Kline said. "How about a soda, Frank?"

"Sure. Thank you, sir."

"Tony, a drink?"

"That would be great."

Jerry and I stepped out of the office after he gave Frank a Seven Up. We each had a drink. "How sick can you get?"

I looked at Jerry. "I've seen a lot of garbage in my time. This takes the ribbon hands down. I'm going to have to do this again. I need a corroborating witness." (I was already formulating the plan, and who my second witness would be). "We're not going to finish this today. The kid has already been through hell reliving this. Let's call his parents, we'll wrap it up, and move on tomorrow."

"I've already got enough for a warrant. The question is going to be how the department wants to handle it. I'll discuss that with the big boys. Everything good with you so far?"

Kline said, "Yes. The tough part is going to be telling the parents. We have to tell them tonight so they can keep an eye on Frank. I'd like to finish this up today, but it will be too much for the kid. If you have any trouble finding a judge to sign off on a warrant, I've got the judge who will be more than happy to help tie these guys in a knot. One more thing," Kline said. "Frank senior, as you probably guessed is connected. He's got motive, means, and opportunity. I'd hate to see him set wheels in motion that can take him down. You might want to watch Frank senior."

I understood precisely what Kline was saying. Delvo could make one phone call back east and we wouldn't need a warrant. I'd be happy to chip in to accomplish that; I really would.

"I know how I want to proceed to make it neat and clean with a bow on it. I have to get approval. If we do it right, the kids won't have to testify in court. These dirt bags will beg to cop a plea."

Kline and I walked back in his office. Frank was sitting still at the desk. "Am I doing okay?"

"You're doing fine," Kline said. "You're the best witness I've had in years."

"You are going to protect me?"

"Of course, we are," I said sincerely. "Nobody is going to do anything to you. You have our word. You're a hero in my book, Frank, a true, true hero."

Kline turned the recorder on. He said we took a short break. The three of us are back on record.

Frank took a drink of soda. "You'll protect me from the police?"

I thought I misheard. "Say that again."

"You'll protect me from the officer?"

"What officer?"

"One of the men in the group was a police officer."

"What do you mean?"

"One day when he sat his jacket down, it opened. I saw his badge."

Just when I thought I had heard it all. "Do you know which police department he's with?"

"Amity. I've seen him on the news."

My head would not stop shaking. Now I understood how they got away with it for so long. The cop ran interference for them. "Was there more than one cop?"

"I don't think so."

"If I were to show you pictures, could you pick out the cop?"

"I'm sure I can."

"We're going to a short break. We've called your parents. They'll be here in a few minutes then we're all going to talk."

"Do you think they'll be mad at me?"

"They'll be proud of you. You're a brave young man," I said. "You're helping to take some very bad people off the street."

I left Jerry and Frank junior in the attorney's office. I had to get some air. I felt dirty, filthy. First a priest then a cop. Where did it stop? I don't know what's worse a dirty cop or a fucked-up priest. I didn't even want to guess which of our cops was a fag child molester.

Getting into a police department is a process and a half. Aside from the book study in the academy, the agility tests, the medical tests, the background checks, there are psychological tests, and polygraphs. There is a written psychological and a one on one psychological. How the fuck this deranged son of a bitch got through all that is beyond me. We needed to revisit the process. We also needed to make sure we were flush with cash. We were going to get the shit sued out of us; and we sure the hell had it coming. And I sometimes wondered why there was so much hatred for police.

When I walked back upstairs, Frank junior, Jerry Kline and I had a brief huddle. The three of us decided it would be best if we all met with the Delvos. We also decided we'd dodge as many legal questions, for now, as we could. While we were waiting for the Delvos, Frank had another Seven Up, I had another double shot of Seagram's and Kline had a scotch rock. Kline left drinks, hard and soft, on the table along with a pitcher of ice water, orange juice, and a bucket of ice. If the situation wasn't so morbid, one would think a party was brewing.

It was still light, but not by much, when Frank senior, and Anita entered attorney Kline's office. Kline greeted the senior Delvo with a handshake and a back slap. He greeted Anita with a slow hug. "Please have a seat."

Anita kept looking at Frank junior, who looked better than I would have been looking under the dire circumstances. The Delvos were Kline's clients so I thought he should kick off the meeting.

He did. "If you'd like a drink, help yourself to anything on the table. It's on the house." Jerry smiled. "What we're going to talk about is going to be very painful. Please understand that as much as it might hurt you, it has probably devastated Frank junior already and will for a long time to come. That being said, the three of us are going to recap our meeting for you."

237

Kline summarized our meeting. Frank senior slammed his fist on the table hard enough to spill water from the pitcher. Nobody moved. He caught himself. For the first time since the meeting began, Frank senior spoke. Looking directly at Frank junior he said, "Son, absolutely none of this is your fault. You are not to blame for any of it. There are some sick people in this world, and you ran in to some of them. I promise you son, I give you all the credit in the world for doing what it is you're doing, which is putting the animals where they belong, and saving some other kids the terrible, terrible pain you're going through. I'll also promise you this, they will pay for what they did."

Devlo and I were both Italian. "I have serious contacts back east," Delvo said, choosing his words carefully. "I can get things done if need be. These sick bastards go away for a long time...." Delvo looked at the tape recorder. He suddenly stopped talking.

I hoped Devlo wasn't inferring that he would take matters into his own hands. I didn't want to pursue that at this time. The family had been through enough for this day.

We talked for a few minutes. Anita, and Frank junior cried for a few minutes. Anita got up from the table walked to junior and hugged him.

Kline took senior Frank aside. They chatted softly and briefly. "We'd like to reconvene the meeting at ten thirty tomorrow morning here. We'd like everyone present."

APRIL, PETER, and ME

It was a long day. It was now evening. It was about to get longer. I phoned April. Immediately I explained to her that this was not a social call, that it was business and it concerned Peter. I assured April that Peter was in absolutely no trouble. I asked her if Peter was in the house. She said he was upstairs in his room doing homework. I asked her not to tell him I was on my way over.

April greeted me at the door in slacks and a t-shirt. She was wearing a bra. She kissed me and leaned in close. I liked close. "About yesterday, I'm sorry we only just begun. I'll explain at a later date."

"You have the right to remain silent, detective. At the moment, I'm more concerned with Peter. Do you want to tell me what's going on?"

I ignored the question. "Is Peter still in his room doing homework?"

She nodded. "Can we meet upstairs?"

"That's fine."

We walked a carpeted staircase. Peter's room was in the far back of a long hallway. His bedroom door was open. He was sitting behind a computer desk apparently writing a school paper. There was a science book leaning against the computer.

I stepped in front of April, walked across the room then held out my hand. "I'm Detective Kano." Thirteen-year-old Peter shook my hand. "Why don't you turn off the computer? I'm sorry to interrupt your studies but this is important. It can't

239

wait. Your mom is going to sit it on our little conference. I want to impress upon you that you are in absolutely no trouble. I also want both you and your mom to understand that you do not have to talk with me. You have the right to an attorney even though you have committed no crime. When we start this meeting, you or your mom have the right to stop it at any time. Is that clear, Mrs. Johnson?"

April looked puzzled. I would have been puzzled too. I couldn't give Frank junior up. I had to be careful. All I wanted to do was loosely verify what Frank junior had told us.

"I understand," April said.

"I've got it, sir."

"This is informal. Nothing is being recorded. I'm not taking notes. Let's begin. Again, anytime you want to stop or if you want a break, just say so. This shouldn't take long then you can get back to your studies."

"Peter, do you belong to a church group?"

Peter stared at his mom then at me. He looked like a large, well-built thirteen-year-old even from behind the desk. I could see his appeal to these demented men.

Peter said nothing. He continued to stare. Finally, he asked, "Do we have to do this in front of my mom?"

I felt sorry for Peter. "Yes, Peter. You're a minor. The mom, in this case, needs to be present." Obviously, Peter was sharp enough to know where this was going from the first question I asked.

"Are you in the eighth grade?" I asked trying to take Peter's mind off the purpose of the meeting momentarily. It failed miserably.

"I want an attorney. I'm not saying another word." The kid must watch plenty of cop shows. He was sharp for a thirteen-year-old.

"Does someone want to tell me what the hell is going on here?"

I remained silent. So did Peter.

April not so much. "What the hell does the church have to do with a detective asking you questions? I'm your mom. Don't jerk me around in a circle. If I have to, I'll call your dad."

Peter started sobbing. "Don't call dad." He wiped his tears with his handkerchief. Little by little enough came out to confirm my strong suspicions. Frank junior's tale was accurate on its face.

April comforted Peter and Peter comforted his mother. Now, two of the boys had told their tale. That was a start.

In the back of my mind, what was I going to do to clean up this mess? It could be done by assembling APEST and raiding the Duffmann house during meeting night. It could be accomplished via the Grand Jury. It could be done by getting a warrant and hiding microphones and cameras on the premises during a nighttime meeting. When they say a cop is on duty twenty-four seven, this is what they mean.

I left April's place after giving here and Peter a loving hug. I felt for both of them. It was dark, approaching eight thirty. I had to go by the police station. I had to pick up photos. I hadn't touched base with Sully, or Mac for I couldn't remember how long, and I had to prepare for a ten o'clock meeting tomorrow at Kline's office with the Delvos. And they say New York is the city that never sleeps.

WHAT THE FUCK?

I drove to the station. I got what I needed then got the hell out of Dodge. I didn't update the brass. I'd wait until after tomorrow morning's meeting. On a whim, I decided to drive to Sully' apartment. I hadn't seen his new digs. I could also update him, and he could update me. Finally, and most important, Sully could probably use some cheering up.

I found the small complex. I drove into the complex and looked for Sully's car. It took me three minutes forty-five seconds to find what I didn't want to find. I observed a familiar Corvette. The license plate read, DCZDMND. What the fuck was Mac doing at Sully's place? I sat behind the wheel pondering my next move.

My next move was to slam my fist on the steering wheel. There was probably a reasonable explanation for Mac being at Sully's place. Maybe she was helping him organize his apartment. Maybe Sully and Mac were debriefing. Maybe Mac was sucking Sully's dick because I couldn't stay hard inside her.

I drove back to my place, made myself a TV dinner, took out a quart bottle of Seagram's, kicked my shoes off, sat down on the couch and turned on the Dodger game. The Dodgers were getting slaughtered. It appeared that I was also getting slaughtered. I'm glad I didn't have time to bet on the game.

I channel surfed. I found a rerun of one of my old favorites, Dragnet. There was Joe Friday in the interrogation room going at it with some Adam Henry. Police work at its finest.

DRAGNET OF YESTERYEAR, POLICE WORK OF THIS YEAR

That was then, and how things have changed. Some punk is standing fifteen feet from you. You tell him to drop the blade. He tells you to go fuck Lassie in the ass. Now he's ten feet from you. You put a round in the ten ring and the next day half the world is out protesting that a white cop shot a black child because the black child pulled out a small knife that he carried to clean his fingernails. The department launches an investigation. People start marching in front of your house. You receive not so loving phone calls. Your mail carrier brings you hate mail. The department assigns you desk duty for God knows how long. The punk dies. Now the shit really hits the fan.

Internal Affairs launches an investigation. The leftist papers are calling for your resignation and your left leg. (Hey assholes, you can have my left leg; it ain't real!) The newspapers dig into your record from the day you were born. They find you once declared bankruptcy before you became a cop. In high school you received a speeding ticket for doing seventy-eight in a sixty-five. You were married at twenty-two and divorced at twenty-six. The left leaners say you were unstable and should never have been hired as a cop, paving the way for a lawsuit against the city, the department and you! The newspapers plaster a picture of this fine young man, in suit and tie, graduating sixth grade.

He never made eighth grade. The punk got kicked out of seventh grade permanently for pulling a blade on his teacher and attempting to assault her. The charges were attempted rape, but the newspapers say attempted assault. Because of his tender age, he's given home probation and a Snickers candy bar. The following year, and now all of fourteen, the

243

punk gets nailed robbing a Rabbi on the street. This time he buys nine months of camp time in one of the County's juvenile facilities replete with swimming pool. The kid comes out of juvie early for good behavior; (actually the County facilities are overcrowded but you ain't going to hear about that).

He makes it another eleven months without getting caught. The newspapers say he was trying to rehabilitate himself but gravitated back to bad company because he lives in a bad area. Get a legit job asshole. Go back to school. That would require balls. You ain't got any! Now he starts taking drugs. You need money to buy drugs. You ain't got no job Bozo. You start robbing on a daily basis to fill your need. You can't find your ass with a mop you're so drugged out.

The newspapers didn't tell you according to the autopsy report that the punk was so high on drugs he probably would have died if you hadn't shot him. They didn't tell you that the "fingernail knife" he pulled on you had a six-inch blade. They didn't tell you he lifted that blade off a druggie in the alley that he stabbed fifteen minutes before he pulled it on you. Ain't life beautiful?

My cell rang. It was the sound of Mac. I really did not want to talk with her. I pictured her and Sully on his couch in his new apartment. Fuck both of them. I downed two doubles and went to sleep on my couch with the TV on. Mac would call it passing out. Fuck her!

244

SECOND VERSE NOT MUCH DIFFERENT THAN THE FIRST

I was in Attorney Kline's office at zero nine fifty-five. The Devlo's were already seated. Kline met me at this office door. We shook hands.

"I want to see if little Frank can pick out the cop who may have participated in the sex ring. I've brought pictures. How's he doing?"

Kline adjusted his tie. "He seems okay. Who knows what the hell is going on inside of him? This couldn't be more shameful, and more painful for Frank. It's horrific. Let's go inside."

I greeted the Devlo family, then I took a seat. "Frank, how are you?"

"I'm okay. Scared, but okay. Will this be the last day?"

Kline nodded. Most likely. He reminded everyone why we were here. He admonished each of us that the meeting was being recorded. Kline had each of us identify ourselves for the recorder.

I kicked the meeting off. "Frank, I'm going to set six pictures in from of you at a time. If you recognize anyone from a picture, please say so. There are no names on any of the pictures." I placed the first six pictures on the table.

For credibility, Kline explained to the Sony tape recorder exactly what we were doing and why we were doing it.

We had one hundred twenty-six staff within our department. This included police, reserve officers, volunteers, and ancillary staff. I had "plain clothes" pictures of each and

245

every one of the one hundred twenty-six in my attaché case. I set six pictures on the table.

Frank studied them carefully. "None of those."

I set six more pictures on the table. "No, none of them."

We were about halfway through the pictures. "Here. Him. He was the one with the badge I saw. This one."

I had placed a number on each of the one hundred twenty-six pictures. The picture Frank junior identified was number 72. "For the record," I said, "let the picture be identified as number 72. For obvious reasons, no picture will be identified by name." I looked at Frank senior. "We're going to run through the rest of the pictures just to be sure."

Frank senior leaned across the table. He wanted to get a look at the picture. I quickly snatched it off the desk and put it in my inside suit pocket. I resumed putting the pictures on the table. Frank did not identify any more police photos. "Good job, Frank. Very good job."

Kline said, "We're going to continue Frank. We're going to make this as brief as possible so you and your parents can be done with it." Kline nodded to me.

"We're not going to go into the detail we went into yesterday, Frank." I looked across the table. He seemed calmer than I would have been under the circumstances. "Did you go to Duffmann's house on other occasions?"

"Almost every other Thursday. Sometimes also for what one man called appreciation dinners."

"Did you have any other partner besides Father Patrick Strayhan?"

"No. Father Strayhan liked me. He wanted me to stay with him." Then Franks added, softly, "He's a priest. I felt safer with him."

"Did you and Father Strayhan do anything else to each other, other than rub each other's penises through your pants?"

"He wanted me to let him put his penis in my mouth."

"Did you let him?"

Frank looked down at the floor, then at his dad. He nodded. "Yes."

"How many times?"

"At least four times on different meeting nights."

"Did he ask you to put your penis in his mouth?"

"Yes."

"Did you?"

"Yes."

"How many times?"

"Four." Tears rolled down Frank junior's cheek. Mom got up and walked out of the room. Frank senior's face was red.

"Let's take a break," Kline said.

We resumed twenty minutes later. Kline and I summarized the meeting. We made sure everyone in the room understood to keep everything under wraps. I told Kline and the Delvos we would keep them updated, that we would be moving as fast as red tape would allow us to move, faster if I dared cut that red tape.

I called April from the parking lot of Kline's office. It was lunch time. "How's Peter doing?"

"He's seems to be going okay. He's like his dad, he's good at hiding things. He's out with friends. I've been finding excuses to call him to check on him. I'm a mom."

"Yes, mom," I joked. "I'd like to talk with you. This is social, not business. Can we meet for lunch?"

"Either that or come over here. Mom's Diner is open for business."

"Sounds good. Half an hour work?"

"Works fine. That'll give me time to put something on. Unless of course…." April didn't finish her thought.

I walked to my car but didn't get in. I called Acting Chief Rolando. "Sir, we need to meet. It's about the ring. We need to move fast. Can I buy half an hour or so of your time about three o'clock this afternoon?"

"My office work?"

"No. I prefer we meet elsewhere. Sully and Mac may be with me depending on how they're doing chasing the money." I was trying to think of where we could meet.

The acting chief beat me to it. "APEST has a secluded office where they meet. It's not well known. How about we meet there?"

"Are these guys closed mouthed? We may need to use them if you approve my plan. But I don't want anything getting out. If the newspapers get a hold of this, the case is fucked and so am I."

"APEST is golden. Every one of them is handpicked and vetted." He gave me the address.

I was thinking fast. Hopefully not too fast. I walked around my car three times as I talked to Rolando. "Let's make the meeting just the two of us. I'll fill Sully and Mac in if the plan is a go. See you at three."

I called Mac. She answered first ring. "I thought you fell off the face of the earth. Where've you been?"

"Working. You?"

"Sunbathing in Hawaii."

"With Sully?"

"Of course, with Sully. I couldn't track you down or I would have invited you." I heard her catch a breath. "We're still doing interviews, but we may have something. I'll keep you posted."

I wanted to ask her if her interviews included Sully at her place. I turned down a red-hot piece of tail that was practically begging to be mounted. "I've got a meeting with the acting chief this afternoon. If things go as planned, I may need you and Sully tonight."

"I wanted a threesome," Mac quipped. "Maybe tonight's my night."

I heard enough. "I'll keep you guys posted, too." I hung up.

APRIL SHOWERS (DAMN, NOT THOSE KIND OF SHOWERS!)

I knocked on April's door. "If you have a warrant, you can come in."

Why is it that the women I know are quick witted? "I have a warrant." I stepped inside. "I'm going to need to search you for weapons." April met me between the hallway and the kitchen. She stepped in front of me. She was wearing a short dark blue skirt and a lighter blue tank top sans bra. She was maybe twelve inches in front me. She bent over grabbing her ankles. Her skirt hiked up. If she was wearing anything under the skirt, the anything was a thong. "I'm not concealing anything detective, honest." She continued to hold her position. She was in amazing shape. The last time I did something like that was in the academy.

I started at her right ankle and worked my way up. All the way up. I ran my thumb straight up as far as it would go. "What big hands you have."

I did the same on her left side with both hands. "In the field, we normally have you face away from the searching male officer, bend over and loosen your bra so we can see you're not concealing a weapon. Since you're not wearing a bra, I need you to stand up straight, face me then pull your shirt up quickly."

April turned, faced me, smiled, blushed, and took her shirt off. She tossed it on the kitchen counter. "No hidden weapons, detective. Am I free to go?"

"You're being detained."

"For what?"

"Decent exposure. Very decent exposure." I had a very hard time (in more ways than one) keeping my eyes off those twins. "Are those stolen property?"

"All mine. I have the birth certificate to prove it."

"You can put your shirt back on now."

She looked down at my crotch. "Is it hard for you to maintain your composure if I keep my shirt off or is it illegal?"

"The former." April stepped closer at the same time I did. Her bare chest was against me. I pressed tighter.

"Is that your baton I feel, or do you care?"

The fact was I was horny as hell. I kissed her on the mouth. We held the kiss. Her mouth opened. I had a warrant to search those premises. I did, slowly, deliberately making sure to search every nook and cranny. "I'm not carrying a straight stick." (What we sometimes call a baton).

"The hell you're not." She pressed against me. I knew April had to feel my hard-on. I slid my right hand up her short skirt grabbing and squeezing her ass cheek. She was firm in all the right places. "Somebody said if you dial 911 you can make a cop come."

I kept squeezing that butt cheek. "Keep doing what you're doing, and you might not need a phone."

I felt her grind against me. I grabbed her and put her on the counter. I lifted her skirt then reached between her legs. I heard a lock turn then a door open. I pulled April off the counter. She grabbed her shirt and we sat at the kitchen table. Peter witnessed absolutely nothing. Mac said God sometimes works in strange and mysterious ways. I believe it.

ONE ACTING CHIEF, ONE BAD ACTING DETECTIVE

This particular APEST office is off the fourteen-freeway about forty minutes north of Los Angeles in Acton. Conveniently, there is a very small airport in Acton and little else. On my drive, I hit light traffic. I had plenty of time to think about Amity's sex ring and the priest. Wouldn't that make a great title for a novel? I doubt anyone would believe it.

I also had plenty of time to think about Sully and Mac, and what the hell she was doing at his apartment. I hoped, for his sake, that she came clean with him. I thought about April. Oh, did I think about April. I thought so hard about April that I had a hard time controlling the steering wheel.

The GPS on my cell phone led me directly to the APEST building. I parked in the rear as instructed by Rolando. I walked to the rear door which was solid steel. I had the code, supplied by Acting Chief Rolando. I started to punch in the five-number code. I stopped. Rolando hadn't arrived. I was a few minutes early.

I walked back to my car. I leaned on the trunk. I called Leo, one of my three bookies. He answered the second ring. "Tony, Tony, Tony, how much of your money can I take tonight?"

"Depends. Dodgers are at the Mets tonight, right?"

"That's a positive."

"Who's pitching for the Dodgers?"

"Kershaw."

"Give me a g-note on the Mets to win. Kershaw is a choke artist."

"I like it baby. More money for Leo. We have Leo in common, Tony."

"What the hell are you talking about?"

"My name is Leo, and you're a LEO, Law Enforcement Officer. We're related."

"In name only friend. In name only." I watched Rolando pull up in an unmarked Mustang. He was sharp. He didn't drive an unmarked Crown Vic. Good thinking, sir. He drove his Ford Explore.

The entire APEST team was out training. We had the building to ourselves. We found an empty office with a couple of chairs and a dusty bridge table. We made ourselves at home. I filled Acting Chief Lee Rolando in on the latest.

"What's your next move, Tony?"

"We have three options, sir, unless you can see another possibility. I don't want any of these kids wearing a wire. I also don't want them going through any more shit. So, we've got to do this fast and hard."

"Option one would be for the APEST guys to hit them all during a meeting night. Then we have to rely on the kids' testimony or get one of the assholes to flip. That's a crap shoot and I don't like it. A second option is round them up one at a time and hand everything over to the Grand Jury. That's iffy also."

"Here's what I like. Tonight, after dark, we get the APEST people, Sully, Mac, and me to enter a couple of houses on Duffmann's street. We tell them we strongly suspect there's a gas leak in a mainline that feeds half a dozen houses on that street. We have trucks, barriers, yellow tape, hard hats, the works. We have to make it as real as possible. Our guys are in hard hats and are either cops clearing the houses or County gas going in to inspect the property.

There's no meeting tonight at Duffmann's so it'll probably be just him we gotta' move out. We'll evacuate several other houses on the street to make it look real. We'll tell them it's a local gas line that broke; that we have to go into the houses to inspect and to locate the leak. We'll get them a good distance from the house. We'll keep them out until we give them the all clear, telling them how dangerous the leak could be."

"Okay, so you got him out, you have other families out, now what?"

"You push them all back to the end of the street behind the barriers. Our guys enter several houses to check for the leak including Duffmann's place. They plant cameras and recorders. We'll need a couple of hours, give or take."

"Do you have the equipment?"

"I need the okay, sir. Once you give me the go, I'll phone Sully and Mac and put them to work. That's the cleanest way of doing it. If I'm right, we get the hard evidence we need, the assholes will cop a plea. I don't want to see these kids go through any more than they've already been through." I looked at Lee. "What do you think?"

"Start calling."

"One more thing. The father of one of the victims, Frank Devlo senior is up for taking out Father Strayhan. It wouldn't break my heart if that happened but that families been through enough. I don't want to see Devlo behind bars for the rest of his life."

254

"Not much we can do about that, Tony. I can't put him under surveillance twenty-four seven."

"One more thing. I slammed a photo on the desk in front of Rolando. Frank Devlo junior identified him as being one of the slime buckets." Lee's face turned sheet white.

BAD TO THE BONE

A priest has no sexual outlet because the church won't let him marry. That, of course, doesn't give a priest the right to mess with kids. It would explain him having an affair with a consenting adult. I can buy into that. In my opinion, the church needs to change its views. The church needs to get real. Times have changed; your thinking needs to change with the times.

How about a cop who exploits kids for his sexual pleasure? What's his excuse? There is a simple answer to that. There is no excuse. Satisfy your urges some other way if you're not getting what you need at home, but kids?

Amity was about to become front page news from California to New York. Late night talk shows would make us the laughingstock of the country. Knowing what I knew, knowing what was about to be public knowledge, made me one embarrassed cop. As I told Frank junior, once it's all out in the open, on the table, the healing process would begin. We had a hell of a lot of healing in front of us.

Amity was involved heavily with community policing. We sponsored, coached, and managed kids' baseball and softball teams. We managed and sponsored football teams. Soccer was a big deal in Amity. We bought uniforms for the teams. We had an Explorer program for the kids. We ran a diversion program for at risk kids called RAPP. Redirecting Attitudes Police Program. In short, we were totally involved, in a positive way, with Amity's kids, our kids. Juvenile crime was down. One reason crime was down is because of our community involvement and our programs that kept kids off the street. I have one question. After this shit hits the news, would you allow your youngster into a program sponsored by our cops? I think not!

INTO ACTION

I called Sully. I brought him up to date. I told him to bring Mac on board. I gave Sully a list of what we needed. I told him we need everything at APEST off the fourteen-freeway by twenty hundred hours. I was taking no chances of anyone at the station seeing something and saying something.

"Got it all?" Sully read it back to me. "I know you can get us the equipment we need. You have access to shit I've only dreamed about."

Sully said, "It's a bit of a time crunch but I'll call in a few favors."

"Put Mac on the line. Listen, I need you to go to work on the warrants." I told her how the warrants had to read. "If you have any problems at all, call this number. That's Jerry Kline's number. He'll expedite for you if you have problems. Questions? Good. Ask Sully one more time if he has questions."

"You did say Jerry Kline, your attorney friend?"

"Don't ask, please. For now, just do as I ask."

"Tony, I hope this works."

"So do I. If we're done here, I want to go home, shower, change and get back here early so we can brief the APEST."

"Not we, Tony. You." Sully said. "You'll do the briefing. You've earned it. To this point, my friend, well done."

258

HOME IS WHERE THE SEAGRAM'S IS

I walked into the bedroom, stripped down to my underwear, ran cold water over my face, finally I went to the living room to find the Seagram's bottle. It was still on the table in front of the couch. So was the shot glass. I poured a shot, downed it. I poured another, ditto.

I started to feel better. I needed a shower. I sat down to collect my thoughts about this evening's "activities." There was a word one my FTO's, field training officers, used to use. The word is juxtaposition. It means everything is in order. Mentally, I needed to make sure we had everything in juxtaposition. No way could I afford to fuck this up. Not with the kids at risk.

I thought about Mac, I thought about Sully, I thought about April, I thought about a shower. I thought about which one I would think about in the shower. Maybe I'd think about both of them. I poured another shot.

The third shot had maudlin written all over it. I loved Mac. She was an incredible individual. Could I deal with the situation over time? I wanted to. As Mac would say, stay in the NOW. Easy for her, for me, difficult. My job demanded I be a forward thinker. Not many men have been in this situation.

I took a long, warm shower. I thought about Mac. I thought about April. All I did was think about them. I got out of the shower and shaved. I thought about Sully and Mac and what the hell she was doing at his apartment. I looked up at the ceiling. I said aloud, "I know God, karma. I know."

259

With all this shit going on, I still loved life. I wouldn't trade it for Kline's Ferrari. Well, maybe his Ferrari and Rhonda Receptionist. I looked up at the ceiling again. "Just kidding, God. I know, I know, Mac told me you'll never give me more than I can handle. If you do, you'll carry me. I know." I swear I heard a voice say, "Relax dummy. I've got your back."

I was showered, shaved, and dressed for an evening out. I'd prefer popcorn and a movie, but this was God's game. Mac had told me nothing happens in God's world by mistake. It's not for me to question it. She also told me that any given time, I'm exactly where God wants me to be. It's not for me to question that either.

I was starting to relax. I called Kline. I owed him the respect of letting him know that we had an operation on the drawing board. Hell, he might be instrumental in obtaining a search warrant.

"Is this a closed-door operation or can a criminal defense attorney join the party?"

"Actually Jerry, this is really a dress rehearsal. Tomorrow's the real deal. As long as you leave your Ferrari at home, you're invited tomorrow. How's that work for you, counselor?"

"I appreciate it, Tony. Here's a motivator for you. Put this thing together, I'll let you drive a Ferrari for three months on me."

"Does your receptionist go with it?"

"For you, she probably would as long as you let her shift your gears."

"I'll see you tomorrow. If anything comes up, I'll call you."

"Thanks, Tony. Be safe."

OPERATION FAITH

Commander Edison made the introductions from in front of the podium in what APEST called the upstairs living room. The ULR, consisted of bridge chairs, tables, big screen television, pool table, portable popcorn machine on legs, and computers. The wood floor appeared to be older than me. The shades were black and pulled down. The lighting was dim, and the mood was serious plus.

Commander Edison introduced me as Detective Kano. I stepped in front of the podium. I could see Mac and Sully seated next to each other. They were in the front row. Mac was wearing a short skirt. As I looked down at Mac, she spread her legs. I could see clearly up her skirt. She was wearing pink panties. I cleared my throat trying to conceal my smile with my hand. "Let's get started."

"I want to thank the APEST team for helping us put this together on such short notice. You're outstanding. This operation has been dubbed Operation Faith. We have a child sex ring operating in Amity. It has, apparently, been in operation for about three years. We are going to close up shop."

"Because this ring includes well known members of the community, it is imperative, I repeat imperative that no one outside this room be privy to this operation. Nobody. The lives of young kids are at stake. This operation will be completed in two stages. Tonight, is stage one."

"The target house is Kevin Duffmann's house. Here's the address. Do not write it down. I repeat, for safety sake do not write down that address. Memorize it. A copy of the floor plan is on your table."

"Does everybody have a copy of that floor plan?" No hands went up. "Look closely at the floor plan. You will see five rooms that are numbered. The living room is labeled LR, and each bedroom is labeled B-1, B-2, B-3, B-4. These are our target rooms. We are going to place hidden video cameras and recorders in those rooms. These recorders are on loan from the FBI and can pick up sound from Nevada. They're also very expensive. The taxpayer paid big bucks for these. I don't want to replace them."

"Tonight's goal is to get those objects in place in Duffmann's house so we have the evidence we need to prosecute. Somebody out there is going to ask how do we do that with the occupant in the house? Good question. The answer is this. Several of us are going to pose as county gas employees. Some of us will knock on doors as cops. The idea is that there is a gas leak from a line that serves half a dozen houses on the street. We'll have a command post set up. We have several trucks that appear to be county gas trucks. We will have barriers at the end of the street. Those evacuated will be escorted behind the barriers and behind the yellow tape. No one is permitted back in until the all clear is given. In actuality, the only person we have to keep an eye on is Duffmann."

"I'm guessing the operation will take a couple of hours. I'll be monitoring the situation from the command post. We have dedicated radios. If for any reason you don't want to use the radio, contact Commander Edison on your cell and he'll relay to us."

"Commander Edison has teamed you up. There will be ten of you. Two of you will take the living room and deploy hidden cameras and recording equipment. Two each for each of the four bedrooms. For those of you who failed math 101, that's a total of ten people. Commander Edison will be with us monitoring from the command post. That leaves five

APEST members. At the back table are five hand selected Los Angeles County Sheriffs. They are under the command of Sheriff's Sergeant Troutmann. Sir, please stand and introduce your team. You'll meet them on your way to your post."

"Here's the game plan. At 2130 hours," I looked at my watch, "which doesn't give us a hell of a lot of time, we will start knocking at doors, explain to people that they will have to leave. They will take pets with them. They are not to lock doors as we have to enter their home to search for the possible gas leak. Once they are out, we will enter. Eight houses have been identified to be evacuated. Those of you entering houses other than Duffmann's, make like you're looking around just in case someone can see inside. You're going to be carrying county gas equipment, so you'll look like the real deal. Any questions?"

"If something doesn't go as planned, and that always seems to happen, we'll improvise. Rendezvous behind the command post at 2130. When the green light is given, hopefully before midnight, we'll meet back here."

"Good luck. Remember vulnerable kids are at stake. Duffmann is a scum bag. Be careful, be diligent, be safe."

THINK, THINK, THINK

Mac taught me that in her program there's a saying, STINKING THINKING LEADS TO DRINKING. If that was the case for non-alcoholics, I was in deep shit. I was thinking about anything and everything. I was thinking about Frank junior and Frank senior. I was thinking about both Peter and Peter. I was thinking about so called Father Strayhan. I was thinking about Duffmann and his damn house. I was thinking about the APEST team. I was thinking about Sergeant Troutmann and his team. And of course, I was thinking about Sully and Mac.

PHASE ONE: OPERATION FAITH

Along with Commander Edison, Mac, Sully, Sergeant Troutmann and I were among the select few who were in the command post. At 2120 hours the four of us walked to the rear of the command post. We joined the APEST team and the on-loan support, including Sheriff's Sergeant Troutmann and his team.

"I'd like to say a quick thank you to everybody here for helping to save some our kids and their families from more emotional damage. This operation will be a success because you are highly professional, and your heart is in the right place. I'd like those who wish to, please join hands with me as we recite the Serenity Prayer. If the ACLU is within earshot, fuck you! Prayer: God grant me the serenity to accept the things I cannot change, the courage to change the things I can, and the wisdom to know the difference. Be safe team. Operation Faith is now a go."

We monitored the activity from the command post. We had cameras and microphones inside Duffmann's house. The pictures were grainy, but we were able to see what we needed to see. The audio was clear. We had cameras outside so we could home in on the movement of the people. Within six minutes, people were exiting their homes. Within thirteen minutes, everyone was out of their respective homes. Within nineteen minutes they were all behind the barricades and the tape. The people were orderly. Our officers were doing their job.

Three trucks, all marked County Emergency Services Unit, drove up near Duffmann's house. On schedule the teams entered the indicated homes.

Sully said, "So far so good."

I responded, "This should be the easy part. Tomorrow might be the bitch."

Mac looked at me. "Is it something I didn't say?"

I shook my head. "We'll talk." The worst part of any operation is the waiting. We were waiting. I hated stakeouts. You could sit in an unmarked unit for hours waiting for something to happen. Sometimes it did, sometimes it didn't. I'd rather be active.

I looked at Sully. "Anything come up with your interviews?"

"We're not sure. We're still working a guy who may know something. We're busting our butts looking for a pea in a sand pit."

Yeah, some sand pit, I thought. You, Mac, and your apartment. I still had empathy for the guy. "How are you doing?"

"Like you said a few minutes ago, accept the things you can't change. I can't change Amy's mind. "

I was watching the street through the one-way glass. It was calm. We continued to wait. I had no idea how long it would take to place the cameras and the audio equipment in the right places.

I had my cell set to vibrate. It was on the table where I was sitting. "Kano."

"APEST three, sir. We found some porn in here and some videos. It looks like they were recording without anyone's knowledge. Do you want me to seize it?"

"No! No! Leave it exactly where you found it but make a mental note. We'll pick it up tomorrow as evidence. If someone sees it's gone, we can fuck up the whole operation."

"That's a copy, sir."

Sully said, "These guys are really sick."

"I thought these whack jobs were wired wrong. These guys deserve to die."

I agreed with Mac at least about the latter part. "If I had my way, I'd wait till tomorrow, hit the house, and put one bullet between the eyes of each of them."

"Including the priest?" Sully asked.

"Especially the priest."

"You'll go to hell for that," he added.

"All my friends will be there."

An hour and ten minutes later we got our first confirmation that the equipment was installed in one of the bedrooms. "Let's do a check, APEST. Stand by."

Our visual and audio specialist ran a check. "How do you read?"

"Loud and clear. How's the view?"

"I can see the spaghetti stain on your shirt."

Twenty minutes later the second team reported in, followed five minutes later by the third team. By 2305 hours all teams had reported in and all equipment was checked, verified, and double checked. We lifted the barriers at 2335 hours, after explaining to the homeowners that everything was safe for them to return to their homes, and we would be monitoring the situation.

We headed back to the APEST barn and quickly assembled to debrief. I set a briefing time at APEST central for 1830 hours tomorrow. I was exhausted.

Mac suggested breakfast. Sully agreed to buy. I begged off. "You two go. I'm tired. I guess I'm getting old. See you tomorrow." I figured that would keep Mac guessing the same way she had me guessing.

KERSHAW GETS POUNDED

Kershaw didn't make it past the third inning in New York. I was five hundred to the good. That was cause for celebration. I poured myself a double.

Phase one was in the books. APEST and Troutmann's team did their job and did it well. If things worked out as well tomorrow, a lot of really bad guys would be off the street, including one fucked up priest.

I was going to buzz April but then I realized it was too damn late. I was to wound up to sleep. My options were limited. There wasn't a damn thing on TV, but I turned it on anyway. Eddie Murphy was getting tossed through a window in Beverly Hills. BHPD was about to arrest him.

Eddie Murphy was funny as hell. He was also a damn good actor. They needed to make another Beverly Hills Cop movie. I watched it until the commercial then walked over to the refrigerator. There wasn't a damn thing in the refrigerator worth eating. As a last resort, I walked back to the living room and poured another shot.

I turned on an all-news channel. That was as depressing as watching commercials. I thought about Kline's half assed offer of law school. I'd probably make a great defense attorney until some sick puke pissed me off. I could see myself getting disbarred for battery on a client. I'd miss the excitement of the street.

I needed to get a few things ironed out and I'd be back in the saddle again. On or near the top of that things-to-get-ironed-out list was Mac. She was eating away at me. Sully was annoying me; Mac was pissing me off. I had no mortgage on her. She was free to do what she wanted. Sully, on the other hand, was my partner. Partners didn't do that to each other. On the flip side, there might be a logical explanation to her being at his place. If there was why didn't one of them mention it? I turned off the television and sat on the couch in the dark. Sometimes it was easier to see the light when you were in the dark.

I fell asleep. I dreamt I was driving a unit, that Rocky was riding shotgun. It was still daylight, but the sun was down. The sky was clear. The shoppers were out in droves walking the boulevard and spending their hard-earned cash. Rocky was on his cell, as usual, talking with Paula. He was laughing. I heard Rocky say into the phone, "I don't know. You know how he is about that." I took a wild guess that he was talking about me and about Paula trying to set up me once again. I looked at Rocky and shook my head.

I made a left turn. The sign said no left turn. I made the left anyway. A sign read Afghanistan. All hell broke loose. There was rapid gunfire from an automatic weapon, a tank was in the background, and somebody tossed a hand grenade at us. Rocky went down covered in blood. I ran over to him. I knelt down at his side. "Buddy, buddy, don't leave me. Wake up, buddy, wake up."

I heard a voice in the background. It was Judge Karma. He was laughing. "I told you not to make a left turn."

I had a second dream that I was back in front of Judge Karma. He wanted to check on my progress. He had garnered reports from God knows who. In my dream I was standing in front of the bench. Judge Karma was reading from the reports. He read the good first then the bad. "You've made progress." the Judge said. "But this bad list is still too long. You need to repent. You can't keep playing with Mac. You have to make a decision. Messing with April while you're involved with Mac is bad, bad, bad. That's like playing Russian roulette with your Glock. Another decision to be made, Tony. You make good, even great split-second decisions in the field. When it comes to your own life, you play games. That's self-defeating and self-destructive. You need to knock it off."

"I'm going to have you back in my court soon, but you won't know when. You are being watched but you don't know by whom. Wake the hell up and smell the gun powder, Tony, before it blows up in your face. Now get the fuck out of my court room and get your shit together before you see me again."

It would have been less frightening to have been in the same room with Mac and April at the same time. What scared the shit out of me was that Judge Karma had his ducks in a row; Tony didn't.

It was daylight when I awoke. I was still tired. I had a very restless sleep. I was exhausted from the case, from both cases, from the damn nightmares, from Mac jerking me around, from not being able to make a decision. I knew this couldn't go on much longer. I wasn't being fair to anyone.

OH FATHER, HOW YOU HAVE SINNED

Early in the day I wrestled with the idea of whether to book the pedophiles at the APEST facility then transport them to Twin Towers or to run them through the regular routine at Amity jail. Once the "raid" began, the newspapers would get a hold of it. Amity Police Department would be overrun with reporters, television crews, outraged community members and church people who would say the cops are arresting innocent people. There was an advantage to setting up booking at APEST office then transporting separately. These guys were sick mother fuckers, but they weren't stupid. None of them would be likely to talk to us without an attorney present. The decision wouldn't be mine to make. I'd run it by Rolando with my recommendation.

We gathered in the same room at APEST at 1830 hours. The same players were present for phase two. I stepped to the front of the room. "Good evening ladies and gentlemen. I want to commend you for yesterday's performance. It went off without a hitch. Give yourselves a well-deserved hand. Thank you all."

"Acting Chief Lee Rolando said after tonight's roundup, there's an open bar. Everything is on the Acting Chief." Rolando laughed.

"Once again, your assignments are on the table. You are either assigned to hitting the house, taking up a position at an exit, or transporting. I want each arresting officer to Mirandize his arrestee. Three officers are assigned to the children. The children will be transported to Lincoln Memorial Hospital for examination. From the hospital, the boys will be released to their parents who will be notified.

The kids will be brought to Amity PD tomorrow for statements. You are to stay with the kids at all times. Every child's safety is your responsibility. Any questions so far?"

"Each of the five who is taken into custody, will be transported right here for booking. We'll have the command post set up for processing. The paperwork can be done here. Probable cause affidavits will also be filled out here. Once booked, and once the paperwork is approved, you will transport your prisoner to Twin Towers."

"Under no circumstances are your arrestees to be together. Transport them separately, book them separately and keep them the hell away from each other. We don't want them comparing notes."

"This one is a safety issue. There has been no sign of a leak. In short, this raid should be a complete surprise. But watch your back and your partner's back at all times."

I paused for a deep breath. "Once the house is clear, another team will collect the cameras, microphones, porn material, and all other evidence. Plan on reconvening here at 1330 hours tomorrow. If something goes afoul, we'll adjust accordingly. Questions? Okay. You have your assigned units. You will converge on the house at twenty hundred hours. Good luck."

Sully, Mac, and I met in an empty office. "So far we're looking good," Mac said.

Sully said, "I'll second that."

I added, "I'll be glad when this is over."

To which Mac said, "This is just the beginning. This case is going to go on and on and on. You're screwing with the church."

"That's wrong, Mac. The church is screwing with kids. Screw with children and you're on the wrong side of the law. No justification, no excuses. Game over. If I thought I could get away with it, I'd fire two rounds from a cold gun; one bullet into Strayhan's head, the other bullet into...." For obvious reasons, I didn't finish my sentence.

Here I was worried about what senior Delvo might do to the dirty priest, and I was thinking the same thing. I wouldn't do it, Delvo might.

KNOCK, KNOCK. WE'RE HERE

Sergeant Troutmann sat in the Command Post. He monitored the computer in room one. Sully had room two, Mac had room three. I had the room that contained Father Strayhan and Frank Delvo junior. I was to give the command for the take down.

Strayhan and Frank junior were on the carpeted floor leaning against the bed. Father Strayhan looked at Frank. He leaned close. "Take off my belt, unzip my pants, and lick me the way only you can do to make me feel so good."

That was all I needed. "HIT IT! HIT IT! HIT IT! HIT IT HARD HIT IT FAST. GO! GO! GO!"

The troops hit the Duffmann house at twenty hundred hours on the money. No fuss, no muss. The precision and timing was a thing of beauty. Because our hidden cameras allowed us to monitor the activity in the house, we knew with precision when to take the place down. Obviously, we intended to "hit the house" before the nightly "activity" began. We felt between cameras, microphones, and statements from the kids, we had more than enough for an indictment. I wanted more. I wanted to break at least one of the sick perps, so we'd get the entire ring to cop a plea. I didn't want a trial. The kids had been through enough. The families had been through enough. I'll give you guess as to which pervert I was going to break.

Everyone was ushered out of the house without issue. The kids were driven to the hospital for examination. The "big five" were ushered out of the house in handcuffs. Fittingly, the last sicko out was Father Patrick Strayhan. The five were carefully searched then searched a second time by a partner officer. We tried to leave no stone unturned.

276

The "second" team entered the house when it was cleared. That team collected evidence. They had boxes of porn, seized computers, condoms, three pair of handcuffs, masks, magazines, bondage equipment and a book of what appeared to be coded names, birthdates, and phone numbers. We had enough to make any sane adult puke.

The five were driven to APEST, the temporary booking station. Their "personals" were bagged for their trip to Twin Towers. I had suggested to the Sheriff's that each be put on suicide watch. Personally, I'd allow them to keep their belt. I didn't give a damn if they ended it. It would save the city, the state money; it would make it easier on the community; most important, the victims would get some solace.

Mac, Sully, Troutmann, Commander Edison and I each "handled" a prisoner. I handpicked Father Strayhan. I escorted him, in handcuffs, to a room with blacked out windows, a couple of chairs, and a card table. "Sit down." I mirandized the so-called priest. "Father, you have sinned. You've made a mockery out of your church. You're an embarrassment. You're as bad as a rogue cop." Those words stung.

Father Strayhan looked me in the eyes. How he was able to do that, I'll never know. "I read you your rights. You don't have to talk to me." I scratched my ear. "Do you have anything you'd like to say? Do you want to talk to me?" I said as sarcastically as I could muster, "If you talk to me. You can earn up to five points toward a trip to Disneyland."

He answered no to both questions. His eyes told me I could fuck a walrus. "I want a lawyer."

"You're going to need a lawyer, Father Puke Pot. But even he isn't going to save your ass. They have a special place in hell reserved for you."

The infamous five as the newspapers would later dub them, including Father StrayhanD (a clever newspaper reporter added the D,) were driven to Twin Towers where they would stay pending arraignment and bond.

Phase two was in the books. Our work had just begun.

MOPPING UP

Now came the part of investigative work I liked least. The paperwork. Police work was built on paperwork. We kill more trees than all the damn advertisements you get in your mailbox annually. Everybody gets in on the action.

An arrest report has to be written for each individual in custody. A probable cause declaration, explaining the reason for the arrest, has to be written. Everybody who "touched" the arrestee has to file a supplemental report. The evidence has to be individually bagged, tagged, listed on an evidence sheet, and put in a locker accordingly or sent off for fingerprint processing or DNA handling. Pictures taken at the crime scene have to be processed. If an automobile was seized during the arrest, you guessed it, the vehicle has to be tagged and processed. The list goes on. If the watch commander finds errors in the report(s), it's back to the drawing board.

If you arrest a guy for driving on a suspended license, in California 14601.1(a) of the CVC, California Vehicle Code, you impound the car, and the police impound yard picks up the car. As the guy on the television would say, "But wait, there's more." To be certain that the car's owner gets back all the possessions that were in his car when you impounded it, you get to fill out what's called a CHP 180 in triplicate. The CHP 180 lists all items in the car including the spare tire if any. Then you get to walk the car and note any damage on the car. One copy goes to the tow truck driver, the other two copies to the WC for approval.

To show you the importance of a proper and thorough vehicle search, an officer who impounded a vehicle, must have been in a hurry. He completed a cursory search of the

279

vehicle, checked off all the proper boxes on the CHP 180, filled in the VIN, vehicle identification number, and checked said vehicle for damage. Up went the car on the tow truck. Off went the driver on his merry way after he signed off on the ticket for 12500(a) CVC, driving without a license.

I'll tell you this. It was not our department. It could have been. The vehicle arrives at the tow yard. Two days later someone at the yard catches a whiff of a foul odor emanating from the vehicle's trunk. They pop the trunk which the officer failed to do at the scene. Yeah, you guessed it. A body! A very dead body!! A very ripe dead body!!! Oops.

Shit happens. Sometimes it's funny. Sometimes a felon gets off because a cop fucked up. Maybe he didn't Mirandize the perp in Spanish. Maybe he neglected to cross a T in his report. Let me ask you this. If a cop makes a paper mistake in the report, why the hell is it sometimes grounds to kick a suspect free? Punish the cop, don't reward the bad guy. Our system, in many ways, is fucked up. Let's repair it.

Once this was behind us, at least once the paperwork was approved and the case was on its way to filing, we could get back on hunting down Ricki's killer. With everything that we had going, and we had almost more than we could handle, we took a hiatus from Ricki. I felt bad about that. But in police work you often had to set priorities. The well-being of these kids was first. Getting these perverts behind bars was a close second.

I called the hospital to check on the wounded deputies. Both deputies were out of surgery. Both deputies were in intensive care. Both deputies were expected to recover. Physically they might recover; mentally, you never recover from something like that anymore than these kids would recover.

More good news, I learned that the reward for the shooter had increased. The city council had put up one hundred thousand dollars. A citizen sponsored a private reward fund. Another seventy-five thousand dollars poured in increasing the reward money to one hundred seventy-five thousand dollars, and still counting. There were still people out there who appreciated and even liked our cops. Thank you!

FIVE DOWN ONE TO GO

At 1330 hours, I took center stage once again to commend the men and women who worked feverishly as a task force to take down these animals. "Let me have your undivided attention, please." The group sat at attention. "I have a couple of questions. Do any of you really give a shit who wins at the Academy Awards?" I heard a chorus of, "Hell no!" "Does anyone really care if the price of milk goes up?" I heard more, "Hell no!" "Does anyone really care that five assholes are behind bars as we speak?" I heard a loud chorus of, "Fuck yes!"

"You, ladies and gentlemen, are responsible for that. You have not only put these puke pots where they belong, you put them there for a long time. I expect that they'll bond out. Some unbelieving church goers will dip into their fat bank accounts and post bond, thinking this might help them one day get to heaven. The fact is we have them dead bang. You have yourselves to thank for that. You have a lot of kids who will have a better life because of your guts, determination, and courage. You have family members who can now let the healing begin. You have a thankful community who will respect you all the more for your dedication. I thank you from the bottom of my heart." I drew a breath.

"We have food and soft drinks, sorry no booze, some of you are still on duty, in the back. I want you to enjoy the food, the drinks, and the fellowship. Oh yeah, one last thing. There is a sixth member of the sex ring who is outstanding. There is a warrant out for his arrest. This may answer a burning question. How could this ring have gone on so long without somebody saying something, without a clue or a hint that something was very rotten in Amity? The answer is former Chief Payne." I paused to let that sink in.

A voice from somewhere yelled, "Are you for real?"

"I'm for real. Chief Payne was one of the players. Whether he somehow had some clue we were on to the ring, we don't know yet. We do know there is a warrant out for his arrest. The Grand Jury will undoubtedly hand down an indictment.

"As we speak, a press conference is in full swing in front of the Amity Station. You can expect a hailstorm of reporters in and around the station for the next week maybe more. If a reporter attempts to buttonhole you, please refer them to Acting Chief Lee Rolando. We need to caution everyone that we do not want to jeopardize what we have worked so hard to build. Thanks again. Enjoy your food."

There it was, plain and simple, a fucking police chief in the center of this child sex ring. How sick can you get? A dynamic duo. A priest and a police chief. It would amaze me if Amity PD survived this shit storm.

I made small talk with a few people in the front of the room then walked to the food area. I was hungry. There was finger food on the table, pizza, sub sandwiches, a ten-foot-long Italian sub, desserts, coffee, iced tea and assorted soft drinks. I grabbed a sub sandwich and an iced tea, found an empty table, and sat down. It felt good to sit. Now I had to unwind without a shot or four of Seagram's.

Walking over to my almost empty table to help me unwind, with a plate full of food and a drink in hand, were who else, Sully and Mac. I thought about Judge Karma. I had a mouth full of tea. It damned near came out all over the table.

Being the smart ass that I can be, I said, "Do you mind if I join you?"

"Thanks," Mac said. "I don't mind if we do."

Sully pulled out a chair. The second he was seated he said, "Are you sure Payne was involved in this shit?"

"One of the kids pulled him out of a six pack. The kid, whose statement we have, saw Payne's badge. He's positive. I had two other kids identify him from a six pack. In total, three off the children went through pictures of every employee of Amity PD. Payne was a winner."

"Jesus. Anybody else we might know?"

"Not that we know of. I think it was basically the five. How many cops do you know who bag a priest and a cop? Apparently, an Arizona department hired the scum bag. He cleared background with them, and he cleared background with us. My best bet is this isn't the first time he's done it. It's the first time he got nailed."

Mac asked, "Do they have any idea where he fled?"

"My guess would be, if he went out of the country, it would be somewhere that doesn't have an extradition treaty with us."

"Is he married?"

I looked at Mac. Damn those eyes drove me crazy. "His wife died of cancer several years ago. This is going to be ugly when the newspapers come out. And you can bet your ass it's already all over the news following the press conference."

Mac wanted to know our next step.

"At this point, most everything is in the hands of the D.A. unless they want our help. The D.A. is going to interview the kids starting tomorrow. The perps all lawyered up. We're at a standstill which gives us a bit of time to look at Ricki's murder. What's going on with you guys and SafeGuard?"

"We've got a shovel into some dirt and we're digging into him. That's about all we've got for now."

I took a bite out of my sub sandwich then asked Sully, "How's the apartment coming?"

"It's boxes and boxes and more boxes. I'm going to need to rent storage space."

"Payne's office is empty, maybe he'll let you stack your stuff in there for a while."

"I don't want my stuff anywhere near Payne or anything Payne's touched in the last fifty years."

"What's with you and Kline? You two have something going?"

I wanted to tell Mac I had nothing going with Kline; then I was going to ask her if she had something going with Sully. Something told me this wasn't the time nor the place. I heard Judge Karma tell me to keep my big fucking pie hole closed.

"The Devlo family has Kline on retainer for his business. Frank junior was part of the sex ring. Kline's helping the family out. The fact of the matter is Kline hates this shit as much as we do. He wanted it shut down and offered to help. He sat in on our interview with the Devlo's." I paused. "And by the way, Kline's Italian."

"I thought you said he was circumcised?"

"Very funny. You been hanging around Sully to long. His real dad died when he was young. He took his stepdad's name which is Kline. His birth dad's name is Lesola."

"Isn't there a crime family back east by that name?" Sully asked.

"Right up there with the Kano family."

Mac just couldn't shut up. "So, Kline's actually Italian. I guess you can't tell what's inside a book by looking at its cover."

"I guess you can't." I stuffed the rest of my sandwich in my mouth, chewed, and swallowed it with a shot of iced tea.

"Tony, we really have to talk."

The worst words you can hear from a woman are, "We really have to talk." I knew what Mac wanted to talk about. She wanted to fill me on her and Sully. I wasn't going to make it easy for her.

"I agree. Now's a bad time."

"I didn't mean now, Tony." She looked at Sully. He wasn't going to go away.

The room started to thin out. I was tired. I'm sure I wasn't the only one who was beyond exhausted.

"Can we set up a time to talk? It's important."

"I'll call you. We'll set something up." I just knew Judge Karma was pushing me into this.

"Please don't wait too long. We're hoping to finish the interview at SafeGuard later today. I'm free after that."

"I said I'll call you. My word's good. If you good people will excuse me, I have to see a man about some money."

WHAT AM I GOING TO DO, ROCKY?

I drove out to the cemetery. At least Rocky was on my side. I felt like everything was coming down on me. I knelt by the Rock's headstone. "Here are the two packs of cigarettes I owe you. But help me out, buddy. I know you know about Judge Karma. Somehow, I can't help but feel there's a connection between you and the Judge. I know I have to straighten out this mess with Mac, now maybe Sully and Mac. I'm so damn confused I don't know what to do."

"This shit is starting to interfere with work. It's starting to pull me down. You know how dangerous that is on the job. I've come to the conclusion that I can't accept Mac as she is or was. It wouldn't be fair to either one of us. Besides, Sully and Mac may now be an item. I know, I know what's coming, Rock. You're going to ask me if Sully's not in my way would I try to make this work with Mac. The answer would still be no. I love Mac, and Mac loves me. We had the best relationship I ever had. We had more crazy fun that I could ever imagine. I'd take Mac over Seagram's. Sex was out of this world. Now I can't even get a hard on with her. Even her damp panties don't do for me what they used to do. Buddy, it's gotta' be the end of the line for Mac and me. It hurts. It hurts like putting down your beloved dog hurts."

I felt tears beginning to well up in my eyes. "The hard part is telling her. Although if she and Sully are together, she sure the shit isn't going to hurt like I'm hurting. If you and Judge Karma say I have to tell her, I have to tell her."

"Thanks, buddy." I sat with Rocky for twenty more minutes. He and the Judge made it come clear for me. Sometimes it's just time to say good-bye.

287

TRUE CONFESSIONS

I had every intention of calling Mac in the morning after breakfast. I poured me a bowl of corn flakes, orange juice, and coffee. I sat at the table, thought, and ate. I finished breakfast. I'd shave and shower then call Mac. I didn't want to talk with her on the phone; that wouldn't be right. We could meet somewhere.

I shaved, showered, and dressed in a sports jacket and slacks sans tie. I splashed cologne on my face. I walked into the living room to retrieve my cell. The phone rang. It was Acting Chief Lee Rolando.

"Tony, good morning. I hope I didn't pull you away from one of your lady friends."

I remained silent, for once.

"First, you did one hell of a job, buddy. You'll be bucking for my position soon. Everybody's talking about how well you handled yourself in all phases. This was a major operation, and you handled it with aplomb."

What the fuck was aplomb other than some fruit? "Thank you, sir."

"Now onto business. I received a call from the priest's attorney, Robert Owens. They want to meet with you today."

That was off the wall. "Has the asshole bonded out?"

"Of course. You know the game. He was out before the paperwork was done, literally."

"I'll give you Owens' number. Give him a call, set something up, then get back to me."

"Two questions, sir. Does he want to meet with just me?"

"Just you."

"Do you have any idea what this is all about?"

"Not a clue. But if the mouthpiece is coming to you, it can't be all bad. Keep me in the loop, buddy. Thanks, Tony."

I hung up. That gave me something to think about. I didn't know Robert Owens. My guess would be he was someone from the church trying to help out so he could score points with God. Before I phoned him, I wanted to think this through.

Strayhan was in a box, gift wrapped with a ribbon around him. He couldn't deny his way out of this. Although he and his slime ball attorney would try anything to dig his way out of criminal charges and invoke the name of God and religion in so doing.

I made myself a second cup of coffee; actually, I poured the water, Keurig made the coffee. It was damn good coffee. I sat at the kitchen table. I sipped the coffee. They wanted to meet with just me. I wasn't crazy about that. But then again, if I could handle Kline, aka Lesola or vice versa, I'm sure I could handle Robert Owens.

I finished the coffee and dropped a dime. (For those of you who are too young to remember "dropping a dime",) I made the call.

When the receptionist connected me, I was polite and to the point. "I'll be happy to meet with you and your client, counselor. Specifically, what will we discuss?" I was getting pretty good at this attorney shit.

"We'll discuss that in my office when we meet, detective."

289

He was cute. But he came to me. "I'm sorry, counselor. I have too much on my calendar to meet today. I'll call you back when it's convenient for me." I had him by the balls, and the sorry son of a bitch knew it.

There was a very long pause and finally, "Okay, detective." Now there was a sigh. "My client wants to talk with you about making a deal."

Deal my ass. He had nothing to offer and I was holding all fifty-two cards, and the jokers. Let him buy another deck. "I don't see what your client can possibly offer."

"I promise you, Detective Kano, once you hear what my client has on the table, you'll deal. Shall we say eleven o'clock my office?"

He gave me the address. "Eleven o'clock your office." This was bullshit but I couldn't leave a stone unturned.

I called the D.A.'s office. I got a friend of mine on the phone. I talked to him about the ins and outs of cutting a deal with this scumbag. I learned that the D.A. would have to approve any deal and very possibly also the judge. He told me to make no promises because the buck didn't stop with me. If I thought Strayhan had something to trade, my line should be, "I'll run it by my boss and the D.A." Basically, I received a twenty-minute crash course in Trump's, The Art of the Deal.

My next call was to Rolando. I brought him up to speed. He underscored what the ADA had told me. He said, "You're getting one hell of a crash course in being a detective, Tony. When you meet with Manny and Mo, if you have any questions or concerns tell the attorney you want five minutes to run it up the chain. Remember, you're in no hurry to deal if indeed he has something to offer. They came to you not the other way around."

"Got it, boss. Thanks. I'll keep you posted."

I hung up. What the hell could the dirty priest have to deal? We had the entire ring dead bang; or so I thought. Could they also have been dealing drugs? Was Payne involved in drug dealing or some other shit? Did Strayhan want to trade Payne for a possible lighter sentence?

Amity was filled with gangs. Gangs, robberies, car thefts, guns and drugs go hand in hand. It was possible that Strayhan had something to offer. If he didn't, his mouthpiece wouldn't have made contact. Owens obviously thought he and his client had something to put on the table. Time would tell.

LET'S MAKE A DEAL

Attorney Robert Owens' office could have fit, with room to spare, in Kline's office closet. They could not have been more opposite. Robert Owens reminded me of Wally Cox, the comic actor who was five foot five if he was lucky and a hundred thirty-five pounds if his pockets were filled with six boxes of nine-millimeter rounds, hollow points of course. Like Cox, Owens also wore thick glasses. We shook hands.

His client, Patrick Strayhan, (I couldn't bring myself to call him Father) sat at a small wooden table. There was a pitcher of water and glasses on the table. No soft drinks, no Seagram's, not even pretzels. Damn.

When we were all seated, I was at one end of the table, Owens at the other, and his client next to him. I needed a carrier pigeon to contact Owens. Fuck him. Without saying a word, I stood up and moved closer. I was now one seat away from Owens, almost directly across from his client. I smiled at Owens, quickly wiped the smile off my face then made eye contact with Strayhan. His eyes immediately fell to the brown carpeted floor.

"Let's begin," Owens said. He grabbed a recorder from somewhere behind him. "We're going to record this session," he said.

I jumped on that like Chinese on rice. "No, we're not. This is preliminary, exploratory, and not for the record." I had no idea what the hell I said, but Malcolm had given me that crash course. "Put the recorder away and make sure it's off, counselor or this meeting is over before it begins."

Owens didn't mouth word one. He set the recorder behind him. I wasn't dealing with a true professional, at least not so far. This guy was no Jerry Kline, Esquire. He finally said, "Anything said in this room stays in this room, detective. Is that clear?"

"Can't do that, counselor. I have my people to report to."

"You're making this unnecessarily difficult, detective."

"No, I'm not, counselor. I'm being honest."

I was on a roll. I wanted to keep the momentum going. "Let's cut to the chase, counselor. Thanks to your client and his sexually sick companions, I have more paperwork to complete at the office than your client has heard confessions. What is it your client has to offer? And keep in mind, this is preliminary. I have to run everything by my boss, and the D.A. and possibly the judge. Again, what does your client want?"

Owens cut to the chase. "Complete immunity from prosecution."

I was stunned. In recent memory the only thing that made my head spin more than Owens' utterance was Mac telling me she was born a guy. I poured a glass of water. "And I want a twelve-inch dick, a ten-inch tongue and girlfriend who's a deaf mute and owns a liquor store. You and your client are dreaming, counselor." I looked at Strayhan. He looked like a scolded puppy. The guy was a pig as far as I was concerned. No way in hell was he not going to do prison time and register as a sex offender.

"Don't you wanted to hear what my client has to offer?"

I drank water. "I'm here. Go for it."

"He'll give you Ricki Montego Valenzuela's killer."

What kind of bullshit was that? Roberto was Ricki's killer; or was he? I'd play his game.

My head started spinning like one those fucking baseball player's bubbleheads you stick on the rear deck of your car. Every time you hit a bump the head bounces every which way. I needed time to swallow and digest this shit. It was good shit if true. But it had to be developed. I lifted the pitcher of water, poured more water, and sipped from the cheap glass. "How can your client be certain he knows the killer?"

"I can't tell you that at this time. I can tell you that if we come to a deal, and my client's information is not accurate, if you don't arrest the killer on my client's information, if he doesn't testify for the prosecution and against the killer, the deal will be dead."

"And for that you want what for your client?"

"I told you before, complete immunity from prosecution."

Fuck that. Maybe he knew who the killer was. How? I'd be damned if I knew. We'd get the killer sooner or later with or without Strayhan's help. "No deal, counselor. We're closing in on the killer," I lied through my pearly whites. "If, and I stress if, your client had workable information, has viable information that we can use in the prosecution of the suspects, in the prosecution of Ricki's killer, your client isn't about to get off with a slap of his filthy fingers. The best I would even consider, and I said consider, counselor, would be a felony sentence, your client registers for life as a child sex offender and is on probation for life."

It was Owens turn to drink water. Strayhan was an onlooker, nothing more. "Would you consider house arrest?"

I looked directly at Strayhan. "No way in hell, counselor."

294

Owens sighed. He looked at his client. "Let's take a twenty-minute break."

I walked down two flights of stairs then walked to my car which was parked on the street next to an expired meter. I had the passenger and the driver's side visor down. Each had a neatly printed cardboard sign that said, Amity Detective on OFFICIAL BUSINESS. Run the plate. Thanks.

I got in the passenger side. I left the door open. I phoned Rolando. As expected, Rolando was unavailable. I called my assistant district attorney buddy. He took my call. I fed him the bottom line from my meeting with Owens and the fucked-up priest.

"Do you believe he can hand you the killer?"

"I don't know. He's not giving me a name nor is he telling me how he knows the killer. They're looking to deal. I'm trying to play hard ball. The priest needs to do time behind a felony, and he needs to register as a sex offender."

"Slow down. You're not sure he isn't bluffing. One way to pull his covers is to tell the counselor you're taking his client in as a material witness. Are you familiar with that term?"

"In general terms."

"Basically, a material witness is an individual that has evidence of sufficient importance that it can influence the outcome of a trial. That fits Father Strayhan. If you decide you want play hardball, fuck with him. His attorney may fold; then again, he may call your bluff. Are you guys on record?"

"No."

"Then it's a crap shoot. I'd feel him out, Tony. Pressure him gently. If you have to give a little to get a lot, go for it. You're talking a one eighty-seven suspect against a sexual predator. Sometimes you have to make a deal with the devil, Tony."

I wasn't making any deals with this cocksucker. And I wasn't about to sell my soul to the devil. I'd have my cake and I'd eat it too. "If you were doing the dealing in this case, Malcolm, what would you do?"

"I'd squeeze but not too tight. Can you nail the killer without the priest's naming him?"

"Eventually."

"In the meantime, is he likely to kill again?"

Malcolm had a point. "I didn't think about that."

"That's okay. You're in a tough situation. Do the best you can. Remember nothing you say or do in that meeting is set in concrete. Everything is subject to the D.A.'s approval; even that may not be binding. I'm here if you need me. By the way, how's Mac doing?"

That was just what I wanted to hear when my head was on the business at hand. "I think she's up the block writing a parking ticket." I didn't stop for a breath. "If I need help, I'll call you. If not, I'll bring you up to date after the meeting."

"Here's my personal cell, Tony. Take it down."

MORE LET'S MAKE A DEAL

I had barely taken my seat when Owens went on the attack. "Did you talk to your people?"

"I spoke with my superiors, counselor."

"Did they school you?"

"Did they 'school' me, counselor? Hell no, they didn't school me. They told me to lock your client up as a material witness."

"Listen, what's said in this room is confidential."

"Show me where that's written. Nobody agreed to that." I decided to play good detective. "Listen counselor, if you want to help your client, let's stop fighting each other. Let's work out a verbal agreement I can take to the D.A. and let's put this show on the road. I'm sure your client would like to put this behind him."

"Fair enough."

I topped off my water glass buying a few seconds of precious time. "Can your client actually put our killer at the scene of the homicide?"

"You're fishing, detective."

"No, I'm not. I'm trying to get concrete information."

"Here's as concrete as we get without a sealed deal. My client can conclusively name the killer of Ricki Montego Valenzuela. No ifs, ands, or buts. My client knows this for a fact. Let me put it this way. My client was not an eyewitness to the killing but he's the closest human to an eyewitness that you're going to find. I can't give you more than that without some kind of offer."

The counselor surprised me. During our break he must have opened a can of ball builders. I had a hunch it was going to be a long day. "Let's try this. If we get a conviction on your client's information, we recommend a sentence of a year and a day; your client is registered as a sex offender; and he's on probation for ten years. If he gets a year, he'll be out in damn near half that time."

"No jail time."

"Can't do it. That's a deal breaker."

"Sit tight." Owens walked out of the room with Strayhan. They weren't gone five minutes. I strained to hear what they were saying. No go. The fact that he took his client outside told me they had to be considering it. He'd likely make a counteroffer. I was on the money.

"Six months at a minimum-security prison of our choice. Five years' probation, and he doesn't register as a sex offender."

"Anything that doesn't include prison or registering as a sex offender is off the table, counselor. Your client had sex with kids. Doesn't that mean anything to you?"

"Look at what my client did for the community over the years."

"And how many kids did he do over the years? I'll let you ask the prosecutor to recommend a facility of your choice but that's as far as I go."

"My client and I need time to discuss this. Can we meet back here at two, tomorrow afternoon?"

I nodded. I knew I was walking out a winner. "Two tomorrow. Same place, same station." I shook hands with Owens. I ignored Strayhan.

On the drive back to the station, I thought about how the priest could positively ID the killer. I also thought about the fact that Strayhan's ability to ID the killer most likely meant the killer was one of the people in the organized sex ring; most likely. The only other possibility that came to mind was that the killer had taken confession with Strayhan; but then Strayhan was bound by church confidentially. I had to laugh at my own reasoning; bound by church confidentiality my ass. Here was a guy who was molesting kids. This prick-less wonder would do anything to save his own ass.

I drove back to the station lot. I sat in the car and called ADA Malcolm. I updated him. He was pleased with the result of the meeting. He told me to stick to my guns. I then went into the station. I found Lee Rolando; he was free. I updated the Acting Chief. He too was pleased. So far so good.

I pulled the file on Ricki. I looked it over again. If Strayhan knew the killer, odds were he either knew the killer from the church or from their little "club" or both. I studied the names of people we had interviewed who said they attended the Church of All Faiths. Zilch. I studied the names of the people from the sex club. Nothing popped. It made no sense. The priest was trying to tell me Roberto wasn't the killer. I didn't know whether I should believe him. Cornered people, like a cornered rat, do crazy, often unexplainable things, and will lie like hell to get out of prison time.

I called the lab. "Do you guys have anything that can link Roberto Vega-Chapa to Ricki Montego Valenzuela's killing?" I knew the answer before I asked the question.

"Nothing yet. We're still working on it."

"Have you found anything that can nail a killer down if we bring him in?"

"Nothing yet."

I was stymied. If Roberto didn't murder Ricki, why did he take his life? Had he loved her that much?

I decided to put my best case for a plea bargain agreement on paper. I moved to the computer room.

I wrote basically what I told Owens in the meeting. The very best I was willing to offer was a year behind bars, five years' probation and registration as a sex offender and child molester. We'd recommend the penitentiary of Strayhan's choice. Of course, none of this was up to me. It still had to pass muster with the district attorney and most likely a judge. The bottom line was Owens' client was going to take it up the ass. I guess turnabout is fair play!

I was now as prepared for tomorrow's meeting as I was going to be. It was quitting time as far as I was concerned. I had put in more hours over the last couple of weeks than I cared to count. None of it was overtime.

I opened my door and went straight for the Seagram's bottle. I was thirsty, tired, wound up and pissed. I could deal with the first three; the last was an issue. Judge Karma told me to deal with it. I would. I needed a few shots first to loosen up my tongue.

I went into the bedroom and stripped down to my slacks and t-shirt. I kicked off my shoes and took off my socks. I walked back to the couch. I poured a double and downed it. The burning felt great. I could feel myself start to unwind. One problem solved. I poured a single shot. The thirst disappeared. Another problem solved. A shower would

300

wake me up. Three out of four makes me rich if I was a baseball player.

I looked up at my white ceiling. Okay Judge Karma, here we go. I grabbed my cell phone off the glass top table. I speed dialed Mac. The phone rang three times then went to voice mail. "I'm sorry I can't take your call. Please leave a message and I'll get back to you."

"Mac, Tony. Call me when you get a chance, please. You want to talk, let's talk." Fuck me, I thought. I tried. I poured another shot of Seagram's and turned on the TV. An Adam 12 rerun was on. If I watched it, maybe I'd learn something.

I didn't hear a damn thing from Mac. I didn't even hear from Sully. I looked up. I said out loud, "Judge Karma, I tried."

I went to sleep to loud sirens. Malloy and Reed were in pursuit. I'm glad it wasn't me they were chasing. I would have passed out behind the wheel.

It was light outside when I awoke. I slept well and I slept through the night. No phone calls, no knock on the door, no one jumping into my bed. Yeah, that bothered me. The Judge could figure that out, I couldn't.

I went to the station late in the morning. I didn't see anything of Sully or Mac. Maybe they were still interviewing; maybe not.

I jumped on a computer with the names of our five child sex stars. I did background checks on all five. One of the five had an arrest for "child annoyance" in New Jersey. The case never saw trial. The youngster wouldn't testify or maybe his parents wouldn't let him testify. There was no other witness. By the time I got finished, all five would have arrest records and all five would be registered sex offenders and in the nation-wide data base.

I was antsy. It was only eleven forty-five. I phoned April to ask her to meet me for a quick lunch. She didn't answer. I left a message. "It's Tony. I called to invite you to lunch. It's about eleven forty-five. At two o'clock I'll be in a meeting. If you want to call me after two, please leave a message. Thanks, April. Have a great day."

I walked out to the lot, got in the unit, and drove around Amity looking for trouble. I couldn't even do that right. I finally went to lunch, alone, at twelve thirty.

SECOND VERSE NOT QUITE THE SAME AS THE FIRST

I was at Owens' office five minutes early. Rhonda Receptionist was at her desk dressed in a top that showed boobs, boobs, and more boobs. The three parts of a female anatomy that starts my clock ticking were a nice tight ass, boobs, and eyes. I knew RR had a great rack. Even sitting down her ass was tight and begged to be squeezed and rubbed. Her eyes were penetrating and invited a challenge. I loved a challenge especially one that was begging me, with her eyes, to unwrap her.

I walked over to her desk. "Vicki, long time no see."

"Did you miss me?"

"I'm back, aren't I?"

"Very funny." She walked around her desk and gave me a long hug. I'm sure she could feel Peter's acknowledgement as well. "You did miss me."

"I told you I did. I'll call as soon as things settle down at work."

"You'd better. I do the billing for Attorney Owens. If you don't call me, I'll bill you for the hug and for giving you my phone number."

"If I call, do I get a reward?"

"Lunch or dinner at the Y or both." Vicki blushed.

The door opened. It was Owens. "Detective, how are you?"

"Better than ever. You?"

"Busy." He waved his arm toward his office. "Let's get this done. My client is here so we're good to go."

I winked at Vicki. She winked back. Peter was standing at attention inside my pants. Vicki let her eyes drop to my crotch. She caught my eye and smiled. I wanted to ask her if she was wearing panties but decided it was best to wait until we took a break.

The office looked familiar. Nothing had changed since yesterday. The water pitcher and the glasses were on the table. I hoped the water was fresh.

"Let's get started," Owens said. "My client is prepared to give you what you need to nail your killer. He'll give you the five w's and how. He'll testify if need be. He'll accept six months of home confinement, probation, and he wants the witness protection program."

I thought, I'll give him the witness protection program. I'll put him in with the general population in the toughest prison I can find.

"And I want a free Ferrari with a big-busted blonde behind the wheel who wants to split a two-million-dollar winning lottery ticket with me. C'mon, counselor, get serious. Your client can take this: one year behind bars, five years-probation, register as a child sex offender, and I'll check on the WPP. In return, I get the killer of Ricki, how he did it, where he did it, and why he did it. He'll testify for us if need be. If he walks, so does our deal. Take it or leave it."

"My client will sweeten the pot, detective. He'll give you a bonus. He'll name one of your own who was involved."

I already had that information. But neither of the two knew that. I had another bargaining chip. "Deal or no deal, counselor?"

"Let's take fifteen. I need to confer with my client."

This was draining. It was less stressful to shoot some punk, fill out a few papers, and let Sheriff's homicide dicks do the investigation. You could be home enjoying a drink by shift's send.

I walked downstairs. I called Malcolm on his private line. "Hey, it's PITA, pain in the ass. Let me run something by you."

Malcolm laughed. "Whatcha' got, big guy?"

I spelled out the deal. "Can we do witness protection?"

"For the right deal, probably."

"We know who our guy is. We're really no closer to the killer. What do you suggest?"

"Here's what I would offer if they balked at your last offer. Give him the one year and one day sentence. Make it six months prison time, and six months house arrest. Everything else stands precisely as you spelled it out."

"Why didn't I think of that?"

"Tony, you're doing an outstanding job. This negotiating shit is like buying a used car. It's a real pain in the ass. Give them hell."

"Thanks. I'll get back to you." I had a few minutes. I called Mac. I got her answering machine. I hung up. I called Sully. I got his answering machine. I hung up. "Fuck it," I said out loud not giving a shit if anyone heard me.

I walked up the stairs and back to Owens' office. He and his client were apparently still behind closed doors. That gave me time to flirt with Vicki. I walked to her desk. I stood next to where she was sitting. Her black dress was hiked up enough that I could see silky, sexy, smooth thighs. I leaned down. My mouth was half an inch from her ear. "Can I ask you a serious question?"

"Shoot, detective."

She had a quick wit that was for sure. "Are you wearing panties?"

She looked at the lawyer's door. It was shut. She hiked up her skirt. Her panties were as blue as her eyes. "Do you want them?"

I stepped away from Vicki's desk just as Owens opened his office door. "Let's try this again, detective."

I was getting too familiar with his office. I was getting too chummy with the chair, the water pitcher and the cheap pictures on the office walls that needed paint. "Your move, counselor."

"My client says no to the deal. He won't accept jail time."

"Last shot, counselor. I consulted with the real suits. Here's my final offer. A year and a day sentence. Six months in a prison that you request. No guarantees the judge will buy it, but we'll recommend it. The other six months are home confinement. In reality, you might do three months behind bars. And you earned those three months. You're going to register for life as a child sex offender. Upon release from home confinement, you'll be on probation for five years. You will accept no position of any kind with a church or any organization where minors are present." I threw in the last requirement because I hated what he did.

I stared the sick priest in the eyes. "If you don't accept that deal, we go to trial. You can face off with all the kids you fucked. You can square off with the parents. You can…."

Owens held up his hand. "Enough, detective. You made your point."

"I don't think I did, counselor. But I'll shut up, for now. I'll give you ten minutes to discuss it with your so-called client. If he turns it down, I'll see the two of you in court." I walked out of the office and immediately to Vicki's desk. I was emotionally and mentally drained.

"You look exhausted. Can I get you a cup of coffee or something?"

"Thanks, babe. I'm good."

"I bet you are. How's it going?"

"Draining. The case is a bitch. What that son of a bitch did is unforgiveable."

"I've been trying to listen through the wall. I pick up bits and pieces." Vicki opened a desk drawer. She handed me a small tan lunch sack. "Put this in your pocket. In case you misplaced my card, my phone numbers in there. I expect a call later."

I had a strong hunch what was in the bag. My best guess was that it wasn't an elephant.

The door opened. "We're ready to go, detective."

GO OR NO GO

"Let's make this easy all the way around, counselor. Will your client accept the deal as I stated it, or do we meet again at trial?"

"My client will accept the deal, detective, providing the Witness Protection Program is acceptable."

"Great." We reexamined the terms that I would present to Malcolm who, if he approved, would run it by the D.A. That was process. I was certain I could get Malcolm to expedite. Assuming it was acceptable, a formal contract would be drawn up then presented to Owens and his client to sign. Once signed, I'd again sit down with Owens and Strayhan and get what I needed to (hopefully) arrest Ricki's killer. "I'll call you later today or early tomorrow, counselor, to let you know if the suits will buy the agreement."

I was sure they'd push this through. Approval meant getting a killer off the street. They say a bird in the hand is worth two in the bush. "My work is done here, counselor. I'm going home to take a shower." I looked at Strayhan. "I need to wash the stench off me."

Owens ushered me out of his office. He wanted to get rid of me. I said good-bye to Vicki, making it obvious I was touching the bag in my pocket. She smiled.

I wanted to touch base with Malcolm and see how we'd get the next step accomplished. But I wanted to do it from home. I really did need a shower, and a drink, maybe half the bottle.

ANOTHER P.O.S BITES THE DUST

I had the news on driving home from Owens office. I heard the usual garbage. Trump said this, Biden said that. Pence didn't say enough, and Kamala was trying to get people to pronounce her name properly.

I was about to turn the radio off when they cut in with a special bulletin. "The shooter of two Los Angeles County Deputies, who were sitting in their parked vehicle when assaulted, has been killed in a shootout with deputies. No police were injured in the shooting. According to early reports, a swarm of deputies attempted to arrest the alleged attempted murderer, who opened fire at deputies from his second-floor apartment in Bell Gardens. When the attempted murderer started firing, other deputies who were waiting outside his apartment, rammed the door off the hinges and returned fire killing the suspect. We have reporters racing to the scene and will bring you updates on this situation as we receive them."

Too damn bad Father Strayhan couldn't be there to give the prick his last rites. Better still, it was a shame Father Strayhan wasn't in the killer's apartment. We could have had a twofer. I drove the rest of the way home with a smile of satisfaction on my face.

MALCOLM IN THE MIDDLE

The first thing I did when I got home was make a note on the magnetic writing pad that I kept on the refrigerator. I wrote Malcolm, then under it I wrote Mac, Sully. Obviously, I had to get in touch with Malcolm to see if the plea deal was going to fly. Next, I wanted to set a date to talk with Mac and set things straight. I wanted the Judge off my case. I also wanted to talk with Sully to get an update on our money chase.

I sat down on my couch. The bottle of Seagram's was waiting for me. I poured a single shot. It tasted good, it felt good, but it didn't help me unwind. I poured shot number two but left it on the table. I got up. I still had my jacket on. I walked to the bedroom closet. As I took the jacket off, my hand rubbed against the pocket. I felt a bulge. I remembered Vicki's gift.

I reached in the pocket and pulled out the small tan lunch sack. I hung up the jacket. I opened the sack. Want to guess? Pale blue silky panties. Most likely the very same ones she was wearing when she hiked up her skirt for me. Exhibit one.

I balled up the paper sack and tossed in the trash can under the sink. I un-balled the pale blue panties. I opened them imagining what and who had been inside those panties. I sniffed the crotch. It was either the raw smell of Vicki's pussy that got Peter aroused or the perfume that she dabbed on those panties; either way it was beyond erotic. I took one last sniff. There was something written on the crotch of those delicious panties. It read, FOR A GREAT TIME CALL 610-547-6547, ASK FOR VICKI.

I walked over to the magnetic note pad. I wrote Vicki under Sully's name. I drank my shot, poured one more to celebrate the possible plea bargain agreement, went into the bedroom,

310

stripped down to my birthday suit, and took a hot shower. Yes, to relieve some of the tension, I played with myself. The quality problem I had was who to think about while I was caressing Peter: Mac, April, Vicki, or a combination of the three.

I got Malcolm on the phone. I ran over the "final" results of the plea bargain negotiation. "What do you think?"

"I like it, Tony. Can you fax me a draft copy? I don't want it on email."

"Sure. I can type it up and fax it to you within half an hour. Do you have a fax number?"

Malcolm gave me his private fax. "If you can get it to me quickly, I'll try to get the D.A. to approve it today. If we can get it approved today, I can get it typed up tomorrow and we can get it signed off later this week, maybe even tomorrow."

"Not a problem, sir. I have a fax machine at my house. I'll go to work as soon as I hang up. Thanks for your help, Malcolm. This couldn't have been done without your help."

"You did a helluva' job, Tony. Anything you need, anytime you need it, call me."

Malcolm had the draft copy thirty-eight minutes after I hung up.

I felt good about what I had accomplished. I felt damn good. Malcolm seemed to be pleased with my perseverance. I was helping to get scum off the street and where they belonged, behind bars. I was learning the detective game. I earned a few minutes of relaxation, or so I thought. I was about to take it up the ass.

THE WAITING GAME

I crossed Malcolm off my list of improvised things to accomplish today. Next up was Mac. A shot and a phone call were in order. "See, Your Honor, I'm not procrastinating. I'm really trying." I dialed. I got her voice mail. I didn't leave a message. I called Sully's private line. I got his voice mail. "Hey partner, give Tony a shout when you get a chance." The visions I had of Mac and Sully made my blood boil.

I didn't erase their names from the refrigerator notepad. My phone interrupted my imagination. It was Vicki. "Did you get my gift?"

"It smelled better than dinner."

"It could be dinner, and dessert. How about tonight at my place?"

"You're going to get your tight little ass and those cute pale blue panties in a wad if your boss finds out. It could be considered a conflict of interest."

"A conflict of interest would be your finishing before me. But I'm sure you're more considerate than that. You strike me as the patient type. You'd wait for me, wouldn't you?"

"Anytime and every time. Are you still at work?"

"Just putting things in order for tomorrow. So, how about tonight?"

"Tonight's not going to work, hon. I have a date with paperwork from today's negotiation session. Can I call you tomorrow?"

"Of course. But what am I going to do about tonight?"

"Seriously, I'm stuck at home with my computer and a fax machine waiting on word about today. I'll call you later and maybe we can solve both our problems on the phone."

"Oooh. I think I might like that. Keep my pale blues handy."

I was rock hard when I hung up. Aloud I said, "I know, Your Honor, I know but what's a guy supposed to do. I can't get a hold of Mac. Besides, if Mac is a dead issue, a guys got a right to move on." I poured another shot. I had bought a book at the mall the other day that I hadn't had a chance to start reading, How Cops Die. The front cover depicted a blue uniformed officer sprawled in front of his police car covered in blood. In his hand was his gun. A car was speeding off in the distance. I opened the book.

I opened the book to the preface. I read, "This book is dedicated to those who wear the badge. This book also recognizes the ancillary staff who support those who wear the badge. To the family members who worry themselves sick every time their husbands, wives, children, sisters, brothers walk out the door, my heart goes out to you."

"There is no more dangerous job than the profession of serving and protecting. There is no sadder or more joyous job than the career of police officer. Every time one of these highly trained professionals gets behind the wheel of his unit, he or she is putting life and limb on the line. From the bottom of my heart, I thank you for your dedication and service. Without you to serve and protect, to keep our streets safe, I would not let my family out of the house.

Unfortunately, today we have handcuffed the very men and women who uphold the law. Who (literally) fight the good fight every day to help ensure our safety and keep our Country free!

313

In 2017, 129 police officers died in the line of duty. In 2019 that number rose to 144. Almost one officer dies every other day. This is an American tragedy.

So, to those who made the ultimate sacrifice, to those of you who forego family holidays, to those who work extended hours, to those who leave their families to care for the needs of others, to those who don't come home from their shift EVER, this book is dedicated to you.

Thank you for what you do. You do it twenty-four seven because you are on duty twenty-four seven. God Bless you and yours. Stay safe."

"Rocky," I said aloud, "this man is talking about you. Thank you, Rocky, for serving and protecting." I closed the book. I poured Seagram's into my shot glass.

The phone rang. It was Malcolm. "I've got good news and not so good news. What do you want me to hit you with first?"

"Give me the not so good news."

"I have preliminary approval but nothing concrete yet. The DA wants to study it tonight. But he likes it. If it's a go, it should be typed up by late tomorrow afternoon. If that occurs, you can meet with your friends tomorrow and get it signed off. Then the real work begins, but not for you. We'll begin building a paper case just in case the plea bargain isn't approved, or it falls apart. It looks like another success for you, Tony."

I thanked Malcolm once again. We were on the right road. I had high hopes we'd soon put Ricki's killer where he belonged, behind bars.

314

A PHONE CALL TO REMEMBER

It started to get dark when my cell rang. I picked it up. "Are you playing with my pale blue panties?"

"Not yet, but I'm sure we can make that happen. Are you playing with anything?"

"Not yet, but I'm sure we can make that happen."

Was there a female in the world who didn't have a smart mouth, or did I just bring out the best in them? "Hey, where are you right now?"

"I'm sitting in front of the fireplace in a black bra and matching panties. I'm sipping white wine and talking with you."

"No kids to distract you?"

"No kids, period."

"No husband to distract you?"

"You looked at my left hand. Did you see a ring or a white circle?"

"Nope. No boyfriend to distract you?"

"I'm two hundred percent yours. What are you going to do about that?"

"The question, counselor, is what are we going to do about that?"

"I'll bite."

"I would prefer you nibble. We don't want to hurt Peter."

Vicki laughed.

"Do you like whip cream?"

"Where?"

"Any and everyplace I'm going to put it." I stripped down to my underwear. I poured a shot. I sat on my couch. "I'm now wearing matching white underwear. I'm drinking a shot of Seagram's. I'm sitting on my couch with feet up on the cocktail table. I have no fireplace. But I do have a can of whip cream." My fantasy was coming to life as was my imagination.

"I want you to take off your bra." I pictured those perky, firm, full breasts with nipples standing at attention. "Do you have pillows on that couch?"

"I do," Vicki responded softly.

"Put a pillow or two behind your head. Make yourself very comfortable. Keep sipping the wine. Is your bra off?"

"Yes."

"Slide those silky black panties off that gorgeous tight body. Tell me when they're off."

I shook up the whip cream can that I didn't have. "Did you hear that? I shook up the whip cream. Are your dirty panties off?"

"Yes."

"Hand them to me."

"Here, Tony."

"Here, Tony, what?"

"Tony, here are my dirty panties. I put them on just for you. I took them off just for you."

"I like those panties. I'm putting them up to my face. They smell sexy as hell, just like you. I'm licking the crotch. They taste so good."

I heard a groan. "You're getting me wet, Tony."

"You're getting me hard, Vicki. Lay back on the couch on your back. I'm going to put whip cream on your big, beautiful boobs. Do you like that?"

"It's cold but because you're doing it, Tony, it feels good."

"I'm spraying whip cream down your body, all the way down. I'm working my way down to your tight, wet, tasty pussy. Is it shaved?"

"There is a landing strip, Tony, just for you, for when you want to put your wheels down and land on my airport. I won't even charge you a landing fee."

"I'm spraying your pussy with whip cream. I'm pulling your pussy lips apart. I'm shooting that delicious whip cream inside that wet, juicy pussy."

"Tony, you're driving me crazy."

"I'm crawling up your body between your legs. I'm licking the whip cream off those gorgeous firm titties. I'm biting so gently on your nipples. First the right then the left. That taste so good, baby. So good. I'm licking my way down your belly eating whip cream all the way down. I'm tasting your sweet juices, your wetness. Oh, so good. I'm spreading your pussy lips so I can bury my tongue deep in your womanhood. Do you like that?"

317

"I can't stand it, Tony. I'm so fucking wet. That feels so good. Your tongue inside me feels so good."

"Turn over on your stomach. Put your face in the pillow. Do you hear the sound of the whip cream can? I'm shaking it up. I'm spraying it up your legs, in the crack of your ass, from top to bottom. Now I'm sucking the whip cream from the back of your legs."

"Oh yes, Tony, don't stop. Please don't damn stop."

"I'm licking the cream off the top of your legs. I'm tasting the whip cream from your ass cheeks. They're so firm and tight. I'm kissing them. I'm eating the last of the whip cream. I'm spreading your ass cheeks wide. I'm licking the whip cream from the crack of your stunning ass. I'm eating the cream. I'm sucking it out of your asshole. I'm kissing your asshole. I'm licking your asshole. That asshole is as sweet as the whip cream. That taste so good."

"Oh, God, Tony. I'm coming, I'm coming. Oh, my God, Tony, I'm coming!"

There was a long silence, long enough for me to pour a shot, drink it then pour another.

"Tony, that was awesome. I mean I really enjoyed it, mentally and physically. I actually got off several times. How about you?"

"I'm fine. I really enjoyed it too. Have you done this before? I mean on the phone."

"No, but there's a first time for everything. Where the heck did you find something like this?"

"I read it in a self-help book." I was trying to be funny. "You don't get out much, do you?"

318

"I owe you one. Next time, maybe it can be up close and personal?"

"I hope so, Vicki."

FLY THE FRIENDLY SKYS

I received a call from Malcom at about eleven o'clock in the morning. Today was supposed to be my day off. Cops, technically, are on duty twenty-four seven. "Great news, buddy. I pulled strings. The D.A. had approved the plea deal. It's full steam ahead. What's the best and safest way to get it to you? I don't want to risk it being intercepted."

"I can pick it up at your office."

"I'll tell you what. Call Owens. See if he and his client are available late this afternoon. If they are, set up an appointment and I'll meet you at Owens' office with the agreement. I'll save you a trip to my office. You're going to need an ADA there anyway."

"I'll call you back."

I called Owens' office. When Vicki answered, I said, "This is Detective Kano. We found a pair of pale blue panties that were somewhat damp on the inside. We were able to trace the DNA back to you."

"Who the hell is this?"

"My God." I felt myself turn red like a traffic light. "I thought this was Vicki. I'm sorry, so sorry." I might be in deep shit.

"It is Vicki, you clown. Are you wearing my panties?"

"I wasn't but I might be now. I just pissed mine."

"Thanks again for last night. I bet you're calling to ask me to dinner tonight."

"Unfortunately, you lose. I'm still tied up."

"Now that can be fun. Aside from enjoying phone sex, and making me come, and come, and come, are you submissive?"

"Sometimes. I need to speak with your boss to see if he and his sleaze-ball client are available late this afternoon to sign the plea bargain agreement."

"Hang on, Mr. Phone sex man."

Owens got on the phone. "Does four o'clock work, Detective?"

"Four o'clock counselor, unless you hear otherwise from me."

I got on the phone with Vicki. "I gotta' go babe. I'll try to call you later. No guarantees. Things are starting to move faster than I can move."

"This is one lady who's glad you don't move fast. Talk to you soon, phone sex man."

I called Malcolm back, gave him the time and address for our meeting. He suggested we meet at three thirty. I suggested the coffee shop downstairs.

I drove to the station. Neither Sully's car nor Mac's car were in the lot. Interesting. I walked inside to check in with dispatch.

"Hey Tony, how goes it?"

"Busy, busy, busy, Sam," which was short for Samantha, although she looked more like a Sam than a Samantha. "I'm here to get some paperwork done," I lied. "Have you seen anything of Sully or Mac?"

"They didn't tell you? They flew to Terre Haute, Indiana on their case yesterday. Don't know when they'll be back."

That hit me like a fucking firetruck. I wondered what the hell that was all about. I vaguely remembered that Paula's parents lived in Terre Haute, and that Rocky's widow, Paula, went to visit them after Rocky's death. I wondered if they went there to talk to Paula about Rocky or something else that had to do with the case. Damn nice of them to let me know. Then again, it may have been something completely different. I know they were involved in interviews at SafeGuard. Fuck it. That was their business. I hoped (sarcastically) they were enjoying the hell out of Indiana. I hoped they had good weather!

SIGN HERE, PLEASE

Malcolm and I met in the coffee shop downstairs from the counselor's office. We went over the paperwork. Malcolm briefed me on what I should say and do. "Tony, you've got this. Say whatever the hell you want; do whatever the hell you want. Get them to sign on the dotted line. Get the name of the killer. Get the hell out of there."

Vicki wasn't in the office. I was disappointed. A stern librarian type lady was behind Vicki's desk. "You must be Detective Kano," she said to Malcolm Tux.

"Actually, I'm Detective Kano. This is assistant District Attorney Tux."

She nodded and remained behind her desk. "You are expected. I'll let Attorney Owens know you're here."

I introduced Malcolm first to Owens and then to Strayhan. I am a hair under six feet tall. Malcolm is an inch or so taller than me. He goes to the gym three times a week; it shows. Shaking hands with Owens, Malcolm looked like Muldoon to Owens Toody. For those of you who don't remember the early sixties television comedy Car Fifty-Four, Where Are You?, Muldoon was the tall, string bean comic cop. Toody was short and squatty. They were inept New York City police officers driving police car fifty-four. They could be anywhere and everywhere in the city. Hence, Car Fifty-Four, Where Are You?

We skipped the small talk. The table had a tan linen cover today. Owens was going all out. In addition to the water pitcher, there was assorted soft drinks, but no Seagram's.

323

I said to everybody in the room, which was the four of us, "I have copies of the agreed upon plea agreement for all of us to review then sign if acceptable, and I trust it will be. Please read it carefully." I had to throw in my attempt at humor. "If you find any typos or spelling mistakes, blame Mr. Tux's secretary." I handed copies of the three-page document to Owens and Strayhan. Malcolm had his copy. I had my copy plus a copy stamped original.

I grabbed a Styrofoam cup and a Coke. I drank and read. The damn thing looked tight and right to me. I re-read. It still looked right and tight. We should be in business.

I sipped my Coke waiting for Owens and his client to finish reading. The attorney must have thought he was an IRS agent. He was going through the damn document with a fine-tooth comb. He hadn't crossed anything out or highlighted anything in red, so it appeared that we were good. It took that clown another ten minutes to get done with reviewing the document. "Give my client and me a couple of minutes to confer. The documents looks like it might work for us."

Malcolm and I took a walk into the carpeted, narrow hallway. "How are things going?"

"Things are good," Malcolm said. "Busy at the office. And busy at home. Marge is pregnant with what I hope will be our second son."

"I guess you are busy."

"We're living the American dream the best one can live these days in California. A kid and a half, a house in the suburbs, a wife, and California's taxes up the wazoo. With overtime, I bring home a damn decent check. When the governor's taxes get finished with me, we barely have enough left over for groceries and condoms so we can eat and don't have any more kids. I guess the illegals need my

324

money more than I do. It's all good. I'd love to get the hell out of California, but I don't see that happening."

"How's it going with you?"

"No wife, no kids, a decent paycheck, enough money, even after taxes, to pay the rent, drink on and make my car payment. Can't complain. Even if I did complain, you wouldn't listen."

"How's Mac?"

"Working hard."

"Are you two as serious as I've heard?"

"You, of all people, should know better than to believe everything you hear. I don't know what the future holds for us." That was an out and out lie. There was no future for Mac and me.

"Who do you think killed Ricki?"

I twisted my face into a question mark. "Hell of a good question. I thought it was obvious from the gate; Roberto Vega-Chapa."

"Motive?"

"She wouldn't let him in her panties. He got frustrated, killed her, then he thought we were coming for him, so he hung himself. Right? Maybe, maybe not. If the whacko priest is telling the truth, we may know soon."

Ms. Librarian stuck her head out the door. "The attorney is ready for you now."

My Coke was still sitting on the table. I let it sit. I looked at Owens.

"My client and I have reviewed the plea agreement. My client is ready to sign off on the document."

Everything we wanted was in the agreement. In exchange for Ricki's killer, in exchange for information on the sex ring, in exchange for Strayhan's testimony against those involved in the sex ring, and his testimony against Ricki's killer, he gets a one year and a day prison sentence. That sentence is split half in prison, half at home. We will recommend a prison of Strayhan's choice, with no guarantee he'll get that sentence. He would get five years' probation after prison release, and will register, for life, as a child sex offender. Also added in the agreement was a clause that stated we would not charge the dirty priest with sex trafficking, which was shaky at best.

"We need signatures from everyone in the room. There is a place for you to sign and date, please," I said. We moved the document around the table. While everyone was signing, I grabbed another Coke. I was the last to sign.

"Now that that's done, let's move on." I looked at Strayhan with disdain. I suppose I could go to hell for wanting to punch a priest in the face. I was probably going to hell anyway. I didn't want to go to jail. Hell, punching a priest in California might be considered a violent felony. I could lose my right to carry a weapon; hence I could say good-bye to my job. I settled myself.

"Let's hear it all, Mr. Strayhan."

Malcolm looked at me with a smile. Owens looked at me. He was poker face. Strayhan wouldn't look at me. He stared straight ahead. I folded my hand on the table. I was waiting for this moment.

Strayhan started to give us the details. He prefaced his comments with. "Forgive me Father, for I have sinned."

I thought, no shit you sick bastard. Save it for the court room. Maybe a jury, if it got that far, would have sympathy for you. As far as I was concerned, you'd find sympathy between shit and syphilis in the dictionary. "Let's move on, shall we?"

"We got involved, shall we say, with the kids a little more than three years ago."

"How did that happen to occur?" I raised my folded hands a few inches off the table. I let them fall back on the table with a shallow thud.

"Forgive me Father, for I have sinned."

"Enough," I yelled startling Owens and Malcolm. The ADA knew I was having my fun. I was so loud I was surprised the librarian receptionist didn't come in to shush us. "Enough, Strayhan. This isn't your fucking church. Get on with it."

Owens looked at me. "Can we show a little respect?"

"Earn it, get it, counselor. Let's go, Strayhan."

"I was involved with one of the young church members…."

"You can name names during the formal interview process, Father Strayhan. Give them general information for now," Owens told Strayhan.

"Apparently, the young man I, uh, befriended, told another boy. The group grew into meetings and more young men. We ended up with four adults and four young men. Duffmann suggested we meet as his place. In general, that's how that began. I'm so sorry, Father.

That was good enough for me, for now. I looked at Malcolm. He nodded. I took that to mean approval.

"Who killed Ricki?"

The dirty priest sighed. "I never meant for that to happen. Ricki and her family were regular church attendees. Her boyfriend was Roberto."

Tell me something I don't already know, I thought.

"Ricki didn't know Roberto was one of our friends. As a matter of fact, Roberto was a dinner guest one night. Before dinner, we were sitting around the living room floor talking about problems and what we could do to solve those problems. Roberto said his girlfriend's mom couldn't make this month's mortgage payment. One of the men offered to make the payment. Roberto said he'd pay him back over time. The man said he didn't have to reimburse him if he'd be his partner that night. Roberto hadn't been involved to this point. He became a member of our group that night and stayed on."

Pay for play. What a sick mother fucker.

"This went on and on."

It was amazing to me that nobody found out, not even a parent. I guess shame and guilt were a tight-lipped secret, especially among kids.

"Two weeks ago, Ricki called me. She asked for confession. We met at the church. During confession she told me she had a problem. She said her boyfriend confided in her that he was selling himself for money and trips, to men, some from the church. She didn't know I was one of those men. I'm so sorry, Father. I didn't know how much she knew. She wanted me to advise her on how to get him out of it and if she should go to Roberto's folks or the police.

"I assured her it would be handled. I asked her for time to consider possibilities."

I looked at Malcolm who looked disgusted. I wanted to puke. I thought I knew what was coming. I don't shock easily. I was shocked.

"I went to Chief Payne, who was one of our group. I asked him what we should do. Payne went to Duffmann. Father, please forgive me. I know not what I did. I'm sorry."

"Continue, damn it."

"This is what you would call a conspiracy. Payne and Duffmann had me call Ricki. I invited her to the church after dark. Duffmann and Payne took her downstairs to supposedly talk with her. They strangled her."

"Were you there when they killed, Ricki?"

"No, I came back upstairs."

"How do you know Payne and Duffmann killed Ricki?"

"Forgive me. I helped them carry her body up the stairs and load it in the back of Chief Payne's police vehicle."

Payne had a take home vehicle, an unmarked slick top black Ford Crown Victoria. "What did they do with the body?"

"They said they were going to drive it to the desert then dispose of it and come back."

"Did you accompany them?"

"No."

"Did Roberto know that Ricki came to you?"

"I don't know if she told Roberto between the time she and I first talked and the second time we met, the night she was killed."

The prick had conspired to commit murder. Under California law, the fag priest was as guilty of murder as the two who had actually killed Ricki. I was sick to my stomach. Under the plea agreement, Strayhan had just screwed two more people, Malcolm, and me.

THE BEAT GOES ON, AND ON, AND ON

I waited until we were downstairs, on the street and out of everybody's ear shot. "I just got fucked bareback by a priest who didn't use Vaseline."

Malcolm shook his head. "You got double teamed by a priest and an attorney. You took it up the ass and in the mouth. But don't sweat it too much. Owens is smarter than he looks. But I'm sharper than he is if I say so myself. It's a learning experience, Tony. You did a hell of a job. He took the lead in the bottom of the eight on a cheap base hit. Yogi said, it isn't over till it's over. We still get to bat in the ninth." Malcolm took his cell from his suit pocket. "Call your station, Tony. Update them so warrants can go out for Payne and Duffmann for murder one."

Malcolm called his office. I called the station to set the warrant in motion and to update Rolando. When he finished his call, I said, "What do we do from here?" I was embarrassed.

"There's a golden parachute. Owens knows this. The priest will pay. Remember, a judge still has to approve this. We may have taken it in the ass, but the priest and Owens just stepped on their own dicks. Once I get a judge to void the agreement, and I will, we'll go for the throat. We'll get the priest on conspiracy to commit murder. The entire agreement will be null and void when I get finished. Don't sweat the small stuff, my friend. When it comes down to it, it's all small stuff. I'd take you on my side any day."

"So, a dirty police Chief, a filthy priest, and kid loving community members. The newspapers are going to have a field day. Actually, it's already started." We were standing next to a newspaper vending machine. You could read the headline through the clear plastic covering the front of the machine, AMITY POLICE BUST CHILD SEX RING.

"It's only just begun," Malcolm quipped. "You'll be famous before this is over."

"Or infamous."

I drove back to the station feeling better about myself because Malcolm assured me that we'd pull the rip cord at will. I was still embarrassed at such a novice mistake. I reminded myself I was a novice.

By the time I returned to the station, warrants were in force for the arrest of Payne and Duffmann on murder charges. Duffmann was out on bail and most likely unaware of the murder warrant. We'd be able to scoop him up like a dog catcher netting a stray pup. Payne, former chief that he was no longer, was probably out of the country. Crime doesn't pay, buddy. You should have learned that long ago in the academy.

When I got to the station, I checked in with dispatch. Rolando has some police conference in central California. Mac and Sully were still screwing around in Indiana, and I needed to file a supplemental report on our earlier meeting with Owens and his client to hand-in to Rolando.

I found a computer and started hitting the keys. It took me less than forty-five minutes to complete the supplemental report, spell check it, and proofread it. I gave myself an A.

I checked with the detectives on the notification to Ricki's mom and Roberto's parents on the pending arrest of Ricki's killer. I was told that already had been done. The department wanted Ricki's mom and Roberto's parents notified by us before they heard it on the news or read it in the newspaper. My work was at a standstill.

I drove home to a waiting bottle of Seagram's. I had two shots then opened the computer. I was five hundred up on my bookie. I checked the night's baseball games. I liked the Yankees over Cleveland. I called my bookie buddy. "Let the five boys ride on tonight's Yankee game. I like the Yankees over Cleveland."

"It's yours, friend. Good luck."

I took a nap.

RING-A-DING-DING, GUESS WHO'S IN A SLING?

It was nineteen hundred hours, seven in the evening when the phone woke me up. That was a great nap. It was the station. "Tony, Chris from the station. I wanted to update you. We picked up Duffmann on a one eighty-seven charge, (homicide). I don't think he was all that surprised when we arrested him. I think it was a relief to him. We're going to ask for a no bail. The guy's obviously a flight risk. Between the sex ring and the murder charge, we should get no bail."

"Listen, we here in detectives want to commend you on the job you did on this case. The kids are out from under, although they'll go through hell for years. The sick bastards will be where they belong. And Payne will get what he deserves. A job well done, my friend. Thank you."

That was a great call. It made me feel better. A shot of Seagram's would make me feel even better. I poured a double.

A shower, a change of clothes and dinner would bring me back from the brink of exhaustion. I wasn't as tired anymore, I was hungry. My refrigerator looked like Mother Hubbard's cupboard; it was empty.

I took a shower and was dressing when the phone rang. It was Chris. "Tony, I got some more news for you. Cochise County Sheriff's Department in Arizona located Payne."

"Awesome news. This case is almost in the books."

"I think, except for the mopping up, the plea bargain, the sentencing, the department has rounded up all parties involved."

"Where did they pick up Payne?"

"In his apartment. But they didn't arrest him."

"Why the hell not?"

"He ate his gun. The coroner took him on his last ride."

"Jesus. Did he leave a note?"

"Nothing. I understand he had so much alcohol in him that if his gun didn't kill him, alcohol poisoning would have."

"Finally, this case has a Hollywood ending."

"Yeah," Chris said. "He saved the state a ton of money. Nice of the sick bastard."

I downed a double in celebration.

AND NOW A WORD FROM....

Two professions that people count on, cops for security, safety, and protection: and the church for spiritual guidance, understanding, and emotional support. It would be a long time before Amity would heal.

I didn't have much that could be done on the murder case. I had completed the majority of my part of the case for now. Sully and Mac were doing whatever the hell they were doing attempting to track down the money. I went from a speeding bullet to hitting a wall, not a really good place for me.

I picked up my cell phone and looked at the ballgames. The Dodgers were in Arizona. I checked the pitchers. The Dodgers looked good. I was about to call a book when my phone rang. It was Attorney Kline. "Hey buddy, I see you cleared the case."

I muttered, "We're well on our way."

"Hell," Kline said, "from what I'm seeing on the news, it's a done deal. One down. Payne decided to swallow something long and hard, again, this time permanently. Game over for him. Duffmann will go down hard for murder one, conspiracy, and sex with a minor, conspiracy, operating a sex ring, and anything else they can toss at him. The priest may get a break if you get a religious jury who might be afraid of going to hell if they hit Father Strayhan too hard."

"I seriously doubt any of them will go to trial; maybe Duffmann. I expect plea bargains across the board." I explained to Jerry how I fucked up the agreement with Father let-me-suck-your-young-stiff-dick. Then I told Kline what Malcolm told me.

"Sharp ADA. He's right on. The judge will tear that plea agreement in pieces. The priest is hung out to dry. How about the four of us go out to celebrate, on me? You deserve it, Tony. Maybe I can lean on you to go to law school. I'll even let you drive the Ferrari."

How the hell do you turn down an offer like that? "Sounds like a plan. Let me know what's good for you."

"I'm thinking a Saturday night would be great. Have you ever been to the Hungry House on the hill overlooking the San Fernando Valley?"

The tip for the valet at that place was more than I could afford. "Not lately."

"Let's do that. How about this. I'm going out of town on business tomorrow. I should be back in a couple of days depending on what shakes loose. I'll call you when I get back. Deal?"

"Sounds good, counselor."

"That'll give you a chance to set things up with Vicki. Have a great day, Tony. Congrats on the bust."

I hung up before I digested his words. How the hell did he know about Vicki? I found my Seagram's bottle. I drank as I punched "call" on my phone next to Vicki. "Panty man. How the hell are you?"

"I'm fine."

"I've been hearing about your escapades on the news. They should be contacting you anytime about a movie contract. You did quite the job cleaning up our not so fine city."

I laughed. "Thanks, Vicki. Hey, how does your boss know about us?"

"What?"

"Jerry wants the four of us to go to dinner when he comes back from some business thing. He made a crack about taking you. How does he know?"

"I haven't the faintest. But why don't you come over. We'll put our heads some place comfortable and see it we can figure it out."

"Are you wearing panties?"

"Do you want me to be?"

"Surprise me. I'll be over in about an hour."

IT'S NOT SUCH A BEAUTIFUL DAY
IN THE NEIGHBORHOOD

Sully and Mac arrived back in town from their "business trip" early Tuesday. I know this because I pulled into the station lot and noticed her Vette parked next to his car; nice.

Not much had happened on the sex ring case since Friday. The D.A. was getting as much down on paper as he could. I had been to the ADA's twice since Friday, and the DA's office once. Everything was in order, or so it appeared.

Two of the arrested sex offenders' attorneys had called the ADA exploring plea options. Duffmann was talking to reporters claiming he was being framed.

Vicki and I were having fun. The Dodgers brought my "bank roll" to a resounding two grand, and I gave serious thought to attempting law school. I wouldn't quit the force if I did decide to go to law school, but Jerry's offer was sure worth consideration.

ADA Malcolm asked me to clarify a question he had relating to the interview with Strayhan and Owens. He asked me for a supplemental report. I had just finished writing the report. I hit the print button and stood by the printer waiting for the report when Sully and Mac appeared.

Sully looked concerned. Mac was smiling. "We're back."

Like I gave a shit. "Welcome home." My voice was dripping with sarcasm.

"Thanks. Want an update? We know what you've been up to. It made the national news. We've been following it. So, congratulations."

Sully added, "Great job, partner."

Partner my ass, I thought. "Thanks." I added a little more sarcasm to my voice.

Mac said, "Why don't we go upstairs. We can brief you in peace and quiet."

I nodded. I was curious at what they had. What had taken them out of town so suddenly? "Works for me."

We found an empty office and settled in. Sully kicked things off. "In digging through paperwork, Mac found a possible link to a person of interest. The guy is and has been a SafeGuard employee for eight years. We've interviewed him three times at SafeGuard. He has a good record with them. He's been promoted three time within eight years. He's well-liked by other employees. His supervisors give him high praise."

I interrupted. "So, what makes this guy a person of interest?"

"Two red flags," Mac said succinctly. "One, he spent six years in the army. Three tours in Afghanistan. His specialty, demolitions." Mac paused to let that sink in.

"Okay, What's the other red flag?"

"When I reviewed his initial application, one of his recommendations was Rocky."

I turned that one over in my mind. "How do they connect?"

"Before I go into that," Mac asked, "Had you ever heard Rocky mention a Rusty Keller?"

I thought for a several seconds. I shook my head. "Never. Tie it up for me."

"According to Keller, Rocky pulled him over on a traffic violation. They got to talking. They attended the same college at different times. They were both sports fans. In short, they hit it off. Keller was recently separated from the army and was looking for work. What he really wanted was to become a cop. He had a previous DUI on his record. You know how that goes."

"Rocky tried to give him an assist. He recommended him for a job with SafeGuard. Keller was hired. He went through the academy at night. Rocky coached him throughout the process. Unfortunately, even with Rocky's recommendation and his positive record at SafeGuard, he couldn't make the background for a department because of his DUI. He stayed on with SafeGuard working his way up the ladder to supervisor. He and Rocky talked on the phone from time to time."

"Okay. I'm sure this is going somewhere. Where?"

"How well do you know Paula?"

"Not well. I had dinner at their house a couple of times. We went out a couple of times together. I heard a one-way conversation in the unit when we were out on patrol. Rocky would talk with Paula when things were quiet. They seemed to have it all together."

"Does this train have a caboose?"

Sully chimed in. "According to Keller, he was dipping his stick into Paula's transmission."

I wasn't liking this one bit. "Is he credible?"

"We think so. Did Rocky ever mention Paula's dad?"

"No. I do know he wasn't close to the family. Since her family lived half a universe a way, there was next to no interaction."

"According to Keller, Paula's dad had a nasty gambling problem. He was into some very bad people for major league money. They were three months in arrears on their mortgage payment."

"Again, does this fucking train have a caboose?"

"We think," Mac said, "there's a possibility Paula was involved. We're bringing Keller in later today for questioning."

I asked the obvious. "If you're thinking Rocky was somehow involved, you're out of your mind; both of you."

Mac ignored my protestations. "Paula is living near Terre Haute, Indiana not far from her folks. Sully and I got approval to make a visit. We never made contact with her. We put a tail on her and did some checking on her, her parents, her friends, her finances, her dad's finances. Unless Keller called her, she probably doesn't know we're interested in her."

Sully said, "Look Tony, at this point everything is speculative. We have to explore all options. Paula did have motive."

"You're fishing."

"Of course, we're fishing. What else can we do at this point?"

"We also went back over the explosion under the armored truck at the scene of the robbery with crime scene investigators. One of our nagging questions was whether the bomb could have been set off remotely."

My ears perked up. I was interested in the answer to that question. "What did they tell you?"

"It was possible. Someone with the proper knowledge could have rigged the bomb to go off with a telephone call from a cell phone. It could be done."

"Do you know how Keller and Paula got together?"

"No. If he comes in, we'll sure the hell know more after we talk to him."

"What makes you think he won't yell for a lawyer?"

"He might. If he has nothing to hide," Mac, asked, "why would he scream lawyer?"

"Point taken. There is no way Rocky was involved. He wouldn't do something like that. Besides, I was driving. If he had been involved, he would have been driving and he would have stayed out of that area. If he was involved, even with me driving, he would have found some excuse to keep me far away from the crime scene."

Sully asked me, "Do you recall if Rocky was on the phone with Paula at the time of the robbery?"

"I can't recall. Was there something about it in my statement?"

"No," Mac responded. "We'll know more after Keller's interview. We'll lean on him."

"How's the interview going to work?" I wanted to know if I was part of the interview team.

"You can watch from the two-way window. Sully and I are going to do the actual interview. We plan on going to SafeGuard about eleven this morning. It's going to be

343

spontaneous. Keller isn't expecting it. He'll be more off balance at the station."

"Anyone interested in breakfast?" Sully asked. "I'm buying."

We headed over to Johnny's Kitchen about two miles from the station. It was small, but quiet and clean. The food was fresh and the owner, John, "bounced" to the tune of fifty percent off for blue suits. We grabbed a booth in the far corner of the eatery so we could watch the door.

"Order me coffee, please," Mac said. "I have to visit the little girl's room."

The minute Mac walked away from the table; Sully opened fire. "Listen, I know how tight you and Rocky were. We've got nothing concrete. Don't let it eat at you."

"Easy for you to say." I wanted to tell Sully to quit calling me partner. I didn't feel like his partner.

"How are you and April doing?"

Maybe he wanted to know if he was free to go for Mac, although I suspected he already had.

"There's nothing there. And to answer the question you haven't asked; I haven't done her." But always put "yet" at the end of a sentence. Mac taught me that from her AA teachings. I didn't mention Vicki to Sully. "How's the apartment coming?"

"I haven't had time for that. Been too busy with the case."

I didn't want him to know I knew Mac was at his place. Obviously, he wasn't going to volunteer anything.

344

Mac returned just as the server put our drinks on the table. She smiled at me then sat down next to Sully. "My woman's intuition tells me Paula was a player. It also tells me Rocky had no idea she was messing around, if in fact she was running around. We'll soon know."

"Is she renting an apartment?"

"She bought a small three-bedroom house just outside Terre Haute. She put twenty percent down and she's current on her mortgage. She's working locally as an office assistant. She's driving a five-year-old Honda Civic. From what we know, she doesn't appear to be hooked up with anyone. She spends time at her folk's house. We haven't found out if Paula's old man is out from under his gambling debt nor if he's still gambling."

I felt a foot brush against my leg. It sure wasn't Sully's. I felt it again. She had brass balls. She's doing Sully and flirting with my damn leg. I pulled away then scooted over out of her reach. The waitress took our order.

TELL ME IT AIN'T SO, ROCK

I had enough time to run out to the cemetery. I didn't stop to buy cigarettes. I ran my hand across Rocky's headstone. I knelt down. "I know you had absolutely nothing to do with this shit, buddy. I also know that if Paula was involved, you had no idea. I just want you to know I'm four hundred percent behind you. Rest easy, Rocky. I'm not about to let anyone screw with you."

ELEVEN FORTY-FIVE
INTERROGATION TIME

Rusty Keller was escorted into an interview room at precisely eleven forty-five Tuesday morning. After he was seated, I took up a position outside the two-way glass. I could hear and see any game of cat and mouse that was being played.

Sully stood off in a corner of the room. Mac had changed into a low-cut white blouse with tight fitting black slacks. As pissed at her as I was, I had to admit that she looked hot.

"I have a tape recorder here that I'm going to turn on," Mac said. "It's so we make sure we get everything down and don't miss anything. Before we officially began talking," Mac said softly as if she was talking to a friend, "let me explain to you that you don't have to have this conversation with us. If you would like an attorney present, we can stop and wait for him to get here."

"I don't need an attorney. I'm good. Let's get on with this." He looked Mac in the eye.

Mac smiled at Rusty Keller who smiled back. He was wearing jeans, black pull over shirt, was smooth shaven. His wide smile showed white teeth. Keller was nearly six foot. He had blonde hair and a tight body. My guess was that he was in his early forties.

"Listen Rusty, I know you probably feel like we're related by now, but we think you might have information that can help us clear this case." Mac was clever. She didn't directly accuse him of anything, but she let him know that they thought he had more information than he was bringing to the game. "Let's backtrack. When and how did you first meet Rocky?"

Rusty appeared relaxed. His fingers were clasped together, and his hands were folded on the table. "A lot of years ago, I don't remember exactly when, Rocky pulled me over for blowing a stop sign. He was cool and calm when he asked me for my license and registration and insurance. We got to talking. It turned out we went to the same college. Long story short, we hit it off. I told him I did three tours in Afghanistan. Turns out Rocky served in Afghanistan. I told him I wanted to become a cop when I called it quits from the service. He encouraged me. I told him about the DUI I told you about. He told me to check out the academy schedule. He gave me his card. We talked on the phone quite a bit, met for lunch a couple of times and he and Paula had me over for dinner three times."

"I applied for a job at SafeGuard. Rocky wrote me a letter of recommendation. I got the job. Less than a year and a half later, I entered the night academy. Rocky would have me over to the house and coach me on some of the academics and some of the physical requirements. He helped me a helluva' lot. It didn't matter. I got through the process up to the background. They'd see the DUI. They were unforgiving."

"I stayed with SafeGuard. I've built a career with them. They're fair-minded people."

Sully remained in the corner like a punished child. He didn't say a word. His arms were folded across his chest.

"How did you get involved with Paula?"

Rusty smiled. "That one was a tiger. She was as two faced as you'll find. When she thought Rocky wasn't looking, she'd flirt with me. Once when I was over at their house for

348

dinner and Rocky was in the bathroom, she set the dessert on the table and "accidently" brushed her hand across my butt. When Rocky was at work, she'd go to the local tavern and shoot pool with the guys. I think she was banging more than pool balls."

"She'd call Rocky constantly when he was at work. He loved it. He thought she couldn't get enough of him. In actuality, she just wanted to make sure he was at work and didn't come home early and catch her screwing around."

"We were in his bed, while she was doing me, she liked to be on top, I guess it was a control thing. She called hubby and repeatedly kept telling him how much she loved him and missed him and to be careful and all that. Then she'd say good-bye and laugh like a fucking hyena. That broad was one bitch, but she was a helluva' good lay."

I was burning up just thinking about it. First of all, Rocky does his best by this prick and he fucks Rocky's wife. Second, Paula was playing Rocky for all he was worth. She was a real bitch in heat. I kept watching the interview.

"How long did you and Paula keep up this relationship?"

"I don't know that you'd call it a relationship. We were definitely having an affair. I found out that she was also messing with guys from the bar who she shot pool with. That was a turn off. I was also afraid Rocky might come home unexpectedly one day and catch us. I didn't want to get my nuts blown off."

"So, you ended it?"

"I guess it was mutual."

"Did you keep in touch?"

"Yeah. I'd even go the bar every so often and we'd shoot a game of pool."

Mac suddenly changed tactics. "If there was an inside person working at SafeGuard who set up the robbery, who do you think that might be?"

Keller's fingers suddenly became stiff. His faced turned ashen. He sat straight up. "I haven't a clue. What makes you think there was an inside man?"

"It had to be someone familiar with explosives. Do you know anyone like that who works or worked at SafeGuard?" Mac asked.

Keller rubbed his chin. Mac was getting the reaction she wanted. Keller's forehead was showing sweat. Sully was watching and smiling. I was admiring Mac's interrogation skills.

"Didn't you do detonation work in the Army?"

Keller nodded. He remained silent.

Mac suddenly dropped a pencil she held in her hand.

Sully spoke up. "How about we take a break? You must be tired. I know I am. I'll buy us a cold drink."

Jesus, Sully, I thought. Not now. She's on a roll.

Sully pushed. "Rusty, we have a couple of vending machines downstairs. You can get a soda and sandwiches and candy. What do you say?"

There was relief on Keller's face. "I can use a break." He stood up.

I got the hell out of the way. I watched the three come out of the interview room and start down the corridor. In another interview room, a blonde lady wearing a grey hat was being interviewed. A female cop was conducting the interview. A male cop walked by as Keller, Mac, and Sully approached. He said to anyone of the three, "Is that Paula in there being interviewed?"

Mac said, "I don't think so."

Keller stopped dead in his tracks. "It looks a bit like her from the back."

Mac reached up and pushed a button. The interview went audible. The answer from the blonde, to whatever the question was, "Understand, the jerk was the lousiest lay on the planet. I'd go down on the son of a bitch, get him hard, he'd put it in and in and out twice, and game over. I'd have to go to the bar and find someone else to screw or I'd never be able to sleep. I'd have to scratch my own itch if you know what I mean."

"The son of a bitch was a real loser. The only thing he was good for was setting the bomb under the SafeGuard armored truck. It was all his idea. He convinced me it was a guarantee. We couldn't miss, Keller told me. He said it was a sure thing. Give me a pad. I'll write it all out for you. Just remember he forced me to do it. He told me nobody would get hurt; nobody. I get the deal if I cop to it first, right?"

The female cop doing the interview said, "You got it, Paula. First come, first served."

Sully reached up and clicked off the volume control. "Still want that break?"

MORE CONFESSIONS

The threesome never made it to the break room. They did an about face after hearing the blonde's haunting words, at least haunting to Rusty Keller. I followed at a safe position and took up my previous position in front of the two-way glass. I hit the volume switch so I could listen to Mac continue what was no longer an interview. This was now an interrogation.

What's the difference between an interview and an interrogation? When cops interview an individual, they're looking for information. When cops interrogate a subject or suspect, they think they have their man, or woman. They just need to prove it.

Rusty took a seat at the same table. Sully stood in the same corner arms folded across his chest. Mac took a seat directly across the table from Rusty Keller. Keller was tense. Mac was relaxed. "Are you as bad in bed as Paula says you are?" Mac cocked her head to one side waiting for Rusty's response. "Fuck that bitch. She doesn't know a dick from a pool cue."

"She said you don't have a dick. She said you have a very slightly enlarged clit."

Rusty put his hands over his face. He sat for thirty seconds. "Let me tell you what really happened. Paula's old man, her father, got into some shylocks for major bread. They were coming down on him, they were threatening to do him major damage, according to that bitch. She needed bread. I had told her I worked bombs in the Army, that I was a specialist. She dreamed this idea of hitting one of the SafeGuard armored trucks on a full payload day. She said it would be easy, that no one would get hurt. It was all her fucking idea. She went

352

to the library. She studied pictures of SafeGuard's specific armored cars. She even brought home pictures for me to study. We did a clay mockup of the damn armored truck. I figured out where to place the bomb, where it blows open the doors. I underestimated the damage."

"We had it all planned. We found "crew members." Everything was set. We were ready. Then that damn cop car shows up unexpectedly; a million to one shot. Her husband happens to be in the police car. Go figure. All hell broke loose."

Mac softened her voice. "How did you rig the bomb to detonate?"

"Easy. I used my cell phone as a trigger. Any novice can get online and learn how to do that within an hour and a half. We got away with over three million dollars; three million spendable, tax free cash. Can you believe that?"

"Paula says you hid the money, that she never received her share."

"Lying bitch. She paid off her father's debt, caught them up on their mortgage and buried the cash in their backyard. Nobody got a piece of that heist except that bitch."

"By that bitch, do you mean Paula Blake?"

"Blake or Princeton which ever last name she was in the mood to use. The deal was we wait a year before we divvy up the money. She figured after a year, if we spent it wisely, no one would catch on."

"I guess in this case, crime doesn't pay."

"It would have if the bitch kept her mouth shut."

"Was Rocky involved in a way, shape or form?"

"Hell no. You gotta' be kidding. Rocky was straighter than a stiff dick."

"You wouldn't know about that, would you?"

"Do all you bitches hate men?"

"Just men who don't know what to do in bed." Mac slid a legal pad across the table. She rolled a pen across the table. "Write it out, Rusty. If you hurry up, and you get it done before Paula, we may cut you a deal with the DA."

Mac walked out of the room. She left Sully leaning against the wall in the corner. I stopped her. "Where's Paula? I'd like a few words with her?"

"My best guess would be somewhere in Terre Haute."

"What are you talking about? Who's being interrogated?"

"Some bimbo from Central Casting who said she could play any roll we wanted her to play for two hundred bucks. Since the WC wouldn't buy into it, each of us is chipping in sixty-six dollars and sixty-seven cents. If you don't have it, you can work it off."

I reached into my pocket. I had collected my baseball winnings. I handed Mac a hundred-dollar bill. "You owe me thirty-three dollars. Keep the change."

"I'll keep the hundred. The change you don't get back is for all the aggravation you've caused me that you're going to regret. Now excuse me, I've got to call Terre Haute and arrange to have Paula picked up. I suspect Sully and I will be on the red eye to Indiana to pick up a prisoner and lots of cash."

THE BEST SCREWING YOU EVER GOT

Mac and Sully gave Keller one hour and ten minutes to write out his statement. When they went back in the room, Mac placed the Sony recorder on the table. "Let's wrap this up, Rusty. Your blonde friend is still writing."

"I'm done. So is that phony haired bitch. I fixed her but good."

Mac looked over Keller's statement. She handed it to Sully. "Looks good to me." He gave it back to Mac.

"Here. Sign it."

Keller signed the document. "I'm curious about one thing. Is Paula's dad okay?"

Mac looked surprised. Maybe the little prick had a spark of decency in him. Mac turned to look at Sully. She smiled then walked back to the table. She put both palms flat on the table. She shook her head as she looked at Keller. Mac shook her head from side to side. "You can't catch a break. Not only are you the lousiest lay in Amity, hell maybe in southern California, you're also gullible. Paula's father is Mormon. The guy doesn't gamble."

"Paula's close to her family. She probably would have left Rocky anyway to move to Indiana. She met a guy online. She's been fucking him. But if it's any consolation for you, you've probably just got the best screwing of your life."

Sully added, "Is this the first time you've been fucked in the ass?"

PRESS CONFERENCE

It's hard to explain the elation a cop, a detective gets when he "clears" a case, especially a high-profile case that takes really bad people off the street and puts them where they belong, in prison safe from harming more people. We had cleared, or just about cleared, two such cases. And the best was yet to come. Oh, was the very best yet to come.

Somehow, I must have made Judge Karma very happy. He was about to bestow on me a priceless gift. No, not a case of Seagram's. Yes, even better than that. Unfortunately, not so much for Rocky, who's beloved was soon to do many years in the pokey.

Sully and Mac did take the red eye back to Terre Haute. They came back to Amity with Paula Blake in hand and in handcuffs, along with the remaining cash from the heist. Paula Blake had just over three million dollars in hard, spendable cash buried in her backyard. It was booked as evidence.

Rusty Keller was hopping mad that he had been tricked. He was pissed that he had been screwed over by a woman, by at least two women. It was a great day all around.

Friday, at fifteen thirty hours, three thirty in the afternoon, Acting Chief Lee Rolando held a press conference in front of the station. It was reminiscent of a scene out of a Hollywood movie. This was very real. The press was at hand. Community members were in front of the station. Off duty police officers were out front. On duty police officers listened to Lee Rolando. Rolando was tall and proud in blue uniform.

356

"My name is Lee Rolando. I am acting chief of Amity. I am here today to reiterate what most of you already know. For at least three years now, a child sex ring has been operating in Amity. Some well- known community members organized and were involved with this child sex ring. It no longer exists. We shut it down."

"Shortly, I will introduce three of our highly trained team who took the lead in putting an end to the heinous organization. Because this investigation is ongoing, and because there is an outside chance that we may have more players than are presently in custody, I will give you one name. It breaks my heart to tell you that former Amity Police Chief Buck Payne was active in the child sex ring. As we were closing in on Payne, and I cannot and will not release further details of his alleged crimes at this time, Payne took his own life. We think we have all involved in custody. We will hold press conferences as we deem they are necessary."

"Moving on. You all remember the horrible SafeGuard armored car robbery that occurred recently. Lives were lost in that robbery, including the life of one of our own, Rocky Blake. During that robbery, Detective Tony Kano lost a leg. Today I am pleased to announce we have arrested the principles in that case and have recovered approximately three million dollars of the stolen cash. Again, because this is still an ongoing investigation, I cannot release names nor can I discuss details of the case."

"With that said, I would like to call up front Tony Kano, Dee Mackenzee and Michael Sullivan. Dee Mackenzee and Michael Sullivan will be joining Amity Police Department on a permanent basis. Tony, you're first up."

I wasn't expecting to say anything. I stepped to the mic. "Thank you, sir. In the course of the SafeGuard armored car heist, my best friend and partner was needlessly and senselessly murdered. This was, without a doubt, the most painful period of my life." I felt the tears welling in my eyes. I couldn't hide the tears, nor did I want to hide the tears. For me it was the beginning of a real healing process.

"I'm thrilled that the perpetrators are where they belong. I'm glad the stolen cash has been recovered. Rocky, may you always RIP. I look forward to continuing to serve the community of Amity. Thank you."

"Dee Mackenzee, please step forward."

"I'm Dee Mackenzee. I appreciate the fact that the department had the faith in me to allow me to be part of the investigation. As a new member of the Amity Police Department, I look forward to serving you. Thank you."

Rolando called Sully forward.

"I'm former FBI Agent Michael Sullivan. As Dee said so eloquently, I thank the department for having the faith in me to assign me to these two cases. It's been an adventure. I'm glad the bad guys are where they belong. I look forward to serving our community with love, devotion, and courage. Thank you. May God Bless the city of Amity, and the Amity Police Department, and all those who wear the badge."

I heard thunderous applause as I took my seat. Then I heard strange words from Acting Chief Lee Rolando. "We will not take questions." The press conference was over. We were free to go about our business. I left Sully and Mac. I went about my business.

YOU'RE A FREE MAN, ROCKY

I knelt at Rocky's headstone. "Guess what, buddy? No cigarettes for you. I think it's time you quit smoking. Nicotine is bad for you. And look at the money you'll save."

"It's officially over, my friend, except for the publicity, the arraignments, the filings, the courts and the sentencing. It's over. Now let's talk about that. It seems you and I have a broken picker when it comes to women. For two cops, who supposedly can read people, we sure can't apply that to women. How can two sharp guys like us, get taken to the cleaners like we have? We're Charlie Harper in reverse."

"I've made a decision, buddy. Mac and I are history. It's over between us. I'll keep a pair of her panties to play with now and then but that's it. I've got April and Vicki to enjoy. I'm looking forward to having fun with each one of them. Who knows what that future may bring. Working around Mac, and Sully may be difficult for a while, but like my manufactured leg, I'll forget, in time."

"As Mac taught me, don't sweat the small stuff; and it's all small stuff. She and Sully can ride off into the sunset together."

"As you know, I have an opportunity to go to law school. That's something I can do at night. Hell, one day I may drive in here in a brand new three 0 eight Ferrari. Wouldn't that shock the shit out of you?"

"As a matter of fact, I might write a book about our adventures. Maybe I'll call it, ROCKY ROAD, or UNBELIVABLE, or PARTNERS. Think of a great name buddy. Let me know. I'll put your name on the cover, too. I'll even give you top billing. You earned it."

359

"Rest in peace, brother. Remember, no smoking."

I got as far as my car. I turned and walked back to where Rocky was at rest. "I can't do it to you, friend." I placed the red and white Marlboro's in the box on Rocky's headstone. "Hell, buddy. At this point, what's the harm? Enjoy!"

ARE YOU FUCKING KIDDING ME, OR WHAT?

I was on my way back to the station when my cell sang HAIL TO THE CHIEF. I debated whether to answer it. It was a violation of the vehicle code to talk on the phone unless you went hands free. I picked up the phone. Fuck it.

"You, Sully, and I need to meet. Sully's place, nineteen hundred this afternoon. Bring Hemlock, you might want to drink it." The connection was broken.

Here we go, I thought. Lower the boom. Tell me about you and Sully. As was about to turn out, I was right on. The reveal WAS going to be about Mac, and Sully. No surprise here. I already had it figured. Like I told Rocky, I had made a decision to call it a day.

I drove home. I had a couple of hours. I could use a shave. I definitely needed a shower. A couple of drinks were in the offering.

I got out of my suit and tie. I walked to the couch with a Seagram's bottle in hand, then set about relaxing. I had earned it. I wanted to spend the evening with Vicki, if she was free, and I suspected that she was more than available. We hadn't yet solidified our relationship for reasons I think Judge Karma understood. I was ready, willing, and more than able. Vicki would have to wait at least one more day.

I poured me a double. It felt good going down. My head cleared. I gave more thought to Jerry's proposition. The more I thought about it, the more I liked it. Maybe there really was a light at the end of the tunnel. And maybe this time it wasn't a fucking train.

I poured another shot, set my phone to wake me up at five forty-five, put a blue lives matter pillow under my head, and closed my eyes. Life was okay.

MESS WITH BULL, YOU GET THE HORNS!

It was 1855 hours when I pulled into Sully's apartment complex. I found Mac's car easily. The Vette stuck out like a fallen tree limb in the middle of crowded highway. Sully's car was parked next to the Corvette. I parked across from their vehicles.

I had yet to visit Sully's place. I wasn't looking forward to this visit. I walked to the door slowly, anticipating the possibilities. How would Mac tell me she was screwing around with Sully? How would he explain what he was doing with Mac to me? Could we still be partners? How would Mac and I handle it? Hell, one way or another the three of us had to work together. Was Amity P.D. large enough to accommodate the three of us? The biggest question of all: did Sully know Mac was formerly a guy?

I knocked on the damn door. I felt like a kid about to go on his first date. My stomach was queasy. Sully opened the door. "C'mon in. Excuse the mess. Between not having time to get this place together, not wanting to get it together, and being lazy, what you see is what you get."

The place looked like a storage facility locker that had been rocked by a California earthquake registering at least a seven on the Richter Scale. I looked past the clutter of boxes to a couple of high back dining room chairs, four to be exact. Mac was seated at one end of the table. She had a small cigar box on the table in front of her.

"When did you take up smoking cigars?"

Her blue eyes looked more ominous than a three fifty-seven locked and loaded. "For once in your stupid life, Tony, sit the fuck down, shut up and listen."

Something told me I didn't want to mess with her right now. Something also told me I might want to know what was in the cigar box. It was the right size to conceal a gun. Judge Karma was screwing with me.

I did as Mac told me. I sat down, at the middle of the table, folded my hands in my lap, and shut up. Sully sat down at the opposite end of the table. I waited for the explosion.

Mac said, "Let's start with the obvious. We need to congratulate each other a job or jobs well done."

Both Sully and I nodded. He got up from the table. We took a short pause. He came back with three water glasses. "Diet Coke for you, my dear," he said to Mac. "Tony, Seagram's for you; and Scotch for me." Sully sat.

"Next," Mac said, "Let's toast to the three of us keeping the streets of Amity safe in the future. So, to the two newest members of Amity P.D., and to the three of us. May we be safe, secure, and successful."

Sully, said, "I'll to drink to that."

I nodded but kept my mouth shut.

"Before we play true confessions here," I said. "How the hell did the two of you get to Paula and the money? I'm really not clear on that."

Mac said, "You've got to work on your patience and your paperwork skills, Detective Kano. Not all detective work is what you see on television. It's not always chase 'em and shoot 'em up."

"Sully and I went back to the beginning. We strongly suspected there had to be an inside person. We also suspected there had to be an outside connection. We started digging into the SafeGuard hiring application because basically we had hit a dead end. We came across Keller's app. In sifting through it, we saw Rocky's name as a reference. We followed up on that."

"We interviewed Keller numerous times. He was too pat at first like he had rehearsed and re-rehearsed his lines. When he told us about the traffic stop, about meeting Rocky, about Rocky going to bat for him to try to help him get into a department, we thought too many coincidences. When he told us about going to dinner at Rocky's and Paula's place, our ears really perked up. When he told us Rocky helped him with academy problems, we thought the link was Rocky. We avoided you because we didn't want you involved until we knew for certain about Rocky. You had enough problems between the sex ring case and little ol' me. Thinking Rocky was involved would have really done you in."

"When bad lay told us about his sorry escapades with Paula, we put the cheese in the trap. The blonde bimbo from Central Casting was Sully's idea. He gets an award for best supporting actor in a police series."

"The shame is that Paula was such a cold-hearted bitch. She was a thief, a player, a fraud, and a taker. Now she's a killer who may well spend the rest of her years behind bars."

She changed the subject abruptly.

"As for you, Tony, did you bring the Hemlock?"

I shook my head. "I thought it might be in the cigar box."

"It is. Do you have any questions, partner?"

365

I didn't like her calling me partner. I kept my mouth shut. I was starting to enjoy the show. "No questions. You told me I had the right to remain silent."

"Okay. Here we go." Mac stood up. She walked to one of Sully's boxes. The box was open. She lifted a framed picture. Mac walked back to the table. She placed the picture in front of me. She walked to the head of the table then sat.

"See anyone in that picture you recognize, dummy?"

I studied the picture. It had to be ten to fifteen years old. "That's you."

"Oh, good for you. You'll make one hell of a great detective. I'm sure. Name the other person in the picture."

"Sully."

"You're pitching a perfect game, asshole." Mac sipped her Diet Coke. "Sully and I are cousins. Family means a lot to me. I have very little family left. I all but begged you to leave Sully alone when you decided to fuck with him. Blood, Tony, is thicker than water. You messed with the bull. I gave you the horns. Actually, my cousin and I gave you the horns."

I was stunned, shocked beyond words. Okay, so they were cousins. She wasn't doing Sully. I took a very large gulp of Seagram's. I looked at Sully. He was smiling. I wanted to drop him like a missed played fly ball.

"When you started that horse shit with the video of Sully and the bumper sticker on the bumper of his car, I decided you needed to be taught a lesson. So, Sully and I want to work. Unfortunately for you, I gave you too much credit. When you get pissed you shove your head up your ass, way up your behind."

"It started with your proposal when I told you I was born a male. You swallowed that like a piece of pizza. So, I continued with that ploy. You kept eating and swallowing. The more indigestion you got, the more Sully and I loved it. Payback is a real bitch. To solidify this payback, we videotaped the proposal, the look on your face, the sheer terror in your eyes, and your look of contempt for me. Sully even borrowed a shotgun mic from the Feds. So not only do we have video, but we also have sound, my dear." Mac got up, walked to the other end of the table, and placed the cigar box in front of me.

"Before you open it, defective detective, let me tell you something and maybe it'll be a life's lesson that will serve you well in the future in and out of the department. If you had put your dick in your pants, which I hadn't expected, had you used your head as I had expected, the first thing you would have done, and I had expected you to do it, would have been to jump on your computer and do a records check." Mac sipped more Diet Coke.

"Open the cigar box, asshole."

I took a long pull from my water glass. I opened the lid of the cigar box. There were half a dozen pictures of Mac at different ages. In all the pictures, she was all woman. At the bottom of the cigar box was a birth certificate. I thought, okay Judge Karma, I had this coming. The birth certificate belonged to Mac. She was born all woman.

I looked at Mac. I looked at Sully. I finished what was left in the water glass of my Seagram's. I wasn't dreaming. This was really happening. I smiled at Sully. I bit my lower lip as I tried to smile at Mac. I was rock hard as I stood up. I couldn't hide Peter's pride. As I walked toward Mac, she stared at my crotch.

"I see you're still thinking with your dick!"

FUN AND FROLIC

It was 2230 hours. Mac and I left Sully to unpack. We went to my place. I thought it would be great if we made up for lost time. We were on the couch. Mac was sipping Diet Coke. I was downing shots of Seagram's. "If you ever decide you want to mess with my family, or me again, remember your lesson. And if you do try it again, you can kiss my ass."

"Did you learn this shit in AA?"

"Actually, in AA we're taught to quit fighting everything and everybody, but we're also taught that we're nobody's doormat."

"Roll over." Mac looked at me with a question in her eyes, but she did as I asked. She rolled over onto her stomach. I slid her short skirt up over her tight round butt. She wasn't wearing panties. I kissed each cheek slowly. "If I do mess with you, I'm paid up. And where are your panties?"

Mac ignored my panty question. "Here's a story for you that should teach you something. A petite, shy librarian marries a strapping outgoing professional football player. On their wedding night, before the quiet, introverted librarian goes into the bathroom to change before going to bed, the football player tosses his tux jacket on the chair. He holds up his pants then says to his bride "put these on." She says, "are you crazy? I can put my whole self into one of your pant legs." The football pro says "that's right. You always need to remember that I wear the pants in our family."

"She thinks about that for less than half a minute. She slides off her tiny pink panties and holds the panties in front of him. Put these on she says. You got to be kidding the big guy says. I'll never get into those. That's right, his bride says, and until your damn attitude changes, you'll never get into my panties!"

"That doesn't apply to me."

"Why is that?"

"Because you're not wearing panties." I rolled Mac over. I took her skirt off. She wasn't wearing a bra either. I ran my tongue slowly over each breast. I took my time. When Mac started to smile, I nibbled at each nipple. As I was sucking on one nipple, I pinched the other nipple. Mac enjoyed a bit of pain which was probably why she was involved with me.

I worked my way down Mac's stomach to her nicely trimmed bush. I spread her lips apart and licked slowly. I buried my tongue deep and played with Mac's clitty. Her eyes were closed. Her face was relaxed. Her smile told me she was beyond content. I spread her legs wide. I ran my tongue around her pussy lips then back inside. Mac was groaning.

Peter was rock hard. Mac wanted me inside her. "Enough fun and games for now. I want you inside me NOW!"

Peter obliged. He was deep inside. He was rock hard. Mac was smiling. "What a difference a couple of days make."

"It was more than a couple of days, bitch. I may have screwed with Sully, but you screwed with Peter and you hurt his feelings."

"He's not acting like his feelings are hurt."

"He gets over things in a hurry. He doesn't like to stay mad. He's learned to let go of resentments."

"I can tell. Back to the old Peter. Don't stop, Tony, damn you, don't stop, don't, don't don't!"

Twenty minutes later, Mac took Peter in her mouth. In two minutes, he was rock hard. In two and a half minutes he slid inside a warm, moist pussy, Mac's warm moist pussy. I was home. We were home. We feel asleep in each other's arms.

I woke up because I had to pee. I mean I really had to pee. I couldn't find Peter. I located Mac. I found Peter. He was hiding in Mac's mouth. She was licking him up and down and sideways. She licked his twins. They weren't identical, one hung lower than the other. She licked and sucked on them gently. She got most of rock-hard Peter in her mouth.

"I got to pee, babe. Let him out. Let him go."

"Ain't going to happen until he's ready."

"You don't understand, angel. I really, really gotta' pee."

"Better not."

"Then let him be."

"He has to finish first. I want breakfast."

"You're going to have orange juice if you don't let him go. Warm orange juice." I didn't think I could come when I had to pee. This could get awkward in a hurry. "Let him go."

"Nope come first."

"I'm telling you, I gotta' pee bad."

"I'm not into that so you better not. Maybe in the next novel we'll try that?"

"You're going to be into that before the next novel comes out if you don't let go of Peter."

After I pee'd, we had the wildest sex we ever had shy of the back of the cop car in the department lot. Where did I pee, you ask? Where do you think?

THREE MONTHS LATER

Life was great again. In fact, life couldn't have been better. The "gruesome threesome" as the department started calling us because we had an uncanny knack for solving cases, worked as a team. We were a two man, ugh, a two-person unit, which meant one month Sully and I partnered, the next month, Sully and Cousin Mac partnered, then Mac and I would be partners. The "odd" person out would work a single person unit.

We worked patrol on an as needed basis, were assigned to robbery division, fraud division, missing person's division; we were assigned to track down warrant suspects, FTA suspects, (failure to appear in court), and were even assigned to homicide division as needed. I was loving it.

Mac went back to school to take more criminology classes working toward her detective shield. Sully was moved into his apartment, which now was clutter free and reasonably clean. His girlfriend took the blame for that.

I was still acting detective, hoping for full time detective status. I was attending night school, you guessed it, toward my law school degree. It was slow but steady, and when need be Jerry was by my side to assist me.

There was only one stunning beautiful, sassy lady in my life. That would be Mac. It was not a question of if we would get married, it was a question of when we'd become a legal team. We bought a house together in Anaheim Hills, a small but quaint two-story brick house in a great neighborhood. We had a small front yard with trees and grass. The backyard was blocked walled. It was a great starter home.

Sully and I exchanged video tapes each swearing there was only the one master tape. All Mac did was laugh when I asked her if there any other copies.

I had to keep up with Mac. Hell, Jerry Kline drove a Ferrari, Mac drove a Corvette, Sully bought himself a 1998 Corvette Pace Car (purple and) yellow. I refused to be out done. I bought a red Pontiac Mera. A Pontiac Mera is a dealer re-body of a Pontiac Fiero. If you looked at the outside of the Mera, any betting man would swear it was a three 0 eight Ferrari. It looked identical. Of course, the inside and the engine were Pontiac. The insurance was cheap. Hagerty, the celebrated class car insurer to the stars, insured her for one hundred eighty bucks a year. It was a flashy looking car. If anything went wrong, it was relatively cheap to repair. The only drawback of the two-seater sports car was that it was so low, like the three 0 eight, that it was a bear for me to get in and out. If Mac was in the passenger seat, wearing a short skirt, she had better be wearing panties when she tried to get out. I'd often "help" her out just to mess with her and to block any pervert's view but mine.

The Mera was so low to the ground that it was almost impossible to flip or roll her. I had been pulled over three times for excessive speed on windy roads. Each time the officer who made the stop and I would talk cars. I had to convince him that the car was not an authentic Ferrari. The dealer re-body Mera was short lived. Ferrari sued Pontiac who had to cease production of the Mera after just two years, nineteen eight seven and nineteen eighty-eight.

As a reward for all our hard work, and in appreciation for our "rides," the department gave us our own parking spaces in the rear of the station's lot. Our spaces had our names painted on the cement curb block. The spaces were wider than the average white lined parking spot, so our cars didn't get dinged. The morale at the station was so high, that not one person complained. It was all taken in good fun.

Mac and I continued our fun and games whenever and wherever we decided we needed to unwind. Sully, and his girlfriend Donna, were an item. She'd accompany Sully on ride-a-longs when she didn't have student papers to correct, or lesson plans to write. Donna was a looker with a crazy side that didn't mirror Mac, but Donna was climbing the ladder rapidly to match Mac. Their first "escapade" was in the back of Donna's truck in the station's lot. Mac and I worked lookout for the coupled couple! That was about to come to a grinding halt as Sully convinced Donna to join the car clique. Donna was actively searching for a sports car.

So, life couldn't get much better. It was fun and games. Even when things got tense at work, we were "goofy" about it. We knew this too shall pass. Suddenly, as great as life can be, there are nails in the street. Judge Karma was about to blow out my tire.

WHO DONE IT?

The city of Glendale, California is a hop, skip and a jump from the Amity off the two-freeway. It's an upper middle-class city that boast nightly entertainment. One of Glendale's upscale night club's is called Scotland Yard. The "Yard" as it was known was owned by two retired LAPD sergeants.

Once every other month they held a murder mystery dinner. Not only did you get to eat and drink, but you also got to attempt to solve a who done it. I had been to a couple of these before, but not at the Yard. They were fun. Sully, Donna, Mac, and I drove to Glendale for a rare night out.

We were seated in a packed house. The lights were dimmed, people were meeting other people. The show had yet to begin. The ambience was friendly. The crowd was upscale. We were relaxed and having fun. "Who's buying?" I asked. "I'm drinking."

"I think you got that twisted," Mac said. "But since you asked, I'll have a Diet Coke."

"I'll have a seven and seven," Donna said. She was dressed in a black dress, white blouse, and high heels. Donna was about five six, blonde, and fortyish. She was a fox. I looked around. We were the best-looking foursome in the place. Now, we just needed to solve the murder when it occurred.

I walked to the bar. I ordered. The bartender gave me a drink tray. I maneuvered between the attendees, wondering if the "suspect" was also on the move. I made it back to the table without spilling a drop of our precious cargo. "Leave the tip on the table. Nothing less than a twenty, please."

Donna wrapped what she could of her arm around Sully's shoulder. "How's school going?"

"So far so good. I can recite the alphabet up to M."

"That's a good start. When do you expect to graduate second grade?"

"If you were my teacher, never."

"You're good," Donna said. "You get an A for brown nosing your teacher."

Mac leaned over to whisper in my ear. "That guy in the corner," Mac said, "Look at the way he's looking everyone over. I wonder if he could be the killer."

"I don't think the action has started yet. And that suspicious character is one of the owners." We shut up and sipped our drinks.

Suddenly the lights dimmed. One of the "crew" took center floor. "Good evening ladies and gentlemen and welcome to Scotland Yard's Murder Mystery Dinner Show. How many of you have never attended a murder mystery?" About a dozen hands went up. "Let me explain what will occur. Sometime before dinner is served, or maybe during dessert, or possibly while you are having coffee or other drinks, someone is going to be killed, murdered. If you hear a gunshot, don't be alarmed. That's our killer at his or her best. If you see someone stabbed, choked, bludgeoned, or otherwise done in, don't take it to heart. It's part of our show. Your job is to figure out who done it. You'll do this by walking around, visiting other tables, talking with our guests. Ask questions, take notes if you wish, work together if you like. We have just one requirement. That requirement is that you have fun. To spice things up, each and every one who names the killer at the end of our show will win two tickets to our next show. The owners of Scotland Yard are two retired Los Angeles Police Department sergeants. They help put the show together so that it is authentic yet lighthearted. Does anyone have any questions?"

"Great. At this time feel free to mix and mingle. The show has officially begun."

Mac and I walked around together. We observed. If we thought we observed someone suspicious, we introduced ourselves, and asked questions. In reality, solving the murder, which had yet to take place, was a monumental task.

We watched the servers bring salad to the tables. That was our cue to return to our seats. "Well," I asked teacher Donna and Former Agent Sully, "Anything yet?"

"I think you're a hired killer," Sully said. "It's in your eyes."

"Actually," Donna added, "I think Mac and Tony are a killer team. They were hired by a New York crime family to off someone who was about to testify against the New York family for operating a money laundering ring."

I was impressed. "Either you watch a lot of crime shows, or you read a lot, or you're connected."

Donna laughed. "All of the above. So far this is fun." We dug into our salad.

During dinner, the Yard suddenly grew quiet. I guess everyone was concentrating on their food. I had ordered fish and chicken. It was delicious. As I forked the last of the chicken into my mouth, I heard two loud shots ring out. A guy three tables away from us fell faced down into his steak. I observed a man in a Columbo like rain jacket running away and out the dining room door. The guy was about five eleven. He had dark hair. He was wearing blue and white

378

tennis shoes. I guessed none of that would matter. I figured he'd come back in the room at some point dressed as most of us were dressed so he would blend in. The games had just begun.

"Got anything, Sully?"

"I was eating. I heard two shots. By the time I looked up, all I could see was the double doors leading out the dining room close."

"Donna?"

"I got as far as you got in the alphabet. I got to the letter M for murder. I didn't even see the doors close. The shot scared the fish right out of me."

"Mac, what did you see?"

"The guy had a little round earring in his left ear. It looked to be gold in color but I'm not positive on that. He was about five eleven to six feet. He had dark hair. He was wearing a rumpled tan rain jacket. He was wearing white tennis shoes. He had a ring on his left hand."

That was pretty amazing observations, I thought. Mac was damn good. "Nice work, detective Mac. Remind me not to kill anyone in your presence."

We finished eating. While we were waiting for dessert, we started our investigation. Sully stuck with Donna. Mac and I worked as a team.

We were looking for the earring. If he took the earring out, he should still have the piercing in his left ear lobe. We walked, talked, and observed. We wanted to catch the culprit, the killer, but what really counted was that we were having fun. "How about another Diet Coke?"

"Sure."

We walked to the bar. I ordered a Diet Coke and a double shot of Seagram's. The bartender dressed in all black was six feet tall and muscular. He wore a black cowboy hat. I checked his left ear. It didn't have a piercing. He put the Diet Coke on the bar then counted out my change. "I also ordered a double shot of Seagram's from Wyatt."

"Sorry sir. We have a three drink max here. You've already consumed more than that."

"Are you kidding me? Let me have a shot of Seagram's." I thought maybe he'd give me one shot. If push came to shove, and it was about to, I could always have Sully or Donna get me a drink. The fact was I was annoyed, bordering on pissed.

There was a small crowd at the bar. Some of those people probably thought this interaction was part of the show. Mac picked up her Diet Coke. She grabbed my arm. "Let's do some detective work, detective."

"I want my drink."

"Sir," Wyatt said, "I need to serve other people. Please take the ladies' advice. Go find the killer." He waved his hand in front of me as if to shoe me away. I lost my cool.

"C'mon asshole. Quit fucking with me and pour the motherfucking drink before I come over the bar and get it myself."

Mac walked away. Wyatt came out from behind the bar to show his muscle. The minute his hand touched my shoulder, I decked him. Within seconds, three bouncers were on me. Within forty-five seconds I was escorted out of Scotland Yard.

THREE DAYS LATER: ARREST WARRANT

Mac was working graveyard shift. I had studied, watched two innings of the Dodger game, which they gave away along with my winnings to date. I had a couple of shots, watched the eleven o'clock news, and fell asleep on the couch.

I found out later that it was two in the morning when the consistent pounding rocked me out of a sound sleep. I still had everything on but shoes. Bleary eyed, and half asleep, I walked to the door. I unlocked and opened it. Four football player sized males, all wearing badges around the neck, stared at me. "Are you Tony Kano?"

I panicked. Mac was at work. What the hell had happened? "I'm Tony. What's going on?"

"You're Tony Kano?"

"I just said I was. What the hell is going on?" Was I still asleep? Was I dreaming?

"We have a warrant for your arrest." Two of them grabbed me, pulled me outside, slammed me against the wall and patted me down none to gently. It took two of them to handcuff me, not because I was resisting, because they were getting in each other's way trying to get the bracelets around my thick wrists.

"I'm a cop, a detective. What's this all about?"

"You have a warrant for assault and battery. You're under arrest. You have the right to remain silent. If you give up that right, anything you say can and will be used against you in a court of law. You have the right to an attorney. If you cannot afford one, an attorney will be appointed for you free of charge. Do you understand each of those rights as I read them to you?"

"Sure."

"Yes or no, please."

"Yes, I understand my right as you read them to me."

Two of the four held me under each arm. "Do you wish to talk with us?"

"Sure, sure. I did what I did. I didn't think Wyatt Earp would press charges. Get me my shoes, please. They should be in front of the couch."

I was hustled to one of the two unmarked units parked at the curb. I was placed in the back seat, and seat belted in. As the driver started the engine to haul my ass to the Glendale Police Department, I realized I had just fucked myself out of a career. Amity would have no choice but to rid themselves of me unless somehow, I could beat this rap. When I got to Glendale, guess who I called. I had to call Jerry Kline.

After booking me, tossing me in a cell, exchanging my clothes for an orange jump suit, I was allowed to make a phone call to Jerry Kline. "Jerry, Tony. I'm in trouble. I'm at Glendale PD. I'm in jail."

"You're drunk."

"I'm stone cold sober."

"What did you do?

"Long story, buddy. Bottom line, assault and battery, I guess. They haven't given me my charges yet. I'm fucked."

"Where's Mac?"

"Working."

"Tell me the entire story."

I went through the whole sad, sorted story. When I finished, I said, "I did it, Jerry. Nobody's at fault but me."

Jerry cut me short. "Save it for the job. Let me see if I can get a hold of this guy. Maybe we can cut some kind of deal."

I AIN'T MONTE HALL, BUT LET'S MAKE A DEAL

I was getting, bored and antsy in the cell. The jailer was friendly enough and sympathetic when he found out who I was. He even agreed with me when I said I was fucked!

I didn't have a watch. It was dark. Two guys in Glendale Police attire approached my cell. The shorter of the two said, "Put this on. You're going to court for a bail hearing." One of the cops unlocked the cell. He handed me another jump suit. Same orange color.

"Do you have something in police blue?"

"Not funny."

It wasn't.

"Turn around. Hands behind your back. Put your palms together."

I was handcuffed for the second time within a matter of hours.

One cop said to the other, "Let's use the parking lot door. Quicker and closer. We don't have to worry about him trying to make a break."

Were these guys Abbott and Costello? There was a damn antique paddy wagon a few feet from the jail door. The back door had a step for getting into the damn paddy wagon. Abbott helped me up and in. He climbed in behind me. The windows had security bars. When I was in and seated, my helper knocked on the partition. I heard the paddy wagon cough then the engine started. We were off.

I couldn't have been in the paddy wagon for ten minutes before it reached the courthouse. I was escorted inside.

I was used to doing this routine on a regular basis but from the other angle. I was doing the escorting. I wasn't used to being the escorted.

I was led through a set of double doors then a second set. We stopped just short of the double court doors. Jerry was standing at the door. "Good news and bad news. I courted up with your victim. He's willing to withdraw all charges."

"Bad news."

"It's going to cost you an arm. I told him you only had one leg. He said he'd leave that leg alone."

"How much?"

"He'll work out a payment plan."

"Let's get this over with." I kicked the door open. The judge in a black robe was seated behind his bench. I had hoped to recognize him. I didn't. I looked to my left to the row of seats. Several Amity cops occupied those seats. More Amity staff occupied the seats to my right.

I looked at Jerry. "You said deal. I made a deal."

I heard the Wedding March. Mac stepped out from the judge's chambers. She was dressed as a prison guard. Sully walked hand in hand with her. Sully left Mac in front of the judge's bench.

Jerry walked me to the bench. I stopped opposite Mac. Jerry smiled at me. "We'll mark this one paid in full."

The Judges name was Carmine. Of course, I thought of Judge Karma. The judge started reading from the Scriptures. I was still in handcuffs.

When the Judge finished his reading, Mac said, "uncuff the stupid son of a bitch." Then she started talking. "There are only two things I have decided I can do with you. One, is kill you. Even though there is no death penalty in California, I thought that probably wouldn't be a viable plan. The second thing I could do was marry you. I have no idea why I love you with all my heart and soul; none. The fact is I want to spend the rest of my life cleaning up every one of your messes. Will you marry me?"

"Not only do I love every inch of you, but I also love your crazy sick mind. I never knew life until we met. As crazy as this sounds, I'll love you forever and always, Peter in or Peter out."

Jerry stepped forward and handing me the ring. I placed it on Mac's finger.

Sully stepped forward and handed Mac a gold band. She placed the band on my finger.

Judge Carmine said simply, "By the powers vested in me by the State of California, I now pronounce you man and wife.

Mac and I walked into the Judge's chambers. Not to solidify our commitment to each other but so I could change. I handed Mac the orange jump suit. "We're keeping this, it's a reminder." She showed me the back of the jumpsuit. It read: Property of DEE MACKENZEE.

We walked out to a sea of blue suits, a round of applause and yelling of glad tidings. Jerry handed me an envelope. "Reservations for a suite at Caesars Palace. Here are the Ferrari keys. There's also some cash in the envelope for gambling if you ever get out of your room. Don't lose the Ferrari at the tables."

Sully walked over to his cousin. "I really want to make some smart-ass remark like how you can marry an asshole like this but it's too late; you already married him."

"When you're in your room, and in your bed, think about our shotgun mics and our hidden video. Enjoy your honeymoon."

The paddy wagon was still parked in the courthouse lot. I looked it over. I looked at Mac. Mac looked at me. We climbed in. As uncomfortable as it would be, why not a paddy wagon? We locked the door from the inside. We began to consummate our wedding vows.

FIVE HOURS FORTY-FIVE MINUTES LATER

We walked into our suite at Caesars, in the middle of the foyer was an actual craps table. The green cloth said, "Place Mac here." I did.

ANOTHER BEGINNING...

Made in the USA
Middletown, DE
11 July 2022

69025247R00223